A Note from the Author:

This novel, like all Darkover novels, is complete in itself. However, for those who have followed the chronology of Darkover, *City of Sorcery* takes place approximately seven years after *Thendara House*, at a time when Terran and Darkovan relationships were at their most friendly; a period which lasted until the time when Dorilys Aillard, known as Cleindori, achieved status as Keeper in Arilinn Tower. Her martyrdom, murder, and the subsequent swing to extreme conservatism under the Regency of Danvan Hastur, ended this period of friendly relations between the two societies, and by the time of *The Bloody Sun*, few Terrans and Fewer Darkovans even remembered that there had been years when Terran and Darkovan had co-existed on such amiable terms.

One of the few who remembered, afterward, that there had been such a time was Magdalen Lorne, of Terran Intelligence; otherwise known as Margali n' Isabet, Free Amazon, Comhi'letziis; Oath-bound of the Guild of Renunciates.

—M.Z.B.

CITY OF SORCERY

Marion Zimmer Bradley

DAW BOOKS, INC.

DONALD A. WOLLHEIM, PUBLISHER

1633 Broadway, New York, NY 10019

Cover art by James Gurney.

DAW Book Collectors' Number 600

DEDICATION

To Donald A. Wollheim
This, as all my books

ACKNOWLEDGMENTS

Although every character and event in this novel is entirely my own invention, the theme and structure of the story were suggested by a novel by the late Talbot Mundy; THE DEVIL'S GUARD, copyright 1926 by the Ridgeway Company. I read it in 1945 or thereabout, and have felt for many years that this kind of Ideal Search or Quest novel should be retold in a Darkovan context.

Also my grateful thanks to my elder son, David Bradley, for preparation of the final manuscript. David went above and beyond the call of duty by retyping, at an hour's notice, from a very imperfect print, the first 15 chapters into a second word processor after the first one had blown up in my face, losing all the early disks and backups. This is why Darkovans are said to hate technology. And thanks to my secretary, Elisabeth Waters, who gave up the use of *her* word processor for three weeks so that we could finish the book on time.

—M.Z.B.

First Printing, October 1984

1 2 3 4 5 6 7 8 9

PRINTED IN U.S.A.

CHAPTER ONE

The messenger was a woman, and though she was wearing Darkovan clothing, she was not Darkovan, and not accustomed to the streets of Thendara's Old Town at night. She walked warily, reminding herself that respectable women were seldom molested in the streets if they minded their own business, acted and looked as if they had somewhere to go; did not loiter, kept moving.

She had learned this lesson so well that she strode along briskly even through the marketplace, looking neither to one side nor the other, keeping her eyes straight ahead.

The red sun of Cottman Four, informally called the Bloody Sun by Terran Empire spaceport workers, lingered at the rim of the horizon, casting a pleasant red-umber twilight. A single moon, like a pale violet shadow in the sky, hung high and waning. In the marketplace, the vendors were closing the front shutters of their stalls. A fried-fish seller was scooping up the last small crispy crumbs from her kettle, watched by a few stray cats; she scattered the crumbs, provoking a cat-scrimmage underfoot, which she watched, amused, for a moment before she hoisted the kettle on its side, straining the fat through several layers of cloth. Close by, a saddlemaker slammed down the front shutters of his stall and padlocked them shut.

Prosperous, thought the Terran woman in Darkovan clothing. *He can afford a Terran metal lock.* Darkover, Cottman Four to the Terrans, was a metal-poor planet. Other vendors were tying their shutters down with ropes and cords and trusting to the night watchman to notice any unauthorized person fumbling with the ropes. A baker was doing a haphazard business selling the last few stale buns in her stall; she looked up as the Terran messenger passed with her quick stride.

"Hey there! Vanessa n'ha Yllana, where are you going in such a rush?"

Vanessa was moving so swiftly that she had gone several steps past the baker's stall before she really heard the words. She stopped and came back, smiling tentatively at the plump woman who was making change for a small boy with a bun in his fist.

"Sherna," she acknowledged, "I didn't see you."

"I could have imagined that," said the baker with a grin. "Striding along as if you were on your way to exterminate a colony of banshees, at the *least*, my dear! Have a bun?" When Vanessa hesitated, she urged, "Go on, take one, there's no sense in hauling this lot all the way back to the Guild-house; it's not as if there were enough left for everyone to have one at supper!"

Thus urged, Vanessa picked up one of the leftover buns and bit into it. It was hearty, made with nut-flour to eke out the grain, and sweet with dried fruits. She stood nibbling, moving automatically to one side as the stall-keeper a few feet away began to bumble about with a broom, sweeping the front of his shop.

"Were you going to the Guild-house, or on some other errand?" Sherna asked.

"To the Guild-house," Vanessa admitted. "I should have thought to come here at once so that I could go through the streets with you." Secretly she was annoyed at herself; where had her mind been?

"Good," Sherna said. "You can help me carry the baskets. But tonight is not a Bridge meeting, is it?"

"Oh, no, no, not that I remember," Vanessa said, picking up one of the breadbaskets. "I have a message for Margali n'ha Ysabet. I cannot see why the Guildmothers refuse to have a communicator in the Guildhouse; it would save sending messengers through the streets this way, especially after dark."

Sherna smiled indulgently. "You *Terranan*," she said, laughing. "So that the noise of the thing can invade our privacy in season and out, to save a messenger the trouble of walking a few minutes' walk in good weather? Ah, your poor abused feet, my heart aches for the lazy things!"

"The weather isn't always so good," Vanessa protested, but the argument was an old one, habitual between the women, and the protests were good-natured.

Both women were members of the Bridge Society, *Penta Cori'yo*, which had been formed a few years ago, when members of the Free Amazons—*Comhi' Letziis*, the Guild of Renunciates—had been the first Darkovans to offer themselves for work in the Terran Headquarters; as medical technicians, as mountain guides and travel-advisers, as translators and language teachers. The Bridge Society offered a home, a place to live, friends among Darkovan women; for Terrans who agreed to live by Renunciate laws, but could not commit themselves fully to the Guild-house, there was even a specially modified form of the Oath. The Bridge maintained homelike quarters for Darkovan women, mostly Renunciates, required by their work to live in the Terran HQ.

It was open to any Darkovan woman who had worked for three of the forty-day moon cycles in the Terran HQ or any Terran woman who spent the same time within a Guild-house. Sherna n'ha Marya, a Renunciate from Thendara Guild-house, had worked half a year as a translator, helping to compile standard works in *casta* and *cahuenga,* the two languages of Darkover. Vanessa ryn Erin, a graduate of the Terran Intelligence Academy on Alpha, had now been four years on Darkover, and had lived in the Guild-house most of the last year, preparing for field work outside Headquarters.

Sherna handed the last of the sweet buns to a woman with a small child in her arms, another clutching her skirt. "Take them for the little ones. No, no," she protested as the woman began to fumble for coins, "they'd only go into the pail for the hens. So, Vanessa, we managed that well, only two loaves to carry back, and the kitchen-women can make us a bread-pudding with them."

"Are we ready to go back to the Guild-house, then?"

"There's no hurry," Sherna said, and Vanessa had been on Darkover long enough not to protest, despite the urgency of her errand. She helped Sherna tie up the front shutters of the bake-stall in leisurely fashion, and collect the scattered baskets.

There was a sudden flurry of activity at one of the gates visible from the marketplace, and a caravan of pack animals clattered over the stones. A cluster of small children playing king-of-the-mountain from the top of an abandoned stall scampered out of the way. A tall, thin woman, clad in the ordinary garb of a Renunciate, loose tunic and trousers tucked into low boots, carrying an Amazon knife as long as a short sword, strode toward them.

"Rafi," Sherna greeted her. "I didn't know you'd be back tonight."

"Neither did I," said Rafaella n'ha Doria. "These

people have been bumbling about the pass for three days. I think the pack animals smelled home, or they'd still be wandering up there looking at the green grass growing and hunting for mushrooms on apple trees. Let me go and pick up my pay. I'd have left them at the city gates, but I'm sure they'd have lost themselves between here and their stables, judging by the way they've behaved all along. And Zandru whip me with scorpions if I ever again accept a commission before it's firmly understood who's bossing the trail! Believe me—I could tell you some stories—'' She hurried off to talk briefly with the head of the caravan. Some money changed hands. Vanessa saw Rafaella carefully stop to count it—even the Terran woman knew what an insult that was, in an open marketplace. Then Rafi came back to them; greeted Vanessa with a casual nod, swung the last of the wicker breadbaskets to her shoulder, and the three women set off together through the cobbled streets.

"What are you doing here, Vanessa? News from HQ?"

"Not much," Vanessa said evasively. "One of our planes from Map and Ex is down in the Hellers."

"Maybe there will be work for us, then," Rafaella said. "Last year, when they sent us out on a salvage contract for a downed plane, there was plenty for everyone to do." Rafaella was a travel-organizer, and was in considerable demand among Terrans who must venture into the little-known and trackless mountains of the northern Domains.

"I don't know if that's what they have in mind. I don't think it's where anyone can salvage it," Vanessa said. The women walked along silently through one of the quieter streets of the city, and paused before a large building of stone, turning a windowless front wall on the street. A small placard on the front door said:

THENDARA GUILD-HOUSE
SISTERHOOD OF RENUNCIATES

Sherna and Vanessa were laden with the baskets; Rafaella alone had a free hand to ring the bell. In the front hall, a heavily pregnant woman let them in, closing and locking the door after them. "Oh, Vanessa, is it the night for the Bridge Society? I had forgotten." But she gave Vanessa no chance to answer. "Rafi, your daughter is here!"

"I thought Doria was still busy among the *Terranan*," said Rafaella, not very graciously. "What is she doing here, Laurinda?"

"She is giving a lecture, with the box which makes lighted pictures on the wall, to seven women who are to be trained as healing assistants, beginning next tenday," said Laurinda. " '*Nurses*,' the *Terranan* call them, isn't that a funny word? It sounds as if they were going to work breast-feeding *Terranan* babies, and that's not what they're being trained for at all. Just caring for the sick and bedridden, and looking after wounds and the like. They must be nearly finished now; you could go in and speak to her."

Vanessa asked, "Is Margali n'ha Ysabet within the house? I am here with a message for her."

"You are fortunate," the woman said, "she is to set out tomorrow morning for Armida, with Jaelle n'ha Melora. They would have gone today, before noon, but one of the horses cast a shoe and by the time the smith had done with her work, it was threatening rain; so they put off their departure till tomorrow."

"If Jaelle is still in the house," Rafaella said, "I should like to speak with her."

"She is helping Doria with the lecture; we all know she has worked among the *Terranan*," Laurinda said.

"Why don't you look inside and see? They're in the music room."

"I will go and put away my baskets first," said Sherna, but Vanessa followed Rafaella toward the music room at the back of the building, and opened the door, quietly slipping inside.

A young woman, her hair cropped Renunciate style, was just finishing a slide lecture; she ticked off several points on her fingers, clicking off a colored slide as the women entered.

"You will be expected to write accurately; they will expect you to read well, and to remember what you read, and to write it down precisely. You will be given preparatory lectures in anatomy, in personal hygiene, in scientific observation and how to record what you observe, before ever you are allowed even to bring a patient a tray of food or a bedpan. You will work as assistants and aides, helping the qualified nurses to care for patients, from the very first day of your lectures; and as soon as you are taught any nursing procedures you will be allowed to do them at once on the wards. Not until your second half year of training will you be allowed to assist the surgeons, or to study midwifery. It is hard, dirty work, but I found it very satisfying, and I think you will too. Any questions?"

One of the young women curled up on the floor listening raised her hand.

"Mirella n'ha Anjali?"

"Why must we have lessons in personal hygiene? Do those Terrans think that Darkovan people are dirty or slovenly, that they must teach us this?"

"You must not take it personally," said Doria. "Even their own women must learn new and different ways of cleanliness when they study nursing; cleanliness for everyday use, and surgical cleanliness for when they must work around people who are very ill, or who have unhealed wounds, or are exposed to disease germs and contagion, are not at all the same, as you will learn.''

Another woman asked, ''I have heard that the *uniforms*—'' she stumbled over the unfamiliar word, ''worn by the Terran workers are as immodest as the wear of a prostitute. Must we wear them, and will it violate our Oath?''

Doria indicated the white tunic and trousers she was wearing. She said, ''Customs differ. Their standards of modesty are different from ours. But the Bridge Society has been successful in creating a compromise. Darkovan women employed by Medic wear a special uniform designed not to offend our standards, and it's so comfortable and warm that many of the Terran nurses have chosen to adopt it. And before you ask, the symbol on the breast of the uniform—'' She indicated the red emblem, a staff with entwined snakes. ''It's a very old Terran symbol indicating Medical service. You will be expected to know a dozen such symbols in order to find your way around the HQ.''

''What does it mean?'' one young girl, not more than fifteen, asked.

''I asked my own teacher this. It is supposed to be the symbol of a very old Terran God of Healing. No one now worships him, but the symbol has remained. Any other questions?''

''I have heard,'' said one woman, ''that the Terrans are licentious, that they regard Darkovan women as being—being like the women of the spaceport bars. Is this true? Must we carry knives to protect ourselves there?''

Doria chuckled. She said, ''Jaelle n'ha Melora lived among them for a time. I will let her answer that.''

A small woman with flaming red hair stood up at the

back of the room. "I cannot speak for all Terran men," she said, "even among the Gods, Zandru and Aldones have not the same attributes, and a *cristoforo* monk behaves differently than a farmer in the Valeron plains. There are boorish men and roughnecks among the Terrans as well as on the streets of Thendara. But I can assure you that among the Terrans in the Medic Department, you need not fear discourtesy or molestation; their Medics are sworn by oath to treat everyone, patients of professional associates, with proper courtesy. In fact, it may disturb you that they will not seem to take any note of whether you are a man, a woman, or a piece of machinery, but will treat you as if you were novice Keepers. As for carrying knives, it is not the custom among the Terrans, and you will not be allowed to bring any weapons for defense into the Medic Department. But then, the Terrans will not be carrying them either: it is forbidden by their regulations. The only knives you will see anywhere in Medic are the surgeon's scalpels. Are there any other questions?"

Vanessa realized that the questions could go on until the bell rang for the evening meal. She said, from where she stood by the door, "I have a question. Is Margali n'ha Ysabet within this room?"

"I have not seen her since noonday," Doria said, then saw Rafaella in the doorway beside Vanessa.

"Mother," she called, and hurried to Rafaella, enveloping her in an enormous hug. Jaelle, smiling, came to her old friend, and the three women stood for a moment embracing.

"It's wonderful to see you, Jaelle. Damn, how long has it been? For the past three years we've kept missing each other; whenever I'm in Thendara, you're out at Armida, and whenever you come to the city, I'm likely to be somewhere north of Caer Donn!"

"It's only luck this time; Margali and I were supposed to leave at noon," Jaelle said. "I have been away from my daughter for a pair of tendays."

"She must be a big girl now, Dorilys n'ha Jaelle," said Rafaella, laughing. "Five, isn't she, or six by now? Old enough to bring her to the house for fostering."

"There's time enough for that," said Jaelle, and looked away, greeting Vanessa with a nod. "I know I met you a few days ago at the Bridge Society meeting, but I have forgotten your name."

"Vanessa," Doria reminded her.

"I am sorry to break up your lecture," Vanessa said, looking at the young women who were putting away the cushions and scattering about the room, but Doria shrugged.

"It's just as well. All the serious questions had been answered. But, they are nervous about their new work, and would have kept thinking up silly questions to be answered until the supper-bell!" She went back to the center of the room, and began packing up her slides and the projector. "How fortunate you came. You can return these to Medic for me tonight, and save me a trip through the streets at night. I borrowed them from the Chief of Nursing Education. You'll take them back when you go, won't you? Or are you spending the night?"

"No, I came here with a message for Margali—"

Doria shrugged again. "I am sure she's somewhere in the House. It's nearly time for the supper-bell. You will be sure to see her there!"

Vanessa had been long enough on Darkover, and lived long enough in Guild-houses, to be accustomed to this casual attitude about time. She was still Terran enough to feel that they really should have sent someone to fetch Margali, or at least told her where to go and find her, but she was on the Darkovan side of town, now; resigning herself, she told Doria that she would be glad to return the slide equipment to the Medic Department for her—actually, she felt it was a considerable imposition, and she was a little annoyed at Doria for asking. But Doria was a sister in the Guild, and there was no courteous way to refuse a request of this sort.

"Is there any news yet about the plane that's down in the Hellers?" Doria asked.

Vanessa was saved from answering by a scornful sound from Rafaella.

"Foolish *Terranan*," Rafaella said. "What do they expect? Even we poor benighted souls without the benefit of Terran science—" She made the words sound like a gutter obscenity—"know that it is folly to travel past the Hellers, at any season, and even a Terran should know there's nothing north of Nevarsin to the Wall Around the World, but frozen wasteland! I say, good riddance to bad rubbish! If they send their foolish planes there, they must expect to lose them!"

"I think you are too hard on them, Rafi," Doria said. "Is the pilot anyone I know, Vanessa?"

"She is not a member of the Bridge Society. Her name is Anders."

"Alexis Anders? I have met her," said Jaelle. "They have not recovered the plane? How dreadful!"

Rafaella put an arm around Jaelle's waist. "Let's not waste time talking of the Terrans, *Shaya*, love, we have so little time together these days. Your daughter is such a big girl now, when will you bring her to the Guild-house for fostering? And then perhaps you will come back too."

Jaelle's face clouded. "I don't know if I can bring her here at all, Rafi. There are—difficulties."

Rafaella's quick temper flared. "So it is true. I did

not believe it of you, Jaelle, that you would go meekly back to your high-born Comyn kindred, when they had cast you off! But then, perhaps it was always certain that the Comyn would never let you go, certainly not when you bore a child to one of them! I wonder that no one has yet called your Oath in question!''

Now Jaelle's face, too, bore the high color of anger; she had, Vanessa thought, the temper associated traditionally, by Terrans, with her flaming red hair.

"How dare you say that to me, Rafaella?"

"Do you deny that the father of your child is the Comyn lord Damon Ridenow?"

"I deny nothing," Jaelle said angrily, "but what of that? You of all people, to reproach me with that, Rafi! Have you not three sons?"

Rafaella quoted from the Oath of the Renunciates:

"*Men dia pre' zhiuro*, from this day forth, I swear I will bear no child to any man for house or heritage, place nor posterity; I swear that I alone will determine rearing and fosterage of any child I bear, without regard to any man's place, position, or pride."

"How dare you quote the Oath to me in that tone and imply that I have broken it? Cleindori is *my* child. Her father is Comyn; if you knew him, you would know how little that means to him. My daughter is an Aillard; the house of Aillard, alone among the Seven Domains, have counted lineage, from the times of Hastur and Cassilda themselves, in the mother's line. I bore my daughter for my own house, not for any man's! What Amazon has not done the same, unless she is so persistent a lover of women that she will not let any man touch her even for that purpose." But Jaelle's anger ebbed; she put her arm around Rafaella again. "Oh, let's not quarrel, Rafi, you are almost my oldest friend, and do you think I have forgotten the years when we were partners? But you are not the keeper of my conscience.''

Rafaella still held herself spitefully aloof.

"No, that office is now filled by that he-keeper of the Forbidden Tower—Damon Ridenow, is that his name? How can I possibly compete with that?''

Jaelle shook her head. "Whatever you think, Rafi, I keep my Oath.'' Rafaella still looked skeptical, but at that moment a mellow-chimed bell sounded through the hall, announcing that in a few minutes dinner would be served.

"Dinner, and I am still wearing all the muck of the pack animals and the marketplace! I must go and wash, even if I am not to be one of Doria's nurses! Come along up with me, Shaya. Let's not quarrel, after all, I see you so seldom now, we have no time to waste in arguing about what we can't change. Vanessa, will you come with us?''

"I think not, I must look for Margali n'ha Ysabet.'' Vanessa watched Jaelle and her friend run up the stairs, and went toward the door of the dining room. There was a good smell of cooking, something hot and savory, the yeasty smell of fresh bread just taken from the oven, and a clatter of dishes where the women helping in the kitchen were setting out bowls and cups on the tables.

If Magdalen Lorne, known in the Guild-house as Margali, was in the Guild-house at all, she must pass through here on her way to dinner. Vanessa wondered if she would know her by sight. She had met her only three or four times, the last time only a tenday ago at a meeting of the Bridge Society within this House.

At that moment, she looked up and saw Magdalen Lorne coming toward her, along the hall from the green-house at the back of the Guild-house. Her arms were full of early melons. At her side, also carrying melons,

was a tall, scarred, rangy woman—an *emmasca,* a woman
who had undergone the dangerous, illegal and frequently
fatal neutering operation. Vanessa knew the woman's
name, Camilla n'ha Kyria; knew that she had once been
a mercenary soldier, was now a teacher of sword-play
in the Guild-house, and knew that she was reputed to be
Magdalen Lorne's lover. That still embarrassed Vanessa
a little, though not as much as it would have done
before she had dwelt for months in the Guild-house and
knew how commonplace and unremarkable it was. It no
longer seemed to her mysterious and perverse; but she
was Terran, and it embarrassed her.

Even before she had come to Darkover, since first
she had gone into training for Intelligence work, Vanessa
ryn Erin had known of the legendary Magdalen Lorne.
She knew most of the story: that she had been born on
Darkover, in the mountains near Caer Donn, before the
building of Thendara Spaceport, so that Magda had
been brought up with Darkovan children and learned the
language as a native. She knew that Magda had been
trained, like herself, in the Intelligence Academy on
Alpha, by Vanessa's own chief, Cholayna Ares, who
had at that time been head of Intelligence Training, and
had only later come to Darkover. She knew that Magda
had, for a time, been married to the present Terran
Legate, Peter Haldane, and that she had been the first
woman to do Intelligence Fieldwork on Darkover; one
of the very few women who had ever done so. She
knew that Magda had been the first to infiltrate the
Guild of Renunciates, had even managed to take the
Oath, and had quixotically insisted on keeping it, even
to serving the full housebound time, which, before the
creation of the Bridge Society, had been required in
unmitigated form even of Terrans. She knew that, a few
years ago, Magda had left the Guild-house and was on

some mysterious detached duty at Armida. This she had known of the legend. But she had met the living woman only a few days ago, and still was not accustomed to her. Somehow she had expected her to be larger than life.

In the Guild-house, courtesy demanded that she use only Lorne's Darkovan name.

"Margali n'ha Ysabet? May I speak with you for a minute?"

"Vanessa? How nice to see you." Magda Lorne, Margali, seemed tall, though she was not much over average height; in her middle thirties, with heavy dark hair cropped short in Renunciate style, shadowing her forehead; she had deep-set, lively gray eyes which rested on Vanessa curiously. "Here, take some of these, will you?" She shoved some of the armload of melons into Vanessa's hands; sniffed, and made a wry face. "Smells like tripe stew. You can have my share. Will I ever forget how I hated it, my first few months here? But maybe you like it, some people do. Never mind, there'll be plenty of bread and cheese, and melons for dessert. Camilla, give her some of those, if you drop them here in the hall we'll be chasing them all over the place— and if any of them smash open, what a mess to clean away! And I, for one, don't feel like scrubbing floors this week!"

Camilla, who was even taller than Magda, loaded Vanessa's arms with some of the melons she was carrying. They smelled sweet and fragrant, with the earthy smell of the greenhouse, but Vanessa resented the intrusion on her mission. Camilla saw her frown.

"What are you doing here, Vanessa? If it is Bridge Society night, I had forgotten."

Vanessa thought, irritably, that if one more person said that to her she would swear out loud. "No—but I have a message for you, Margali, from Cholayna n'ha Chandria." Vanessa used the Guild-house name, and Magda shook her head in puzzlement.

"Damn the woman, what can she want? I talked with her three days ago, and she knew I was leaving. Jaelle and I should have gone this afternoon. In case you'd forgotten, we have children at Armida."

"It's an assignment. She said it was important, possibly a matter of life or death," Vanessa told her.

Camilla said, "Cholayna doesn't exaggerate. If she said *life or death,* she meant it."

"I'm sure of it," Magda said, frowning. "But do you have any idea what it's all about, Vanessa? I don't want to get hung up here. As I said, I'm needed at Armida. Jaelle's daughter is old enough to be left, but Shaya's not quite two years old, and if I stay much longer in the city she'll forget what I look like!"

"I couldn't say," Vanessa evaded, carefully not saying that she didn't know. She had been briefed on why Magda had left the Guild-house, and something from the most secret and classified files had been made available to her about Magda's work at Armida, but not nearly enough to understand it.

She could not imagine any conceivable reason why an Intelligence Agent of Magda's status should want to burden herself with a half-Darkovan child, and like all women who are childless by choice, she judged Magda harshly. Although she admired the legend, she was not yet accustomed to the living reality of the woman. Walking at Magda's side, it confused her to note that Magda was actually an inch or two shorter than she was herself.

"It's not all that late. Have we time for dinner here? No, I suppose if Cholayna said life or death, she means exactly that. Let me go and tell Jaelle n'ha Melora that I may not be able to leave at first light, after all." But her face was grim as she started up the stairs.

"Let me tell you, Vanessa, if this is a nonsense of some sort, Cholayna will wish she had never learned the way to the Guild-house. I'm leaving tomorrow, and that's that!"

She smiled suddenly as she started up the stairs, and for the first time, Vanessa sensed, behind the matter-of-fact woman, the powerful personality who had become the legend.

"Oh, well, if it had to come, what better time? At least I'll miss the tripe stew."

CHAPTER TWO

It was pitch-dark now, and raining, spits and slashes of sleet in the nightly rain. The streets were all but empty when Magda and Vanessa finally crossed the square facing the entrance to the Terran HQ and gave passwords to the Spaceforce man in black leather uniform. He was bundled to the neck in a black wool scarf, which was not regulation, and there was a heavy down jacket over the uniform which was not regulation either, but on this particular planet, at night, should have been. Magda knew they winked at it, but that wasn't enough; they should have changed the rules to authorize it.

And they think the Darkovan people are unwilling to change their primitive ways!

Magda did not know most of the new Spaceforce people now. Even a year ago, she would have introduced herself; now it seemed pointless. She would be going back to Armida in the morning; that was where her life was laid now. She had remained accessible to Cholayna to help in the founding and implementing of the Bridge Society, but now it was working well on its own. And now she had a child to bind her further to Armida and the Forbidden Tower. Cholayna Ares, Head of Intelligence on Cottman Four, would simply have to get along without her.

If she thinks she can send me into the field at a moment's notice, she can simply think again.

Magda had lived so long under the Darkovan sun that she flinched at the bright yellow, Earth-normal lights as they came on inside the main HQ building. But she stepped into the elevator without hesitation. She had acquired a certain impatience with these Terran conveniences, but she wasn't going to walk up forty-two flights of stairs to make her point.

At this hour the sector given over to Terran Intelligence was dark and deserted; only from the office of Cholayna Ares was there a gleam of light, and Magda realized that if Cholayna awaited her in the office, instead of sending for her in her comfortable living quarters, there was something very important in the wind.

"Cholayna? I came as soon as I could. But what in the world—this one or any other—is so important that it couldn't wait until morning?"

"I was afraid that by morning you would be gone," Cholayna answered. "I wasn't eager to send a messenger after you to Armida. But I would have done it if I had to."

Cholayna Ares, Terran Intelligence, was a very tall woman, with a shock of silver-white hair in astonishing contrast to the darkness of her black skin. She rose to greet Magda; gestured her to take a seat. Magda remained standing.

"It's good of you to come, Magda."

"It's not good at all, you didn't give me a choice," Magda retorted irritably. "You said something about life and death. I didn't think you'd say that lightly. Was I wrong?"

"Magda—do you remember an agent named Anders? Alexis. She came here from Magaera two years ago.

Basic Training in Intelligence; shifted here to Mapping and Exploring.''

"Lexie Anders? I didn't know her well," Magda said, "and she made it very clear she didn't want to know me any better. Later, when I suggested that if she wanted to know how to relate to the women here, she join the Bridge Society, she laughed in my face. I must admit I've never especially liked her. Why?''

"I think you were too hard on her," Cholayna said. "She came here and immediately found herself up against the Lorne Legend." Magda made an impatient gesture, but Cholayna went on, imperturbable.

"No, no, my dear, I'm perfectly serious. You had done more, on a world where in general it was impossible for a woman to accomplish anything at all in intelligence work, than Anders had accomplished in her first three assignments. Whatever she did, she found herself competing with you, and in consequence she knew she was outclassed before she began. I wasn't at all surprised when she shifted to M-and-Ex.''

"I can't see why she thought she had to compete—" Magda began irritably; but Cholayna brushed that aside.

"Be that as it may. Her plane went down over the Hellers three days ago. We got a message that she was lost, couldn't navigate—something wrong with the computer compass. Then nothing. Dead silence, not even a tracking beam to the satellite. Not even a signal from the black box.''

"That seems very unlikely," Magda said. The "black box," or automatic recording device in a mapping plane, was supposed to keep sending out signals for retrieval, at least with the newer models, for at least three years after the plane went down. Magda knew Alexis Anders well enough to know that she would not have allowed herself to be sent out with anything less than the very newest in equipment.

"Unlikely or not, it happened, Magda. The plane was giving out no signals, the black box and tracking recorder were silent, the satellite couldn't trace a thing."

"She crashed, then?" Magda felt cheap; she had not particularly liked Lexie, but she wished now she had not spoken quite so unkindly of the woman—now, presumably, dead.

Of course, there had been Terrans who had survived the crash of a Mapping plane, and found shelter, and in at least one case, Magda knew, a new life, and a new home. But not in the Hellers, the wildest, most unknown, trackless and uninhabited mountains on Darkover; perhaps the worst on any settled or inhabitable planet. It was almost impossible to survive in the Hellers, at least in winter, for more than a few hours, without special survival gear. And beyond the Hellers, as far as anyone knew (and now the Empire knew Cottman Four considerably better than the Darkovans themselves), was nothing; only the impenetrable mountain range known as the Wall around the World. And beyond the Wall, nothing but barren icy wastes stretching from pole to pole.

"So she's presumed dead, then? Too bad." Anything further would be hypocrisy. Lexie had disliked Magda quite as much as Magda had disliked Lexie.

"No," said Cholayna, "she's down in Medic."

"You recovered the plane? But—"

"No, we *didn't* recover the plane, do you think I would have brought you across the city in a rush like this for a routine rescue or debriefing?"

"You keep telling me what it isn't," Magda said, "but you haven't given me any idea, yet, what this is. . . ."

Still, Cholayna hesitated. At last, she said, quite formally, "Magda, I remind you that you are still a sworn Intelligence Agent, and are covered by the Official Secrets Provision of Civil Service—"

"Cholayna, I can't imagine what you're talking about," Magda began, and now she was seriously annoyed. What was all this rigmarole? She had never questioned her Oath to Intelligence, except during the painful identity crisis of her first half-year among the Renunciates. There had then been no Bridge Society to help in this kind of transition. She had been the first.

"You know, I fought to keep you on inactive duty status, instead of accepting your resignation," Cholayna said deliberately. "One of the tenets of intelligence work, and this applies to all Empire planets, incidentally, not just Darkover, is this: when one of ours goes over the wall—goes native, acquires a native spouse and children—the rule of thumb is that it makes him a better agent. Although there is always a question in the record about any decision he might make which could possibly create a conflict as to where his personal interest lies. I'm sure you know that."

"I could quote you pages of regulations about it," Magda said dryly. "I was prepared for this. I assume it applies to me because I've had a child, though as far as you know I'm not married. Right? Well, you're wrong."

"Are you married, then?"

"Not in any way you'd recognize under Terran law. But I have sworn the Oath of Freemates with Jaelle n'ha Melora: by Darkovan law, that creates an analogy to marriage. Specifically, it means that if either of us should die, the other has both a legal right *and a legal obligation* to foster and act as guardian of the other's child or children, exactly as a wife or husband would do. Specifically this oath overrides, by law, any claim of the children's fathers. So for all practical purposes, the situation is identical with marriage. Is that clear?''

Cholayna said, her voice hard, ''I'm sure Xenoanthropology will find it fascinating. I'll make sure they get it from the records. But I wasn't inquiring into the details of your private life.''

''I wasn't giving them.'' Magda's voice was equally unyielding, although in fact Cholayna was one of the few people alive to whom she might have given such details if asked. ''I was apprising you of the legal situation. I assume, then, that those standard assumptions about Empire men with a native wife and children apply to me, and I am expected to behave accordingly.''

''You assume wrongly, Magda. Yes, on the books, it's true; but in actual practice—and this is classified information I'm giving you—on the occasions, and incidentally they are very rare, when a woman goes over the wall—classified practice is to deactivate her intelligence rating immediately. The reasons given for this are numerous, but they all boil down to the same thing. Official Intelligence policy assumes that a man can maintain an objective detachment from his wife and children, more easily than you or I could, because of—Magda, remember I'm quoting, this isn't my personal belief—because of her deeper involvement. Presumably, a husband can detach himself from a wife easier than vice versa, and the children are, again supposedly, closer to the woman who bore them than they are to the man who fathered them.''

Magda swore. ''I should have expected something like this. Do I have to tell you what I think of the *reish?*'' The Darkovan word was a childish vulgarity, which meant literally *stable-sweepings,* but her face twisted in real anger as she said it.

''Of course you don't. What you think of it and what

I think of it are very much the same, but what either of us thinks, is completely beside the point. I'm talking about official policy. I was supposed to accept your resignation the first time you handed it in.''

"I suppose it's also in those extremely confidential and classified private files that I am reputed to be a lover of women?" Magda asked with a wry twist of her mouth. "I know the *classified* policy regarding lovers of men, among Terrans—legally they're protected by official policies of non-discrimination. Practically, you know and I know that they're hassled on any pretext anyone can find.''

"You're wrong," Cholayna said, "or at least it's not true in every case. There's a legal loophole: a man who is living with a wife and children, no matter what his private preference, cannot officially be classified homosexual. In practice, he's covered, and can fight any such action. You covered yourself against any such action when your child was born, Magda. Nobody really cares whether you married the father or not. But by immunizing yourself from *that* kind of persecution, you invoked the other one: now it's assumed that you are completely unsuited to Intelligence work because your loyalty would be to your child or children, and to the man who fathered them. I should, according to the Code, have accepted your resignation the first time you handed it in.''

"I would have been perfectly agreeable to that," said Magda.

"I know. Goodness knows, you've given me opportunities enough," Cholayna said. "You've handed it in so regularly every season that I've wondered if it's just your way of celebrating Midsummer and Midwinter! But I still think I'm seeing a little farther than you do. We can't afford to lose qualified women this way.''

"Why are you telling me all this?"

"By way of explaining to you why this request is unofficial, and why, just the same, you have to listen to me, and help me. Magda, you have the ultimate weapon over me; you can tell me where to go and what to do when I get there, and according to regulations I have no recourse at all. The legal situation is, you've gone over the wall, and I have no right to call you in. But I'm bucking regulations because you are the one person who might be able to make sense of what's happening now."

"And so, finally, we come around to it," Magda said, "the reason you hauled me out on a rainy night—"

"All nights here are rainy, but that's beside the point, too."

"Lexie Anders?"

"Ten minutes or so before her plane went down, she transmitted a message via satellite; she was approaching the Wall Around the World, and was preparing to turn back. Her final message said she'd spotted something, like a city, which she had *not* found on the radar map. She was descending to five thousand meters to investigate. Then we lost her, and the plane. Nothing more. Not even the black box, as I said. As far as HQ or the satellites know, the plane vanished, black box and all, right out of the atmosphere of the planet. But Lexie Anders appeared this morning at the gates of the HQ, out of uniform, without her identity cards. And her mind had been wiped. Wiped clean. Complete amnesia. Magda, she can hardly speak Terran Standard! She speaks the native language of her home planet— Vainwal—but on the baby-talk level. So obviously, we can't ask her what happened."

"But—all this is impossible, Cholayna! I don't understand—"

"Neither do we. And that's an understatement. And it's no use questioning Anders, in her condition."

"So why did you send for me?" Magda asked. But she was afraid she knew, and it made her angry. Although as far as Magda had ever known Cholayna had no *laran*, the woman seemed to sense her annoyance and hesitated; then, as Magda had known she would, she said it anyhow.

"You're a psi-technician, Magda. The nearest one we have, the only properly trained one this side of the Alpha colony. You can find out what really happened."

Magda was silent for a moment, staring angrily at Cholayna. She should have expected this. It was, she thought, her own fault for not breaking a tie that had ceased to have any meaning. As Cholayna had reminded her, she had tried to resign from Terran Intelligence, and Cholayna had dissuaded her; Magda, she said, was best qualified to build closer communications, ties, a bridge between the world of Magda's birth and the Darkovan world Magda had chosen for her own. Magda had wanted this too: the Bridge Society was living proof of her desire to strengthen that tie. Yet when Magda had left the Guild-house to become part of the only *laran* circle of trained psychics which worked its trained matrix circle outside the carefully surrounded, safeguarded precincts of a Tower, she should have known this problem would again become acute.

It was not that the Empire had no command of psi techniques. Not as common, nor as well developed as they were on Darkover. Few planets in the known universe had the displayed skill, the taken-for-granted potential of telepaths and other psi-sensitive talents which the Darkovans called *laran*. As far as was known, Darkover was unique in that respect.

But these talents, it was now known, were an ineradicable part of the human mind. Although there were still a few determined skeptics—and for some reason, determined skepticism was a self-fulfilling prophecy, so that skeptics rarely developed any psi skills of any kind—where there were humans, there were the psi skills which were part of the human mind. And so there were trained telepaths, though not many, and even a few mechanical psi-probes had been developed which could do much the same work.

"Only there are none on Darkover; none nearer than the Intelligence Academy on Alpha," said Cholayna, "and we've got to know what happened to her. Don't you understand, Magda? We've got to know!"

When Magda did not answer, she drew a long breath, loud in the room. "Listen, Magda, you know what this means as well as I do! You know there's nothing out there beyond the Hellers, nothing! So she signals she's spotted something out there, and then she goes down. Nothing on the satellite picture, no black box, no plane recorder—nothing. But if there's nothing out there, she's still gone down with her plane. We've lost planes from Map and Ex before this. We've lost pilots, too. But she didn't go down. Something out there grabbed her—*and then gave her back! In this condition!*"

Magda thought this over for a moment. She said at last, "It means there has to be something out there; something outside the Wall Around the World. But that's impossible." She had seen the weather-satellite pictures of Cottman Four. A cold planet, a planet tilted strongly on its axis by the presence of the high himals of the Hellers, the Wall Around the World, amounting to a "third pole." A planet inhabitable only in a relatively small part of one continent, and elsewhere a frozen wasteland with no signs of life.

"You're beginning to see what I mean," Cholayna said grimly. "And you're trained in what the Darkovans call *laran.*"

"I was a fool ever to let you know that!" Magda knew it was her own fault for retaining even this fragile bond. When she had outgrown the ties of the Guildhouse, she should have done what Andrew Carr had done before her, and allowed the Terrans, perhaps even the Renunciates, to think her dead.

In the Forbidden Tower, she had found a home, a world of others like herself, who belonged nowhere else in worlds that demanded they define themselves in narrow categories. Callista, Keeper, exiled from her Tower because she could give up neither her human love nor the exercise of the powerful *laran* for which she had nearly given her life. Andrew Carr, Terran, who had discovered his own powers and found a new world and a new life. Damon, exiled from a Tower, the only man who had had the courage to demand what no man had been allowed in centuries: he had become Keeper of the Tower they called Forbidden, and fought for the right to establish his Tower in the open. There were others who had come to it, outcasts from the regular Towers, or those who despite talent would never have been admitted to a Tower; and now, among them, herself and Jaelle.

And she had been foolish enough to let Cholayna know something—*anything,* of this. . . .

"You want me to psi-probe her, Cholayna? Why can't you get a technician out from Alpha? You could send a message and have one here in a tenday."

"No, Magda. If she stays like this, she could drop into catatonia and we'd never know. Besides, if there is something out there, we have to know it. *Now.* We can't send another plane up until we know what happened to that one.''

"There's nothing out there," Magda said, with more harshness than she intended. "Satellite pictures don't lie."

"That's what I've always said." Cholayna stared at the lighted panels on her desktop; when Magda said nothing, she got up and came around the desk and grabbed Magda's shoulders. "Damn it, something happened to her! I can understand the plane going down. I've never tried to fly over the Hellers myself, but I've talked to some who have. What scares me is how she got back here, and the condition she's in. If it could happen to Lexie, it could happen to anyone. Not a single person in Mapping and Exploring, or anywhere else outside the Trade City, is safe until we know what took her and her plane—and how, and why—*they*—sent her back. You've got to help us, Magda."

Magda walked away from Cholayna, and stared out at the lights of the Spaceport below. Up here, she could see the whole of Terran HQ, and across the city to the Old Town. The contrast was definite, the glaring lights of the Terran Trade City, the dim scattered lights of the Old Town, already all but dark at this hour. Somewhere in that darkness lay the Guild-house and her friends, while out beyond the pass that was just a blacker darkness against the night sky lay the estate of Armida, a little more than a day's ride north, where was her new world. If only she could consult with one of them, with their Keeper Damon, with Andrew, who like herself had fought the battle between his Terran self and his Darkovan world. But they were *there*, and she was *here*, and it was her own unique predicament and her own unanswerable problem.

"I'm the last person Lexie would want mucking around in her mind, believe me."

Cholayna said, and there was no possible answer, "She wouldn't want to stay like this forever, either. She's down in Medic, in Isolation. We haven't wanted anyone else to know what happened."

Some day, Magda thought, it was going to occur to the Terran HQ personnel that there were some things even they couldn't control. She didn't give a fundamental damn whether the Terrans kept up their pretense of omnipotence. But there was a fellow human being, a woman, caught up in the gears. She said, more roughly than she intended, "Let's get on with it, then. But I'm not a trained psi-technician, so don't blame me if all I can do is make things worse. I'll do my best. That's all I can say."

CHAPTER THREE

Magda hated to ring the night-bell at the Guild-house; it meant that someone would have to be roused, come down the stairs and open the bolted door. Yet she preferred that, inconvenient as it was, to accepting Cholayna's offer to find her a place to stay either in Unmarried Personnel Living Quarters, or even in the Bridge Society Hostel, where some of the Darkovan nurses in training had their lodgings.

She stood shivering on the steps, for even in high summer it was chilly at this hour, listening to the clang of the bell inside. Then she heard a long scraping of the heavy bolt, and at last the door opened grudgingly, and a young woman's voice asked, "Who is it? Do you want the midwife?"

"No, Cressa. It is I, Margali n'ha Ysabet," Magda said, and came inside. "I am truly sorry to disturb you. I'll just go quietly up to bed."

"It's all right, I wasn't asleep. Someone came for Keitha just a little while ago. Poor girl, she was out all day, and had just gotten to sleep, and a man came for her, his wife was expecting her first, so she'll be out all night, too. Someone suggested in House Meeting a few moons ago that the midwives should answer all the night bells, because most of the time, night calls were for them."

"That wouldn't really be fair," Magda said, "they deserve to sleep when they can, if only because they lose so much sleep already. I apologize again for waking you. Do you need help with the bolt?"

"Thank you, it really is too heavy for me."

Magda came and helped her to fasten the heavy lock. Cressa went off to the night doorkeeper's room, and Magda went slowly up the stairs to the room she had been given to share with Jaelle during this stay in the House. She paused at the door; then turned away, went to a nearby door and knocked softly. After a moment she heard a muffled response, turned the knob and went inside.

"Camilla," she whispered, "are you asleep?"

"Of course I am, could I talk to you if I were awake?" Camilla sat up in bed. "Margali? What is it?"

Without answering, Magda came and sat on the edge of the bed, where she slumped, letting her head fall wearily into her hands.

"What is it, *bredhiya*?" Camilla asked gently. "What did they ask of you this time?"

"I don't want to talk about it." Her sensitivity was so high—she had been using *laran* at such a level—that she could almost hear Camilla's thoughts as if the woman had spoken them aloud:

Oh yes, of course, it is because you do not want to talk that you come and wake me instead of quietly going to sleep in your own room!

But aloud, Camilla said only, "You missed dinner here; did they at least feed you in the Terran Zone?"

"It's my own fault. After all these years using *laran* I should have known enough to demand something to eat," Magda said, "but I wanted to get away, I couldn't wait to get away. Cholayna did offer—"

Camilla's eyebrows went up in the dark. "You were

using *laran* in the Terran HQ? And you don't want to talk about it. That does not sound like what I would expect of Cholayna n'ha Chandria.'' She slid out of bed and drew a heavy woolen wrapper over her warm nightgown, scuffed her long narrow feet into fur slippers. "Let's go down to the kitchen for something hot for you.''

"I'm not hungry," Magda said wearily.

"Nevertheless, if you have been using *laran*—you know you must eat and regain your strength—''

"What in all of Zandru's hells do you know about it?'' Magda snarled. Camilla shrugged.

"I know what all the world knows. I know what the little children in the marketplace know. I know *you*. Come downstairs; at least you can have some hot milk, after that long walk in the cold. Take your boots off, though, and put on your slippers.''

"Damnation, Camilla, don't fuss at me.''

Again the indifferent shrug. "If you want to sit in wet clothes all night, please yourself. I suppose one of the young nursing trainees would be delighted at the chance to nurse you through lung-fever. But it is hardly fair to go clumping around through the halls after midnight in heavy boots waking everyone who sleeps on the corridor because you're too lazy to pull them off. If you're simply too tired, I'll help you.''

Wearily, Magda roused herself to pull off her boots and soaked jacket. "I'll borrow one of your nightgowns; I don't want to wake Jaelle.'' Somehow she took off the wet clothes and got herself into a heavy gown of thick flannel.

"We'd better take these down and dry them; there will be a fire in the kitchen," Camilla said. Magda was too weary to argue; she put her wet clothes over her arm and followed Camilla.

She was still shivering as they went down the corridors and the silent stairs, but in the Guild-house kitchen, the fire was banked, and near the fireplace it was warm. A kettle of hot water was hissing softly on its crane; Camilla found mugs on a shelf while Magda raked up the fire and spread out her wet garments. Camilla poured Magda some bark-tea, then went into the pantry and cut cold meat and bread, laying them on the kitchen table next to the bowls of rolled grains and dried fruits, soaking for the breakfast porridge.

Magda sipped listlessly at the hot bitter tea, too tired to look for honey on the shelves. She did not touch the food, sitting motionless on the bench before the table. Camilla made herself some tea, but instead of drinking it, she came around behind Magda. Her strong hands kneaded the tight muscles in the younger woman's shoulders and neck; after a long time Magda reached out and took up a piece of the buttered bread.

"I'm not really hungry, but I suppose I should eat something," she said wearily, and put it to her lips.

After a bite or two, as Camilla had expected, the ravenous hunger of anyone who has been working with *laran* took over, and she ate and drank almost mechanically. She finished the bread and meat, and got up to ransack the pantry for some leftover cakes with spice and sugar.

When her hunger was satisfied, she leaned back, turning the bench round so that she could put her feet up on the rail that guarded the fireplace. Camilla came and sat beside her, putting up her own feet— long, narrow, somehow aristocratic—on the rail beside Magda's. They sat together, neither speaking, looking into the bed of coals. After a time, Magda got up restlessly and put more wood on the fire, causing flames to flare up so that flickering shadows played on the walls of the cavernous kitchen.

She said, at last, "I'm not really a psi-tech, not the way they think of it in the Terran Zone. I'm not a therapist. The work I do at Armida is—is different. What I had to do tonight was to go into someone's mind, someone who's normally head-blind, and try to—" She wet her lips with her tongue and said, "It's not easy to explain. There aren't words."

She looked around hesitantly at Camilla. She had known the woman at her side for years, and had long known that Camilla had, or had once had, *laran*, though Camilla herself denied it. Magda was one of the few people living who knew all of Camilla's story: born of Comyn blood—no trace of which was visible now except for the faded, sandy hair which had once flamed with the same Comyn red as Jaelle's—Camilla had been kidnapped when barely out of childhood, and so savagely raped and abused that her mind had broken. Magda did not know all of the details; only that for many years, Camilla had lived as a mercenary soldier, even her closest associates unaware that she was not the rough-spoken, rough living man she seemed. After some years of this, Camilla, wounded and near death, had revealed herself to a Renunciate: Kindra, Jaelle's own foster-mother. She had found herself able, in the Guild of Free Amazons, to take up again, painfully and with great self-doubt, the womanhood she had tried so long and so hard to renounce or conceal.

Once or twice, when their barriers were down to one another, Magda had become certain that Camilla retained some of her family's heritage of *laran*, whatever that family might be. She was sure that Camilla bore the blood of one of the Seven Domains, the great

families of Darkover, even though she concealed her
laran.

It was not impossible that Camilla knew, without
being told, how difficult the thing was that the Terrans
had asked her to do.

"Do you remember meeting Lexie Anders at the
special orientation meeting they gave for the new women
working in the Terran Zone?"

"I do. She was very scornful of the notion that the
Penta Cori'yo had anything to offer Terran women.
Even when the other women in the Bridge Society
pointed out that, after all, Terran women could hardly
go to the Spaceport bars for recreation in the City, and
that this would give her friends and associates, and a
place to go when she could not stand being cooped up
in the HQ anymore—"

"And I know, if Lexie doesn't, that that's one reason
women employees haven't been very fortunate on
Darkover, unless they were brought up here and feel
comfortable with the language and the way women are
expected to behave," Magda said. "I remember how
rude and casual Lexie was at the reception. She made
us all feel like—well, like natives, crude aboriginals;
that we should all have been wearing skin loincloths
and bones in our hair."

"And you had to go into *her* mind? Poor Margali,"
said Camilla, "I do not imagine her mind is a pleasant
place to be. Not even, I should imagine, for her. As for
you—"

"It wasn't only that," Magda said. Briefly, she repeated to Camilla what Cholayna had told her about the
lost plane, and about Lexie's mysterious reappearance.
"—So I told her, I'm not a trained psi-tech, and don't
blame me if I make things worse," she said, "and then

we went down to Isolation, in Medic, where they had been keeping her.''

Magda had not remembered that Lexie Anders was such a little woman. She was loud-voiced and definite, with such an assertive stance and manner that it was shocking to see her lying flat against her cot, pale and scrubbed like a sick child. Her hair was fair, cut short and curly; her face looked almost bruised, the blue veins showing through the skin. More distressing than this was the emptiness in her face; Magda felt that even Lexie's aggressive rudeness was preferable to this passive, childish pliancy.

Magda had learned a little of the dialect of Vainwal during her years in training on Planet Alpha, in the Intelligence Academy. "How are you feeling, Lieutenant Anders?''

"My name's Lexie. I don't know why they're keeping me here, I'm not sick,'' Lexie said, in a childish, complaining tone. "Are you going to stick more needles in me?''

"No, I promise I won't stick you with any needles.'' Magda lifted a questioning eyebrow at Cholayna, who said in an undertone, "The Medics tried pentothal; they thought if this was simply emotional shock, it might help her to relive it and talk about it. No result.''

Magda thought about that for a moment. If Lexie Anders had been, at one moment, in a plane about to crash in the frozen wastelands surrounding the Wall Around the World, and in the next moment, was outside the Spaceport gates of Thendara HQ, the emotional shock alone could have reduced her to this condition.

"Do you know where you are, Lexie?''

"Hospital. They told me,'' she said, laying her curly head down tiredly on the pillow. "I don't feel sick at all. Why am I in a hospital? Are you a doctor? You don't look like a doctor, not in those clothes.''

"Then—you don't remember anything that happened?" Magda had once watched Lady Callista deal with a case of shock: a man who had seen four members of his family killed in a freak flood. "Can you tell me the last thing you remember?"

" 'Member—a kitten," said Lexie with a childish grin. "It ran away."

"You don't remember the plane?"

"Plane? My dad flies a plane," she said. "I want to fly one when I grow up. My cousin says girls don't fly planes, but Dada says it's all right, some girls fly planes, they even pilot starships.''

"Certainly they do." Magda remembered a brief ambition of her own (about the time she found out the difference between her parents and the parents of the Darkovan children around her, with whom she had grown up) to be a starship pilot. She supposed most tomboy girls had similar ambitions, and briefly it created a bond of sympathy.

"Lexie, suppose I were to tell you that you have forgotten many things; that you are all grown up, and that you did fly a plane; that you are here because your plane crashed. Will you think about that, please? What would you say to that?"

Lexie did not even stop to think. Her small face was already crinkled up in a jeering laugh. "I'd say you were crazy. Crazy woman, what are you doing in a hospital, trying to act like a doctor? Is it a crazy hospital?"

Magda's brief moment of liking and sympathy for Lexie evaporated. An unpleasant child, she thought, who grew up into an even more unpleasant woman. . . .

Yet she remembered what Callista, training her in the arts of matrix work, had said about this kind of thing:

They abuse us because they are afraid of us. If anyone is rude and unpleasant when you are trying to help them, it is out of fear, because they are afraid of what you will try and make them see or understand. No matter how deeply their reason is hidden, something in them knows and understands, and fears leaving the protection of shock.

(In the Guild-house, before the fire, hours later, Magda again recalled and repeated these words, so deeply absorbed in her own memories that she did not see Camilla's facial muscles tauten, nor the tense nod with which she acquiesced. There were many things Camilla could not, or chose not to remember, of her own ordeal.)

Magda ignored Lexie's rudeness. From around her neck, she took her matrix stone, carefully unwrapping the layers of shielding. She rolled the blue stone, hidden fires flashing from its depth, out into her palm. Lexie's eyes followed the moving colors in the jewel.

"Pretty," she said in her babytalk voice. "Can I see it?"

"In a minute, perhaps. But you must not touch it, or you might be hurt." For an out-of-phase person, particularly a nontelepath, to touch a keyed matrix could produce a serious and painful shock; worse, it could throw the operator of the matrix, keyed to the stone, into shock that could be fatal. She held the psi-sensitive crystal away from Lexie's childishly grasping fingers and said, "Look into the stone, Lexie."

Lexie twisted her face away. "Makes my head ache."

That was normal enough. Few untrained persons could endure to look into a keyed matrix, and Lexie's psi potential was evidently very slight. Magda realized she should at least have asked for a look at Personnel Records on Lieutenant Alexis Anders, to know her determined level of psi ability. They did test Terrans for such things now. It would have been useful to know.

But they had not, and there was no way to do it now. She held the matrix before Lexie's eyes. "I want you to look into the stone, so that we can see what is the matter with you, and why you are in the hospital here." Magda spoke deliberately, her voice friendly but firm. Lexie pouted like a child, but under Magda's commanding voice and posture, finally fixed her eyes on the shifting colors of the stone.

Magda watched until her face relaxed. She was not sure how an ordinary psi-tech would handle this, but for the best part of seven years she had been intensively trained in the uses of a matrix. The words of the Monitor's Oath, demanded of any telepath soon after being entrusted with a matrix, briefly resonated in her mind: *Enter no mind save to help or heal, and never for power over any being.*

Then she made contact, briefly, with Lexie Anders's mind.

On the surface, it was a jumble, a confused child not knowing what had happened. On a deeper level, something shivered and quaked, not wanting to know. Gently Magda touched the child-mind (a hand confidingly tucked into hers, as a little girl holds the hand of an older sister; she let the warmth linger for a moment, wanting Lexie to trust her).

Who are you? It's scary, I can't remember.

I'm your friend, Lexie. I won't let anyone hurt you. You're a big girl now. You wanted to fly a plane, remember? Let's go, let's find the plane. The first time your hands touched the controls. Look at the plane. The controls are under your hands. Where are you, Lexie?

The young woman's hands curved reminiscently as if over the controls she had mastered. . . .

Abruptly the childish plaintive voice lisping the dialect of Vainwal changed; became crisp, accurate, Terran Standard spoken with the precision of those to whom it was an acquired second language.

"Anders, Alexis, Cadet Recruit, reporting as ordered, Ma'am."

It was no use to try to bring her along with verbal commands. Simple hypnotic suggestion would have brought a less traumatized subject to present time; but Magda had already seen how Lexie's conscious intellect and even the unconscious mind refused the level of mere suggestion. With the matrix, Magda could bypass that resistance. Again she slipped into the younger woman's mind, seeking the child who had walked with her hand in hand, trustingly.

Lieutenant Anders. When did you get your promotion?

A tenday after I was moved to Cottman Four. I decided to move over to Mapping and Exploring.

Magda was prepared to ask, directly in Lexie's mind, why the younger woman had made the transfer application. Surely Cholayna had done her, Magda, a monstrous injustice when she had spoken of the Lorne legend and the inability of Lexie to compete with the more famous older woman. But she stopped herself. Was this truly relevant to Lexie's problem, or was she, Magda, simply indulging a desire to explain and justify herself? Gently she re-established the rapport; but the childish acceptance was gone. She regretted it, regretted the image of the little sister walking beside her, hand in hand.

Tell me about your work in Mapping and Exploring, Lieutenant. Do you like your work?

Yes. I love it. I can work alone and nobody bothers me. I didn't like it in Intelligence. There were too many women. I don't like women. I don't trust them. Always ready to stab you in the back. You can trust a plane. Does what you tell it to, and if anything goes wrong it's your own damn fault. Her face was almost animated.

Slowly, carefully, Magda insinuated herself into Lexie's memory. This was not ordinary amnesia, where selectively the mind chooses to reject an intolerable burden. It was total rejection. Magda's mind intertwined with Lexie's; she had never held the controls of a plane, large or small, but now her hands covered Lexie's and she shared the full-round vision to all points of the compass, the frozen mountains spread below, the precise definiteness of every motion and idea. She was moving farther north, she was about to set a record if the damned plane would cooperate. Her skill was such that the maddening surges of crosswinds and updrafts only bounced her a little where any other pilot would have been battered. Then—

Lexie Anders screamed and sat bolt upright in bed. Magda, knocked out of the rapport, stood staring, her eyes wide.

"I crashed," Lexie said, in her most precise Terran Standard. "The last thing I remember was going down. And then I was here, at the HQ gates. Hellfire, Lorne, are you involved in Medic too? Isn't there any pie on this whole planet you don't have your fingers into?"

"So what did you tell them?" Camilla asked at last.

"I didn't have any reasonable explanation," Magda said. "I grasped at the usual straws. I told Cholayna that it was just possible that when the plane went down, Anders developed a sudden surge of previously unguessed-at psi-potential, and teleported herself back here. It's not at all unheard-of, under life-and-death threat like that, to find someone doing something they'd never have believed a remote possibility. I did something like that once, myself—not physically but mentally."

She and Jaelle, in a cave on a hillside, with Jaelle desperately ill, after miscarrying Peter Haldane's child. Escape had seemed impossible. Somehow, she never knew how, she had reached out and touched rescue—had called for help and had, somehow, been answered.

"That kind of thing doesn't show up in test labs because you can't fool the subconscious mind; hypnosis, or what-have-you, may make their conscious mind think they're in danger, but down underneath, they know perfectly well there's no real threat." She sighed, thinking of how, for a brief time, she had actually liked the child Lexie had been.

"But you don't believe that explanation," Camilla said.

"Camilla, I knew it was a lie when I said it."

"But why should you lie? What had really happened to Lexie Anders?"

Before she answered, Magda reached for Camilla's hand. She said, "My fourth night in this house, my very first Training Session as a Renunciate, do you remember? That same night there was a meeting of a society called the Sisterhood. Do you remember that I lost track of what you asked me, and you scolded and bullied me for not paying attention to what was going on?"

"Not particularly," Camilla said. "Why? And what has the Sisterhood to do with Lexie Anders?" She reached across the bench and picked up her cold tea, sipping at it.

Magda said, "Let me make you a fresh cup," took

both mugs, and poured the tea. She went to refill the kettle.

At last, knowing she was delaying, she said, "During that meeting, I saw—something. I didn't know then what to call it, I thought it was a—a thought-form of the Goddess Avarra. Of course, at the time, I thought I was hallucinating, that it wasn't really there."

Camilla said, "I have seen it too, during meetings of the Sisterhood. You know that the Renunciates were formed from two societies: the Sisterhood of the Sword, who were a soldier-caste, and the priestesses of Avarra, who were healers. I believe the Sisterhood invokes Avarra in their meetings. Again—what have their religious practices to do with Lexie Anders?"

Magda stood braced against the table, leaning on her fists. Her face was drawn and distant, remembering. She said, and it was no more than a whisper of horror, "Twice more, I saw—something. Not the Goddess Avarra. Robed figures. A whisper of—of a sound like crows calling. Once I asked: *Who are you?*"

Camilla asked, her voice dropping in response to the frozen dread in Magda's, "Did they—was there any answer?"

"None that made any sense to me. I seemed to hear—not quite to hear, to *sense*—the words, *The Dark Sisterhood*. Something—" Magda wrinkled up her face, tensely; it was tenuous, like trying to remember a dream in daylight. "Only that they were guardians of some sort, but couldn't interfere. And just as I was about to reach the point where Lexie relived and remembered the crash, I saw that. Again."

Her throat closed, her voice was reduced to a thready whisper. "Walls. A city. Robed figures. Then the sound of crows calling. And nothing. After that—nothing."

CHAPTER FOUR

Camilla turned away and banked the fire. She felt carefully about the legs of Magda's breeches to see if they were dry.

"Leave them for a few minutes more," she said.

"Camilla! You know something of the Sisterhood; what are they?"

Camilla was still fussing with the half-dried clothing.

"If I knew," she said, "I would be like Marisela—sworn to secrecy. Why do you think those people don't make it, whatever it is that they know, part of the regular Training sessions? Secrets, bah! Once Marisela tried to get me to join them. When I would not, she was very annoyed with me. Weren't you angry when Lexie refused to join the *Penta Cori'yo*?

That was different, Magda thought, even though she could not define how. She was not accustomed to defending herself against Camilla, not anymore.

"You don't like Marisela?"

"Certainly I like her. But I refused to make her the keeper of my conscience and of course she has never forgiven me for that. But when first she insisted I should join them, she did tell me something of the original purposes of the Sisterhood. Most of it is what you would expect from the Oath, the usual business about women as sisters, *Men dia pre' zhiuro, sister and mother and daughter to all women*—but there is more; it is to give teaching in *laran* to those who were not born Comyn and thus are not eligible for training in the ordinary Towers. She even tried to frighten me— threatened me with all kinds of dreadful consequences if I was not willing to swallow her kind of medicine for my ills.''

"That does not sound like Marisela," Magda said.

"Oh, believe me, she did not say it in those words. She didn't bully me, or say do what I suggest or you will have to suffer all kinds of things—no, it was more a matter of being afraid for me. More a matter of—*Let me help you, you poor thing, or you cannot imagine how dreadful it will be.* You know the kind of thing I mean." Magda heard the unspoken part of that, *and you know how much I would hate that kind of thing,* just as clearly as she had heard what Camilla had said aloud. She knew Camilla trusted her enough not to take advantage, or she would never have allowed that.

"Among other things, Marisela tried to tell me that an untrained telepath is a danger to herself and to everyone around her." Camilla's scornful look showed what she thought of that.

But that is perfectly true, Magda thought, remembering her own training. And the attempt to block her own *laran* had all but destroyed Jaelle. If Camilla had done so unharmed, it would have taken such iron control, such perfect self-discipline—

But Camilla *did* have both iron control and perfect self-discipline; she had had to have them, or she could never have survived what had happened to her. And if she had the strength to survive all that—not unscarred, but simply to survive—then she had the control and discipline for that too. But Magda was not surprised that Marisela did not believe it.

"At that time—after I was—changed, and recovered," Camilla said, almost inaudibly, "Leonie offered me this. She said something of the same sort—that I had been born into the caste with *laran* and therefore could not survive without that teaching. I honor Leonie—she was kind to me when I greatly needed that kindness. She saved more than my life; she saved my reason. For all that, I would have been more comfortable with the bandits who so misused me; at least, when they violated me, they didn't pretend they were doing it for my own good."

Magda did not say a word. Only twice in the years they had known each other had Camilla referred to the trauma of her girlhood, which had made her what she was; Magda had some idea what it had cost Camilla to say this much, even to her. Abruptly, Camilla jerked the drying tunic and undervest off the rack and began vigorously to fold them.

"Like Jaelle, I was asked to join the Sisterhood. And like Jaelle, I refused. I have no love for secret societies and sisterhoods, and what I know, I reserve the right to tell as I choose, to whomever I choose. I think most of what they believe they know is superstition and nonsense." She pursed her mouth and looked grim.

"Then how do you explain what happened to me, Camilla? Out there in the Kilghard Hills, in that cave. I know what happened, because it happened to me. We were marooned. Jaelle was dying. We would both have died there in that cave in the hills—I cried out for help. And I—I was answered. Answered, I tell you!"

"You have *laran*," Camilla said, "and I suppose the Terran from the Forbidden Tower—what is his name, Andrew Carr? I suppose this Andrew Carr heard you and answered."

"Ann'dra." Magda deliberately used Carr's Darkovan

name. "Yes, he has *laran*. But what prompted him to go looking for me in the first place? For all he knew, I was in Thendara, snug in the Guild-house as a bug in a saddlebag. Instead he sent out a search party for us and found us in time to save Jaelle's life."

"Ferrika," said Camilla. "She is a member of the Sisterhood. And so is Marisela. Marisela knew you had gone, and knew the state Jaelle was in. And Ferrika is midwife at Armida—"

"She is more than that," Magda said. "She is a full member of the Tower Circle."

Camilla looked skeptical, and Magda insisted, "She is, I tell you, as much as I am myself."

Camilla shrugged. "Then, there is your answer."

"And the vision I had? Robed women—crows calling—"

"You said it yourself. You were desperate. You believed Jaelle was dying. Desperate people see visions. I don't believe there was anything supernatural about your answer at all."

"You don't believe that a—a cry for help of that kind can be answered?"

"No, I don't."

"Why not?"

Camilla's lips were set in a hard line. "Don't you suppose that I—prayed? I cried out for help with all my strength. Not only for human help, I cried out to all the Gods and to any supernatural forces that might have been hanging around to help me. If they could have heard you, where were they when I cried out to heaven, or even hell, for help? If they heard you, why did they not hear me? And if they heard me, and did not answer—what sort of Gods or helpers were they?"

Magda flinched before the unanswerable bitterness of that.

Camilla went on, without interruption, "You had a vision, *bredhiya*." She used the word, which meant originally *sister*, in the intimate inflection which could make it mean *darling* or *beloved*, and was used only in close family intimacy or to a sworn lover.

"You had a vision, a dream; it was your Ann'dra who heard you. Or perhaps, Marisela, who sent word to Ferrika that a sister was in peril."

Since that was certainly possible, and was in any case more rational than her own belief, Magda did not try further to convince her. Camilla's face relaxed a little; she went on.

"The Sisterhood, I have heard, was designed to do for women what the *cristoforo* brethren at Nevarsin do for men. But unlike the Nevarsin brotherhood or the Comyn, the Sisterhood—so I am told—do not exact piety nor conformity in return for their instruction. There is an old tale, a fable if you will, but some of the Comyn believe it, that the *laran* of the Seven Domains is because they are the descendants of Gods." Camilla's scornfully arched eyebrows told Magda what the *emmasca* thought of that. "It did not suit them that the common folk should have this gift, or believe they have it, or be trained to use it if, as sometimes happens, they have it though they were born outside the sacred caste. I do not know what will happen to the Comyn when they fully get it through their minds that *laran* appears even in Terrans like your Andrew Carr. To do them credit, if it is brought to the attention of Comyn that a commoner possesses *laran*, they will sometimes have him trained— usually in one of the lesser Towers like Neskaya. I don't doubt at all that your Andrew could—"

"You keep calling him *my* Andrew. He isn't, Camilla."

Camilla shrugged. She said, "Do you want more tea? This is cold." And indeed, despite the fire on the hearth, a thin skin of ice had begun to form on Magda's tea. "Or would you rather go up and sleep?"

"I am not sleepy." Magda shivered; the memory of what she had seen in Lexie's mind was still alive in her, and she wondered how she would ever manage to sleep. She got up and poured boiling water into her mug; tilted the spout toward Camilla. The older woman shook her head.

"If I drink any more, I will never sleep! Nor will you."

"Why should I sleep? I had hoped to be away at daybreak, and now I cannot. Cholayna has asked me to stay until this is resolved."

"And of course you must do as Cholayna commands?"

"She is my friend. I would stay if you asked me; why not for her? But I would like to get back to my child."

"A few more days will not weaken the bond, *bredhiya*." Camilla's face relaxed and she smiled. "I would like to see her—your daughter."

"The journey to Armida is not so long as all that, and for all your talk of being old, Camilla, I know perfectly well that you could be off tomorrow to the Dry-Towns, or to Dalereuth, or the Wall Around the World itself, if you had some reason! Why not ride back with me when I go, and see my little Shaya?"

Camilla smiled. "I? Among those *leronyn*?"

"They are my friends and my family, Camilla. They would welcome you if only as my friend."

"One day, then, perhaps. Not this time, I think. Shaya—we called Jaelle so, as a child. So she is Jaelle's namesake? What does she look like? Is she like you, your daughter?"

"Her hair curls like mine, but not so dark; her eyes are like mine, but Ferrika thinks they will darken as she grows older. To me, she has a look of my father: I know she has his hands. Strange, is it not? We renounce our fathers when we swear the Oath, yet we cannot wholly renounce them; they reappear in the faces of our children.''

"Perhaps it is as well I had no daughter. I would not have cared to see in her the face of the man who renounced me before ever I renounced him! Your father, though, seems to have been a remarkable man, and I dare say you have no reason to resent the likeness. But what of *her* father? I had assumed, of course, it was the same Lord Damon Ridenow who fathered Jaelle's child— Comyn lords are encouraged to breed sons and daughters everywhere, as my own real father did. It's odd that although my mother was with child by a man far above her own station and was then married off in consequence to a man far below it, still both of them were too proud to accept that I might be pregnant with the child of one of the rogues who—well, enough of that. But as I was saying—it seemed reasonable to me that it would be Lord Damon who fathered your child, as he did Jaelle's.''

Magda laughed. "Oh, Damon is not like that. Believe me, he is not. Jaelle chose him for her child's father, but it was *her* choice. Damon is very dear to me, but he is not my lover.''

"That Terran then? Your Andrew Carr, Lord Ann'dra? He is of your own people. I could understand that— well, as much as I could ever understand desire for a man.''

"At least you do not condemn it, as do so many women of the Guild, as treason to the Oath.''

Camilla chuckled. "No, I lived for years among men, as one of them, and I know that men are very like women—only not, perhaps, so free to be what they are.

It's a pity there's no Guild-house for them. Jaelle has talked to me, a little, about Damon. But *is* it this Andrew, then?''

"I love Andrew," Magda said, "almost as much as I love Lady Callista. When first I decided that I wanted a child, we talked of it, all three of us.''

She knew she could never have explained to Camilla what the bond was like within the Tower. It was nothing like any other bond she had ever known. In many ways she felt closer to Camilla than to any other human being; she wished that she could share this with her, too. But how could she make Camilla understand? Camilla, who had chosen to block away her *laran* and live forever as one of the head-blind. It hurt to feel Camilla's mind closed to her.

The bond of the Forbidden Tower had reached out to take her in; she had become a part, mind and body and heart, of the Tower circle there. Until Jaelle's child was born, she had not really known how much she wanted a child of her own. They had grown so close, all of them, that for a time it had seemed natural that she too should have Damon's child, so that her child and Jaelle's might be truly sisters. Yet even more than with Damon, she shared a close bond with Andrew Carr: like herself, Andrew had found that the world of the Terrans could not hold him.

"In the end, though," Magda said, "Andrew and I decided not. It was really Andrew's choice, not mine. He felt that he would not want to father a child that he could not rear as his own, and I would not give up that privilege to him. I chose my child's father because, though we felt kindness toward one another, he was someone from whom I felt I could part again without too much grief." She was silent, her eyes faraway, and Camilla wondered what she was thinking.

"I will tell you his name, if you ask me, *bredhiya*. He has his own household, and sons of his own; but he promised, if I bore a son and could not care for him, that he would foster him and give him such a start in life as he could. If I had a daughter, he swore he would make no claim on her. His wife was willing—I would not do such a thing without his wife's consent."

"I am curious about this paragon," Camilla said, "but you are welcome to your secrets, my dear." She rose again and felt the legs of Magda's breeches. "Cover the fire. It is time, and past, that we were in bed. Even if you need not ride at daybreak, there are things I must do tomorrow." She put her arm around Magda as they went silently up the stairs; and not until she was on the very edge of sleep did Magda realize that Camilla had really said nothing about the Sisterhood, after all.

A day or two later, she found Marisela, the Guild-house's senior midwife, enjoying a rare moment of solitude in the music room, idly strumming a *rryl*. But when Magda apologized for her intrusion and would have gone away again, Marisela set down the small lap-harp, and said, "Please don't go. I haven't really anything to do with myself, and I was only killing time pretending I could play. Do sit down and talk to me. We never see each other these days."

Magda sat down and watched as Marisela put the instrument into its case.

"Remind me to tell Rafaella that a string has broken; I took it off, but could not replace it. Well, Margali, do you just want to chat, or do you want to ask me something?"

Magda asked, "Do you remember when I was first in the house, during my housebound time? In my first Training Session, I saw a vision of the Goddess Avarra.

I know it came from the Sisterhood. And now again I have encountered—Marisela, will you tell me something about the Sisterhood?''

Marisela fiddled with the clasps on the instrument case.

''There was a time,'' she said after a moment, ''when I felt you were ready for the Sisterhood, and would willingly have had you among us. But when you left the Guild-house, you went elsewhere for the training of your *laran*. For that reason, I do not feel free to discuss the secrets of the Sisterhood with you. I can tell you nothing, my dear. I am sure you are as well among the Forbidden Tower as with us, and if there was ever a time when I resented your choice, it was long ago. But I am sorry. I may not talk of this to an outsider.''

Magda felt a sense of total frustration. She said, ''If these people who call themselves the Dark Sisterhood reached out to me, how can you say I am an outsider? If they spoke to me—''

''If they did,'' repeated Marisela. ''Oh, no, my dear, I am sure you are not lying, but when this happened, you were under great stress. This much I can say: the Sisterhood are those who serve Avarra; we on the plane which we call physical life, and they, the Dark Ones, on the plane of existence known as the overworld. I suppose—in such extremity—if you have the talent of reaching out into it, they might hear you from the overworld and relay a message. You are strongly gifted with *laran*; you may have reached Those Who Hear, and they may have answered you from where they dwell.'' Deliberately, she changed the subject.

''But now, tell me what you have been doing with yourself these last few years. I haven't really had a chance to talk with you since your daughter was born. Is she well and thriving? Was she a big, strong baby?

You told Doria that she was weaned—how long did you
feed her yourself?''

"Something less than a year," Magda replied, not
really sorry to abandon the frustrating topic, and perfectly willing to satisfy the midwife's professional interest.
"When she began to cut her teeth, I was quite ready
and glad to say to her, if you are big enough to bite,
you are big enough to bite bread!''

With an unexpected pang of homesickness she missed
her daughter, the small wriggling body in her arms,
snuggled sleepily in her lap, struggling to escape being
combed or dressed, scampering naked from the bath . . .
"She is very strong and seems to me very intelligent
and quick, very independent for two years old. She
actually tries to put on her own clothes. Of course she
can't yet; gets stuck with her tunic over her head and
yells for her nurse to come and get her loose. But she
tries! She says *Mama*, but she doesn't always mean me,
she says it to Jaelle, to Ellemir—''

"I have never met the Lady Ellemir, but Ferrika and
Jaelle have spoken of her. I always thought you would
have no trouble in bearing children. Did you have a
difficult time?''

"I had nothing to compare it with. I thought it hard,''
Magda said, "but not nearly as bad as it was for
Jaelle.''

"I have never had a chance to ask Jaelle about it.
Was it difficult for her? I expected that if she had one
child, she would want another.''

"She did; but Ferrika advised against it. Cleindori is
thriving; she was five last Spring Festival.''

"What a very peculiar name for a child, to name her
after the *kireseth* flower!''

"Her name is Dorilys; it is a family name among the
Ardais, I understand, and Lady Rohana was Jaelle's

foster-mother. But she is golden-haired, and her nurse dresses her always in blue, so that Ferrika said one day, she looks like a bell of the flower all covered in golden pollen. She is so pretty no one can deny her anything, so of course she's dreadfully spoiled; but she has such a sweet disposition, it seems to have done her no harm. She is very quick and clever, too, already the other girls pet and spoil her, and the boys all treat her as a little queen.''

"And I dare say you do homage, too," Marisela said, laughing, and Magda admitted it.

"Oh, she has always been my special darling. When Shaya was born, I expected Cleindori to be jealous, but she isn't. She insists that this is her very own little sister, and wants to share everything with her. When Shaya was only two months old we found her trying to dress the baby up in her own best Holiday tunic, and I have forgotten how many times we had to remind her that it was very nice to be generous, but that Shaya could not eat spice-bread or nut-cake till she had her teeth!''

"Better that the natural rivalry should take that form, than jealousy," remarked Marisela. "She has decided to rival you as mother, instead of Shaya as baby.'' It was not the first time Magda had been surprised at the woman's psychological insight. It had been a salutary lesson for Magda, who had thought for a long time that a non-technological culture would have no advanced psychological knowledge. But of course, if Marisela belonged to the Sisterhood, whose special province was to train the *laran* and psi skills of those outside the normal system of the Towers, it was not at all surprising. Magda's own awareness of mental processes had increased a thousandfold when she began to explore her *laran*.

"And the father," Marisela asked, "did he follow custom and stay with you for the birth?"

"He would have done, if I had asked him," Magda said, "but since he agreed to make no claim, it was Jaelle I asked to be with me; Jaelle, and Lady Callista." She had never told anyone—although Marisela would certainly have understood—that in the profound helplessness and power of birth, it had somehow been Camilla she had wanted with her. She would never tell that to anyone, not even to Camilla. Instead, she changed the subject.

"But tell me now what our sister Keitha is doing. I understand she studied midwifery both at Arilinn and with the Terrans—"

"And she will go next month to Neskaya, to teach the midwives the new skills she learned from the Terrans; and after that, to Nevarsin, to establish a Guild-house of midwives in that city. The *cristoforo* brethren do not like it, but there is nothing they can do. They can hardly say that they wish women to die in childbirth when they can be saved, can they?"

Magda agreed that they could not, although they might like to; but the choice of subject was an unfortunate one, as it reminded her of what Camilla had said of the Sisterhood: that they had been formed to do for women, in the darkest years of the Ages of Chaos, what the *cristoforo* brethren had done for men—to keep a little learning alive despite Chaos and ignorance. And it also reminded her that Marisela had refused to tell what she knew.

CHAPTER FIVE

"There's no reason you should have to stay here," Magda said. "This is my problem, and Cholayna doesn't need you. You could go back to Armida and to the children."

Jaelle shook her head. "No, *breda*. As long as you have to stay, do you think I would leave you here alone?"

"It's not as if I were exactly alone," Magda pointed out to her. "I have Cholayna, and everybody in Bridge if I need them, not to mention a whole Guild-house full of our sisters. I'd really feel better about it if I knew you were with the children, Shaya."

Jaelle n'ha Melora laughed. "Margali, of all the arguments you might have given me, that is the one least likely to make any impression! How much time do I spend with either of the children? I should be there to give her an admiring hug at bedtime? As long as Ellemir is there, and her nurse, and Ferrika—with a whole houseful of nurses and nannies, with Ellemir to supervise them and Andrew to spoil them, I doubt if they know we are gone."

This was true, more or less, and Magda knew it. If anything, Jaelle was far less domestic, and less interested in little children, than was Magda herself. Jaelle loved Cleindori—as who did not?—but since the little girl had been weaned, spent little time in her daughter's company.

She thought again, as she had thought before, that Jaelle had really changed very little since they had met: a small, slight woman with hair only slightly faded from its early tint of new-minted copper; she had the fragile look of many Comyn—Damon had it, and Callista—but Magda knew it was deceptive, and concealed the delicate strength of ancient forged steel.

In many ways, Jaelle is the strongest of us all. They say the Aillard women have always been the best Keepers; perhaps the post of Keeper was designed for their kind of strength. But Jaelle's strength was not *laran.* Perhaps they did not yet know what her true strength would be.

We are both at the age, Magda thought, *at which a woman should have decided what she wants to do with her life. I have outgrown first love, first marriage, early ideals. I have a child, and have recovered my strength and health. I have work I love. I have made some decisions—I know many of the things I do not want to do with my life. I have developed my* laran *and I know that my love and my strongest emotions are given to women. But I am not yet really sure what it is given to me to do with my life.* And this disturbed her so much that she had no heart to argue with Jaelle.

"Stay if you wish. But I can't imagine wanting to stay in the City when you could be out in the country, at Armida."

Jaelle looked up toward the skyline, where the Venza Mountains overshadowed the pass that led down into the city. "You feel it too? I would like to be out again on the trail. I have done my duty to clan and family, and when Dori is only a little older, I shall send her to be fostered as a daughter of Aillard. And then—oh,

Magda, aren't you eager to be in the field again, traveling in the mountains? Rafaella wants me to come back
to work with her; she's talking about some new special
project for the Terrans, but won't tell me any details
until I promise I'll join her. It would be hard to leave
the Tower, and I would miss it, but—couldn't I take a
year away, just to travel again? It's been so long! I
never spent so long in one place in my whole life as I
have spent at Armida! Five years, Magda!''

Magda smiled indulgently. "I'm sure they would
give you leave to spend a year in the mountains if you
wished."

"I heard the other day that there is an expedition
going to climb High Kimbi. It's never been climbed—"

"And probably never will be," Magda said. "Not by
either of us, in any case. You know as well as I do they
wouldn't have women along, not even as guides. If
there are still men who think women unfit to be part of
anything facing danger or demanding courage, they are
the men who go out climbing mountains."

Jaelle snorted. "I led a trade caravan over the Pass of
Scaravel when I was not yet eighteen!"

"*Breda*, I know what you can do on the trail. And
Rafaella is listed in Intelligence Services as the best
mountain guide in the business! But there are still men
who won't use women guides. The more fools they."

Jaelle shrugged philosophically. "I guess if we want
to climb High Kimbi, or Dammerung Peak, we'll have
to organize our own expedition."

Magda laughed. "Forget the *we* part, Jaelle. *You*
would have to do it. That one trip across Scaravel was
enough to last me a lifetime." Even remembering, she
shivered at the thought of the cliffs and chasms of the
Pass of Scaravel.

"Talk to Camilla. She'd probably be delighted to go out and climb anything inaccessible you can find."

"And knowing you, you'll be right beside her." Jaelle laughed. "You talk about being timid, but when you're actually in the field—I know you better than you know yourself."

"Whether or no," Magda said, "for the moment we are in Thendara, and here we will stay, for the next few days, at least."

"We should relay a message to Armida, though. They'll be expecting us," Jaelle reminded her. "They should be told that we are all right—not murdered by bandits on the trail, or something of that sort."

"No," Magda said morosely, "only murdered here in Thendara, by bureaucratic nonsense! Shall we get in touch with them tonight?"

"You do it, Magda, you're a far better telepath than I am."

"But they will want to hear from us both," Magda said, and Jaelle nodded soberly.

"Tonight, then, when it's quiet."

But that night there was an Oath-taking in the house. Although neither the new Renunciate nor her Oath-sisters were known to Magda or Jaelle, they could not in decency absent themselves from such festivities in their own house. Afterward there was a party with cakes and wine; Magda, knowing what lay ahead of her, drank sparingly. She spent most of the evening with Camilla and Mother Lauria, and found herself agreeing how very young the new Renunciates appeared. It seemed that the woman who had taken the Oath tonight, and her friends who had witnessed the Oath, were just children. Had she and Jaelle ever been as young as that? Apart from the Oath-mother, an older woman was always chosen to witness the ceremony, and it seemed incredible to see Doria, whom Magda remembered as a girl of fifteen sharing her own housebound time, described as an older woman.

Rafaella was there, and spent much of the latter part of the evening talking with Jaelle; Magda did not begrudge Jaelle the company of her old friend and partner, but, watching Rafi drinking heavily of the pale wine from the mountain vineyards, she hoped Jaelle would not be led into drinking. It was late before they could get away to the room they shared—but that was just as well. The atmosphere was quieter at night, with most people sleeping; much matrix work, in the Towers and outside them, was done between sunset and sunrise.

"What was Rafi talking about?"

"Some new project from Mapping and Exploring—a survey in the mountains. She wanted me to promise I'd come." Jaelle looked regretful as she pulled off her low indoor boots and untied the laces of her tunic. Magda sat on the bed to remove her own.

"Did you promise?"

"How could I? I told her I would have to consult you, and also the folk in the Tower. I do not think she knows we have sworn oath as freemates, and I had no opportunity to tell her."

"Perhaps it is as well not to tell her."

"You told Camilla."

"But Camilla is not jealous. Rafaella and I have worked out a pact for mutual co-existence—we even manage to like each other most of the time—but she is jealous of our closeness, Jaelle."

"Rafi and I were never lovers, Margali. At least, not since I was a little girl. She was really not much more. And now, at least, Rafaella is certainly a lover of men.

What may have been between us when we were young girls does not seem that important to me, and I cannot believe it is important to her." Jaelle shivered, standing barefoot on the icy floor, and quickly pulled her nightgown over her head.

"That is not what she is jealous of." Magda wondered why Jaelle could not see it. "What she envies is that we work together, that we share *laran*. And that is closer than any other bond." She hurried into her warm nightgown and warmer robe, for the Guild-house was not well-heated at night. "Will you monitor, Jaelle, or do you want me to do it?"

"I will. That's about my level of skill." Jaelle had no illusions about her competence working with *laran*. She had spent half a lifetime blocking away her psychic gift, submitting to the training only when the *laran* could not be excluded from her consciousness. Now, she knew, she could achieve only the minimal level of training: sufficient to keep her from being, in the phrase so often used about untrained telepaths, a menace to herself and everyone around her.

Jaelle was, and was glad to be, an integral part of the group of telepaths and psi workers, loosely allied, who worked outside the ordinary structure of matrix workers on Darkover, and in defiance called themselves the Forbidden Tower. But she would never achieve sufficient competence to call herself matrix mechanic or technician. Sometimes when she watched Magda, born a Terran, and now the most skillful of technicians, she was painfully aware that she had cast away that birthright, and could now never recover it.

They were both wearing warm, fur-lined robes, fur-lined slippers. Magda wrapped herself in an extra blanket. Psychic work withdrew heat from the body. If the worker stayed out too long on the astral planes known collectively as the overworld, it could result in painful chill.

Jaelle took her matrix, from the tiny leather bag around her neck, and carefully stripped away the protecting silks. The blue stone, no larger than the nail of her little finger, glinted with pallid fires.

She spoke aloud, though it was not really necessary; from the moment Magda had taken out her matrix, they had been in contact.

"Match resonances—"

Magda was aware first of the physical heat and mass of Jaelle's body, though she did not look at the other woman; her eyes were fixed within the matrix, seeing only the moving lights in the stone. She sensed the living energy fields of Jaelle's body near her, the pulsing spots where the life currents moved. Then, delicately, she moved to match the vibration of her stone to Jaelle's, feeling it as a point of—was it heat, light, some indefinable energy moving in the room? Nothing so tangible as these. She felt her heartbeat altering slightly, pulsing with the ebb and flow of the energies of the matched stones, knew that the very blood in her veins and arteries moved in cadence with the other woman's.

She sensed, like a hand passing over her body, the monitoring touch of Jaelle, scanning her to make certain that all was well in her body before she withdrew her consciousness from it, aware of everything, even noticing the graze on her ankle where she had skidded the other day on a pebble, the slight clogging of her sinuses— she must have encountered something in the HQ today to which she was mildly allergic; she noticed it, as Jaelle moved energies to clear the condition.

Neither spoke, but she picked it up as Jaelle finished:

Ready?

I'm going out.

Magda let her consciousness slip free of her body and looked down, seeing herself lying apparently unconscious on the bed they shared. Jaelle, blanket-wrapped, sat beside her. With total irrelevance, she thought. *That old robe of mine is really getting too old and grubby, I shall have to have a new one before long. What a pity I hate sewing so much.* She could have requisitioned a new one from Supplies, in the Terran HQ, but she had lived in the Guild-house too long to see that as a workable solution.

Then she was up and out of the room, finding herself alone in the gray and featureless plain of the overworld. After a moment, Jaelle stood beside her. As always in the overworld, Jaelle seemed smaller, slighter, more fragile, and Magda wondered, as she had wondered before, whether what she saw was a projection of the way Jaelle saw herself, or whether it reflected the way in which, for some reason, she had always felt protective, as if Jaelle were younger and weaker than herself.

Around them stretched grayness in every direction, colorless and without form. In the distance, figures drifted. Some of them, Magda knew, were their fellow pilgrims on the non-physical planes of existence; some had merely strayed from their bodies in dreams or meditation. She could see none of them clearly as yet, for she had not yet marked her own path with will and purpose.

Now, in the clearing dimness as what looked like fog dispersed, she could see faint landmarks in the gray. First, foremost, she saw a shining structure, rising tall on the plain, which she knew to be the landmark made on these planes by the thought-form called the Forbidden Tower—shelter from the nothingness of the astral world. Her home, the home she had found for her spirit, shared with those who meant more to her even than the Sisterhood of the Guild-house. She still observed meticulously every provision of the Renunciate Oath; she was a Free Amazon not only in word but in spirit. But the Guild-house could no longer contain the fullness of her being.

With the speed of thought—for what she imagined in the overworld was literally true—she was standing beside the Tower itself. Simultaneously she was inside it, in what appeared to be, complete in every detail, the upstairs suite in the Great House of Armida. She had come so late to this work that she had never quite accustomed herself to how time and space behaved on this plane.

All four of the rooms were empty—she could see them all at once, in a way she did not understand—but somewhere, there was the blue glow of a matrix where someone of the Tower kept watch. And then, without a moment of transition, Callista Lanart-Carr was beside her.

Magda knew rationally that Callista was not as beautiful in body as she looked in the overworld. In this case at least she was seeing Callista through the eyes of the spirit and through the eyes of her love and veneration for this woman who was at the center of the heart and spirit of the Forbidden Tower. In reality (but what, after all, was reality, and which was the illusion?)—on the material plane of existence, Callista Lanart-Carr, once Keeper at Arilinn, was a tall, frail-looking woman, her red hair faded almost to silvery gray, though she was not much past thirty; her body was sagging from the three children she had borne, and her face was lined and careworn. Yet on this plane, at least for Magda, Callista had the radiant beauty of early youth.

Magda knew that she did not speak, but speech and sound were irrelevant here. It seemed to her that Callista cried out a joyful greeting.

"Magda! Jaelle! Oh, we have been expecting to see you—"

And suddenly they were surrounded by the others of the Tower circle, Ellemir and Andrew and Damon, summoned quickly from dreams or sleep. Damon's brother Kieran was there too, and Kieran's son Kester, and Lady Hilary Castamir-Syrtis, who like Callista had once been Keeper in Arilinn. It seemed to both Magda and Jaelle that for a moment they were encompassed in an instant love-feast of greeting, made up of all the kisses and embraces and tenderness they had ever known, without time or the limits of the body, and it lasted (in reality, Magda knew, a split second or less) a long time.

At last, reluctantly, the intensity of loving communion ebbed (although Magda knew in some deeper reality that it would always be a part of her, always renewed and reassuring), and Ellemir said, "But my dears, we expected to have you here more than a tenday ago. I know the weather in Thendara is harsh sometimes, but I have heard of no storms, even in the pass. What has happened?"

With a humorous question from someone—Kester? —wanting to know what pleasures of the big city kept them away, friends, lovers—something like a swift reprimand for this intrusion from Damon—Ellemir's ill-concealed wonder that anything could keep two mothers from their children—Andrew's special enfolding of Magda in something that was very private between them, a bond of shared experiences stronger than love—

"Cholayna had need for me, and Jaelle stayed to keep me company," Magda told them, and swiftly shared the knowledge of the downed plane in the Helles. Something might have drifted through into the overworld.

She felt Andrew's surge of anger like a dull flame of colors, crimson and burnt orange, surrounding the outline of his body; she could sometimes see this even when they were both in their bodies. Here it was unmistakable.

"They should not have asked it of you, Magda." *Damn the Anders woman, nothing was worth doing that to you. That is like the Terrans, their damnable Need to Know, regardless. They have no idea of human needs—*

"That's too strong, Andrew. Cholayna made a point of telling me I could refuse."

Andrew dismissed that. "You should have refused. I'll bet you didn't find out anything worth knowing."

"I did bring Lexie back," Magda defended herself. "She might have stayed like that indefinitely! And there was more." On an impulse, she shared quickly with Callista the image with which she had come away from Lexie's mind.

Robed figures, deep hoods. The sound of crows calling, drifting through a silence deeper than the depths of the overworld . . .

Momentarily she could sense that Callista did not find it new, not quite.

I have encountered strange leroni *in the overworld, now and again,* Callista's memory reached them all at once. *Not often, and only a glimmering. Once when I was very ill*—her mind edged away from the ordeal in which she had been made Keeper at Arilinn—*and again when I was trapped in the other planes of the overworld and could reach nothing familiar. I remember the call-*

*ing of strange birds, and dark forms, and little more.
Your friend—Alexis?—if, in extremity, she teleported
herself from the crashed plane, she may have crossed
some strange places in the overworld. I truly do not
think it was more than that, Margali.*

"But what of the crashed plane? And no trace of it
found—"

"I have a theory for that, too," said Damon, and the
familiar sensation of warmth, strength, protection *(their
Keeper, closer than a lover, the figure around whom
the Forbidden Tower had gathered, the only one in all
the Domains who had had the courage for this, to
restore Hilary and Callista to full strength in spite of
the laws which forbade a failed Keeper from ever again
taking up her* laran, *their shelter and their strength and
their lover and their father all at once) . . .*

Again the disparity from what Magda knew as
"reality" and how Damon appeared here in the overworld: in real life, a small, dark-haired, insignificant-
looking man with fading hair and tired eyes, showing
his age—he was a good twenty years older than Andrew,
who was somewhat older than Ellemir or Callista. But
here where the things of the spirit were made manifest,
Damon appeared to be a tall, strong and imposing man,
who gave the impression of a warrior. It had taken a
warrior to resist the power of Leonie Hastur, the Keeper
of Arilinn, who ruled all the Towers in the Domains
with the same iron hand with which her twin brother,
Lorill Hastur, ruled the Domains. Damon had won from
Leonie, in a psychic battle against terrible odds, the
right to establish what was now called, defiantly, the
Forbidden Tower.

"I have a theory about the disappearance of your
plane," Damon said. "If the Anders woman truly sum-

moned up, from latency in her mind, a new psi skill and teleported herself—and that's not impossible, I saw Callista do it when we were imprisoned among the catmen—the pure energy had to come from somewhere. She did not, of coure, have a matrix,'' Damon added. The matrix stones were crystals which had the curious property of transforming thought-waves into energy without transition by-products.

''Somehow, as she summoned the strength to translocate, to teleport herself, she used the kinetic mass of the Terran airplane for the energy requirement. That energy couldn't have come from nowhere, after all. In effect, she disintegrated and atomized the plane and utilized that immense energy for the strength to make the teleportation possible. No wonder they couldn't locate the plane, even with satellites. It doesn't exist anymore. It's disintegrated.''

''I think that's a little far-fetched, Damon,'' Andrew argued. ''Where would she get the strength, let alone the knowledge, to do that? If she was a trained psi-tech, even from some other world and some other tradition, I suppose she might have managed it. But a complete novice—possibly head-blind? I can't imagine it. She would have needed help.''

''Maybe she had help, from those stray *leroni* Callista mentioned; she might have crossed someplace in the overworld, and there found such help,'' suggested Kieran.

''Does it matter?'' Ellemir asked practically. She was always the pragmatic one. ''It's gone, and I suppose it doesn't matter how or why unless the Terrans get a bee in their bonnet about mounting a salvage operation to try to find if there's a record in—what did you call it, the black box?—of whatever it was she spotted beyond the Wall.''

"They'd have a lot of fun with that," Andrew said, with dry irony. "I used to work for M-and-Ex. There's nothing out there, nothing at all."

"Let them look," Lady Hilary said with the equivalent of a shrug. "It will keep them busy and out of trouble. Some of the Terrans may be very nice people—" and her affectionate look encompassed both Magda and Andrew. "But what do we care what foolish quests they may attempt? When are you coming back to us, dear sisters? We miss you. And the children—"

She broke off, for the little group where they were gathered had suddenly been enlarged by two others.

Kiha Margali—it was like a gentle tug at Magda's arm, and Cassilde, a girl of fourteen, fair-haired and blue-eyed, was immediately enfolded in Magda's embrace.

And Magda felt the surprise in the circle. None of them had known that Callista's eldest daughter had gained access to the overworld. Young children did not, as a usual thing, have much *laran*—although Cassilde was approaching the age at which any latent *laran* she might have would be surfacing at any time.

Am I dreaming, Mother? Kihu—am I dreaming? Or are you all really here?

"Perhaps you are only dreaming, *chiya*," Damon said gently, and again his thought, wordless, embraced them all, *But she is old enough, we must begin teaching her properly*.

But even as their warm welcome enfolded young Cassie, there was a cry and a clamor for attention.

Mama! Oh, I called you, and see, you have come—

Jaelle enfolded Cleindori in her arms, but the child's confusion astonished them all. Cassilde, at the very verge of puberty, might well have gained access to these non-material planes of thought and spirit; that

Cleindori could have done so at five years old was preposterous.

Cassie, my darling, even if you have skill for this, you should not attempt it until you learn the proper way to safeguard yourself, Callista admonished her, gently; and Andrew added, in his kindest and most fatherly tone, *Even if you can come here, child, you should not bring Cleindori with you.*

"I didn't," Cassie began, and simultaneously Cleindori clamored, "Cassie didn't bring me, I came all by myself, I love Auntie Ellemir, love her lots, but I wanted *you,* Mama, and you stayed away so long, so long! I called you and you came, and I can *too* come here without Cassie bringing me, I come here lots, I can even bring Shaya here, *look!*" Cleindori was crying with loud anger.

And Magda saw her two-year-old daughter, night-gowned, her dark hair tousled from the pillow; she said sleepily, "Mama?"

Half-unbelieving, Magda took the child into a close embrace. Although their bodies were separated by a three days' journey, it felt as if she were holding the actual child in her arms, the snuggling warmth of the little body, the small sleepy head on her shoulder. Ah, she had missed her, how she had missed her! But Shaya, at least, was here only in a dream. She would wake tomorrow, remembering that she had dreamed of her mother; Magda hoped she would not cry.

"Now this is enough!" said Ellemir, with firm authority. "We see what you have done, Cleindori, but this is not allowed. Take Shaya back to bed at once. And you, Cassie, you should go back to bed, too, you are not strong enough to stay out of your body this long. Tomorrow, I promise you, if no one else here will teach you to do it properly, I will do so myself. But for now, you must go back.''

Cassie vanished. But Damon took Cleindori gently from her mother's arms. ''Listen to me, daughter, I know you are only a very little girl, but since you have done this, we must acknowledge that you are old enough to do it. Do you know where you are, *chiya*?''

''It's the gray world. I don't know what you call it. I think it's the place I go when I dream, isn't it?''

''That and more, little one. Have you been here before?''

Cleindori struggled to find words. ''I don't remember when I couldn't come here. I always came here. I think I was here with Mama and Shaya before I was born. When Auntie Ellemir told me about how babies came, before Shaya was born, I was surprised, because I thought they came from the gray world. Because I used to talk to Shaya before she was a baby. She was all grown up here, and then suddenly she was a baby and couldn't talk to me anymore except when we were *here*.''

Merciful Evanda! Magda thought. In childish words, Cleindori had explicated a metaphysical theory that was beyond her, and probably beyond all of them; except perhaps, Callista and Damon, who had studied these things.

Damon certainly understood. He hugged the small girl close and said, ''But in that world down there, my darling, you are only a little girl, and your body is not strong enough for you to spend much time here. Do you remember Aunt Margali telling you that Shaya could not eat nut-cake till her teeth were grown? Well, *your* body is not grown enough for this, Dori. You must stay in it until you know just how to leave it. You must come here only in dreams, little one; and especially you must not try to bring Shaya here until she is able to come and go without your help. Remember how you watched the chickens pecking their way out of the shell, and you wanted to help?''

She nodded soberly. "I did try to help one, and it died.''

"Then you know why you must not help Shaya do anything she is too young to do. She too may stray to this level in dreams. You may ask her to try to dream with you. But no more.''

"But when we're dreaming we can't stay here long enough.''

"No, but you can stay here as long as you are able, and it will not harm you. But you must not come here except in dreams, my daughter. Will you promise me that?''

She looked into Damon's eyes, and Magda, still deeply in rapport with Damon, saw the child's eyes, and they were not like a child's eyes at all.

Then Cleindori said with unusual meekness, "I promise, Dada.''

"Then both of you, back to sleep," said Damon with a gently banishing gesture, and both children vanished into wisps of dream. Extending her awareness, Magda could see the children in their cots, side by side, fast asleep.

Damon sighed. "She is *too* precocious! I knew it must come, but I never guessed it would come so soon!''

But before either of them could see further into his thought, he enveloped them all again in his concern and kindness. "You must stay in Thendara as long as you are needed. Believe us, we have been taking better care of the children than you might think, from *this*!''

The gray world was breaking up now into wisps of fog. As Magda felt herself withdrawing from it, knowing that soon the overworld would merge into normal sleep, and tomorrow this whole encounter would seem hardly more than a dream. For a moment, she felt all of them close and encircling her. In the wispy grayness she saw and briefly embraced Ferrika (the midwife had been out at the far end of the estate, waking and dozing by the bed of a woman in labor, and could not withdraw her waking consciousness even to greet her sisters), and also Colin of Syrtis, Lady Hilary's husband (a brief, sweet moment, momentarily rousing again a passion that had burnt away to embers even before Shaya was born) and then once again, for a sudden long moment, suspended between time and space, she came face to face with her daughter.

A dream. . . .

But of course there is some reality where Shaya is not a child at all. I must always remember that—remember that she is more than just the baby I held in my arms and nursed and cherished. Mothers who forget this do dreadful things to their children, she thought. And then it was all gone into the formless grayness and she was slipping down into her empty half-frozen body.

She crawled closer to Jaelle, hugging the other woman in her arms for warmth. For a moment, roused on a level that was not physical at all, as such work often left her aroused and excited, it seemed to her that she would like to make love to her freemate, all the tender little rituals of touching and reaffirming what was so strong between them. But Jaelle was already deeply asleep.

We do not need that now, when we can have this, she thought, feeling again the exultation of the moment when they had all been around her with that closeness stronger than any other known bond.

And then, with a longing that was both sweet and sad, she wished that she could share this bond too with Camilla.

Do we make love, Camilla and I, because we cannot share this? And why has she refused this for so long? A little ruefully, she remembered what Damon had told Cleindori, and realized that it was a lesson she too must remember.

As she drifted down into sleep, real sleep, Magda thought, I hope I can remember all this when I wake up!

CHAPTER SIX

A few days later, Cholayna asked if Magda would address a group of women recruits to HQ services. She was glad to accept: at least it gave her the illusion that she was doing something useful.

She had never been really comfortable with public speaking— few Intelligence agents were; their training essentially prepared them for work outside the public eye. The newcomers to Darkover struck her as being very young; it was hard to remember that most of them were older than she had been when she was first sent into the field with Peter Haldane.

Two of the young women recruits were from Communications; Magda had worked there for a time, while it was still too difficult for women to operate independently as intelligence agents on a world with such rigidly structured gender roles as Darkover. Two were from Spaceforce itself. She wondered if these women had known, before they came here, that they could operate only inside the HQ Sector itself. Three were from Mapping and Exploring, and three more from Intelligence, Magda's own service.

"And now," Cholayna said after a few preliminary remarks, "I have brought someone here to speak to you all. I'm sure you already know her by reputation; she practically wrote, single-handed, all the documentation for fieldwork on this planet. Magdalen Lorne of Terran Intelligence.''

Magda was nervous enough not to have noticed who was in the audience, but as she made her way forward through the group of women she heard a small, almost scornful sound. She wondered, with a certain resignation, why Lexie Anders had chosen to attend this session. These women knew her only in terms of the *Lorne Legend*, for which she was not responsible. Whatever she had done, at the time she had done it, she had only been doing what any of them might do; simply muddling her way, from day to day, as best she could, through whatever she was given to do. She wondered, a little bitterly, how many other ''legends'' were simply victims of luck and circumstances.

She spoke only briefly, saying she could hardly give an impersonal assessment of Darkover; it was her home world, and she had been fortunate enough to be allowed to remain. She did warn them about some of the difficulties they would encounter as women working here, and ended by inviting them to attend the meeting of the Bridge Society. She answered several questions about languages and dress from the young Intelligence workers; but when the women from Mapping and Exploring asked technical questions about the planet, she said pleasantly, ''I'm sure Lieutenant Anders can tell you more about that than I. Anders is an expert in that field. Lexie—would you take over?''

She felt, as Alexis came up from the back of the room, that she had done her duty. If Lexie still held any grudge against her, it was Lexie's own problem, not hers. There would always be people who didn't like you and that wasn't always your fault.

She left Lexie to answer the technical questions, and went down to the main cafeteria for something to eat.

Every now and then she had a craving for foods she could find only in the Terran Zone. She was looking about for a seat, tray in hand, when a voice said behind her, "We don't often see you here, Mag. You're looking well. What brings you today?"

"Cholayna asked me to talk to a group of her young recruits," Magda answered, turning to face the Legate. "Hello, Peter, it's nice to see you."

"If I'd known you were going to be here, I'd have asked you to stop by my office; I'm glad I ran into you." Peter Haldane took her tray and led the way to an isolated table for two. Magda, about to protest, shrugged and held her peace. Whatever the Legate had to say to her, better he said it here, informally, than officially in his quarters.

There was constraint in his voice as he asked, "And Jaelle—is she well?"

"Oh yes, certainly." After her own marriage to Peter had ended, Peter and Jaelle had been married, briefly and disastrously, for half a year. For a long time after that, Magda had not felt comfortable with Peter. She and Jaelle, after all, had chosen one another in a way that excluded Peter himself, and not many men could tolerate or understand that. . . .

But that had all been a long time ago. Peter now seemed her earliest friend, one who shared an otherwise irrecoverable childhood. Like herself, he had grown up with Darkovans before the Terran HQ had been built in Thendara. In the intervening years, she had come to feel that their early marriage had been because Peter had seemed the only person alive that she could talk to, and vice versa. Everybody else either of them knew was either Terran or Darkovan, defined by that difference.

That had not, in the end, been enough to build a marriage on. Nevertheless, she felt they should manage

to remain on good terms, despite the different directions
their lives had taken.

Peter, like herself, had suffered all the pains of divided loyalties. That would, she hoped, give him a
greater understanding of the Terrans over whom he
must now serve as Legate. He had always belonged in
the career diplomatic service anyhow and never, really,
in Intelligence; and Magda had known it before he had.

Like Lexie, he was always competing with me, she
thought, and since no one had ever accused Peter Haldane of having any trace of *laran,* she was shocked
when his next words were, "You know Lieutenant
Anders, don't you, Mag?"

"Certainly I do," she said, abandoning her attempt
to finish a dish of custard. "Why do you ask?"

"I suppose Cholayna's kept you up to date on the
way she set us all by the ears here, with her plane going
down?"

She lifted her eyebrows at him. "Then it wasn't your
idea to have Cholayna call me in as a psi-tech for her?"

His blank look was answer enough. "You? A psi-
tech? It would never have occurred to me. I gather from
that, then, that you know all about it?"

"I know the plane went down and that she ended up
here. Even with a mind-probe, that's all I found out. Is
there something more I should have known?"

Peter answered with another question. "Then she
hasn't come to you with her latest wild idea?"

"Peter, I'm the last person Lexie would have come
to. She's never liked me. I've hardly spoken to her,
except that night Cholayna called me in. All I know is
what I found out then."

"Well, in a word—Anders is convinced there's a real
city out there. She's sure what she saw before the plane
went down was not a hallucination, or a radar angel or

mistaken ground signal, but a real city. Why not? Every developed planet in this galaxy has an installation which TI can, if necessary, conceal from radar and sky-spies. Why not this one?''

Magda thought that over for a minute.

"I can't imagine it," she said. "You know, and I know, the Darkovans have nothing like that."

"You mean, nothing like that *as far as we know*."

"No, I mean *nothing like that*! Peter, I've been working in a matrix circle now for six years. If there was anything like that in the Domains, believe me, I would know."

"What about *outside* the Domains?"

"Your own satellite reports tell you, that's impossible! Ask anyone in Comm or M-and-Ex."

He bit his lip. "Nothing, you mean, that can be detected. How do we know we can detect everything? The available technology on Cottman Four couldn't handle it, no. But that means nothing. Unofficial sources from outside Empire Civil Service could have set up a base here for some reason—mining, perhaps, or—''

"I can't believe it, you're talking Space Pirates!" Magda said, almost laughing.

Predictably, he reacted with annoyance. "Must you always make fun of everything *you* didn't think of?"

"If I was making fun, Peter, it wasn't of you," she said, now completely serious. "It's only—I can't believe anything like that could have been set up there without being discovered by satellite, or space sensors; it's hard to believe it could be done at all, though I suppose nothing's impossible. Is that what Lexie believes?"

"Yes. And she wants to mount an expedition to find it. I thought she might have come to you because you were working in Intelligence here, and because she knows your Free Amazons are the best mountain guides on the planet.''

"As I said, Peter. I'm the last person she'd come to.''

"But if she did—''

"I'd tell her the idea's completely mad. We have years of satellite observations to tell us there's nothing—all right, nothing observable—outside the Domains. And I'll bet there's nothing, period. That area must have been uninhabitable since—well, I'm no expert on geology and crustal movement, but—certainly for a geological eon. Probably since the Hellers rose out of the sea bed. As for mounting any kind of expedition, the logistics of it would be all but impossible, even *with* all the resources of Terran Intelligence behind it. Jaelle could tell you better than I what the difficulties would be, but I know enough to know it's impossible, and so do you.'' They had, after all, been in the field together, traveling as Darkovans. "To begin with—you'd have to cross the Hellers, and when you get beyond Nevarsin, the country's all but unknown. We have no operatives in Intelligence who know the trails or the languages. There are catmen tribes up there, and—and God knows what else. Banshees—perhaps nonhuman cultures—I don't think it could be done, at all. Certainly I wouldn't try it.''

Peter looked skeptical. "If she should come to you, that's what you'll tell her?''

"Believe me, Peter, she won't. Anyhow, Anders isn't Intelligence, she's Mapping and Exploring.'' Legally, Intelligence was responsible only to the Terran Empire Head Centre, while Mapping and Exploring was under the sole authority of the Legate of the planet. "She'd have to get your permission, not Cholayna's. Even if you thought Cholayna would do something like that behind your back, Peter, she'd send one of her own operatives, not Lexie.''

She did not know if Peter was convinced, but he had reason to know she had always told him the truth. She hoped he knew she always would. They exchanged a few more commonplaces and parted in friendly fashion. But as Magda walked across the city to the Guild-house, she wondered if that was why Lexie had chosen to attend her lecture.

A few days later, as Magda was leaving the HQ, Doria joined her at the Gates.

''Are you going to the Guild-house? I will go with you. I have a message from my mother for Jaelle n'ha Melora.''

''Let me take it for you,'' Magda said, glancing at the sky. ''It will save you a long walk in the rain.''

Doria colored slightly. ''I am sorry—Rafaella said I was to give it only to Jaelle herself.''

Magda shrugged. There was a time when she and Rafaella had actually been friends, but she could never count on the other woman's friendliness. She would become accustomed to thinking of her as friendly, even presume on it a little—then discover without warning that Rafi was behaving as if she disliked her. But since she genuinely respected and admired Rafaella, she accepted her as Jaelle's friend, if not her own.

The two women set off side by side, walking swiftly, the hoods of their capes drawn against the rain. ''Are you staying much longer in the city, Margali?''

''I hope not. There is really not much for me to do here. I know Jaelle would like to go back to work with Rafi, and Rafaella would like that too, but that would have to be her own decision.''

They turned into the square where the Guild-house stood. Doria was about to ring the bell when the door opened and Keitha stormed down the steps, swearing aloud.

"Keitha, what's the matter?"

"Doria? Oh—well—it's not your fault, but when I see your mother again—"

"What? What *is* the matter, Keitha?"

"I leased a horse from Rafaella, since I have none of my own, and sometimes, when I am summoned to a confinement outside the City walls, I must have one. I wanted to make it a formal arrangement, but she said, no, she had a dozen ponies in the stable, eating their heads off, not getting enough exercise, and I was welcome to use one whenever I needed one to ride."

"And you are angry with her for that?"

"No," said Keitha, "but I asked her to lease me one formally, just so this wouldn't happen! Now all her horses are gone, and I must hire one in the market or go afoot."

"Take mine," Magda said, "you know which it is, Keitha, the black." It had been a gift from Shaya's father. "I won't be wanting it tonight."

"Thank you, Oath-sister." Keitha hurried back into the house, and Magda and Doria watched her run toward the back door leading to the courtyard and stables. Doria whistled in surprise.

"What, all Rafaella's horses gone? I can't understand this! She must have had a—a large commission, unexpectedly, if she couldn't leave a horse for Keitha! It was really very thoughtless of her not to warn Keitha before-hand." Frowning, Doria went in search of Jaelle, while Magda went to hang her cloak, by now thoroughly soaked, on one of the drying racks in the kitchen.

By the time she had dried the wet cloak and hood, the women were already coming into the dining room, so Magda stayed to help put bowls and mugs on the table. When everyone had been served, she slipped into her customary seat beside Jaelle.

"Did Doria give you her message?"

"Yes, but I cannot imagine what can be in her mind," Jaelle said. She looked troubled. "It was the last thing I expected after all these years. We aren't children anymore."

"What is wrong, Jaelle?" With her freemate so troubled, it was more than Magda could do to keep her resolve to stay entirely out of it.

"The message was only a few words, not even written down: *There is a letter for you in the old place.* Magda, that goes back a long way—to when I was only a little girl, Kindra's fosterling. Kindra used to take me with her on long trips, and Rafi and I wouldn't see each other for long periods of time. So we used to have a secret, private letter drop at the old saddlemaker's in the Street of the Four Winds."

Magda shrugged. "Why not? I suppose most children do that sort of thing at one time or another."

"Rafaella wasn't a child, she was older than I—but, well, I thought it wonderful that an older girl would play games with me. Rafi and I have always been— close. You know that."

"Indeed I do," Magda said. The sympathy she felt was very real. As a Terran child, isolated among Darkovans, she had always been an outsider.

"But now we are not children, we are not even young girls, I am a grown woman with a child of my own, and Rafaella is older than you are! Why should she revert to this childish nonsense?"

"Oh, Jaelle," Magda said, "don't worry so about it. Perhaps she wants to confide in you, or to assure herself that you are still close enough to her to do something silly and childish for her. A way of—re-establishing that old closeness. She doesn't trust me not to come between you.''

"And that *is* silly and childish,'' Jaelle said, still looking pale and troubled. "We're *not* children, and does she truly think she can come between freemates? I am ashamed of her, Magda. She can hardly want me as a lover after all these years. But if she does not understand that I will always be her friend—then she is sillier than ever I thought her.''

"Don't worry,'' Magda reassured her, "you'll see, she simply has something she wants to tell you privately.''

"But she ought to know I *always* respect her confidences,'' Jaelle fretted. "I am really afraid she's gotten herself into trouble of some sort—''

Magda shrugged. "I wouldn't think so. If she felt free to leave the city and take all her horses, leaving poor Keitha to borrow mine—''

"*What?*''

"Jaelle, didn't you know?''

"No, all day I have been recopying some old archives for Mother Lauria. The paper on which they are written is disintegrating, because the ink they used in those days was so acid. They are only about a hundred years old, but they are falling to pieces. And I've nothing else to do here. So I've been shut up all day in the library—''

Briefly, Magda told the story.

"It's really not like Rafi to be so thoughtless. What can she be thinking of?'' Jaelle's smooth forehead drew into lines of puzzlement. "I think I should go at once to the saddlemaker's, Magda.''

"Tonight? You're out of your mind,'' Magda said. "Listen to the rain and wind out there!'' It sounded like one of the summer gales which blow down through the pass from the Venza Mountains, striking Thendara with rain and high winds and sometimes, even in high summer, sleet or snow. Jaelle frowned, listening to the wind slamming the shutters against the windows.

"Whatever it is, Rafi is out in it." She pushed aside the untouched piece of nut-cake on her plate and went toward the hall. Magda followed.

"You can't go out alone in this weather on some hen-brained notion of Rafaella's—"

Jaelle turned and caught her arm. "Come with me, then. I have a feeling that this may mean trouble, Magda—more trouble than Rafaella being jealous or wanting to play girl's games."

With a sigh of resignation, Magda nodded, and caught up the cloak she had so painstakingly dried. Camilla appeared in the hallway behind them.

"Going out? In this weather? Are you both quite mad?"

Jaelle told her what had happened. Her face was pale and drawn.

"Camilla, come with us. You are Rafi's friend too."

"As much as she will allow," Camilla said. Sighing, she took down a battered old cape. "Let's go."

Wind and rain slammed into the hall as the three women went out into the night.

CHAPTER SEVEN

The rain poured down as the three women walked swiftly toward the marketplace. Magda was angry at herself for having allowed the hostilities between them to go on for so long. Jaelle's small triangular face was hidden under her hood, but it seemed to Magda that she could see pale anger there.

Camilla strode beside them, gaunt and silent, and the rain sloshed in puddles under their feet and flapped their capes around their faces. The marketplace was empty, pools of icy water making a miniature landscape of lakes and small rocky shores. Stalls, tightly locked and boarded, rose like islands over those shores.

"She's not here. The saddlemaker's stall is closed," Camilla said. "Come home, Jaelle, there's nothing that can't wait till tomorrow."

"I know where the saddlemaker lives." Jaelle spun abruptly on her heel, heading toward a dark side street. Camilla and Magda exchanged a single despairing glance and followed her.

Magda felt she would like to shake Rafaella until her teeth rattled. She was also angry at Jaelle, who was for catering to Rafaella by tearing off into the Old Town at this godforgotten hour.

The wind was icy, even through their capes, striking hard down the back of her neck. Magda spared a thought for Keitha, riding outside the city. But Keitha would be warm inside a house, with a good fire they would build up for heating water. Magda had never had the slightest wish to be a Medic or even a Renunciate midwife, but at least tonight Keitha knew where she was going and why and what she was going to do when she got there. And that was more than the others knew.

Jaelle stopped before a small weatherbeaten house, spoke briefly to someone who came to answer the bell, and after a time, a fattish old woman came to the door.

"Why, it's our little Jaelle, and all grown up, aren't you? Yes, your partner left you a letter, and I brought it home here, afraid, I was, someone would put it away somewheres I couldn't find it. Now, dear me, where'd I leave it?" The woman dug in several of her capacious pockets like an owl trimming her feathers, hunching herself and digging about. "Ah, here we are—no, that's an order for Lady D'Amato's saddle. This—ah, yes, here you are, *chiya*, won't you come in, and your friends too, and have some sweet cakes and cider by my fireside, like you used to?"

She held out a somewhat grimy fold of paper, sealed with a colored wafer.

"No, I thank you, I must try and catch up with Rafi before she is too far out of the city," Jaelle said, and turned away, her mouth set into a grim line. Magda could see her scanning the letter's front, but it was too dark to see or read.

"Here." Camilla seized Jaelle's shoulder, steered her toward the spill of light from the open door of a wineshop on the corner. The place was humming with talk, crowded with mercenary soldiers and Guardsmen, but though some greeted Camilla with a nod and a word or two, none of them attempted to hinder the tall *emmasca* as she led her friends to a table at the rear. A thick-bodied lamp was swinging over the table. Camilla quieted Jaelle's attempt at protest with a word.

"They know me here. No one will bother us. Sit down and read your letter, Shaya." She jerked her head at the round-bodied woman who hurried toward them. "Just wine punch, and privacy at this table, Chella." Camilla flung a coin on the table, and as the woman scurried off to obey her, said deliberately to Magda, "She's not much now, but you should have seen her ten years ago. Skin like rich cream, and the softest neck I ever tried to bite. Her hair was long enough to sit on, then, and the color—it made you want to hang it with silver, and believe me, she knew it. But she's a good soul for all that."

The woman, coming back with the hot wine, giggled softly and ran her fingertips lightly across Camilla's hand. Camilla smiled up at her and said, "Another time, Chella. My friends and I need to talk. Make sure nobody gets any notion that we want company, will you, Chella?"

Jaelle tore open Rafaella's letter and moved it under the light. As she read, she frowned, and finally said, "She's gone raving mad." She tossed the letter to Magda.

Reluctantly, Magda took the letter and read:

Dearest Shaya,

I've been trying to get you to come back to work with me long enough. Now it's time to stop talking about it, and do something. I'm leaving this at the old place as a way of reminding you of the good times, but this is bigger in every way. There might even be a chance at the special expedition we used to talk about. Lieutenant Anders thinks she is using me for the big discovery she thinks *she* can make. It's the other way round, really. But I'll give the woman value for her money, and so will you.

Remember when we were girls, Kindra's old legends of the secret city far away in the Hellers, where an ancient Sisterhood watches over the affairs of humankind? There's a chance it may not be legend after all. Remember the legends used to say that if you found your way there, and you were sufficiently virtuous, they would teach you all the wisdom of the universe. I wouldn't give a catman's tooth for wisdom, and I probably don't have the virtue to qualify, either.

It could be a dangerous business, but the legends all agree on one thing: they won't, or aren't allowed to interfere in human affairs, and if you find them, they aren't allowed, by their laws, to kill. Their city is supposed to be filled with copper and gold and rare old books of wisdom. They say all the wisdom of the *cristoforos* came from them, but the *cristoforos* only got a little of it. Yet everyone says the *cristoforos* are the custodians of all wisdom!

So I don't have to tell you what I'm doing. The Terran woman wants information for HQ, which she says will make her famous. As for me, I'm betting on some of that copper coin and gold. Forget the wisdom. If I get there, and get out again, I guarantee I'll have something a lot better than some old books and fancy words. But I need your help. I can't do this alone, and there aren't that many women in the Guild-house now that I can rely on, except you.

I need trade supplies, extra-warm clothing, and a few more horses and pack animals. Try to persuade a couple of the Guild-sisters to come along, too—not goody-goodies like Doria or Keitha, but someone who can travel hard, live rough, chew leather and take orders. And whatever you do, *don't* run and blab all this to Margali! For once, love, keep something good to yourself. Remember your old partner— and bring all the horses and trade goods you can get your hands on. It will be a rough trip, but believe it, it will be worth your while. Think of making your daughter independent of her father, even if he *is* Comyn!

I'll wait for you for three days where we had to slaughter the chervines that time with Kindra. Don't fail me! Get on the road at once, so we can be over the Kadarin before the weather breaks.

I know you, and I know how you must be longing to be on the road again. I'll be waiting for you, Oath-Sister! With my love,

Rafi

Magda dropped the letter on the table and took up the smoking cup of hot wine punch that the bar woman had set before her.

She said, "It's not Rafi who's gone mad, it's Lexie Anders."

"Most likely both of them." Camilla picked up the letter, raised an eyebrow toward Jaelle. "May I?"

"Please do."

As she read, Camilla snorted. At last she said, "Legends! Why doesn't she go off looking for the Hidden City, the one with the spice-bread trees all hung with candied fruit . . . I thought Rafi had more sense."

"She's going to get herself into terrible trouble," Magda said. "Of course the responsibility is Lexie's, but that doesn't mean Rafaella can get away with this. Even if such a place had ever existed—"

"Oh, it may well exist," said Jaelle unexpectedly, and Magda turned on her.

"You never said that when Callista and I were talking about strange *leronyn* from other parts of the Overworld—"

"To be perfectly truthful, Magda, I hadn't associated the two. I never thought of the Sisters of Wisdom as robed figures with calling crows. When I was a little girl in the Guild-house, and first heard of the Sisterhood, I used to wonder if they came from the Hidden City. Kindra talked of it to me a time or two, when we were traveling together—a city inhabited by wise-women, perhaps descended from the old priestesses of Avarra. The city is said to be on an island, or it was, once, when the climate was different from today's. If you find it, they have to take you in. They can tell you everything you need to know—how to make a fortune, if that's what you want, or mystical wisdom about the purpose of your life, if *that's* what you want. Kindra said she had met women who had been there, so it never occurred to me that it was a legend. If you put all the stories together, there may well be something to them. That doesn't mean I think the place is *accessible*. According to Kindra, they would do everything they could to keep anyone from finding it. Everything except kill, Camilla's right about that part of the legend. And if you actually *did* find it, they were obligated—oh, none of this makes any sense, I can't imagine why the Terrans should meddle with any of it, or why Rafi would have anything to do with it if they did!"

Magda, heartsick, said, "I'm afraid that's my fault. Lexie, I think, would do anything, anything at all now, to get ahead of me, to make her mark in Terran Intelligence in a way I couldn't hope to equal. I swear I never intended to set myself up as a legend, I wasn't trying to grab *any* glory! She accused me of wanting it all, once, saying I didn't leave anything for anyone else to accomplish—''

"Oh, the woman's a fool," Camilla said, "you did what was set in front of you. If she can't understand that you aren't competing with her—"

It was something very different that was troubling Jaelle. "If she does this, Rafaella will end by being blackballed by the Terrans. She would never work for them again. And what will happen to Lieutenant Anders, Magda, if she does this against official advice?"

"The best she could hope for would be to be shipped offworld," Magda said. "At worst, she could be thrown out of the service, and serve her right. Unless she made such a major discovery that they'll—that must be what she's hoping for, to make a discovery for M-and-Ex that's so spectacular they'll overlook her disobeying Standard Orders. That's not unknown in the history of the service, either. Peter told me she was thinking of doing this, but I told him it could hardly *be* done, even with all the resources of the Empire behind her."

"Evidently," Camilla said, "she's *not* trying it with them behind her. Which is just as well, Terrans aren't welcome in the Hellers, and a big expedition wouldn't find anything, except, probably, more trouble than they could manage. But half a dozen women, well-provisioned, with good luck and good weather, might manage it. Kindra always said she'd like to try it, Jaelle, but when she took you in as a fosterling, she waited for you to grow up, and died before she ever had the chance." After a minute, Camilla added, "Rafaella would know about that. Rafi was her kinswoman. I'm surprised that she'd try to take a Terran on such a trip, though."

"I'm not," Magda said. "The Terrans have the resources, the money, maps and so forth, to mount expeditions like that. If, in all these years, Rafi hasn't found any women, even in the Guild-house, who were willing to try, I'm not surprised that when a woman of the Empire brought it up, she'd be excited about the possibility. I *am* surprised Lexie dragged Jaelle into it. And I'd want more evidence, that it was real, not just an old story."

But had Lexie been able to provide more evidence than Magda had read in her mind? Magda realized, with sudden horror, that she was jealous; that she was thinking, *This should not have been brushed aside by the Terrans, this should have been given to* me, *Magda Lorne!* She was, after all, the first woman to do underground field-work on Darkover. If something this big was in the wind, what right did they have to let Lexie take over?

Magda was shocked at herself. This was the very kind of thing which had precipitated Lexie Anders's hostility in the first place. And far from sending Lexie off on an exciting chase for a legendary city, Peter Haldane had specifically refused to authorize any such thing.

Or had he? Maybe calling Magda in with a blunt prohibition from the Legate's office would be the perfect cover-up for Terran Intelligence to go out looking for the same thing. Was it even ethical for Magda, sworn to the Guild-house, to see Terrans led into the heart of the most carefully guarded women's secret on Darkover?

No, this was nonsense, she was only giving credence to Marisela's absurd intimations of mystical sisterhoods and cosmic secrets.

"I don't know why I am worrying about it," she said. "It's impossible. Suicide. Even with luck and good weather—neither of which are easy to find in the Hellers—it can't be done."

And even if it were possible, even if Cholayna sent for her and asked her to take it over, she would have refused. "Totally impossible," she repeated, again, hunting for conviction in the words.

"I don't know about that," Camilla said. "Assuming Kindra was right, and there really is such a place—if it has ever been done, *ever*—it could be done again. But I don't think Rafi could do it. *You* might, Jaelle. Or might have, once. I don't know if you've still got it in you, after seven years of soft living out at Armida."

Magda said angrily, "That's not the point, is it? Of course, that's what Rafaella wants to do, to lure you to go with her, drag you into the trouble that she and Lexie are making for everyone. She's counting on your sense of loyalty and your friendship. She thinks you'll go off after her the way you pursued Alessandro Li when he took off into the hills on his own. Then she can get you back, which is what she wants—"

"I thought you said you were not competing with her, Magda. Should I let her go alone, to get into trouble in the Hellers, or die there?"

"Then—you're going to do what she wants."

"She was my partner for all those years. But there's no reason to drag you into it, Magda."

"Do you think I'll let you go by yourself, and make trouble for yourself with the Terrans, and—" She stopped, looking into Jaelle's glowing eyes. She said, "That isn't the point, either, is it? You *want* to go! Don't you? You want to be back on the road, and any excuse is good enough."

"Magda—you don't understand—" Jaelle sighed, and said, "I haven't any right to want to go. But it drives me mad that Rafi is free to go and I am not. Besides—"

"You are free to do whatever you think you should do," Magda said, realizing almost in despair that Jaelle was almost echoing her own thoughts. She added, "I should have been straight with Lexie. I should have told her about my own experiences with these people. Whether or not they're real, or from some other plane of existence, if I had been willing to share that with her, tell her how and why I encountered them, perhaps she would have understood—"

Magda now felt she understood: Lexie, like herself, had encountered these mysterious ones, the same dark-robed Sisterhood who had reached out to rescue herself and Jaelle. It was they who had sent Lexie back, as they had sent help to her . . . She knew Camilla did not believe it, but she had been there, and Camilla had not. But Lexie had had the courage to go in search of them, and she had not.

"The legend is very specific," Camilla said wryly, "that if you go looking for them and you are not qualified for admission, you'll wish you'd never heard of them. Somehow I don't think Rafaella's desire for riches is qualification enough. I'll bet on Rafi to bluff her way in, maybe. But not to get out again."

"Can't you see?" Jaelle's eyes were bright. "Those two, they aren't the right ones to go."

"And we are? Oh, come, Shaya—"

"I don't think it's coincidence that all this has happened," Jaelle argued. "In any case, Rafaella has put the safety of their expedition in my hands. She has asked me to catch up to her with more horses, trade goods, warm clothing—I can't abandon her."

"And—perhaps if I tell Lexie what I know of these— these mysterious ones, she'll have a better chance." Magda hesitated. "And I have access to other information she could not get, special security information, what little *is* known about the country in the Hellers beyond Nevarsin—"

And yet, in her heart, Magda knew Lexie would never see it that way. To Alexis Anders, the well-meant attempt to help would be no more than the Lorne Legend standing in the way again.

Hellfire, Lorne, is there any pie on this planet that you don't have your fingers in?

"Neither of you are being honest," Camilla said wryly, "yet both of you feel yourselves summoned to this mysterious city. As for me—my motives are perfectly clear." She glared at them and said, "*I* will go to this mysterious City of Sorceresses, but I at least am honest about my reasons. These people are supposed to be able to tell you the purpose why you were born, and—" She looked around, daring anyone to challenge her. "I have reason to question the Fates. If the Goddess has demanded of me that I suffer these things, then do I have no right to demand of the Goddess that she, or these mysterious women who pretend to do her will, account to me for my life? I choose to seek out this mysterious city, and there demand of the Goddess why she has treated me as a toy."

And despite the angry, half-flippant way in which Camilla phrased her words, Magda knew that they were a threat. And in any confrontation of that sort, Magda would bet on Camilla to come off best.

Jaelle shoved her chair back; thrust the letter, which had been lying on the table, into the pocket of her breeches. "When do we start?"

Magda felt as if she had been caught in the track of one of the Terran earth-moving machines, the kind used to transform a green hill lush with trees and plants, into leveled, bare ground, a stripped place where a spaceport could rise, or anything happen. Jaelle had never taken her protest seriously at all. Yet she had tried, fairly tried, to assess the rights and wrongs of this. Or had she?

"She said she'd wait three days," Magda said. "I'll go in the morning to the HQ and get maps from Intelligence; I have access to satellite overflight pictures, and the computer time to have them blown up into scale maps."

"And I'll make arrangements for horses and trade goods," Camilla said. "I have contacts now. You don't."

And the children? Magda thought. Yet she had been wondering, only the other day, why there seemed nothing now worthy of her energies. She found herself remembering an old Terran proverb: *Be careful what you pray for, you might get it.*

The rain had stopped when they came out of the wineshop, and Magda looked up to the skyline, where the high ragged teeth of the Venza Mountains rose clear. A small moon was just setting over one of the peaks.

They would be going up that way, then northward, past the Kadarin and into the deeps of the Hellers, to Nevarsin and beyond. She had never been so far into the unknown wilds. Her two companions were, with the skill of experienced mountain guides, already planning the stages of the journey.

If there was one thing she had learned when she left the Guild-house for the Forbidden Tower, it was never to assume that her life was settled or would follow an orderly track from now on. She listened to Camilla, scowling and talking about the difficulty of finding mountain-hardened horses at this season, and realized that she was also mentally rummaging through her wardrobe for the warm clothes she would need long before they got into the Hellers.

CHAPTER EIGHT

At first light, Camilla went off to see about horses, pack animals and saddles.

Magda, who could do nothing until regular work hours in the HQ, went into the dining room, where cold sliced bread and hot porridge were laid out for breakfast. As she ate, she tried to think what she should do first.

As an agent in the field, she had had access to the most sophisticated fly-over photographs, and to the elegant equipment which could, from a photo taken at eighty thousand meters, generate a map sophisticated enough to distinguish a resin-tree from a spice bush.

There were few Darkovan maps. Few traders came and went in the Hellers, and when they did, they followed trails their grandfathers had known. Beyond Nevarsin, little was known: a frozen plateau, wilderness. The maps from photograph work would help. But not, Magda thought, enough.

Jaelle came down, already dressed for the road, in riding breeches and boots. Magda had never before seen her wearing the long Amazon knife, like a short sword, of a mercenary or soldier. She slid into the seat beside Magda.

"I'll go and see about trail food," she said. "And you should have a riding cape. You'll need it when we get into the mountains; no jacket is ever really warm enough. Do you suppose we can get some Terran sleeping bags? They're better than what we can find in the market.''

"I'll arrange it.'' Extra warm socks, she thought, special gloves, sunburn cream, sunglasses. . . . A little group of women, readying themselves for work in the market, came in and dipped up bowls of porridge. Sherna raised her eyebrows at Jaelle.

"Dressed for riding? You're away, then?''

"As soon as we can get away. Taking a caravan north.''

"If you see Ferrika at Armida, give her my greetings.'' Sherna finished her porridge and went into the kitchen for the loaves for the bake-stall. She turned back to ask Magda, "Are you going with Jaelle, Oath-sister?''

Magda nodded, feeling raw-edged; she knew it was all meant kindly, but one of the few things she still found difficult about Guild-house living was the way everyone intruded on your private life.

She had never seen Jaelle at the work for which her freemate had been trained. She was astonished at the swift efficiency with which Jaelle plotted packloads, ran down lists of items.

"Maps, sleeping bags, perhaps some packaged high-energy Terran rations, they'd be better when we get into the mountains. Camp stoves and concentrated fuel tablets. I'll leave everything from the Terran Zone to you.''

"I may have to tell Cholayna—''

Jaelle sighed. "If you have to, you have to. She's met Rafaella, hasn't she?''

"Rafaella is listed with Mapping and Exploring, and in Intelligence, as the best of the available—'' Magda stopped, swallowed down *"native"* and finished, "Darkovan guides. Not the best of the *woman* guides, just the best of the guides. She's worked before this with mapping expeditions. Naturally Cholayna knows her. She probably recommends her to all of the bigger expeditions.''

Jaelle nodded. "Rafi told me once that she likes working with Terrans. They get the best equipment and they never try to argue about the bills. They either agree to pay, or tell you it's too much and go somewhere else. They don't bargain just for the fun of bargaining. Also, they tip better.''

There were, Magda thought, not a few Darkovans like that: working for the Terrans, secretly despising them. Since her first year in the Guild-house, she had had the same curious relationship, compounded almost in equal parts of affection and dislike, with Rafaella.

She said, "Sherna told me the other day that she dislikes trading with Terrans for that very reason—they take all the fun out of being in business. They won't bargain, just yes or no, take it or leave it.''

"I know what she means," Jaelle said, "the Terrans have no sense of humor. Neither does Rafaella. That's why she gets along so well with them.''

"Why should anyone carry their sense of humor into the marketplace?''

"It's a game, love. It all comes out about the same— maybe a few *sekals* difference, but everybody gains face and everybody thinks they get the best of the bargain.''

"I can't see the fun in that sort of thing. I like to know what I'm being asked, and say yes or no to it, not play games for hours every time I want to buy a basket or a pair of boots!''

Jaelle touched her freemate's wrist affectionately. "I know. You're a lot like Rafi, you know? I suspect that's why you two don't get along very well.'' She pushed away her porridge bowl. "Don't forget sunglasses.

We'll be traveling on ice once we're halfway through the Kilghard Hills, even at this season.''

As she made her way through the city, Magda reflected that Jaelle and Camilla seemed to be taking it for granted that they were going on; that there was no question of catching up with Lexie and Rafaella to bring them back from this unsanctioned expedition, but to join it.

It's my fault. I shouldn't have told her what I had found out about the Sisterhood. That was what started it. She too had wanted to know what was behind the mystery. The difference was that she would never have thought of going off on her own to find it.

I'm not adventurous. Maybe that's why I shouldn't have come between Jaelle and Rafaella. Jaelle has never been quite content to settle down in one place.

She gave her ident numbers to the Spaceforce man at the gate, and caught herself sounding almost furtive. *What's the matter with me, I have* clearance *here, I'm an accredited agent, and for all anybody knows I'm going about my regular duties! Actually, it* is *my business to stop Lexie going off into unmapped, unexplored parts of Darkover without authorization!*

In the hostel of the Bridge Society, she had begun keeping a few Standard uniforms: the access codes wired into the collars allowed her to come and go in the Headquarters building without constant identity and security rechecks. She greeted the young Darkovan nurses getting ready for the day shift there, went quickly to the locker she kept, and changed into uniform—the dark tunic and tights with the red piping which cleared her for any area except Medic and Psych. Monitors clicked ACCEPT as she went swiftly along the corridors to the major Mapping room. She found a free terminal and requested a satellite picture taken during overflight past Nevarsin. She could read the picture well enough to purse her lips and whistle silently at the terrain.

And Lexie believes there is some sort of city out there which has managed to screen itself from satellite or radar imaging? The woman's insane.

If the mysterious city of the Sisterhood existed—and Magda had an open mind about that—it must be in some inaccessible part of the overworld. Yet ever since she had known Jaelle, she had heard tales of Kindra n'ha Mhari, Jaelle's foster mother, who had guided Lady Rohana into the Dry-Towns. She had been a legendary explorer and mercenary. If she said she had known women who had actually been inside this legendary city, who was Magda to say it didn't exist?

She touched controls which would generate, from the satellite photograph, a somewhat more detailed computer-diagrammed map, one which would not require her own expertise with Terran formulations to decipher. She studied it on the screen for a time, requesting slight clarifications here and there until it resembled the Darkovan maps she had seen in Rafaella's collection, then asked for a hard copy. The laser-directed burst-printer moved silently, and in under half a minute the map slid out. She took it and studied it again for a long time, seeking errors, comparing it with other pictures on the screen; making absolutely certain that it was the very best that she could get.

In her early years with Intelligence, Magda had traveled with Peter Haldane over much of the Seven Domains, and into the foothills of the Hellers. She had made some of the early maps herself, though Peter had been better at that; her own gift was with languages. As she looked at some of the roads (on any planet but Darkover, they would have been classified as cattle trails), memories began resurfacing from that half-forgotten time . . . How young she had been then, how boundlessly energetic. Had she and Jaelle actually crossed the Pass of Scaravel, almost four thousand meters high? *Yes*, she thought grimly, *Jaelle has the scars to prove it*. And once, she and Peter had gone in disguise to the City of Snows, Nevarsin of the *cristoforos*. . . . After a moment, she sighed and turned again to the terminal, requesting yet another review of available maps northward from Nevarsin.

She studied the few narrow tracks that led into the wilderness. The plateau was over two thousand meters high; the passes might be expected to be short on oxygen; certainly there would be banshees—those blind, flightless carnivores that moved with a terrible tropism toward anything that breathed, and that could disembowel a horse with a single stroke of those dreadful claws. In the unexplored areas marked in cross-hatching on the maps, there would be unknown dangers. Some of the passes were far higher than Scaravel; most of what was shown was covered in the pale blue cross-hatching that meant, *Unexplored—no hard data*. If what they were looking for really existed, it would be somewhere there.

Needles in haystacks, anybody?

There must be more to the legends than that. If women Kindra knew had come and gone, it must be possible, not easy but possible, to track down information, to buy it, bribe those who knew—

But that would all have to be done on the Darkovan side. She had pretty well exhausted Terran sources at this point. She got SUPPLY on the terminal, requisitioned sleeping bags, solid fuel for camp stoves, sunglasses and sunburn cream—none of these items was at all unusual; any agent of Mapping and Exploring, Survey or Intelligence who was going into the field requisitioned the same things. Even if they hadn't been credited to Magda's personal account instead of being requested without charge as *work related expenses*, they would hardly have blipped a CAUTION flag at Auditing. Still, as a personal expense, she would never, ever have to explain why she had wanted them.

She wondered if Lexie, too, had covered her tracks in this way. Alexis Anders, like herself, had been trained in the Intelligence Training College on Alpha; but Lexie was younger than she was, and had considerably less experience in this sort of thing.

After a minute, Magda opened up the terminal again and entered the access code for Personnel.

As she had expected, she was challenged twice; but her clearance levels were such that she was able to determine that Anders, Alexis, M&E Special Duty Pilot, had put in for vacation time and had requisitioned certain mountaineering equipment. *Very interesting,* Magda thought as she cleared the screen.

She would have to make the trip down to Supply to pick up the things she had requested, even though payment had already been automatically deducted from Magda's credit at HQ. Indeed, it had nearly cleared her account: detached-duty pay was not very good. Only the bonuses Cholayna had arranged for her recent work with the Bridge Society had enabled her to pay for them at all.

Well, it'll be worth it. That's what matters.

She specified the kind of packaging she wanted, queried the prices of some other items—Jaelle could probably get them cheaper in the Old Town—and prepared to return to the Bridge hostel to change into what, when she was in the Terran Zone, she still automatically thought of as *field disguise*. As she shut down the terminal, she looked round to see Vanessa ryn Erin standing in the doorway of the room.

"I thought it was you. What did you want with Lexie's records, Magda? Curiosity isn't a valid reason for snooping in Personnel Files, you know. I'd thought better of you."

"If you talk about snooping, what were you doing snooping on what *I* was doing?"

"Personnel is my job, Magda. Not yours. Come on—explain." Vanessa paused, gazing coolly at Magda. "I'm dead serious. I can have you psy-probed for less cause than this."

Magda, who detested lying, had meant to tell her the truth; but now she realized that, to protect herself, not to mention Jaelle and Camilla, it would be better to think up a good lie, one that would satisfy Vanessa's conspiratorial imagination; and, like many people who are almost compulsively truthful, Magda couldn't think of one. It made her angry. She thought, *I can't just stand here blinking my eyes like a little girl caught with my hands in the cookie jar!* And of course, she did exactly that.

At last she said, "I wanted to know what Lexie was doing. I saw her at the Bridge Society meeting, but after an ordeal like that, I was curious to know if she was really well again." Then it occurred to her what she should have said in the first place. "She seems to have gone off with Jaelle's partner: we needed to know which way they'd gone. Jaelle missed a message from Rafaella, and—"

"As you discovered, she has put in for vacation time," said Vanessa. "When I spoke to Cholayna, though, I got the impression she'd given Lexie an assignment, which was how she got the equipment on a cost-free basis. She hired a Renunciate guide, and she's going into the Kilghard Hills to study women's folk dancing."

"So that's—" Magda stopped herself. She said flatly, "I don't believe it."

"Why not? It's nice, easy work, a good way to get what amounts to a paid vacation. We've all done that kind of thing."

For the next half year, Magda regretted that she had not simply allowed Vanessa to believe that. It was such a simple explanation, and would have saved an enormous amount of trouble—if Vanessa had actually believed it.

Instead, she drew a long breath of disbelief and indignation.

"What kind of hare-brained imbecile do you think me, Vanessa? There are Renunciate guides, yes, who would accept a commission to take a Terran woman alone into the hills to study folk dancing, or ballad styles, or the *rryl*, or the basket-weaving of the forge folk. But Rafaella? It was Rafaella who led the Mapping expedition to Scaravel! It's Rafi they ask for when they want someone to coordinate ninety men, five hundred pack chervines and half a dozen half-trained mountain guides! Come *on*, Vanessa! Do you honestly think Rafaella n'ha Doria would accept a commission to take one Terran woman on a little Sunday excursion to scribble down the differences between a *secain* and an Anhazak ring-dance? Possibly, just possibly, if they were lovers and wanted an excuse to get away together. I can't think of any other reason. Knowing Rafaella, I don't believe it for a minute—though I don't know anything about Lexie's love-life, come to think of it; but I'd bet you a week's pay she's completely heterosexual. Or didn't you see the look on her face when I introduced Jaelle to her as my freemate?"

Vanessa shrugged. "I hadn't thought much about it. I just thought she wanted to get into the hills. After all, Magda, Lexie *did* train as an Intelligence agent. I thought, after the crash, this could have been the only assignment she could get. She knew she'd need a Renunciate guide, and I suppose she simply asked for the best one on the list."

"And Rafaella accepted, just like that? Nonsense."

Vanessa burst out, angry, defensive, "I didn't stop to think about it at all until I got a buzz that someone was snooping in her file! After what she's been through, Lexie's certainly entitled to put in for vacation! It's not a crime to hire a guide who's over-qualified, is it? As long as she can pay Rafaella's fees! Maybe Rafaella just wanted some easy money, or to get the better of a foolish off-worlder who's willing to pay four times the—" Vanessa stopped dead, and said, thoughtfully, "Or maybe Cholayna assigned her to study folk dances as a cover, and she's going into the field to do something much more important and serious—"

"Now," said Magda, "you're just beginning to catch up with me."

"But—would Cholayna do that without consulting Personnel, to certify that Lexie was fit—stable enough, for that kind of thing? That's the point, Magda. That's *my* job! With a breakdown and amnesia so recently—I'd demand a consult from Medic and Psych before she went out again. And so would Cholayna! Although Cholayna does tend to—make up her own mind, about people—" She stopped, and Magda, knowing what she was reluctant to say, said it for her.

"You were remembering that *I* was supposed to have been fired, or allowed to resign—weren't you, Vanessa? Of course. And there are plenty of times when I wish she hadn't fought for me. And damn it, *this is one of them!* The fact is, Vanessa—I think Lexie's pulled a fast one, and she may just have pulled it on Cholayna, too.''

Suddenly it occurred to her that she was sharing with Vanessa a secret that was not hers to share, one that belonged to Jaelle and Camilla. If her purpose was to keep Rafaella out of trouble, or keep Lexie from getting into a part of Darkover where Terrans were not entitled to go, what she had just said was inexcusable.

But Vanessa's anger was not, as Magda had thought, directed at her. It frightened Magda that she could so clearly see what Vanessa was thinking: Vanessa was a Terran, head-blind, she was not even supposed to be *able* to read Vanessa's mind; yet there it was, clear as could be: *Lexie has a right not to join Bridge Society if she doesn't want to, but she has no right to try to manipulate all of us because she thinks we're fools who have gone native—or something like that! Doesn't she understand that Magda and Cholayna are my sisters, and that if she puts something over on them, she's tangling with me as well?*

But aloud, Vanessa said only, "Let's go up and ask Cholayna.''

CHAPTER NINE

Almost since she had known her, Magda had wondered about Cholayna's secret of relaxation. Cholayna never seemed actually to be doing anything, whether you went into her office in the HQ, or whether you sought her out in the special offices of the Alpha Intelligence Academy. Yet judging by results, one would suppose she spent all her time in frenetic activity.

Today was no exception: Cholayna was lying back in a comfortable chair, her narrow feet higher than her head, her eyes closed. But as Magda and Vanessa came into the office, she opened them and smiled.

"I thought this would be your next stop," she said. "What do you want with the satellite maps, Magda?"

This was why I told Jaelle that I might have to tell Cholayna what was going on. She always knows.

Vanessa, however, allowed Magda no chance to answer.

"I don't suppose you'll tell me, if it's Classified," she said, "but is Lexie's assignment, studying folk dances, a cover for some kind of official Intelligence maneuver?"

Cholayna looked mildly startled. "No, it's just a bit of xenoanthropology. I had to okay it because any time a Terran goes into the field—which in effect means anywhere more than ten kilometers outside the Old

Town—Intelligence is supposed to clear it, make sure they won't step officially on anyone's toes. I could see that after the shock she'd had, she wouldn't be much good as a pilot without a fairly extended rest. So I okayed it. There isn't, after all, a great deal of formal Intelligence work here—why do you think I *picked* this place? I spend ninety-nine percent of my time preparing undercover ops for work in linguistics and xenoanthropology. Which Magda set up before I ever got here." She smiled at Magda, who returned the smile. Vanessa looked suspicious, but Magda was enough of a telepath to know when she was being told the truth.

"So it's not a cover for that expedition Peter Haldane says she wanted to lead into the Hellers?"

"Oh, that." Cholayna chuckled. "Lexie admitted she'd been fairly spaced when she came back, didn't know what she was doing for the first few days. In fact, she wanted me to make sure what she said to him didn't go into her permanent record. She knows Peter and I are old friends. Then she said she needed a good rest, and would like to get out into the mountains. Don't think I don't know when I'm being worked for a free vacation on company time, but Lexie's competent, and she's entitled to the same perquisites as the rest of us. So I told her to find herself a qualified guide from the Bridge Society, and cleared it for her with Xeno-An."

Magda opened her mouth, but again Vanessa spoke first.

"You see, Lorne? You see? I told you so—"

Cholayna put her feet down on the floor. "*What* is going on?"

"Cholayna—what would you say if I told you that the guide Lexie engaged was Rafaella n'ha Doria?"

"Knowing what Rafaella charges," Cholayna said, "I would say that Lexie made a very poor bargain. I know at least half a dozen women who would take her on such a trip for half—no, a quarter of Rafi's standard charge—''

But then she stopped. It was frightening: Magda actually felt the information penetrate through the outer layers of Cholayna's lazy good nature. For the first time since her training-school days she saw the sharp intelligence behind that façade.

''In the name of a million fire-eating demons, what are those two up to?'' Cholayna sat back a little, eyes narrowing.

''I think,'' said Vanessa, ''that Lexie has found a way of getting the expedition she wanted, without going through the formalities. At the very least—it makes a fool of you and your department, Cholayna.''

Cholayna's face tightened, and the bushy silver eyebrows bristled above her dark eyes. ''I should have known. I trained Lexie and I ought to know when she's being devious! So, that's why you wanted the maps. But what do you suppose they're looking for?''

Magda handed her the letter. Cholayna glanced at it, very briefly, then tossed it back across the desk.

''Hmm. Looks like an exceptionally private sort of letter. But knowing you, you wouldn't show it to me without a good reason. Why don't you just tell me *that*, instead?''

Magda detailed the contents of the letter.

Cholayna frowned. ''Chasing fairy tales doesn't sound much more like Lexie, actually, than studying folk-dancing.''

''Oh, it's more than that. Lexie saw them—or thinks she did—and under the same type of circumstances that *I* saw them.'' Drawing a long breath, Magda explained what she had seen in Lexie's mind when she had probed it: robed women, voices, the calling of crows. Cholayna listened, tapping her long fingers restlessly against the glass surface of her desk.

Magda finished: "I always believed that, if they existed, they existed only in the overworld. But Camilla said that Kindra knew women who had been there. Marisela knows something about them, too, but she won't tell."

"And you're going after them?" Cholayna sat up briskly. "All right. I'll arrange clearance for all the maps you need. Get Supply, Vanessa, it won't take me more than—" She consulted a chronometer. "Half an hour to be ready to ride."

Magda stared. "Cholayna, you can't—"

"*Can't* isn't a word you use to me," Cholayna reminded her, but she was smiling. "Think, Magda! If Alexis Anders's theory is correct, and some other planetary influence has set up a radar-impervious, satellite-blinding station here, it's not only my business to know about it, we could all be fired, or worse, and Peter and I could be court-martialed if we didn't know about it. What do you think I'm here for? And if you're right, and it's some secret of the Sisterhood—do you think I want some spoiled brat from Map and Ex, someone so arrogant about this planet that she wouldn't even join Bridge, meddling with it? Quite apart from the diplomatic difficulties—if any non-Darkovans are going to be meddling in the Sisterhood's business, better you and me than Lexie, hmm?"

This was all so true that there was nothing Magda could say. Still, she remonstrated.

"You knew when you came here that you couldn't work in the field, Cholayna. Riding with us, you wouldn't even be safe, everyone would know you were not native." Almost alone among planets settled by man, Darkover, one of the "lost colonies," had been settled by a commune from the British Isles and was almost exclusively caucasoid.

Cholayna replied, "Out in the wilderness, what does it matter? They'll think, if we meet anyone who thinks anything at all, that I'm deformed, burnt or tattooed by Dry-Town slavers, perhaps; or—as some of the women in the Guild-house thought at first—that I have a terrible skin disease. Or that I'm nonhuman." Cholayna shrugged. "Talk to Supply, Vanessa. I should check Magda's supply list first, there's no sense in duplicating. Do you have enough sunburn cream and extra sunglasses?"

Once, Magda had barely escaped being caught in a stampede of the wild chervines, antlered analogues of deer, used as pack or dairy animals, who roamed the Kilghard Hills. She felt something like this now. She wondered what Camilla and Jaelle would say.

Cholayna excused herself, and went swiftly to her quarters; came back with a surprisingly small pack of personal possessions.

"Everything else, except boots, I can get from Supply. They'll be waiting for me at the gate. Let's go. Maps ready, Vanessa? I spoke to my subordinate; she's ready for indefinite takeover. I told her it was Cosmic Top Secret, and not to mention it to Haldane until I had been gone a tenday. She probably thinks she can wriggle her way in enough to become indispensable while I'm gone, and I'm sure she thinks I care one millicredit. Let's go." She slung the pack over her arm.

"Wait," said Vanessa. "I'm going, too."

"Don't be foolish, Vanessa. You can't—"

"It's you who's being foolish," Vanessa said, "but you haven't any monopoly on it. First: I have been climbing since I was sixteen years old. I led an all-woman climbing team in the first ascent of Montenegro

Summit, on Alpha. That was one of the factors in sending me here; I know all about severe climates. And you've got to admit that when it comes to climate, Darkover is something really unusual—*especially* in the outer Hellers. Second: I am also a member of Bridge, and what Lexie is trying to do makes a mockery of everything Bridge has done on Darkover, so it's as much my business as hers, or yours. And third—" She held up a hand as Cholayna tried to interrupt her. "If you want to be perfectly technical about it, Personnel has a right to pass on anybody's psychological and physical fitness to go into the field. Just try to leave without me. I'll make sure—no, the Legate will make sure, neither of you get out of the HQ gates."

"This is a fingernail's breadth from blackmail," Cholayna murmured.

"Damn right." Vanessa stared, facing her down. After a moment, Cholayna burst out laughing.

"Shall we all be mad together, then? Ten minutes, Vanessa. We'll meet you at Supply."

Cholayna kept the parka hood of her down jacket, with its priceless ruff of offworld fur, drawn close about her face as they crossed the city. The assigned meeting place was a tavern they knew; at this hour it was half-filled, a few Guardsmen enjoying a noonday pot of beer or a dish of boiled noodles. A smaller circle of Guardsmen were standing at the front, playing darts, but after a moment Magda saw Camilla's tall, lean figure at the center of the group, knife in hand.

"Come on," one of them shouted, "prove it, put your money where your bragging mouth is!"

"I hate to take your money," Camilla said in her gentle voice, and let the knife fly. It landed directly in the center of the dart, slicing feathers from the haft, which split, driving into the board to wedge so tight against the dart's metal pin that a hair could not have been threaded between them. There were gasps of amazement. Laughing gaily, Camilla picked up a dozen coins lying on the bar and shoved them into a jacket pocket before she went to retrieve her knife. She saw Magda at the door, and went to meet her.

"Showing off again, *bredhiya*?" Magda asked.

"They never will believe a woman can throw a knife faster and straighter than they. When I was a mercenary, I used to earn all my drinking money that way," Camilla said, "and this time, I needed some money. I cleaned myself out buying travel supplies this morning. Good thing I brought two extra horses." As simply as that, she accepted Cholayna's and Vanessa's presence, and led them to a back booth where Jaelle waited.

"I ordered soup and bread for all of us. We might as well have at least one hot meal before we get on the trail." She barely glanced at Cholayna as she added, "It doesn't meet your criteria for edibility, Cholayna, I know you try not to eat anything that ever moved of its own accord, but you'll have to get used to that on the road, anyhow."

It was as if she had known all along that Cholayna and Vanessa would be coming with them. Perhaps she had. Magda knew that she would never ask, and that Camilla would never tell her.

CHAPTER TEN

It was still early afternoon when they left the city behind, and before sunset they had crossed Dammerung Pass. It was neither especially high nor steep, but as they began to descend, Camilla, who had set a stiff pace, looked appraisingly at the two Terran women.

"You're in fair shape, Vanessa. Cholayna, you're reasonably soft, but no worse than these two—living soft at Armida all these years, having children—nothing worse for your wind! You'll harden up fast enough on the trail."

They took the road north, traveling at the fastest pace the pack animals could sustain. In the last lingering red light, Cholayna threw back her hood; she looked happy, and later said to Magda as they rode side by side, "I'd forgotten what this was like! After seven years behind a desk in Administration, and fifteen years teaching before that, I thought I'd never get out in the field again. I hadn't really realized what it would mean, coming to Darkover. I stayed because I thought I was doing good work, especially with the Bridge Society. But it's good to be back in the field. It's been so damned long."

She must have been one hell of a Field Operative, if they gave her a post in Training School, Magda thought, and not for the first time, wondered just how old Cholayna was; but it would not have occurred to her to ask.

The sun set, and the swift-falling night which gave Darkover its name dropped across the Venza Mountains. There was no rain; Camilla, taking advantage of the rare good weather, pushed the pace as hard as she could. It was nearly midnight when she signaled a halt. They set up camp quickly by lantern light, and Cholayna kindled a small fire to heat water for hot drinks, though they ate only bread and cold meat from their packs.

"We can get fresh food in the villages for a few days, and save the trail food," Camilla said, chewing a handful of dried fruit. "After that we'll be in the hills; and villages where we can get provisions may be three or four days' ride apart."

"How do we know which way we are going, or shouldn't I ask?" Vanessa's voice was quiet in the darkness beyond the fire; it was Jaelle who answered.

"Margali told you about the letter? Rafaella said she would wait three days at the place where we slaughtered the chervines. She knew I would remember that. It was ten years ago; we were young girls, traveling with Kindra. We ran out of food and water and killed the animals rather than leave them to starve. The fresh meat let us get along without water. But it was a near thing. I haven't been that hungry since, and I hope I never am again."

She cast a quick look at the dark sky. "We'd better turn in. This weather may hold another day, but when it breaks, it's likely to break for good. North of Dammerung Pass, we'll be in the foothills. I'd rather not spend a tenday holed up in a snow cave! And, if we want to catch up with Rafaella, they're traveling lighter than we are."

Jaelle had done this work for years; there had been many times when her life, or the lives of a dozen other people, had depended on her judgment about the weather.

Without discussion, Vanessa went to help Camilla with the horses, while Cholayna started pulling out the sleeping bags.

They slept in a ring, feet to the last coals of the dying fire. Magda, looking into the unusually clear night at the rarely seen stars of the Darkovan sky, wondered what Rafaella would say, if they did catch up, about having the Terrans with them.

As if Magda had spoken aloud, Jaelle said, "She did tell us to bring along a few people who could travel hard, live rough—"

"And take orders," Magda said wryly. She couldn't see either Vanessa or Cholayna doing that.

And what if they did not catch up to Rafaella? Only a dangerous trip through the wildest unknown country on Darkover, where Darkovans themselves never went, seeking a city that might not even exist. Her back ached and she was no longer accustomed to hard riding. She thought of Shaya, and had a sudden picture in her mind, like a vision, of her child peacefully sleeping at Armida.

What am I doing here? I have a family now, a child, a home and work I love, and here I am heading into wild country chasing a dream, a legend, wild geese. . . . The memory of Damon's eyes, Callista's chiding face, seemed to reproach her. *Why have I involved myself in this madness? I should have left it to Jaelle—Rafi's her partner, Rafi doesn't even like me. And Cholayna's career is at stake, it makes sense for her to be here.*

In the morning, she decided, she would tell them all firmly that it wasn't her business at all, and set off toward Armida and her loved ones and, most of all, her daughter.

Yet, as she fell asleep, she couldn't help but feel again the excitement of the unknown trail ahead, leading up into territory where no Terran had ever set foot, and quite probably no woman except the unknown *leroni*. That night her dreams resounded with the calling of crows.

Four days north from Thendara, the weather broke, and by noon heavy flakes began drifting slowly from the sky, each one as big across as Jaelle's palm. Jaelle swore softly as she rummaged in her pack for mittens and a warm hood.

"I'd hoped we'd get across Ravensmark Pass before the snow set in. There's always nasty going along those ledges. I should have taken the longer route through Hammerfell, but I gambled on the weather, hoping we could gain a day and catch up with Rafaella. Somebody told me in the last town that some of the road was washed out over Ravensmark in the summer floods. In good weather it wouldn't matter. In this—" She stopped and stood, watching, as if trying to see through the thick flakes.

Vanessa asked, "Should we go back then and catch up on the road to Hammerfell?"

Jaelle shook her head, causing a loose strand of auburn hair to tumble from her hood. "Too late for that. We'd lose two days now. And we have no way of knowing which way they took. Magda, have you any idea?"

Magda caught what she was thinking; she was doing it all the time now, almost automatically. She ought to be accustomed to it by now; she remembered how she had used her *laran* to track Jaelle through hills like these, years ago. But she shook her head.

"I'm not close enough to either of them for that."

"But you actually probed Lexie's mind," Jaelle protested, "that might make a bond."

"I'm not sure I want a bond like that," said Magda wearily; but she closed her eyes and tried to see Lexie; and for a moment, she had a fleeting glimpse of Lexie, her head covered with a Darkovan hooded cape, leaning forward over a pony's neck . . . Snow seemed to blot out the vision, she did not know whether it was the snow falling now, or some other storm in some other place, could not tell whether it had been memory or imagination or a true picture from her *laran*.

She said, doubtfully, "I think I saw—they have been delayed by a storm? I'm not sure." Even with the whole of the Forbidden Tower matrix circle around her, she knew the same uncertainty would have remained: present—where Lexie was now—or a flash from past or future.

"I'd do as well guessing," she sighed, "and you could make a better guess about Rafaella than I could."

"I've been trying to do that," Jaella told her, "but I don't like it. We were so close, for so long, it's as if I was using that closeness to spy on her. And she has no *laran* at all, she would never understand."

Magda heard also what Jaelle didn't say; this was not the first time her Comyn birth, the heritage of *laran* they could never share, had come between them, disrupting their long partnership, even their brief time as lovers. Rafaella could have forgiven Jaelle everything except this, that she had returned to bear a child to a Comyn lord—had taken a place in that mysterious world in which Rafaella could have no part. Magda thought Rafaella could even have forgiven Jaelle for that, if Jaelle had had to leave all of her Renunciate world behind. What she could never forgive was that Magda, a Terran, had followed Jaelle where Rafi herself could not.

"Trying to track them with *laran* is foolishness,"

Vanessa said, so impatiently that for a moment Magda wondered if she had been thinking aloud. Then she remembered what Jaelle had actually said, about trying to follow Rafaella with the psychic bond between them.

"Maybe one of you can do it, maybe you can't, I don't see why you should waste time trying. Is it important to know if they came this way?"

"Only to know how near they are to the meeting place she left the message about," Jaelle said. "If they had good luck and good weather, traveling light, they could be at Barrensclae already—that's where we slaughtered the chervines—and we've got three days to catch them there."

"How far is it?" Camilla asked. "I'm not familiar with the place."

"In good weather? Ten hours, once we cross Ravensmark. In this? Your guess is as good as mine. A day, ten days, never. If we hit avalanches, we might not make it at all."

"Avalanches?" Cholayna craned her neck up toward the pass, invisible in the flying snow. "How high *is* Ravensmark?"

"Eleven thousand forty."

"Meters? Good God! You can't call that a *pass!* That's a mountain all by itself."

"No, eleven thousand forty feet—"

"What's that in civilized numbers?" Vanessa demanded.

"I can't be bothered to figure all these numbers for you," Jaelle snapped, "I have important things to worry about, such as how in the names of all the goddesses we're going to get these horses across here if the road's been washed out from the summer floods! There's a long stretch where the road has never been good for more than one pony's width, a washout there could mean losing half our baggage. Do you want to hike through the Kilghards in a backpack and no spare boots? I don't.''

''I've probably climbed worse,'' Vanessa said. ''Believe it or not, Jaelle, there are other planets with snow and high mountains in the Empire. If you're not able to get over a pass without your mystical psychic powers—''

''Now listen here—'' Jaelle began.

''Hold it! Both of you,'' Camilla ordered. ''If we're going to stand here arguing about what we're going to do, let's use the time for something practical while we wait. Vanessa, hunt out the grain. We'll feed the animals. Then if we decide to start over the pass, they at least will be well fed and in good shape. Jaelle, have you been over Ravensmark before this?''

''Twice. It's easier this way. Coming down from the North, you're more exposed to the wind. But this direction isn't exactly a picnic. I really am worried about washouts, and with snow in the pass—if Vanessa is really as experienced as she claims, she wouldn't take it lightly either.''

''I never said I was taking it lightly,'' Vanessa quibbled, ''but I do feel, the worse it is, the more sense it makes to get over it before the snow gets any deeper. If Jaelle doesn't feel comfortable leading the way, I'll try.''

''I know the way, and you don't,'' Jaelle said. ''If it can be led at all, I'll lead it. I'm not worried about getting across myself, on foot. The chervines can make it, it's their kind of country, after all. And I think the ponies probably can. But I tell you, those ledges are *narrow*. Even at the best, you don't cross Ravensmark on horseback. It makes Scaravel look like the Great Northern Road. Even with washouts, I'd try it in decent weather. But if we get a hard freeze, and there's glare ice—I'm not actively suicidal, and I don't imagine you are."

"That bad, huh?" Vanessa looked at Jaelle in silence for a minute. When at last she spoke, to Magda's relief, there was not a trace of argumentativeness in her voice.

"What are our options, then? If the risk is that great—what alternatives do we have?"

Jaelle considered this for a moment. She looked at the thickening snow, and said, "If we don't cross it tonight, it probably can't be crossed at all until after next spring-thaw. That's why it's the least traveled pass in the Kilghard Hills. Once there's glare ice on those ledges, I wouldn't cross it for all the copper in Zandru's tomb. We'd have no choice except to go back, and go round by Hammerfell."

"*Can* we cross it tonight?"

"I think I could get across in daylight," Jaelle mused, "though I might have to lead the horses across one by one. If you're used to mountain-style ice-climbing, you probably could. And I'd bet on Camilla. I'm not sure about Magda, but she did get across Scaravel in the dead of winter, and I wasn't any help even when the banshees found us. But—" She turned and looked at the one remaining woman.

Cholayna looked straight into Jaelle's eyes. "I'm not afraid."

"That has nothing to do with it. It's not your courage I question. It's your balance, your skill, your head for heights. Magda has no head for heights at all, but she knows I do, and she'll take orders. What about you? Ravensmark is about the worst trail you can imagine, and then some. Vanessa has done some climbing for the fun of it, so I know she won't panic when the going gets rough—and believe me, it's rough enough that I get scared myself, and I don't usually scare. If you lose your nerve when we're in the neck of the pass, along those ledges—what then? We won't be able to turn around and go back, not at that point. Once we're halfway over, it's too late. I think we're going to have to go around. I honestly can't be sure you'll make it, and I don't want to risk all our lives on your nerves."

Cholayna opened her mouth to protest, and shut it again. At last she said, "Fair enough. I'm the weak link. Do you want me to turn back, and let the rest of you go on? Because what you're saying is, the rest of you can make it without me. And if you turn back and go around—there wouldn't be much chance of catching up with them in time—right?"

"If we go round by Hammerfell," Camilla said, "I doubt we'd catch up with them this side of Nevarsin."

"And if we—or you—go on, you have a good chance?"

"A chance," Jaelle said. "Not a good chance. There's that, too. I could risk all our lives and push across Ravensmark, and we might *still* lose them. I don't know if it's worth pushing you all this way for such a bare chance. I'm no gambler—never have been."

"Forget about me," Cholayna said. "What do you want to do?"

Jaelle turned on her angrily. "That's not a fair question! How can I forget about you? You're *here*! Do you think I want your death on my conscience?"

"I shouldn't have come, should I?"

"Too late to worry about that now," Camilla said, while Jaelle hesitated, too polite to answer. "Done is done. I can see why you wanted to come, why you had to. Sending you back alone would be just as dangerous as trying to drag you across Ravensmark, so forget about it. Just shut up and let Jaelle think what's right to do.''

Cholayna shut up. It must, Magda thought, have been the first time in twenty years that Cholayna had been treated like a nuisance, a liability. It was Jaelle who must make the final decision. Quietly she went to the saddlebags, dug out rations and shared out handfuls of dried fruit and meat bars.

''Whether we cross or go back, we won't have time for a meal in the neck of the pass. We fed the horses, which makes sense. Eat.'' She handed Jaelle some of the meat-and-dried-fruit mixture, and Jaelle put some of the stuff, absentmindedly, into her mouth and chewed.

Cholayna nibbled on a raisin, and Camilla said, ''Eat some of the meat, too. Whatever we do, in this cold you need something solid.''

Cholayna sighed, put the dried meat into her mouth with visible distaste. What Camilla had said was right, and Cholayna knew it, but Magda, watching her struggle to keep from spitting out the detested and unfamiliar food, felt considerable sympathy for her. Cholayna Ares was used to giving orders, not taking them; and while she might be willing to take them on important things which were obviously a question of all their lives, she would, sooner or later, refuse to take orders about personal matters.

Vanessa looked at the sky, from which the color was already beginning to fade as the snow thickened. ''So what are we going to do? If we're going to try to cross, we'd better not waste any more time. And if we're not, shouldn't we get under cover?''

Magda knew that Jaelle had no taste for making such decisions. Yet they were all turning to her, demanding it. She wished she could shelter her friend in her arms and protect her. But for better or for worse, the decision was Jaelle's.

Jaelle finished the mouthful of dried meat and fruit, swallowed once or twice, and sighed. "I don't know what to say. I swear I don't! Vanessa, what do you think?"

"I'm not as familiar as you are with the place. I'm not familiar with it at all. If you want to try, I'll follow. We can give it a good try."

"Magda, what do you say?"

"I'm willing to take the risk, if you think it can be done."

"I know that," Jaelle said, and now she sounded irritable. "I'm asking what you think Cholayna's chances are of making it, and whether it's worth pushing on, with the risks what they are; or if we should play it safe, turn around and head for Hammerfell. Or would you take her round by Hammerfell, and Van and I go over, try to catch up, and wait for you at Barrensclae?"

"Maybe you should ask Vanessa," Magda temporized, half joking. "Personnel is *her* job. I think we should all go ahead, or all go back together and go round. If she goes back, I shall have to go with her. What about it, Cholayna? Do you want to try? I see no point losing three days or so, but only you know if you're willing to risk it. But if Jaelle thinks I can make it, you probably can."

"I'll try," Cholayna said, with the ghost of a smile. "And I promise not to lose my nerve. Or, if I do, I'll keep my mouth shut about it."

Jaelle shrugged. "All right. Let's go before the snow gets any thicker and has a chance to freeze. If we can get through before there's ice on the ledges, it will be a lot more workable. One word of advice—and this goes for you too, Magda. Keep your eyes on the trail and don't look down."

CHAPTER ELEVEN

At first the road led upward between hills, steep but not yet menacing. The snowflakes had grown smaller, no longer hand-sized, but the smaller flakes came down thickly, and Magda knew this meant the snow would continue to fall. There were still a few hours of grayish daylight.

Jaelle led the way, muffled in cloak and hood, thick scarf tied over her face; Camilla came after, with two chervines broken to a tandem rein; then Cholayna, at the center, on the smallest and most-sure-footed of the mountain ponies. Magda came behind her, riding a horse and leading one of the chervines. Vanessa, mountain-wise but unfamiliar with the trail, brought up the rear.

As the trail led upward, it grew fainter and steeper. Parts of it were trodden deeply into old mud, rocks lining the path underfoot, and patches of last winter's snow clinging beneath the thick tree-hedges that lined the road. It was very silent, even the animal's hooves sounding muffled underfoot, and the snow continued to fall. Upward and still upward; now there were places where the trail all but disappeared between trees and rocks. The chervines did not like it, and whickered uneasily as they picked their way. After an hour's riding—though it seemed like more—Camilla signaled

133

a halt, got down and took the two tethered-together pack animals off the tandem rein.

"They won't be able to make it like this. Cholayna, you take the lead rein on this one. He'll follow the other, she's his mother and they've worked together for years. He won't run off and get lost, but he needs a rein to follow." She climbed back into her saddle. Her face was muffled in a scarf and heavily smeared with cream against the burning of the wind. Cholayna had the same cream on her face; it looked grotesque against the darkness of her skin, as if she were checkerboarded black and white.

When they started upward again, the path was so steep and so narrow that the chervines were lurching upward as if they were climbing steps. Magda kept feeling that she would slip backward off her horse as the animal's quarters strained up under her saddle. She thought, *We'll never make it*. A few minutes later, Jaelle signaled a halt. Her figure was blurred through the thickening snow, which was no longer melting as it fell but sticking to the ground, still no more than a thin white sifting; rocks and mud showed patchy black through snowy lace.

Jaelle slid to the ground, hanging the reins on the saddle; she came back, picking her way down over the rocks in the narrow space between the trail's edge against the mountain, and the horses and pack animals. She spoke to Camilla as she edged past, and Camilla dismounted and came after her. Magda heard her say to Cholayna: "It's too steep even for your pony. You'll have to get down. Walk close to your horse and hold his bridle. He'll find the way better than you can." She steadied the older woman as she clambered out of the saddle. "Is the altitude bothering you?"

"Not yet, just a little short of breath."

"Well, take it easy. There's no point hurrying. There's bad going ahead, but no danger here. Are you all right, Magda?"

Magda could feel her heart pounding with the altitude, but so far she was in no trouble. She was not so sure about Cholayna, but so far the Terran woman was keeping the pace well enough, and they were gaining height so slowly that there was time to adjust to the altitude. Her ears felt tight, and she yawned, feeling them pop.

"How are you doing, Vanessa?" Jaelle faced the younger woman at the back of the line.

"So far, so good. What are we? About halfway up?"

"Close enough. The hard going starts up there." Jaelle pointed and Magda sighted up along the path to where a crag hung over the narrow path and, as far as she could tell, the road disappeared and dropped off to nowhere.

Vanessa surveyed it, frowning. Jaelle said, "There are steps. Broad enough and low enough, the horses and chervines can make them if the snow doesn't get any more slippery. It's one of the bad spots. I'm going on ahead; let my horse follow if she will, but wait till I signal if it's all right. I want to be sure there are no nasty surprises up here, while it's still light enough to see." She turned and went upward along the narrow trail, half disappearing from sight as the pathway dipped; they could see her red cap bobbing along, then nothing. Camilla said tensely, "I should have gone up with her."

"She knows what she's doing," Magda said. After a minute or two, Jaelle reappeared and beckoned them forward. Camilla took the lead reins of one chervine, letting her horse follow as he would; Cholayna the other. Magda dismounted, taking the reins of horse and chervine, one in either hand, until the trail grew so narrow that she was forced to go ahead, leading her horse and letting the mountain-bred chervine pick his way as he could. Once she found herself edging a tight curb, looking over a dizzy cliff into gulfs of space. The trunks of tall trees thrust up below at crazy angles on the mountainside, and she looked down into their topmost branches. She clutched the lead rein tight and was careful not to look down again.

Ahead of her, where the trail made its sharpest turn, she saw Camilla holding out her hand to Cholayna.

"Hang on. Let the horse go. She'll find her way all right. Don't look down. It's a little steep here. One long step up. That's right. Fine." Cholayna's legs disappeared around the corner. Camilla's voice came, reassuring her.

"It's a bit slippery, Margali. Careful."

She set her boots down with extra care, scrambling for a hold; rounded the blind corner and found herself on broad, low rock steps. One of them crumbled away perilously close to a sheer drop of at least fifty feet and then vanished into blurred snowy treetops. A little dizzy, her ears ringing, she heaved herself to her feet, scrambled up another step and found herself on firm ground, her horse lunging upward after her. She came up on the broad rock plate above, where the wind of the heights tore at her hair. She struggled to re-tie her hood, hearing Cholayna's harsh breaths close behind her. Vanessa pulled herself nimbly up beside them.

"Whew! That's a mean one. And you say it gets worse?"

"Unless there are bad washouts, we can probably handle it," Jaelle said, "but let's get along. There's not more than an hour of daylight left, and the snow's beginning to stick. There are some places we couldn't possibly manage in the dark.''

The upward path was less steep now, but wound close to the side of the mountain, just wide enough for a woman or a pony. Cholayna, at Camilla's advice, walked on the inside of the trail, hugging the rock cliff and clinging to the pony's bridle. Magda would have liked to do the same; she edged as close to the cliff as she dared and did not look down. Once she heard a *kyorebni* scream, and the great carrion-bird loomed close to them; the pony lunged with fright and Magda struggled with the rein, trying to quiet the animal, herself terrified by the huge beating wings, the evil glinting eye which looked for a moment straight into hers, and then was gone; she saw the bird careening off into the wind below her and quickly turned her head and stared at the solid rock of the cliff.

Vanessa, behind her so close that Magda could feel her body's warmth, muttered, ''What in hell was that?''

Magda said briefly, in Terran Standard, ''Lammergeier. Near as makes no difference.''

They bent their heads against the wind. It was strong now, whirling the snow in stinging, biting needles. Every step now strained the muscles of Magda's thighs painfully against the upward slope, and the snow, half an inch thick now under her boot soles, was wet enough to slip underfoot. She could hear the animals panting hard, their breath like hers, coming in white clouds against the white snow.

Upward and upward; then she heard Jaelle's shout:

''Washout ahead. Hug the cliff and let the horses find their own way!''

Ahead, she saw Cholayna inching her way past a giant's bite taken out of the edge of the roadway, so that the path narrowed to a few inches. Trying to steady her breathing, Magda flattened herself against the cliff and placed each footstep with extra caution, closing her eyes against the temptation to look down into the dizzying expanse of snow beneath, blotting out the valley below. She felt Vanessa's hand on her elbow, steadying her.

"All right, Miss Lorne?"

How absurd that sounded, in these wilderness surroundings. She thought, *I'll have to speak to her about that*, and concentrated on placing her feet with care. The chervine picked its way carefully along, shaking its antlers against the thick snow.

Her heart was thumping now. *No more than thirty-four hundred meters, that's not all that high, I must be in worse condition than I thought. And we're not even near the top yet.* Her world had narrowed, the precarious rocky road under her feet, the soft snorting of her horse, the soft clicking of the chervine's hooves muffled by snow. Somewhere above them a rock rattled loose and bounced over the trail ahead and Camilla called back softly, "Careful. Look out for falling rocks along here."

Her eyes blurred; she felt herself swaying, perilously close to the edge. No—she was not dizzy, what was she picking up? Cautiously she made her way along the cliff until she was beside Cholayna. The woman's dark face was gray-white, and when Magda took her gloved hand, it seemed that she could hear the manic thumping of Cholayna's heart.

"Altitude getting to you?"

"Just a little. Not—used to—heights like this." Cholayna, too, kept her eyes averted from the drop edge; although Camilla kept looking over, with curiosity and interest, and Jaelle plodded along at the very edge in a way that sent shivering spasms through the muscles of Magda's thighs and buttocks. Vanessa strolled along as unconcernedly as if she were on an escalator in the Terran HQ.

Magda said to Cholayna in an undertone, "I don't care for this kind of trail myself. You don't *have* to look over the cliff, though. Hang on here if you want to." She felt Cholayna's hand clutching at hers and tried to feel calm, to quiet Cholayna's panic. "It's safe enough. Just don't look over the edge."

"I keep feeling—I'll slip and go over—" Cholayna whispered.

"I know. I get it too. It's not much farther now," Magda added, though she did not have the faintest idea how far it was to the top. "Just take it one step at a time. It's wider than an ordinary staircase and that wouldn't bother you. You're doing fine."

She heard the other woman sigh. "It's all right. It got to me for a minute, that's all. I hate being the weakest link this way."

"Well, if it weren't you, it would be me," Magda said. "All right, now?" She turned her attention to her chervine, but continued to watch, unobtrusively, as Cholayna moved slowly upward through the gathering dark.

I hope we get there before it's much darker, she thought, gritting her teeth against the cold that made her cheekbones ache. Already she could barely see the path under her feet, though the whiteness of the snow made it easier to see where the path actually vanished. Once her foot dislodged a loose rock at the very edge of the trail and she heard it rattle down for what seemed an endless time before it was out of earshot. One step, then another, steeper one, then another and another.

She edged round another sharp switchback where the

trail was almost invisible. She bumped softly into Cholayna, motionless before her.

"I can't see the trail anymore!" the older woman gasped.

Neither could Magda, really. "Follow the horse. She can see better than you can." But she wondered how far Jaelle thought they could go on in this dim twilight, with the wind high enough that it was coming at their faces almost horizontally, mixed with needles of sleet.

She could not really see ahead, but she could feel the animals gathered around her on a widening of the ledge, a hollowing out of the overhanging cliff into something like shelter. Vanessa came up with them and they stood gathered in a circle.

Jaelle said, "No way we can get over tonight. We have to bivouac somewhere, and this is the safest place."

Vanessa asked, "Do we have lights with us?"

Jaelle shook her head. "No use, in this. The trail's just too bad underfoot. We'll have to risk snow-freeze on the ledges. In daylight, when we're all fresh and strong, we'll try again. Listen to that!" she added. The wind was howling down from the crags above them, and from somewhere came a long, eerie scream—the cry of a banshee. Magda shivered, remembering her only encounter with such creatures, in the Pass of Scaravel. She hoped this one was a good long way off.

Jaelle said, "Let's get set up. No room for a proper camp, but the overhang gives us some shelter. Chervines on the outside. They're more sure-footed than horses."

Magda got a fire lighted to melt snow for hot drinks, though there was no space for much cooking. By the time the drinks were ready, the sleeping bags were spread in the shelter of the ledge. The cold was so fierce, snow hissing past the lantern in white streaks, that they crowded together close under piled blankets,

Magda and Vanessa to either side of Cholayna. The older woman's fingers were stiff and shaking as she took off her boots, and her feet looked pale and swollen. Vanessa took them in her lap to warm them in her hands.

Cholayna began to protest. Vanessa said, "Cholayna, I'm an old hand in the mountains and know more about feet and frostbite than you've ever heard of. Drink your tea."

"I'm not thirsty. I don't think I can swallow."

"All the more reason. Go on, you have to. At this altitude, you have to force fluids, because the body tries to shut down peripheral systems to protect the torso, which is why your feet start to freeze. That's right, wiggle those toes as much as you can! Your body starts to eat its own muscle tissue, you see, that means forcing fluids so your kidneys don't shut down. That's the first lesson in surviving high altitudes—not that this is so high, but it's higher than you're used to. Drink that up, and eat." She handed Cholayna a bar of dried fruit, sticky with nuts and honey. Dutifully, Cholayna tried to eat, but Magda could see that she was too weary to chew. She took Cholayna's ration and soaked the dried fruit in the hot tea, making it softer and easier to swallow, a trick she had learned long ago on the trail. She loaded the tea with extra sugar and gave it back to Cholayna.

"Just get it down—don't bother about how it tastes."

"Same to you, Magda," Jaelle reproved dryly. "You've forgotten yours. Finish that before you lie down."

Magda nodded, acknowledging the reproof. She was too tired to rummage in her pack for clean socks, but she did it anyway, and took her boots into the bottom of the sleeping bag. Jaelle and Camilla slid a filled water bottle inside their bag, keeping it from freezing with body heat. They spread extra blankets over all the sleeping bags, huddling together to conserve the last bits of warmth.

Vanessa had chosen the outside edge; Cholayna between her and Magda, with Jaelle and Camilla curled up against them. Magda was too tired to sleep; one by one she heard the other women drop off with soft-breathing slumber, but she lay awake, hearing the soft rasping of Cholayna's breath, Jaelle coughing a little in her sleep. She could sense Camilla's shivers: she was the thinnest of them, with the least body fat; and though Magda knew the *emmasca* was tougher than copper wire, she resolved to speak to her about warmer clothes. At higher altitudes this would be serious, and Camilla had a great deal of emotional investment in proving her own toughness; she might not want to dress more warmly than, say, Vanessa, who had, though she was slenderly made, the normal extra layer of fat on a human female. Camilla didn't, and had a phobia about calling attention to the fact.

Magda turned over cautiously without disturbing the women to either side, and wondered if she was going to sleep at all. She should really try. She composed herself mentally for some of the disciplines she had learned in matrix work; then decided that she would, before she slept, check in briefly with the Forbidden Tower circle— her family. They should know where she was, and that she would not be returning home as soon as she had promised.

Although if we do get over this damnable pass tomorrow, and catch up to Lexie and Rafaella, I'm going back to Shaya as soon as I can!

Jaelle was deeply asleep. *No need for her to come along.*

Briefly, Magda monitored her body, checking to be sure the circulation was adequate in fingers and toes; there was always a small but distinct danger involved in leaving the body under these conditions.

Then she was out of her body and standing in the gray and faceless plain of the overworld, swiftly looking round for the landmark of the Forbidden Tower, sending out a silent call to Callista.

But there was no sign of the Tower. And then, in the grayness, a strange and unfamiliar face slowly took shape before Magda's eyes.

It was a woman's face, old, with deep-set eyes under eyebrows that were all white; a wrinkled forehead beneath braided hair as white as the eyebrows. Devoid of the benevolent peace Magda always associated with wrinkles and age, this woman glared—and although there were no words, Magda felt the angry challenge.

Go back. You may not pass here.

"By whose authority do you challenge my freedom of the overworld?" Magda called up in her mind a clear picture of the Tower and of Damon, its Keeper.

The old woman threw back her head and emitted what Magda could only characterize as a series of yelps, though after a moment she knew they were intended as mocking laughter.

That one doesn't cut any ice out here, you'll have to do better than him to get by out here! You ought to turn around and go right back, girl, get back to your baby, you had no business leaving her anyhow! What do you girls think you're at anyway, climbing around out here? Heh-eh-eh! Think you're tough and strong? Proud of yourself for getting up this little hill, heh? You haven't seen anything yet, chiya! (The word was tinged with scathing contempt.) *Pack of girls and a couple of old ladies without the honesty to admit they're too old to*

*take it anymore! Oh no, you won't get through when the
going gets rough! Suppose you think you know the way,
the passwords? Well, try it, just try it, that's all. Heh
heh heh, heh-eh-eh-eh-eeeee!*

With her head thrown back, the white braids jiggling
with scornful laughter, the horrible old crone shook her
fist at Magda. Magda knew that she was betraying her
fear, for in the overworld it was impossible to conceal
one's real feelings; nevertheless she said firmly: "Old
mother, you cannot deny me my place here."

*And what are you doing out here, leaving your child
and all?*

Magda's instinct to answer, *What business of yours is
it?* was tempered by some knowledge of the laws by
which the overworld worked. You could not avoid a
challenge; nor was this her first, though never had she
faced anything like this hideous old woman. So she
answered, "I am following a call of duty and friendship."

*Hah! You're no friend to either of them that's gone
ahead; you don't have the guts to do what they do,
jealous, that's all.*

Magda considered this and answered, "That doesn't
matter. My friends are worried about it, and I am going
for their sake."

*Heh-eh-eh! Not good enough! I knew it! What you
have to do on this quest, you have to do for your own
reasons, can't follow no one else out here. See? I knew
it. Get back!* She raised her hand, and it seemed that a
bolt of blue fire struck Magda between the breasts. Pain
lanced through her heart, and she felt herself falling,
falling. . . .

The gray world was gone. Magda shivered inside her
sleeping bag, back in her body . . . Or had she ever left
it? Had she not simply fallen asleep, the whole encounter been a bizarre dream dramatizing her own mental

conflicts about this strange and unwanted quest? She could hear Cholayna moaning softly in her sleep, and Jaelle muttering, "no, no," and wondered if her friend was having nightmares about ledges and cliffs.

Should she try to go back at once into the overworld? She had been told that such a failure should immediately be challenged again, that it was like being thrown from a horse: you must at once mount and ride again. But had she ever been in the overworld at all, had she not simply fallen asleep? She knew it was unwise to attempt psi work when you were overtired or ill, and the ordeal of the climb and her tremendous fatigue made it unsafe.

Firmly summoning the disciplines she had been taught, she began to count herself quietly down into sleep. She could not afford to lie awake with the crossing of Ravensmark before them tomorrow.

CHAPTER TWELVE

Jaelle crawled to the edge of the rock overhang and looked out. "Snowing harder than ever," she said grimly. "I don't think we're going anywhere in this!"

"I have to go out anyhow. I'll check the animals," Camilla said, climbing over her. When she returned, she was scraping at her boot distastefully. "Step carefully when you go out; with ten animals out there, it's like a stable."

"Well, there's a snow shovel in one of the loads, if you feel like shoveling it clean," Jaelle said, and went out. She came back grimacing. "Snowing like Zandru's sixth or seventh hell. And guess what?"

Vanessa, kneeling at the back of the ledge to light a fire, turned to rummage in her own pack. She tossed a small packet at Jaelle and said, "Be my guest. There's an old maxim on women's climbing expeditions: whatever's going to happen will happen at the worst possible time. You're lucky. Usually it happens just above seven thousand."

"It's not the worst possible time," Magda said, "it could be a nice clear morning and you'd have to go out and lead the pass. Crawl back in your sleeping bag, Shaya, and I'll make you a hot drink."

Complying, Jaelle said, "I don't suppose you brought any golden-flower tea?"

"Whatever that is, I don't think so," Vanessa said, "but I have some prostaglandin inhibitors in my medikit." She dug out some tablets while Magda was making porridge, heavily fortified with fruit and extra sugar. Cholayna got a heavier sweater from her pack and pulled it on. She was shivering.

"I'd like a good stiff drink."

"At this altitude? You'd be roaring drunk before you could drink three sips!" Vanessa said. "Try a caffeine tablet instead." She handed them around with the porridge; only Camilla refused.

"Does it look as if it would clear any time today?"

"I've no idea," Jaelle said. "I know what's worrying you: if we get two or three feet of snow, we're really in trouble. The pass isn't the kind we can get through with snow up to our knees or worse." They could all hear what she did not say aloud, that going back past the narrow ledges of the washed-out area would be as dangerous as trying to go ahead. And with every hour that passed, their chances of overtaking Rafaella and Lexie grew less.

They ate porridge, and afterward Vanessa and Camilla repacked the stacked loads. The sky remained gray, but the snow grew no heavier. It seemed to Magda that it was slowing, if not stopping.

Camilla said once, staring out over the cliff edge, "There are devils in this place. Was I the only one to suffer Alar's own nightmares?"

"It's the altitude," said Cholayna. "My head is splitting. I dreamed I was in that damned city Lexie was talking about, and there were a dozen women with horns and tails and false-face masks like the demons of my ancestral tribes, all trying to make me crawl through a needle's eye before I could come in. They said I was too fat, and they were squeezing me through and burning off what hung outside the edges.''

"Bad dreams are the rule at this altitude," Vanessa said. "I dreamed about *you*, Cholayna. You were telling me that if we ever got back I'd have to take a demotion of three grades for insubordination."

Jaelle chuckled. "I dreamed my daughter was a Keeper, and she was telling me that because I had deserted her, I'd never be competent enough to work on my own. Then she was trying to give me lessons in monitoring, only instead of a matrix it was a chervine turd and I had to turn it to stone.''

They all laughed, except Camilla, who frowned and stared at her clenched knuckles. "What I dreamed I will not say. But there are devils in this place.''

"Altitude and cold," said Magda briskly. "You're too thin. Another layer of heavy underwear ought to take care of it.''

Hours crawled by. Toward noon, there was a vagrant glimmer toward the south, and Jaelle said, "I think the sun's trying to come out. We ought to get along if we can.''

"Want me to break trail?" Vanessa offered, as they crawled out of their sleeping bags.

"No, thanks, really, I'm fine. Your pills are wonder workers, I never felt better. Truly, Vanessa, I'm not just trying to stay ahead. If I need help, I'll say so, I promise. But I know the way and you don't. I can manage. Believe me, if I get chilled or over-tired, I'll let you take the lead, but even with me leading, a lot of the landmarks aren't going to be visible." She slung her pack over the pony's back. "Let's get the loads on. Cinch them well, the footing's likely to be bad.''

There was a thick heavy silence around the ledge as they cinched loads and packs. In the damp heavy air, even the small sounds made by the animals seemed unreal. The snow was firm and crunching softly underfoot, and not as slippery as Magda had feared. She looked back down the trail they had come up. It seemed to her that they were very high, but above them the trail went on, curving around rocks and disappearing.

Jaelle put one hand on her pony's rein; she had tethered the chervine to it so that the pack beast had no choice but to follow. Camilla took the reins of the next three animals, and began climbing after Jaelle. Here the trail was steep but by no means impassable.

Magda gestured to Cholayna to go before her, and waited until the Terran woman was several steps up the trail before setting her animals on the way and beginning to climb. Up and up the trail led, and as they climbed the sun came out. There was a clear view, where the trail curved, of a whole range of hills beyond; the path led steeply upward, against the sharp rock cliff, to a notch between two peaks.

"Ravensmark," Jaelle said, pointing, and started up toward it.

Magda climbed. She felt fresh and strong, but though she climbed steadily for hours, the pass seemed no nearer. About every hour, Jaelle called a halt for rest, but even so she was tiring, and after three or four rests, she called Vanessa forward to take the lead.

"As soon as we're through the pass, I'll lead again. There's a nasty bit just below the top, on the other side."

Vanessa nodded assent. Jaelle dropped back beside Camilla, who looked like a thundercloud.

"Want to take the rear? I don't feel up to it," Jaelle said, and Camilla went quietly back along the trail to take up the rearguard, pausing to ask how Cholayna was doing.

"It helps to be able to see where we're going."

Magda felt she would rather not see. She kept her eyes away from the edges.

As Camilla passed Magda on her way, she paused to draw a deep breath. "We'll be past the worst soon. From there, it's downhill."

Magda was almost too short of breath to nod her gratitude for that. With the sun out, it was more cheerful, but the snow was beginning to melt and the going was more slippery. For the final steep haul upward to the pass, she had to stretch herself to the utmost; she could hear her breath whistling loudly in her lungs as she struggled up the last bit to stand between Jaelle and Cholayna in the throat of the peaks.

Jaelle swore under her breath; pointed.

"That used to be the trail," she said. Now the pathway downward was buried beneath tons of rock and shifting gravel, half hidden in the snow.

"Washout, rockslide, the gods alone know what else under there. Old rotten ice from the peak must have crashed down on it in the spring rains, and that part of the trail is gone for good."

"So what do we do now?" Vanessa asked. "Can it be crossed at all?"

'Your guess is as good as mine. Lightweight, climbing, I could get across it. The chervines could probably get down. Look—" She pointed. "Down past that clump of trees, the trail's fairly good again. At least there *is* some kind of trail! The rockslide covered about five hundred meters, more or less, with rocks and rubble. It's steep, and it looks nasty. It's probably not as bad as it looks—"

"Unless all this loose snow starts sliding down again. It looks as if there might be loose rocks, too, which could start avalanching down when we set foot on it,"

Camilla said, coming to join them. "No wonder we had nightmares back there." The women stood looking down, while Magda and Cholayna, knowing they could contribute nothing to the discussion, stood silent, looking down at the chaos of snow, rock and old ice heaped up below them where once there had been at least the semblance of a trail.

At last Vanessa suggested, "Jaelle, you and I could rope up and scout the way down on foot. At least we'd know then whether it's solid enough underfoot to bring the animals down after us. With the snow this deep, it's likely to be frozen hard enough underneath that it won't start sliding too fast. That was a damned hard freeze last night."

Jaelle thought that over for a minute, then she said, "I don't see any alternative. Unless someone else has a better idea?"

Nobody did. It was clearly obvious that the only other choice was to turn around, retrace their steps over Ravensmark and detour through Hammerfell. They had certainly lost any chance of catching up with Rafaella at Barrensclae.

"If we'd known," Jaelle said grimly, rummaging through a load, looking for her ice axe, "we could have taken the Great Northern Road directly to Nevarsin."

"And if the Duke of Hammerfell had worn a skirt," Camilla said, "he might have been the Duchess."

"Jaelle, hindsight is always twenty-twenty vision," Cholayna reminded her. "We did the best we could. The important thing is that we're here, and so far we're safe."

Jaelle said, with a twitchy small grin, "Let's just hope we can still say that tonight. Vanessa, give me the rope. Do you want to lead down, or shall I?"

"I don't see that it makes any difference. We can

both see where the road ought to be, and isn't. I'll start.'' She snapped the buckle of a body harness around her waist, tested the free passage of the rope through it, and took a firm grip on her ice axe.

"A few feet of slack. That's right.'' She placed her feet gingerly on the snow and rubble and started to pick her way down; went over the edge, slid, and the rope went tight. Magda heard Cholayna's breath go out in a gasp, but after a minute Vanessa called up, "I'm all right, lost my footing. Tricky here. Let me find a solider step. Hang on tight.''

Presently her head reappeared, climbing up.

"This way won't go. There's a drop-off of forty meters just below here, I'll have to scout over this way.'' She went slowly leftward, picking her footing with caution. This time she managed to keep her feet under her; after a time, it began to look rather like a trail. Jaelle handed the rope to Magda.

"You and Camilla belay me from here.'' She started after Vanessa, picking her way carefully in the rut of Vanessa's trail. Camilla came and stood behind Magda, ready to hold the rope hard if either of the women below them should slip. They were out of sight now. Magda, Camilla holding her firmly round the waist, felt her breath coming hard. Part of it was fear; the rest was helplessness. She was no good here: she had no climbing skills, no mountain-craft. All she could do was hang on and trust her freemate.

"That's enough,'' Camilla said softly—or had she spoken aloud? Was it the silence, the isolation of the mountain trail, where no other minds intruded, that meant that Magda did not need to shield against the low-level telepathic jangle of cities and crowds, and so made it seem that she was almost constantly in communion with Camilla's mind? She didn't know, and her

mind was on something else anyhow. But she leaned
back against Camilla's hands, firmly bracing her and
holding her weight, as the rope stretched taut, holding
the climbers below. Her throat and nose were painfully
dry; the cold dryness of the heights dehydrated sinuses
and mucous membranes, and all she could think of was
how much she wanted a drink. It must have been harder
still for Jaelle and Vanessa, fighting ice and loose rock
below.

The rope slackened, and for a moment Magda
panicked, fearing a broken rope, a fall. . . . Then a
ringing call came up from somewhere below them.

"It's all right. It will go this way. I'm coming up."
It was Jaelle's voice, and after a long time she reappeared,
climbing carefully up from below.

Vanessa came after, bent over and breathing hard.

"I want a drink," she said, and Cholayna found the
water bottle and passed it to the climbers.

When Jaelle had recovered her breath, she said, "It's
all right; not even very steep. There's one bad place
where there's loose rock; we'll have to lead the horses
over one at a time, very carefully, so they don't slip. It
would be damned easy for any of us to break a leg
there. But everywhere else it's solid underfoot, and we
kicked away what we could of the loosest stuff. Below
there, the trail starts again. It's narrow, but it's *there*. I
think we can make it. But I'm going to take Cholayna
across that stretch myself." She took another drink,
gasping. But at Camilla's concerned look, she said
only, "I'm fine, don't fuss," and Magda knew better
than to display any concern.

"Hunt out some bread and cheese; we should eat
lunch here," Vanessa said, "and if anyone has any
little personal things to attend to, do it here. There's no
place below to step off the trail."

"As I recall," Cholayna joked, "there's no trail to step off of."

Jaelle carefully redistributed loads on the pack animals as they munched a few mouthfuls of bread and cheese. At last they were ready to start down. Jaelle took the leading reins off of the chervines' bridles.

"They'll follow the horses. But they can find the way better than we can." She started down. "Let me get about forty feet along the trail and then come after me, Magda. Then you, Camilla, and Cholayna. I'll come back for the extra horses. Vanessa, you stay behind in case anyone gets into trouble, all right?"

"Right."

Magda picked up her horse's reins and started down the narrow trail Jaelle was re-making—no more than a scattering of foot- and hoof-prints. The snow was hard, and the snorting of the chervines picking their way along after her sounded loud. She placed each foot carefully; her horse whinnied and tried to hang back, and she felt nervous about pulling on the rein.

"Come along, there's a good girl." She patted the horse's nose, encouraging her gently. When they had gotten a little farther down the trail, she heard Camilla's and Cholayna's footsteps behind her; then again the loose, crowding chervines. One of them bolted up around the newly rutted trail in the snow; the small bells on its load jingled wildly as the spooked beast galloped downward. Magda hoped the straps on its load would hold and that they would be able to catch it at the bottom. She heard Camilla's breath jolt out hard in a curse; looked back and called, "You all right?"

"Turned my foot on a stone. All right now."

With a quick look behind, Magda saw Camilla was walking unevenly, but there was nothing to be done about it for the moment. They were lucky it was not worse. She felt a stone roll under her own foot, and narrowly escaped turning an ankle as she jolted down hard and unevenly. The horse scrambled more than once to stay balanced.

Jaelle was waiting a few steps ahead. "This is the beginning of the bad patch. I'm going across with my horse. Wait till I call you, then come across, slowly and carefully, understand?" Her face was patched red and white with exertion and there was a narrow band of sunburn across her nose. Magda was glad to rest for a moment; she watched Jaelle picking her way, leading the horse . . . Then Jaelle was across, and waving her ahead. She came across, feeling with her boots for firm patches, twice feeling rocks slip and roll down beneath her. She found that she was holding her breath as if even breathing hard would dislodge the loose gravel and ice. Once she slid to her knees with a little shout and found herself suddenly looking over a sheer cliff; but she mastered the queasy nausea, clawed herself backward and upright again, and went on, It seemed there were no sounds, not even of her own breathing, until a hand, extended, met hers, and she was safe beside Jaelle.

"All right, love?"

"Fine." Magda could hear little but her own breathing.

"Tether your horse. I'm going back across for Camilla's. You come along and lead Cholayna's—or—can you manage that?"

Magda's breath caught at the thought of crossing that hellish stretch of loose rubble and rock not once more, but twice. But Jaelle thought she could do it. She nodded. "Let me catch my breath a little, first."

Jaelle hobbled the horses; hung their reins across the

saddles. "I'll go first. Watch where I step. I've been across it four times now. Looks worse than it is, love."

Magda was still shaky, but this time the crossing was easier. They waited for Camilla and Cholayna to arrive at the far edge of the loose rocks; everyone waved at everyone else, and then Magda and Jaelle crossed again with the horses. Almost all of the chervines were across by now, though they lurched and nearly fell, scrambling up again on their thin hocks, tossing their heads and whickering in distress. But they all arrived safely, Vanessa last, white-faced, clinging to the rein of her horse.

"What's wrong, Vanessa?" Cholayna asked.

"Ankle." Now they could see that she had been supporting as much of her weight as she could holding on to the horse; abruptly she let go and sank to the ground. Camilla came and tried to pull off her boot, but in the end they had to cut through the heavy leather to remove it. The ankle was swollen, with a great purplish-red patch on the ankle-bone.

"This is worse than a sprain," Camilla said. "You may have knocked a chip of bone out of the ankle."

Vanessa made a wry face. "I was afraid of that. Probably needs X-raying, but there's no good thinking about that here. There are spare boots in my rucksack—"

"You'll never get them on," Magda said. "Take my spares, they're four sizes bigger. Never thought I'd be grateful for having big feet."

Vanessa let out her breath in a gasp as Cholayna came to examine the foot.

"Wiggle your toes. Fine. Does it hurt when I do this?"

Vanessa's answer was loud, profane, and affirmative.

"Nothing broken, I'd say. Just a really bad bruise and a lot of swelling. Are there elastic bandages in that medikit?"

"There's one in my pack," Jaelle said. She went and found it, gave it to Cholayna and said, "It probably needs bathing and all kinds of things, but there's no good trying to stop and make a fire here, so bandage it up and we'll round up the chervines." The beasts were scattered all up and down the next half mile of the downward trail. "Camilla, you turned an ankle too, didn't you? Is that okay? Any other casualties?"

Camilla's ankle, examined, proved to be only strained a little; nevertheless, Jaelle told her to bandage it up and give it a rest.

"Magda will help me round up the chervines. We're not more than a couple of hours from Barrensclae. With Avarra's mercy, we'll be able to ride most of the way from there."

While they were catching and quieting the scattered pack animals, Magda spotted a scrap of something which had no business on that trail. She caught it up and called softly to Jaelle.

"Look here."

Jaelle took the brightly colored scrap of plastic from her; yellow, with a torn letter at one edge. "Packaging?"

"From standard high-altitude emergency rations, yes."

"Lexie's?"

"Who else? Anyone who saw this, though, must have known she wasn't going out to study folk dancing. At least now we know they *did* come this way."

Jaelle nodded and thrust the scrap into a pocket. "Maybe they lost time here, too. Let's go and find out if they're still waiting for us. They do need the things we're bringing—extra warm clothes, trade goods—they'll do better in the Hellers if they wait."

"Then you'll be going on, if we do catch them? You actually think they'll find that—city?"

"Don't you, Magda?" Jaelle looked surprised and hurt. "You're coming too, I thought—?"

"I suppose so," Magda said, slowly and not at all sure. She could deal with Rafaella, who had been both friendly and unfriendly and would probably only accept her for Jaelle's sake, and then only if it was her best hope of continuing the search. But Lexie? Magda could hear her now.

Hellfire, Lorne, are there any pies on this planet you don't have your fingers in?

CHAPTER THIRTEEN

Barrensclae was well named, Magda thought; a high plateau, without grass or trees, rocky rubble lying loose, and a few stone ruins where once there had been houses and stockpens. She wondered why it had been abandoned, what had impelled the farmers who had lived here to pull up and go away. Or had they all been murdered by bandits in one of the blood-feuds that still raged in the Kilghard Hills?

She put the question to Jaelle, who shrugged.

"Who knows? Who cares? It can't have been much or we'd have heard a hundred different stories already."

Camilla said, with a grim smile, "If they just went away on their own, it may have been the only sensible thing they ever did. I'd be more interested to know why they ever thought of settling here in the first place."

Cholayna said the obvious: "If Lexie and Rafaella were ever here, they're not here now."

"They might be hunting. Or exploring." Jaelle rode slowly toward the abandoned stockpen, near a house which still had some semblance of roof clinging to the old stones. "We slaughtered the chervines here, and slept three nights in that house. If Rafi left a message, it would be here."

Camilla looked at the sky, lowering gray; the night's rain would begin soon. "We'll spend the night anyway,

I suppose. No sense going much farther, and Vanessa's ankle needs looking after. There's something like a roof on this, too. I suggest we look inside and see if we can camp there.''

"Any reason we shouldn't?" Vanessa asked. "I mean, the original owners seem to be *very* long gone. What could stop us?"

"Oh, just little things, like—no floor, mold, bugs, snakes, rats, bats." Camilla ticked them over on her fingers, laughing. "On the other hand, we might just find Rafaella's pack animals and their various belongings stored there, in which case—"

Magda was not sure whether she hoped they would find the women there or that they would not. When they managed to swing the heavy door inward from the hinges, the place was suspiciously clear of all the things Camilla had warned against: the old stone-paved floor was dusty but not filthy, and there seemed to be nothing lurking about.

"This place *has* been used recently," Cholayna remarked. "They were here, and not long ago."

"I wouldn't be so sure," Jaelle warned, "anyone could have used this place. Travelers, bandits—it's possible they were here, but we can't be sure."

It looked to Magda like a good place for bandits: she remembered encountering bandits in a travel-shelter once, years ago. She had not thought about bandits on this trip, and wished she had not had the idea brought to her attention just now.

There was no point in letting it worry her. Camilla could certainly manage three times their weight in bandits, and would probably rather enjoy the opportunity to try.

"That's not what's worrying me," Jaelle said. "There are only two of them, and one a *Terranan* greenhorn."

"Don't you believe it," Cholayna said. "Lexie had

the same unarmed-combat training as Magda. And Rafaella's no weakling."

"Bandits travel in packs," Jaelle said. "Fair fights aren't what they're noted for." Just the same, she brought in her saddlebags and dumped them on the stone floor. "Cholayna, why don't you make a fire so we can look after Vanessa's ankle."

Before long the fire was blazing, and Cholayna was making what use she could of the medikit. She still suspected that Vanessa had knocked a chip of bone loose from her ankle, but there was nothing they could do about it here.

"At least there's no shortage of ice," Cholayna said, looking out into the snow. "Cold packs until the swelling goes down; after that, hot and cold alternately. A proper medic would put it in a cast, but it's probably not dangerous without one. It's going to make walking hard for a few days, but since Jaelle says we can probably ride most of the way from here, it could be worse. At least you're not in danger of being lamed for life if you don't get proper Terran treatment."

Unasked, Magda pulled out the cooking kit and started making soup from the dried meat in their supplies. A hearty aroma began to steal through the old stone house. Toasting did wonders for the hard journey-bread, too. Soup, cooked grain-porridge, and a kettle of hot bark-tea—it was the first real hot meal they had had since leaving Thendara, and it greatly revived their spirits.

When they finally crawled into their sleeping bags, Magda soon knew all the others were sleeping peacefully. Still she lay awake, troubled without knowing why. She could not help feeling that this whole trip was somehow a reflection of her failures—with Lexie, Vanessa, Cholayna, and, perhaps especially, Rafaella. Somehow, she had made Lexie feel that she must compete with what some people in the HQ insisted on calling the "Lorne Legend"; had said the wrong things to Vanessa and Cholayna or they would not have been here; without meaning to, she had come between Jaelle and Rafaella . . . But whatever the unknown dangers of the road, Jaelle was right, they could not turn back.

The next morning, Vanessa's ankle was swollen to the size of a peck basket, and she was running a fever. Cholayna dosed her with salicylates from the medikit, while Magda and Camilla repacked the loads to redistribute weight and Jaelle went out to search the terrain for any signs of the passage of the other women. She came back late in the day with the carcass of a chervine calf slung over her back.

"We can all use fresh meat. Vanessa particularly needs the extra protein." She set about skinning and butchering the carcass with an expert hand; Cholayna turned her eyes away, but Vanessa watched with fascination.

"Where did you learn to do that?"

"Leading mountain expeditions. We don't have a lot of fancy packaged rations available," Jaelle said, "and hunting skills are one of the first things you learn to feed yourself in the wilds. I could bring down a full-grown animal before I was fifteen years old, and if you're killing your own meat, you have to be able to skin it and cut it up and dry it for the trail, too. We'll eat as much of this fresh as we can. I'll roast a haunch for supper, but it's too small to dry properly. What we can't eat, we'll put out for the *kyorebni* before we leave." She looked regretfully at the delicate dappled skin of the little animal. "Hate to waste this hide, I could get a nice pair of gauntlets out of it if we had the time to tan it."

Cholayna shuddered and kept her eyes even more averted than they had already been; but she said nothing. It must, Magda thought, be difficult for her all round, taking orders when she was accustomed to giving them, and resigning herself to being the oldest and the weakest. This assault on her ethical principles—Magda knew Cholayna had never eaten meat, or anything which had once lived, before this—must be the final trial. But she had kept silent about it, which could not have been easy.

By the next morning, the worst of the swelling was gone from Vanessa's ankle, and Jaelle, looking uneasily at the sky, said they should press on. Cholayna felt that Vanessa should rest her ankle for another day, but Jaelle was uneasy about the weather and studied Magda's maps for a long time, seeking an easier route.

"We'll head straight north, but we'll go around by the trail instead of going straight over the ridge. They have enough of a start on us now that it's very unlikely we'll catch up with them this side of the Kadarin; more probably not much before Nevarsin," Jaelle said.

With horses and chervines well rested, they started again, along trails that did not need to be negotiated on foot. There were flurries of snow as they rode, and it was damp and cold; they all dug out their warmest sweaters and underclothing. At night the sleeping bags were dank and clammy, and even Cholayna drank the hot meat-soup gladly.

On the third afternoon, the trail began to rise again, each hill steeper than the last, and finally Jaelle said that on the upward slopes they must dismount and walk to spare the horses the extra weight—except for Vanessa, who was still unable to bear her weight on the injured ankle.

"I can walk if I have to," said Vanessa, brandishing the thick branch Camilla had cut for a walking stick that morning. "I don't need special treatment, either!"

"Believe me, Vanessa, I'll tell you if it's necessary for you to walk. Don't try to be heroic," Jaelle added. "If we end up carrying you, we'll never get through."

They were slogging up the fourth or fifth of these hills—Magda had lost count in the dreary dripping fog—when her foot turned under her, and she lost her footing, fell full length and slipped backward, sliding down the steep path, scraping against rocks, ice and tough roots in the way. She struck her head, and in a flash of pain, lost consciousness.

. . . she was wandering in a the gray world; she heard Jaelle calling her, but the hideous old woman was there, laughing . . . wherever she turned, though she ran and ran, always the old crone was there with that terrible screaming laughter that was like the cry of some wild bird, arms outstretched to shoo her back, force her away . . . suddenly Camilla was there, knife drawn to protect her, facing the old woman; her knife struck blue fire . . .

There was something wet on her face; cold moisture was seeping into her collar. She raised her hand—it felt heavy and cold—to push it away and it turned into a damp cloth. It was like fire on her forehead, which felt as if it had been split with an axe.

Camilla's face looked down into hers; she was pale, and it seemed to Magda that she had been crying. *Nonsense,* she thought, *Camilla never cries.*

"*Bredhiya,*" Camilla murmured, and her hand clasped Magda's so tightly that she winced, "I thought I had lost you. How do you feel?"

"Like hell. Every bone in my body feels as if it had

been beaten with a smith's hammer," Magda muttered. She discovered that she was undressed to the waist. "Hell, no wonder I'm cold! Is this standard treatment for shock?"

She tried to make a joke of it, but Jaelle bent over her and said, "I undressed you to make sure you didn't have any internal injuries. You scraped all the skin off one arm down to the elbow, and you may have cracked a rib. Try to sit up, if you can."

Magda pulled herself carefully to a sitting position. She moved her head cautiously and wished she hadn't. "What did I hit, a mountain?"

"Just a rock, Miss Lorne," Vanessa said. It sounded so absurd; Magda had meant to protest before this. Vanessa asked, "Are you cold?" and put her shirt onto her. Her arm, she discovered, was bandaged heavily over some slick and foul-smelling ointment.

Camilla draped a warm cloak around her. "It will be easier than trying to get your jacket on over the bandages and won't rub the sore spots so much," she said, pulling Magda's jacket around her own lean frame. "Do you feel sleepy?"

Magda tried again to shake her head and didn't. "No. Sleepy is the last thing I am."

"Do you think you can go on?" Jaelle asked. "There's no place to camp here, but if you can't—"

Magda managed to pull herself upright with Camilla's help. Her head was still splitting, and she asked for some of Cholayna's painkillers, but Cholayna shook her head.

"Not until we know how serious your concussion is. If you're still wide awake when we stop for the night, you can have some. Till then, nothing that might depress your breathing."

"Miserable sadist," Magda grumbled; but she too

had had basic emergency training, and knew about head injuries.

"Look on the bright side," said Cholayna, "now you get to ride uphill along with Vanessa, while the rest of us slog along on foot."

Magda found it almost impossible to haul herself into her saddle, even with Camilla's help, and when the horse began to move, she wished she were walking; the motion was nearly intolerable. The snow was wet now, half rain and half snow, and clung thickly, soaking through her cloak. She rode in dreary misery, every footfall of her horse jolting as if the beast were actually stepping on her head; and the uphill path was so steep that again she felt as if she were slipping backward off her saddle. Without being asked, Camilla came close and took the reins from her hand.

"*Bredhiya*, you just hang on, I'll guide your horse. Just a little further now. Poor love, I wish I could carry you."

"I'm all right, Camilla. Really I am, it's only a headache. And I feel so foolish, falling like that and delaying all of you this way."

"Look, here we are at the top of the ridge. Now we can all ride again, and if you can't sit in your saddle, *bredhiya*, you can ride double with me. My horse will carry two and all you need to do is lean against me. Do you want to do that?"

"No, no, really, I'm all right," Magda said; and though she knew it was unfair, the older woman's solicitude embarrassed her—partly because she knew that it must be embarrassing to the other women, especially Vanessa, who could not understand the bond between them. "*Please* don't fuss over me so, Camilla. Just let me alone, I'm fine."

"Please yourself, then." Camilla touched her heels

to her horse's side, and went to the head of the line beside Jaelle. As soon as she was gone, Magda regretted her words and wished Camilla was still beside her; what, after all, did it matter to her what anyone thought, after all these years? Discouraged, her head aching, she clung to the reins and let her horse find his own way down the hill.

As she rounded a turn in the downhill road, past a huge stand of conifers, she could see lights below. A little village huddled in the valley, just a crossing of the narrow road; first an outlying farm or two, then a forge and a stream dammed for a mill, with a granary warehouse, a windmill and a few small stone houses, each surrounded by a patch of garden.

"I wonder if there is an inn in this place?" Camilla asked.

Children and women and even a few men had come out to the roadside to watch as they passed; a sure sign, Magda knew from her years in the field, that the place was so isolated that the appearance of any stranger was a major event.

Jaelle asked one of the women, heavy-set, imposing, in clothing somewhat less coarse than the rest, "Is there an inn where we can spend the night and command supper?"

She had to repeat the question several times, in different dialects, before she could make herself understood, and when the woman finally answered, her own dialect was so rude a patois of *cahuenga* that Magda could hardly understand her. She asked Camilla, who had returned to ride beside her, "What did she say? You know more of the mountain languages than I do."

"She said there is no inn," Camilla said—speaking pure *casta* so that they would not be understood if they were overheard. "But there is a good public bathhouse, she said, where we could bathe. She also offered us the use of a barn which is empty at this time of year. They look like a fine lot of ruffians to me, and I would just as soon not trust any of them, but I don't know what alternatives we have.''

Vanessa had heard only part of this. ''A bathhouse sounds like exactly what we need most. I'm sure my ankle, and your arm, can use a good long soak in clean hot water. And bathhouse or no, these people look dirty enough that I'd rather sleep in one of their barns than their houses. Or, for that matter, their inns. Lead me to the bath!''

The woman who had appointed herself their guide led the way, a small procession of children following. Cholayna said, ''I had not expected to find amenities like this outside Thendara.''

''There are hot springs all through the mountains,'' Magda said. ''Most little villages have bathhouses, even if every house must fetch water for drinking from a common well. And they have separate soaking rooms and tubs for men and women, so you need not worry about differing customs of modesty.''

Vanessa shrugged. ''I am used to mixed bathing and bathhouses on my own world. It wouldn't bother me if the whole village bathed in one big pool, as long as they changed the water occasionally.''

''Well, it would bother me,'' Camilla said, and Jaelle chuckled.

''Me, too. I was brought up in the Dry-Towns, after all.''

She turned to haggle with the woman, who seemed to be the proprietor of the bathhouse and a sort of headwoman of the village, over the bathhouse fee. It seemed exorbitant to Magda, but, after all, this village was very isolated, and the hire of the bathhouse to

occasional travelers was, no doubt, their only source of
coined money. At least, Jaelle told her, she had managed to secure the place for their exclusive use that
evening, and had arranged with the headwoman for a
cooked hot meal to be brought to them; the fee also
included use of the barn to stable their animals and
spread their sleeping bags. Because it was a stone barn,
with no stored hay, they had permission to make a fire
there. They went to deposit their goods, unsaddle the
horses and off-load the pack beasts before they went to
the bath.

"How is your head, Magda?" Cholayna asked. "How
do you feel?"

"Better for the thought of a bath."

"Wide awake? Then you can have some pain pills,"
Cholayna said, and dug some tablets out of the medikit.
"Is something wrong, Camilla?" For the woman was
standing over their loads, scowling.

"I do not trust these people," said Camilla, still
speaking *casta*, although they seemed to be quite alone.
"It looks like the abode of bandits. If we are wise, we
will not all go to bathe at once; we should not leave all
our goods unguarded."

"Most hill-folk are so honest, you could leave a bag
of copper unguarded in the center of the square, and
find it there untouched when you returned half a year
later," Jaelle reminded her, "except that they might
have put up a little shelter over it so that the bag would
not be destroyed by the winter rains."

"I'm perfectly aware of that," Camilla said testily.
"But have you been to this particular village before?
Do you know these people, Shaya?"

"Not really. But I have been in many, many mountain villages very like this one."

"Not good enough," said Camilla. "All of you, go

off to bathe. I will stay here and guard our goods."
And though they argued, she would not be moved from
this stance. Finally it was agreed that Jaelle and Vanessa
would go and use the bath first, and that Magda, Cholayna
and Camilla would bathe in a second shift, which meant
that one person in each party would be unwounded,
healthy, and skilled in the use of weapons.

"I am still not pleased," Camilla grumbled, as Jaelle
and Vanessa went off to the bathhouse, carrying clean
clothing over their arms. "These people would cut our
throats for the scented soap! The idea might well be to
split up our party so that we cannot defend ourselves
properly. We should have camped outside the village,
and set guard."

"You have a terribly suspicious nature, Camilla,"
Cholayna reproved gently, kneeling on the floor to light
a fire. "I for one will be delighted to get a bath!"

"And so should I, in any decent place. Or do you
think I am fonder of dirt than a Terran? But here, I
would feel safer sleeping in the muck of the road."

"Camilla," said Magda quietly, out of earshot of the
others, as they looked for fresh clothing in their packs,
"is this a premonition, is this your *laran*?"

The woman's face was tight-lipped and closed. "You
know what I think of that. If it were so, would not you
or Jaelle have known it, you who are *leroni* of the
Forbidden Tower? It needs no *laran* to know that a
ruffian will be a ruffian. *Laran*!" she snorted again,
crossly, and turned away.

Magda felt troubled, for she respected, with good
reason, Camilla's intuitions; but the party was already
split, and her head and injured arm ached dreadfully, so
that she felt unwilling to forgo the prospect of a bath.
She felt she would even endure an onslaught by bandits
if she could get a bath and a good hot meal first.

CHAPTER FOURTEEN

There was a little sound in the corner of the room. Within seconds Camilla had her knife out and rushed to the hidden space behind the door; she came back dragging someone by the wrist: a woman, not young, her dark hair braided carelessly down her back. She was no different from any of the people of the village except, Magda noticed, that she seemed personally clean.

"Who are you?" Camilla growled, gripping the woman's wrist so hard that she flinched and squealed, and emphasizing her words with a flourish of her knife, "What do you want here? Who sent you?"

"I didn't mean any harm," the woman said, with a little yelp of fright. "Are you—are you Shaya n'ha M'lorya?"

The name *Jaelle* was a Dry-Town name, very uncommon in the Kilghard Hills. Magda herself called Jaelle, mostly, by the *casta* version of her name, and had given it to her daughter.

"I am not," Camilla said, "but I am her oath-sister; and this—" indicating Magda, "her freemate. Speak! What do you want with her. Who are you?"

The woman's eyes swiveled furtively to stare at Cholayna. Magda thought, *No doubt she has never seen anyone with a black skin before this, maybe she has just come to gawp at the strangers. But then how would she know Jaelle's name?*

"My name is Calisu'," the woman said. "There are no Renunciates in our village. The headman won't have it. But some of us are in—in sympathy." She pulled the loose hair away from her ear, revealing a small earring; the secret sign, Magda knew, recognized for hundreds of years, of women in sympathy with the Guild-houses, who for one reason or another could not legally commit themselves. Lady Rohana herself had worn such a hidden ornament, and Magda was sure not even Dom Gabriel had known why. Seeing it, Camilla's grip loosened somewhat.

"What do you want? Why were you sneaking around like that?"

Calisu'—the name, Magda remembered, was a dialect version of Callista—said, "Two Renunciates passed through our village ten days ago. They asked for the village midwife, saying one of them suffered from cramps, and when they came to me, asked if—if I wore the earring."

That was Rafaella's artifice. Not in a thousand years would Lexie have thought of that.

"And then they wanted me give this message to Shaya n'ha M'lorya. But if'n you're her freemate, I can give it to you? If they find me here—"

"You can give the message to me," Magda said.

"She said—they'll meet wi' you at Nevarsin Guild-house."

Camilla said, "But there isn't—"

Magda kicked her shins and she fell silent. Calisu' wrenched her arms free from Camilla's grip, scuttled toward the door and was gone.

Camilla strode after her. She struggled with the ancient mechanism, which was rusted and could not be

properly bolted shut again. Finally she sighed, and said,
"Put some of the loads in front of it, so we'll hear if
someone tries to get in again. I was afraid this would
happen. No, no, not you, you shouldn't be lifting things
with your head—"

"I seldom do," said Magda, "that's not my *laran*,
I'm sad to say I have to use my hands." But she
stepped back and let Cholayna and Camilla pile loads in
front of the side entrance. Camilla said moodily, "You
heard her. What does it mean? There is no Guild-house
in Nevarsin, it's a city of *cristoforos*. How can we meet
them when—"

"Shaya will understand," said Magda. Her head was
splitting in spite of Cholayna's pain pills, and she wished
that Jaelle would return so that she could go and have a
bath and lie down.

Listlessly she found clean underclothing and thick
socks, a heavy sweater and woollen breeches to sleep
in. Jaelle and Vanessa came in; they had even washed
their hair, and Jaelle's coppery locks were curled up in
tight, damp, frizzy ringlets.

"Just what the weary traveler needs," Jaelle said,
elaborately stretching her arms and yawning. "Now,
when that meal comes—I saw it cooking; smelled it.
Roast fowl on the spit, and mushrooms in a casserole
with redberry sauce." She licked her lips greedily.
"This is a better place to stop than I thought. Go along,
you three, get your baths. But don't be too long or we'll
eat all the mushrooms. I wonder if this village makes a
good mountain wine?"

"If not," Cholayna joked, "I shall complain to the
headwoman."

The bathhouse was an isolated stone building, from
which issued wisps of steam. When they went inside,
the bath attendant gave them little three-legged stools to

sit on and asked with rough deference if the ladies had their own soap and sponges. She scrubbed them well, clucking at Magda's injured arm, and even managed not to stare too long or too inquisitively at Cholayna. Then she ushered them down the steps into the stone-lined pool filled with steaming hot water. Magda sighed with pure pleasure, feeling the scalding heat drawing the pain from her wounded arm, and lay back so that she was covered to the neck.

"Feels good," Camilla agreed, and Magda remembered that she too had hurt her ankle, though not as seriously as Vanessa.

"Are you really all right, *breda*?"

"Nothing hot water and a good night's sleep wouldn't cure. *If* I felt safe about getting it here," Camilla muttered, softly so the bath attendant wouldn't hear. "Careful, let's not say anything serious, it may be her business to carry tales. No, I trust *none* of them, no farther than I could kick a statue uphill."

Under the surface of the water, Magda sought Camilla's hand and pressed the long fingers between her own. She was ashamed of how she had behaved in the afternoon. Had she really been willing to hurt Camilla's feelings because of what Vanessa might think? Why should it matter? She sat holding Camilla's hand, silently, and in the quiet comfort of the bath, she slowly began to pick her friend's fear, her suspicion.

She could understand both. In the days when she and Peter Haldane, then married, had explored from the Kilghard Hills to the Plains of Arilinn, they had encountered their share, or more, of bandits and outlaws. They had had more than enough narrow escapes—although they had survived, when others had not. Those had been the days when the so-called "Lorne Legend" was in the making. Poor Peter, in a sense it was unfair; it might as well have been called the Haldane Legend, for he had done as much as she in the matter of gathering information about territories and boundaries, recording linguistic variables and social customs—all the basic information for Intelligence. The difference was that Magda had done it on a world, and in a milieu, where women found it almost impossible to go into the field at all, let alone accomplish anything meaningful there; and so Magda had gotten most of the credit and all the attention.

But Peter had had his reward: he had become Legate, and he was a good one, concerned, fair, committed to the world he loved. She had chosen another path, and different rewards.

"Magda? Don't fall asleep here, there is a good supper waiting for us."

"No, I'm not asleep." Magda pulled herself upright in the steaming water, blinking. She felt almost dangerously relaxed.

Camilla squeezed her hand underwater, and said in a whisper that could not be heard inches away, "*Z'bredhyi, chiya*." Magda returned the pressure and whispered, "I love you, too." But because they were not alone, she turned to Cholayna and said aloud, "I suppose they are waiting for us, they may not serve supper till we're all there. I suppose we should get out, but I could stay here all night."

Cholayna looked at her fingers, beginning to wrinkle like dried fruit in the steaming water. "We'd end up a great deal smaller, I think." She pulled herself to her feet, and the bath attendant brought a towel to wrap about her. Camilla followed, and Magda saw that in the hot water, the old scars on her back and side were clear white, standing out against her fair skin reddened by the heat. She saw the bath attendant notice them, and

Cholayna actually opened her mouth to speak. Magda could almost hear her: *In the name of the secret gods, what happened to you?* before she realized that neither Cholayna nor the attendant had said a word. In the peace and relaxation of the bath, once again she was picking up unspoken thoughts.

Reluctantly, Magda hauled herself out of the hot, relaxing bath, and wrapped herself in the thick towel provided by the attendant. It felt wonderful to dress in clean clothes from the skin out.

"Now for some of that good roast fowl, and maybe the mountain wine Jaelle was talking about."

Cholayna pursed her lips. "I don't want to sound like a nervous foster mother, Magda, but if you really have concussion, you shouldn't drink any wine. How is your head?"

Magda, though the hot water had relaxed the muscles of her neck and she felt much better, admitted that the headache was still there, a dull hard pounding despite the pain pills.

Camilla said, "She's right, Margali, you really should stick to tea or soup till we're sure about your head," and Magda, inching her sweater over the throbbing bump on her skull, shrugged.

"I'll have to make do with good hot food and fine company, then. Lucky Vanessa, she only bashed her ankle, she can have a hangover if she wants to. I really could use a drink, but I'll defer to your medical knowledge."

It was a shock to go out into the cold again. The fierce wind had blown the snow into deep drifts; they hurried across the narrow space between the buildings. In places the snow had drifted so high that it came up over their boot-tops, icy, chilling the new warmth of their feet. They were glad to see the blazing fire inside the barn allotted to them. The building was so large that it was not exactly warm, but at least they were out of the wind.

Vanessa and Jaelle had made the beds up, and the place looked clean and inviting, almost homelike; though it was hardly like their own homes, with horses and chervines stabled at the other end. An ample supply of hay had been brought in for them, which gave a clean healthy smell to the surroundings. Almost at once, serving women began to parade in with dishes and smoking platters; in addition to the roast fowl, there was a haunch of roasted chervine with its sizzling layer of good-smelling fat, and rabbithorn stewed in wine. There were long rolls of bread, hot from the oven, with plenty of butter and honey, a savory casserole of mushrooms and bland but nourishing boiled whiteroot, and the promised redberry sauce.

"Why, this is really lavish!" Cholayna exclaimed.

"It ought to be. Enjoy it. We paid enough for it," Jaelle said, as they gathered around, sitting on piled-up loads and packs, digging in with a good appetite—all except Cholayna. The older woman ate some of the boiled whiteroot, and tasted the redberry sauce with appreciation, but after valiantly trying to eat the piece of roast fowl Jaelle had carved for her, she turned pale and put her plate aside.

"What's the matter, *comi'ya*?" asked Camilla.

Cholayna said faintly, "It looks—still looks too much like the—the living animal. I'm sorry, I—I tried. When it's just a—a bar, or a slice, I can manage it, but—but this is a *wing*!'

"You need the protein," Vanessa said. "Hunt out some emergency rations. You can't make a meal on mushrooms and redberry sauce."

"I—I'm sorry." Cholayna apologized again, and found

the load containing the packaged Terran rations. This was forbidden in the field, lest some unauthorized observer should catch sight of the obviously alien packaging, but Magda had not the heart to reprimand her; she looked so sick. Cholayna had had a hard few days, and she supposed that if you really applied the rules strictly, even the elastic bandage on Vanessa's ankle would be against the laws of Intelligence work.

On the other hand, if the head of Intelligence for Darkover can't break a rule when there's hardly even anyone to know she's done so—

"Never mind," Camilla was saying, "have some of the wine, at least. It's very good. They certainly aren't skimping on us, I'll say that for them! Shaya, tell me—there isn't a Guild-house in Nevarsin, is there?"

"Goodness, no!" Jaelle laughed, raising her winecup to be refilled for the third time. "Keitha used to talk about starting one there, remember? There is a hostel where some women lived while they were copying some of the old manuscripts from the Monastery of Saint Valentine, years ago, but that would hardly count." She frowned. "Why, Camilla?"

"There was a message." She told about Calisu', her earring and her relayed words, and Jaelle frowned.

"Rafi evidently thought it would mean something to me, but—oh, wait!" She broke off and said, "When we were girls, traveling with Kindra, there was a place where we used to lodge. It wasn't an inn; women can't go to public inns in the Hellers unless they are properly escorted by their menfolk. There was an old dame who made leather jackets and boots to sell—that was where I learned to make gloves and sandals, in fact."

"Oh, of course," Camilla said. "I went there once, and one of the young girls taught me to embroider gloves with beads! I remember old Betta, and all her wards and foster daughters!''

"She took in all the female orphans she could find in the city, and brought them up to work for her, but instead of getting them married off, as virtuous *cristoforo* matrons do with their girl apprentices, this old dame used to teach them a trade and encourage them to set up business for themselves. Some of them went off and got married anyway, but some of them are still in business and living in the old woman's house, and others, old Betta sent them south with us to the Guild-house. Kindra used to say, when there *was* a Guild-house in Nevarsin, we should get Betta to run it for us. I think she's dead, but four of her adopted daughters are still running the place, and Guild-women were always welcome there. Certainly, that is where Rafi would lodge."

She drained the winecup, looked wistfully at the bottle, and sighed.

"Oh, finish it if you want to," Camilla chuckled. "You can drink Margali's share."

"Yes, have it by all means," Magda said; her head was spinning and she felt dizzy, though she had not even touched the wine. Jaelle resolutely pushed it away.

"I would have a head worse than hers tomorrow if I drank any more, already I'm falling asleep where I sit. Let's get to bed."

And in fact the dishes were all but empty; the bones of the roast fowl were scattered, only a few scraps of gravy remaining on the platter which had held the roast chervine. After the fatigue of the day, the bath and the heavy meal, Magda was sure they would sleep well tonight. Her head still throbbed, and she wobbled when she got up to go to her sleeping bag.

Camilla protested. "Aren't we going to set watch?"

Vanessa yawned hugely. "Not I. An offense to these

good people's hospitality. I'm going to—'' Another vast yawn split her words. "Sleep."

Jaelle, drawing off her boots, looked up seriously at Camilla. "Truly, do you think we should set a watch, aunt?" She used the old affectionate word of her childhood, and it made Camilla smile; but the other woman said, "Truly, I do. Even if most of these people are good, trustworthy and hospitable, it is possible there are rogues among them. I will stand first watch myself."

"I will let you, then," Jaelle said, and went to crawl into her sleeping bag. Almost before the others had their boots off, she was fast asleep and snoring. Magda thought, *She must be even more tired than we realized. Of course all the weight of the trip has been on her. I must try to bear more of the responsibility.*

She felt so dizzy, her head pounding, that she asked Cholayna for another of the pain pills, and Cholayna gave it to her, rather reluctantly. "You really should not. After a bath and a meal like that one, I am sure you will sleep well enough without it."

"I won't take it unless I find I cannot sleep," Magda promised. Cholayna pulled off her boots, wrapped her pale halo of hair into a crimson scarf, and crept into her sleeping bag. Camilla, yawning, settled down on one of the loads, her knife across her knees.

Vanessa lowered the light of the lantern to its lowest point. "Camilla, wake me after an hour or so. You need sleep, too. We should try to make an early start."

"In this?" Camilla gestured, and in the silence they could hear the rattle of snow blowing against the frame of the building and the wind howling around the corners. "We'll be lucky to get out of here by day after tomorrow."

"Well, maybe it will stop during the night."

"Maybe Durraman's donkey could really fly. Go to sleep, Vanessa. I'll watch for a few hours, at least."

Vanessa's sleeping bag—now that they were not in the wilds, they were using the Terran single bags rather than the doubled ones from the Guild-House—was spread next to Magda's. After a moment, Vanessa asked softly, "Are you asleep?"

"Not nearly. I thought I'd fall asleep right away, but my head really aches. I think I'm going to take Cholayna's pill after all."

"Miss Lorne—may I ask you something? Something really personal?"

"Of course," Magda said, "but only if you stop calling me Miss Lorne. Vanessa, we are sisters of the Guild-house. What would please me most would be if you would call me Margali. It really is my name, you know, it's not just an alias, or the name I use in the field. My parents named me Margali. I was born on Darkover, in these mountains; though I've been away from them for a long time. No one ever called me Magdalen till I went to the Intelligence Academy on Alpha. I worked so long for the HQ that I'm quite used to Magda now, but I really prefer Margali."

"Margali, then. I—I have some trouble understanding women as freemates. Jaelle is your freemate, yes? But you and Camilla—"

"Camilla is my lover, yes," said Magda deliberately. "The Oath of Freemates is something else. Jaelle and I swore that oath, which is legal for women, so that we could be guardians of one another's children. Jaelle and I—perhaps no one brought up under Terran laws could understand. We have been lovers, too; but Camilla and I—I said you wouldn't understand."

"I don't. I would like to understand. What—what is it like, to love a woman?"

Magda laughed. "What is it like to love? To love anyone?"

Vanessa was asleep at her side. Jaelle still snored softly; she had, Magda reflected, drunk far too much. Cholayna, though coughing a little, was fast asleep. But Magda could not sleep, though she felt as sick and dizzy as if she had finished the bottle of wine herself. She wanted to take Cholayna's pill, but was restrained by the thought that if her concussion was serious, she probably should not. From where she lay, she could see Camilla, the long knife resting across her knees; but even as she watched, Camilla's head sagged forward; she started, pulled herself upright with a jerk—then sagged again, asleep.

And suddenly, as if she had read it printed in letters of fire, Magda knew. She never knew whether it was *laran* or something else, but she knew.

The wine had been drugged. And probably some of the food as well.

Cholayna didn't eat much of their food. She may not be drugged. I should wake her at once and tell her.

But Magda could not make herself move, feeling sicker and dizzier than ever. She thought, in terror, *I am drugged too!* She tried to force herself to move, to wake, to scream out to Camilla, to Cholayna.

But she could not move.

CHAPTER FIFTEEN

Magda fought against the sluggishness of her brain, struggling to move. She tried to reach out with *laran* to Jaelle—*Shaya, wake up, we have been drugged, it's a trap, Camilla was right!* She tried to pull herself upright, to crawl over to her freemate and shake her from her drugged and drunken sleep; Jaelle had drunk more of the drugged wine than any of them.

And no wonder. She has carried the fullest weight of this trip, all the way, and now when she has relaxed, now that she will let herself sleep, I may not be able to wake her at all.

Jaelle was probably so deeply drunk and drugged as to be unrousable. If she could reach Camilla, though, and waken her. . . . Magda fought against her weakness and dizziness, her throbbing head and sickness, concentrating on the pain. She gave thanks to the Goddess that she had not swallowed Cholayna's last sleeping pill, or she would now be sleeping alongside her drugged friends; and the folk of this village would be able to come and steal their loads, and perhaps cut their throats, at their leisure . . . or whatever else they might have in mind.

Cholayna had drunk little of the drugged wine, eaten almost none of the food. She might be the easiest to rouse . . . Magda tried to raise her head, clench her fists, anything. Pain lanced through her forehead like blinding knives, but she did force her head a little up from the packload which served her as pillow. Bracing herself with her hands, feeling so sick she was sure she would vomit, she managed to pull herself up inch by inch to a sitting position.

"Cholayna," she whispered hoarsely, but the Terran woman neither stirred nor answered, and Magda wondered if her voice was audible, if she had really even moved at all, whether this was one of those dreadful nightmares where you are convinced that you have gotten out of bed and gone about some business or another while in actuality, you are still motionless, fast asleep . . . Magda managed to get her fist up to her forehead and struck herself on the temple. The resulting flood of pain convinced her that it was real.

Think! she admonished herself. At Cholayna's advice, she had drunk none of the drugged wine, and they would hardly have drugged every dish; probably she had had relatively little of the drug, and Cholayna even less. *If I can only reach her!*

If only Cholayna were one of the Terrans who were gifted with *laran*! As far as Magda knew, she was not. Struggling against weakness, sickness and tears, Magda somehow crawled over Vanessa; deep in drugged sleep, Vanessa muttered in protest.

"Damn it, lie down and go t' sleep, le'me sleep . . ."

She was closest, easiest to reach. Magda tried to shake her, but could manage only a weak clutch at Vanessa's shoulder, and her voice was no more than a thick whisper.

"Vanessa. Wake up! Please, *wake up!*"

Vanessa stirred again, turning over heavily, dragging sleepily at her heavy, makeshift pillow as if to pull it over her face, and Magda, her *laran* wide open, sensed the way in which the other woman retreated further down into dreams.

They had been ready-made victims for the people of this place. That dreadful washed-out pass, the unpeopled wilderness of Barrensclae—and then a hospitable village, a bathhouse, good food and plenty of wine. Most travelers would sleep the sleep almost of the dead at the end of such a trail, even without whatever devilish drug the villagers used to make sure.

Vanessa was sleeping almost as heavily as Jaelle. She had drunk plenty of the drugged wine, after the long ordeal of traveling on her damaged ankle. It would have to be Cholayna, then. Even in her desperate struggle, head throbbing and her body and brain refusing to obey her, Magda felt a surge of hysterical laughter bubbling up at the thought of what Vanessa might think if she woke up suddenly and found her, Magda, sprawled over her like this. But she could not make her limbs obey her enough to get up and walk or go round, and so she had no choice but to crawl over her.

If I can just get her awake at all, I'll take my chances on whether she screams rape, Magda told herself sternly; but although Vanessa muttered, and swore in her sleep, and even struck out feebly at Magda once or twice, she did not wake. Now, however, Magda was close enough to grab Cholayna's shoulder.

"Cholayna," she whispered, "Cholayna, wake up!"

Cholayna Ares had eaten little, and had drunk almost nothing, but it had been a long and exhausting trip and she was sleeping very heavily. Magda shook the older woman, weakly, and struggled to make herself heard for several minutes before Cholayna abruptly opened her eyes and looked at Magda. Now fully awake, Cholayna shook her head in disbelief.

"Magda? What's the matter? Is your head worse? Do you need—"

"The food—the wine—*drugged!* Camilla was right. Look at her, she would never sleep on watch that way—" But Magda had to fight to even make her tight, shaky whisper heard; it sagged and wobbled in the worst possible way. "Cholayna, I mean it! I'm not—drunk, not crazy—"

Something in Magda's urgency, if not in her words, penetrated; Cholayna sat up, looking swiftly about the barn. Once again Magda, shaking and unable to coordinate what was happening, saw the emergence of the woman who had been put in charge of training Intelligence agents.

"Can you sit up? Can you swallow?" Cholayna was on her feet in one swift movement, hunting in her pack for a capsule. "Now, this is just a mild stimulant; I hate to give it to you, really, you may have a concussion, but you're conscious and they're not. Try to swallow this."

Magda got it into her mouth, managed to force the capsule down, dimly wondering what the effect of Terran stimulants would be when mixed with whatever drug the villagers had used. *This could kill me,* she realized. *But then, that's probably better than what the villagers have in mind. . . .*

Steadying Magda with one arm, Cholayna stepped toward Camilla, sitting on the packload fast asleep with her knife across her knees. She bent, shaking her roughly.

Camilla came awake fighting, striking out with the blunt end of the knife; but blinking, recognized Cholayna and pulled back. "What the—?" She shook herself like a wet dog. "In hell's name, was *I* sleeping on watch?"

"We were drugged. Certainly in the wine, maybe in some of the food too. We'll have to be on guard for—whatever they have planned,'' Cholayna explained. Magda's head was clearing; it still throbbed, but the ordinary pain was manageable, as long as she did not have to cope with the dizzy blurring of thought and motion. Cholayna offered Camilla some of the same stimulant she had given to Magda, but Camilla, fisting sleep from her eyes, refused.

''I'm fine, I'm awake. Zandru's buggering demons! I suspected something like this, but I never thought the food would be drugged! The more fool I! I wonder if that midwife— Calisu'—I wonder if they sent her to soften us up and disarm our suspicions?''

Cholayna was opening her medikit again. ''I wonder,'' she said, ''if Lexie and Rafaella are lying somewhere with their throats cut.''

Magda shuddered. She had not even thought of that. She said, ''I don't think a woman who wore the earring would have done that to her sisters—'' But after she said it, she realized she could not be sure the earring had not been stolen.

Cholayna had found an ampoule in the medikit, but cursed softly. ''I can't use this, Vanessa's allergic to it, oh *hell!*''

''How else would she know about the Nevarsin Guild-house?''

''She may not have known there wasn't one, though; or that Jaelle would interpret it that way. It may have been like saying 'at the fish markets in Temora'; anybody could assume there'd be one on the seacoast. What do they say—'It needs no *laran* to prophesy snow at midwinter.' The whole thing could have been made up out of whole cloth, except for Shaya's name.''

''Only one thing's sure,'' Cholayna said, ''we weren't drugged out of rustic kindness, to give us a good night's sleep. Let's stop talking and see if we can wake up the others. Magda—do you know Jaelle's endorphin type?''

''Her what?''

''You don't, then,'' Cholayna said in resignation.

Camilla was shaking Jaelle, furiously but fruitlessly. Jaelle fought and mumbled, opened her eyes but stared without seeing, and finally Camilla hauled her and her sleeping bag into a corner.

''She might as well be in Hermit's Cave on Nevarsin Peak, for all the good she'd be in a fight right now!''

''It's just luck we're not *all* in the same state.''

''Cholayna,'' Camilla said, ''if I ever say one more word about your chosen diet, ever again, kick me. Hard. Can we get Vanessa part way awake?''

''I can't,'' Cholayna said.

''Could she fight, anyway, with her ankle the way it is?'' Magda asked.

''Well, it's up to us,'' Camilla said. ''Let's try and move her where she won't be hurt if it comes to fighting. No, Margali, not you, sit down a minute longer while you can. You know you're as white as a glacier?''

Cholayna shoved Magda down on the packload where Camilla had slept, and together they hauled Vanessa out of the way behind the stacked loads.

''Are there bolts on the doors that we can draw? It might slow them down a little.''

''I checked that even before we had dinner,'' Camilla said. ''No wonder they have us in a barn instead of an inn. No one expects to be able to make a barn secure.''

''Do you think the whole village is in on this?''

''Who knows? Most of them, probably. I've heard about robbers' villages,'' Camilla said, ''but I thought it was a folk tale.'' They were all speaking in strained whispers. Camilla went to the main door and opened it a crack, cautiously peering out. The wind and snow tore into the room like a live animal prowling; the door almost got away from her and she had to manhandle it shut with all her strength.

"Still snowing and blowing. What hour of night *is* this?"

"God knows," Cholayna said, "I don't have my chronometer. Magda warned me not to bring any item obviously of Terran manufacture that isn't openly sold in Thendara or Caer Donn."

"It can't be very late," Magda said, "I hadn't been fast asleep at all. Not more than an hour can have gone by since we turned in. I should think they'll wait a while longer to be sure."

"Depends on what drug they gave us, and how long it takes to do whatever it does, and how long it lasts," said Camilla. "We might want to keep half an eye on Shaya and Vanessa, just in case they start choking to death." Magda shuddered at the matter of factness of Camilla's voice as she went on, "If it's fast acting and short-lived, they'll be here any minute. If we're really lucky, they'll trust it completely and send one man to cut our throats, and we can arrange something else."

She made a grim, final gesture with her knife. "Then, while they're waiting for him to come back and give the signal to pile up the loot, we high-tail it out of here. But if we're not lucky, the whole village could come in with hammers and pitchforks." She strode to the concealed entrance where Calisu' had come in to give her message. The wind was not so high here, but still it tore through the room. Camilla looked out into the blowing snow, and drew a harsh gasp of consternation; Magda expected her to slam the door shut, but instead she darted out and, after a moment, beckoned.

"Here's the answer to one question," she said grimly, and pointed.

Already covered by a layer of drifted snow, the woman Calisu' lay on the ground, her dead eyes staring at the storm. Her throat had been cut from ear to ear.

Camilla slammed the door and swore. "I hope the headman's wife goes into labor tomorrow with an obstructed transverse birth! Poor damned woman, they may have thought she warned us!"

"Are we going to leave her body lying there?"

"Got to," Camilla said. "If they find it gone, they'll know we *are* warned. Hellfire, Magda, you think it matters to her anymore where her body lies?"

"Do you think it's early enough that we could simply escape—sneak out of here before they come?" Cholayna suggested.

"Not a chance, not with Jaelle and Vanessa still dead to the world. One chervine bleat and they'd be on us. They're probably sitting around in that inn they told us didn't exist, whetting their knives," Camilla said gloomily. She stood with her hands on her hips, scowling, thinking it over. "Stack all the loads against the back door—" She pointed. "Slow them down. We'll be ready for them at the front. Magda, are you all right?"

"I'm fine." Whether it was Cholayna's stimulant or the adrenalin of danger, Magda had no idea, but she felt almost agreeably braced at the thought of a fight. Camilla had her knife out. Magda made sure that her dagger was loose in its sheath. It had been a long time since she had faced any human enemy, but she felt it would be a good and praiseworthy deed to kill whoever had cut the throat of the harmless midwife.

She began to help Cholayna stack the loads, but Cholayna stopped. "I have a better idea. Get the loads *on* the animals. Have them all backed up against that door. Then, when they come at us, if Jaelle and Vanessa are awake by then, we can ride out right over them! If not—we can get free, as soon as the first attackers are out of the way.''

''Not much hope of that,'' Camilla said, ''but you're right; we have to be able to get the hell out of here without stopping to load and saddle up the animals. We'll do that, but keep an eye on that front door, because that's where they'll come.''

''Stack up a few loads against it,'' Magda suggested.

''No, they'll know we're warned then, and come at us with knives ready. If they come in here thinking we're all asleep and ready for the slaughter, we can get the first couple of them before they have much of a chance at us. Anything that shortens the odds against us is fair under these circumstances.''

Camilla started hoisting loads onto chervines, while Magda saddled her pony and Jaelle's. Cholayna went to help Camilla with the packloads, taking away everything before the door, and Magda knew, with a shiver down her spine, that Camilla was clearing the space for a fight. She had seen Camilla fight; had fought once at her side. . . . Her head still throbbed faintly, but otherwise everything seemed blindingly lucid, everything she saw sharp-edged and fresh. She started to put a saddle on Camilla's horse, realized it was Vanessa's saddle which was larger, and made the exchange, saying to herself, *I'll be saddling up chervines next if I'm not careful.*

The horses were saddled; the pack animals loaded. *If they do kill us, at least they'll have some trouble getting at our stuff,* she thought, and wondered why she thought that it mattered.

Camilla hunkered down where she could face the door, her fingers just resting on her sword. The Renunciate charter provided that no *Comhi' letziis* might wear a sword, only the long Amazon knife, by law three inches shorter than an ordinary sword; but Camilla, who had lived for years as a male mercenary, wore the sword she had worn as a man, and no one had ever challenged her.

She grinned at Magda. "Remember the day we fought Shann's men, and I said you had dishonored your sword?"

"Will I ever forget?"

"Fight as well as that and I'm not afraid of any bandit in the Kilghard Hills."

Cholayna, half-smiling, leaned against the wall nearby. "Do you hear something?" she asked suddenly.

Silence, except for the high whistle of the blowing snow and wind roaring around the eaves of the building. Some small animal rustled in the straw. After the frantic activity of the last few minutes, Magda felt let down, her heart bumping and pounding, the metallic taste of fear in her mouth.

Time crawled by. Magda had no idea whether it was an hour, ten minutes, half the night. Time had lost its meaning.

"Damn them, why don't they come?" Cholayna's voice came tight through her teeth.

Camilla muttered, "They may be waiting till we put out that last light. But Zandru whip me with scorpions if I'm going to fight in the dark, and if we have to wait till morning, so be it. I'd just as soon they never came at all."

Magda wished that if there was going to be a fight, it would come and be over with; but at the same time, she was remembering in sharp-edged detail her first fight, feeling the appalling pain of the sword slicing along her thigh and laying it open. She was, quite simply, terrified.

Camilla looked so calm, as if she actually relished the notion of a good fight.

Maybe she does. She earned a living as a mercenary for God-knows-how-many-years!

Then, in the silence, she heard Cholayna's breath hiss inward, and the Terran woman pointed at the door.

Slowly, it was pushing inward, the wind howling around the edges. A face peered around the edge; a round, scarred, sneering face. Immediately the bandit saw the light, the cleared space and the women awaiting him, but even as his mouth opened to give a warning yell, Cholayna leaped in a *vaido* kick, and his face burst, exploding blood; he fell and lay still.

Camilla bent to drag the man, unconscious or a corpse, out of the way; another bandit rushed in after him, and she ran him through expertly. He fell, with a short hoarse howl. The man who pushed in after him got his neck broken by a swift slam of Magda's hand.

"You haven't forgotten *everything*, anyway," Cholayna whispered approvingly.

There was a lull, and then the man whose belly Camilla had split groaned and began screaming again. Magda cringed at the terrible cries, but did nothing. He had been ready to cut all their throats as they slept. She owed him no pity; but as Camilla stepped toward him, her knife raised to silence him once for all, he fell back again with a gurgle, and the barn was almost silent again.

There are certainly more of them out there, thought Magda, *sooner or later they'll rush us all at once.* They had been lucky: Magda had killed her man, and the one Cholayna had kicked, though possibly not dead, had at least had all the fight knocked out of him. . . .

The door burst open, and the room filled with men, yelling like so many demons. Camilla ran the nearest one through, and Magda found herself fighting with her knife at close quarters. Cholayna was in the center of a cluster of them, fighting like some legendary devil or hero, kicking with frequently deadly accuracy. Magda's next opponent ran in over her dagger and drove her backward, off-balance; she felt his knife slice into her arm and kicked out wildly, then slammed her other elbow into the base of his throat and sent him flying aside, unconscious. She could feel hot blood trickling down her arm, but another bandit was on her already, and there was no time for pain or fear.

One of them, running toward the horses, literally stumbled over Jaelle; he bent swiftly with his dagger, and Magda flung herself on him from behind, shrieking a warning. She pulled her knife across his throat with a strength she had never imagined having, and he fell, half-beheaded, across Jaelle—who woke, staring and mumbling uncomprehendingly.

As quickly as that, it was all over. Seven men lay dead or unconscious on the floor. The rest had retreated, possibly to regroup, Magda did not know which or, at the moment, care.

Jaelle muttered, plaintively, "What's going on?"

"Cholayna," Camilla ordered, "get into your pack, try to get one of those pills of yours down Jaelle and Vanessa! That was just the first onslaught, they'll be back."

Jaelle blinked and Magda saw her eyes come into focus.

"We were poisoned? Drugged?"

Cholayna nodded, imperatively gesturing for Jaelle to swallow the stimulant capsule. Forcing it down, Jaelle exploded, "Damn them! They had the nerve to *haggle* with us over the price of the food and wine, too!" She got out of her sleeping bag, tried to haul Vanessa to her feet; then gave it up, and grabbing up her knife, Jaelle came to join Camilla. She still looked groggy, but the stimulant was taking effect.

Magda thought, *We were lucky with the first fight, and Cholayna is one hell of a scrapper for her age! Nevertheless, there's no way the four of us—even if Vanessa could be waked in time—we can't kill off an entire village! We'll die here . . .* But was that so, she wondered; now that the villagers knew the women would be no easy pickings, could they bargain for their lives? Looking at Camilla's face, she knew the swordswoman would entertain no such notions; she was prepared for a fight to the death. What other defenses did they have?

They would probably rush them all at once. Magda was aware of pain now in her wounded arm, and her head was beginning to throb. The man Camilla had gutted began, unexpectedly, his terrible moaning again; Camilla knelt and quickly cut his throat.

Cleaning the knife on the dead man's ragged coat, Camilla stood up, fingering her sword. Magda felt she could almost read her mind, knowing the mercenary's code of honor. Camilla was more than ready to die bravely. *But I don't want to die bravely,* Magda thought. *I don't want to die at all. And I don't want Cholayna's and Vanessa's lives on my conscience if I don't! Is there any alternative—?*

Then, with a dreadful sense of *déjà vu,* she saw a face peer round the door, as if they had returned to the very beginning of the fight.

Think, damn it, think! What good is it having laran *if it can't save your life* now!

A bandit rushed at her, knife upraised. She struck hard, felt him crumple away under her—but they were outnumbered. Desperately she reached out with her *laran,* remembering an old trick; suddenly seeing, like an image painted behind her eyes, the fireside at Armida, and Damon telling them about a battle fought with *laran,* long ago.

Jaelle! Shaya, help me!

Jaelle was fighting for her life with a bandit in a red shirt. Magda reached desperately, wove an image, saw the bandits recoil; above them in the barn a demon wavered, no Darkovan demon but an ancient devil out of Terran myth, with horns, tail, and a mighty stink of sulphur . . . The line of men broke and surged back. Then Jaelle linked with her, the minds of the freemates locking into one; and suddenly a dozen fanged demons armed with swords faced the bandits. The villagers faltered again, fell back yet again, and then with a howl, turned and ran. Some even threw down their weapons as they went.

Vanessa chose that moment to sit up. Staring about the barn with bewilderment, she saw the demons, emitted a strangled squeak and buried her head in the blankets.

The stink of sulphur still lingered. Cholayna ran quickly to Vanessa, urging her to get up. Camilla said, "That ought to hold them for a while! Not for long, though. Let's get out while we can!"

Swiftly they scrambled to their horses, Vanessa still shaking her head and mumbling dizzily. Magda checked her bleeding arm. Nothing, she supposed to worry about; though blood was still oozing slowly from the cut. *If a vein was severed,* she told herself, *it would be a steady flow, and if the artery had gone, I'd have bled to death already.* She tore a strip from the bottom of her undertunic once she'd clambered into her saddle; she tied the tourniquet swiftly, anchoring it with her teeth to keep both hands free.

Clumped together on their horses, chervines on lead reins, they moved toward the door. Jaelle said, "Wait—"

and Magda felt the touch of her *laran*, "let's make sure they don't get in here for a good long time. . . ."

Magda looked over her shoulder at the face and form of the Goddess, dark robe glittering with stars, jeweled wings overshadowing the dark spaces of the barn, her face haloed and her eyes piercing, sorrowful, terrifying. She did not envy the villager who tried to use that barn again, even for an innocent purpose. Where had she found the image in her mind? On the night of that first meeting of the Sisterhood?

They rode together out of the barn into the wind and blowing snow. A few villagers huddled together, watching them go, but made no move to stop them. Maybe they still saw the demons she and Jaelle had created.

All at once, Magda was fearfully sick and dizzy. She held to her saddle with both hands, trying to avoid falling from her horse. Her wounded arm—the same arm she had scraped raw in the fall, she realized for the first time—stung with pain, and her head throbbed as if every pulse of her blood were a separate stone hurled at her forehead; but she clung to the saddle, desperately. The important thing was to put as much space as humanly possible between themselves and that miserable, damnable village. She tried to hang on with one hand and pull her scarf over her face to protect her eyes a little from the stinging wind—without much luck. She bent forward, huddling her face into the neck of her jacket, riding in a dark nightmare of pain. She hardly heard Camilla's voice at her side.

"Margali? *Bredhiya*? Are you all right? Can you ride?"

Isn't that what I'm doing? Would it make any difference if I said I couldn't? she tried to say, irritably; but her voice would not obey her. She felt that she was fighting the reins, fighting the horse that would not

obey her. Later she knew that she had fought and tried
to hit Camilla when the older woman lifted her bodily
from her horse and into her arms. Then Magda's mind
went dark and she fell into a dark dream of screaming
demons pinioning her to a cattle-stall while a banshee-
faced *kyorebni* tore with a fierce beak at her arm and
shoulder; then it pecked out her eyes, and she went
blind, and knew no more.

CHAPTER SIXTEEN

She was wandering in the gray world; alone, formless, without landmarks. She had wandered there for a hundred thousand times a hundred thousand years. And then, into a universe without form and void, there were voices. Voices curiously soundless, echoing into her throbbing brain.

I think she's coming around. Breda mea, bredhiya, *open your eyes, speak to me.*

No thanks to you, if she is. This was Jaelle's voice, and it occurred to Magda in the formless grayness that the emotion which formed and inhabited and throbbed in Jaelle's voice now was anger; right-down, gut-level, honest wrath. *You say that you love her so much, yet you do nothing to help. . . .*

There is nothing I could have done. I am no leronis, *I leave that to you. . . .*

I have heard you say that before, Camilla, and I believe it no more than I did then. If it is your fancy, as it may well be your privilege, to say at all times that you were born without laran *and to maintain it when it harms none but you, so be it; but with her very life at stake—*

*Her life? Nonsense; the goddess be thanked, she breathes, she lives, she's waking—*breda, *open your eyes.*

Camilla's face came out of the grayness, pale against a clear, cold starry dark. Magda said her name shakily. Behind Camilla she could now see Jaelle; and then the fight and its aftermath came back to her.

"Where are we? How did we get away from—from that place?"

"We're far enough away that it's not likely they'll come after us," Cholayna said, somewhere out of Magda's sight. "You've been unconscious for four or five hours."

Magda raised her hand and rubbed her face. It hurt. Camilla said, "I am sorry, Margali—I had no alternative. You would not let me take you off your horse to carry you before me on my saddle—you seemed to think I was another of those creatures from the village." She touched, tenderly, the sore spot at the point of Magda's jaw. "I had to knock you out. While you were healing her, Shaya, couldn't you have done something about that?"

"You don't know anything about it." Jaelle's lips were still tight and she was not looking at Camilla.

Her fingers strayed to the narrow crimson seam of the knife scar along her own face. She said, "I have repaid you for this, at least." Years ago Magda had discovered her own *laran* in helping Lady Rohana to heal it. Then she asked, "How do you feel?"

Magda sat up, trying to assess how in fact she did feel. Her head still ached; apart from that, she seemed quite all right. Then she remembered.

"My arm—the knife—"

She looked curiously down at her arm. It had been skinned raw in the fall, later laid open by the bandit's knife, but there was only a faint pale scar, as if long healed. Jaelle had called upon the force of her *laran* to heal the very structure of the cells.

"What else could I do? I slept through most of the fight," Jaelle said lightly. "And Vanessa didn't really get herself awake until we were an hour outside the village; I don't think she really believed there had been a fight until she saw your arm, Margali."

"Was anyone else hurt?"

"Cholayna's nose was bloodied, but a handful of snow stopped that," Camilla said, "and one of the bastards cut open my best holiday tunic, though the skin was not much more than scratched under it. Jaelle's ribs will be sore for a tenday where you squashed that bandit against her chest." Magda vaguely remembered, now, trying to pull a bandit off Jaelle and cutting his throat in the process.

It was blurred, like a nightmare, and she preferred that it should stay that way.

"We were lucky to get out of there all alive and well," Jaelle said. "Camilla, I owe you an apology."

"Nine times out of ten you would have been right and the place as safe as a Guild-house," Camilla said gruffly.

"And still you insist you have no *laran*?"

Camilla's pale narrow features flushed with anger. "Drop it, Shaya," she said, "or I swear by my sword, I will break your neck. Even you can go too far."

Jaelle clenched her fists and Magda felt the anger again surging up in both of them, like tangible crimson lines of force woven into the air between the women. She strained to speak, to break the tension, but realized that she could hardly sit up, hardly manage a whisper.

"Camilla—"

Jaelle let her breath go. "Hellfire, what does it matter? You heard the warning, kinswoman, call it what you will. I don't doubt it saved all our lives. That's what matters. Vanessa, is the tea ready?'' She set a steaming mug in Magda's hand. ''Drink this. We'll rest here till it's light enough to see our way.''

''I'll stand guard,'' Vanessa offered. ''I think I have had enough sleep for a tenday!''

''And I will stand guard with you,'' said Jaelle, sipping from another mug. ''These three have a fight behind them, and they deserve some rest. We'll off-load the beasts till morning, too. Cholayna, is there any dried fruit?''

Cholayna gestured toward a saddlebag. ''But you can hardly be hungry, after that meal—I didn't think any of us would be hungry for three days!''

But Magda knew, watching Jaelle gnaw on dried raisins, the fierce hunger that succeeded the depletion of *laran*. Camilla took a handful of the raisins too.

''You girls stand watch. You missed the real fun,'' she said, spreading her blankets beside Magda and Cholayna. Magda suddenly felt anxious about Camilla. She was not a young woman, and that had been a dreadful fight. And Camilla had been so worried about her that she had probably not troubled to look after herself. Yet she knew if she inquired, Camilla would make it a point of honor to insist there was nothing wrong with her.

Cholayna, lowering herself to her spread blankets, hesitated.

''Shall I cover the fire? It might show us up to—to anything that's prowling in the woods.''

''Leave it,'' said Jaelle. ''Anything on four legs, the fire would scare them away. Anything on two legs— Goddess forbid—we might as well see what's coming after us. I don't want anyone—or anything—sneaking up on me in the dark.'' She laughed, nervously. ''This time Vanessa and I will do the fighting and let *you* sleep.''

Magda did not feel sleepy, but knew she should rest. The healing skin on her arm itched almost to the bone. The fire sank lower. She could see Vanessa, seated on a saddlebag; Jaelle was somewhere out of her sight, but Magda could *feel* her pacing boundaries of their camp, protecting it, as if she spread brooding wings over it . . . *dark wings of the Goddess Avarra, sheltering them.* . . .

For so many years she had thought of Jaelle as younger, fragile and vulnerable, to be protected as she would have protected her child; yet from the first Jaelle had assumed leadership of this journey, taken responsibility for seeing all of them safe. Her freemate had grown; it was time for Magda to stop thinking of Jaelle as less than her equal.

She is as strong as I, perhaps stronger. It is high time for me to realize that I cannot, I need not, carry all the weight alone. Jaelle, if I let her, will do her share. And more. . . .

They took the road northward, cutting across wild country by little-known trails toward the Kadarin, avoiding main roads and villages. After five days of travel they came on a better-traveled road; Jaelle said that she would rather keep away from main roads, especially with Cholayna with them. ''Even this far north, gossip may have run into the hills that among the Terrans in Thendara there are some with black skins, and I would as soon answer no questions about what we are doing with a Terran in our company. Renunciates raise enough question in these hills, without a Terran woman as well. Vanessa could pass for a mountain woman, some of the forge-folk have animal eyes. Nevertheless we must ford the Kadarin, and for that we must go to one of the main fords or ferries; last spring's floods have made the less-traveled fords too dangerous.''

"I'll risk anything you will," Vanessa said.

"Never mind; Cholayna, just keep your hood around your face and don't answer any questions. Pretend you're deaf and dumb.''

"I should have stayed in Thendara, shouldn't I? I'm just endangering all of you," said Cholayna with a touch of bitterness, but Jaelle made an impatient gesture.

"Done is done. Just keep your wits about you and obey orders, that's all I ask.''

And for a minute Magda wondered if her freemate was actually glad to see the Terran woman, head of Intelligence, for a change taking orders rather than giving them, if Jaelle was pleased to have Cholayna under her command. Then she absolved Jaelle, mentally, of that pettiness. She herself might have felt that way, at least for a moment; Jaelle was all too obviously only worrying about the safety of the group.

And in fact there was probably less danger for any of them, even if Cholayna *was* recognized as Terran, at the large populated fords and ferries, than in some remote village where the Kadarin could be forded in secret. They had had enough of remote villages for one trip.

Half a dozen caravans were at the ford before them, and Camilla, who was wearing a short down jacket, her ragged gingery hair and scarred gaunt features hardly identifiable as a woman's, made some excuse and rode along the stacked-up groups awaiting the ferry. She came riding back looking disappointed.

"I had hoped to see Rafi here, with the Anders woman, perhaps."

Jaelle shook her head. "Oh, no. They are a long way ahead of us, kinswoman."

Camilla tightened her mouth and looked away, her eyes veiled like a hawk's. "That's as it may be; there is always the chance. Are we going to ford, or pay the ferryman?"

"Ford, of course. I don't want anyone getting a good look at Cholayna; there's a proverb in these hills, inquisitive as a ferryman's apprentice. What's the matter, afraid to get your feet wet?"

"No more than yourself, *chiya*. But I thought we were in a hurry."

"We'd have to wait an hour for the ferryman, with all those people ahead of us; we can ford as soon as that man and his dogs and his chervines are all across," Jaelle said, watching the badly organized group ahead of them, a pair of young boys urging dogs and chervines into the water with sticks and menaces, women in riding-skirts clinging to their saddles and squealing; something frightened one of the nervous riding-beasts in midstream, and one of the women was out of her saddle and floundering in the water; it was an hour before the ford was clear again, and Jaelle paced the bank restlessly. Magda could see that she was itching to get out there and show the men how a well-organized caravan forded a river. Their mission permitted no such indulgence.

"Never mind," Magda said as they started leading their pack animals into the trampled mud at the near edge of the ford, "you can get out there and show them how a Renunciate guide takes her crew across."

Jaelle grinned, abashed. "Am I as transparent as that?"

"I've known you a long time, *breda mea*."

They went in orderly fashion, Jaelle leading with the foremost of the pack animals on a lead rein, then Magda,

Vanessa, Cholayna muffled like a *leronis* in Magda's spare riding-cape, and Camilla bringing up the rear. They had, she reflected, forded the Kadarin more easily than if they had waited for the ferry, which was now caught in one of the eddies of the ford, while the ferryman and his sons, swearing and shouting, were trying to pole it free.

They left the ferry behind, and the Kadarin, and rode away into the mountains.

At first the slopes of the foothills were gentle, and they rode on well-marked trails, every slope leading between deep canyons filled with conifers and cloud. Jaelle led, setting the fastest pace the horses could endure. This was home country for the chervines, and they headed into the fiercest winds with pure pleasure.

Gradually the hills began to rise higher, the passes now leading between naked rock. Jaelle was careful not to be caught above the treeline after dark, but at night, cuddled in their doubled sleeping bags for warmth, Magda shivered at the savage shrilling cry of banshees in the frozen passes, a cry which could, she remembered, paralyze any prey within range.

"What in hell is that?" Vanessa quavered.

"Banshee. You read about them, remember? They probably wouldn't come below the treeline except in a specially hard winter when they were starving. This is still summer, remember?"

"Some summer," Cholayna grumbled. "I haven't been warm since we forded the Kadarin."

"So eat more," Magda suggested. "Calories are heat, as well as nourishment." Cholayna was tolerating the pace, the cold and the altitude better than Magda had hoped; *she must have been one hell of a field agent.* Though as the passes grew steeper, more like chervine trails to climb, and they were forced to dismount and walk or climb up the steeper slopes—past Nevarsin they might have to abandon the horses altogether, and ride chervines—the Terran woman's face seemed pinched, her eyes daily deeper sunken in her head. Camilla was hardened to rough travel, and Vanessa sometimes acted as if the whole trip was something she had organized for the fun of it, her own special climbing holiday. This attitude sometimes got on Magda's nerves, but since Vanessa's mountaincraft had helped them over some of the worst stretches, she supposed Vanessa was entitled to enjoy herself.

Ahead of them lay the Pass of Scaravel, more than seven thousand meters high. On the fifth day past the Kadarin, they camped on the lower slope of the road up into Scaravel, after daylong travel in thin flurrying snow that cut visibility to a few horse-lengths ahead. Camilla and Vanessa had grumbled about this, but Magda was just as well pleased; she could keep her eyes on the trail and was not confronted at every turn with the sight of bottomless chasms and dizzying drops off sheer cliffs. The path was slippery in the snow, but not really dangerous, she thought, only dimly realizing how hardened she had grown to roads that would have had her sweating blood only a few tendays ago.

"There's still light," Vanessa argued, "it's less than three or four kilometers to the top. We could still get across."

"With luck. And I'm not trusting to luck any more," Jaelle said testily. "There are banshees above the treeline here, as I have good cause to remember. Want me to introduce you to one in the dark? It's easier to get over in daylight. And we could all do with some rest and hot food."

Vanessa glared and for a moment Magda was sure

she would continue the argument, but finally she turned away and began to unsaddle her horse.

"You're the boss."

"I want all the loads unpacked and redistributed before we start out tomorrow," Jaelle ordered. "We've used up a considerable amount of supplies; and the less weight the animals have to carry, the easier to get across Scaravel—and through the mountains beyond. There are passes beyond Nevarsin which make Scaravel look like a hole in the ground."

Magda came to help with the loads, while Camilla started a fire in the camp stove and Cholayna began unpacking rations. They had fallen into a regular camp routine by this time. Soon a good smell of cooking began to steal through the camp.

"Snowing harder," Camilla said, surveying the dark sky. "We'll need the tents. Come and help me set them up, *breda*."

They had made it a habit that whenever they set up tents they should alternate, changing tentmates every camp; Magda would have preferred sharing quarters permanently with either Camilla or Jaelle, but she understood Jaelle's insistence that they should not divide themselves into cliques or teams; that this had been the ruin of many expeditions. Tonight Magda was sharing the smaller tent with Vanessa, while Camilla, Cholayna and Jaelle were in the larger one. Vanessa, changing her socks before dinner, dug into her personal pack and began to attack her hair with a brush.

"I think I'd face bandits again for a chance at a bath," she said. "My hair feels filthy and I'm grubby all over."

Magda agreed with her that this was one of the greatest hardships of the trail. "There will be a women's bath-house in Nevarsin, though," she said, "and perhaps we can find a washerwoman for some clean clothes.''

"Ready to eat, you two?''

"Just brushing my hair,'' Vanessa said, tying a cotton scarf over her head. Camilla was ladling stew onto plates and handing it round; they sheltered under the tent flaps, sitting on saddlebags, to eat. Magda was hungry, and cleaned up her stew quickly, but Cholayna was simply pushing the food around on her plate.

"Cholayna, you are going to have to eat more than that,'' Camilla said. "Really, you must—''

Cholayna exploded. "Damnation, Camilla, I am not a child; I have been looking after myself for the best part of sixty years, and I simply will not be badgered this way! I know you mean well, but I am sick and tired of being endlessly ordered about!''

"Then you should act as if you knew how to look after yourself as a grown woman,'' Camilla snarled. "You are behaving like a girl of fifteen on her first excursion from the Guild-house! I don't care how old you are or how experienced in other climates or among the Terrans, here you do not know how to care for yourself—or you would be doing it. And if you cannot be trusted to eat properly, then someone must make sure that you do it—''

"Hold it, Camilla—'' Jaelle began, and Camilla turned on her.

"Don't *you* start! I have been holding back from saying this for a tenday now. It is not fair; if Cholayna neglects herself and gets sick, she can endanger us all—''

"Even if this is true, it is not your place to say it—'' Jaelle began, but now Camilla was in a rage.

"At this point I care nothing whose place it may be! If the leader says nothing, then I will. I have been waiting for days for you to do your duty and speak to her about this, but because this Terran woman was once your employer you have not had the courage or the common sense to speak a single word. If that is how you see your duty as head of this expedition—"

"I do my duty as I see it," Jaelle said, at white heat, "and I am not a girl to be lessoned by you—"

"Listen to me, both of you," Cholayna interrupted. "Settle your places in the pecking order somewhere else, and don't use me as your excuse! I am trying to eat as much as I can of your damned filthy food, but it's not easy for me, and I don't need reminding all the time! I will do the best I can; leave it at that, will you?"

"Just the same," Vanessa said, "what they said is true, Cholayna. You act as if they had no right to say it. But on an expedition like this, politeness is not as important as the truth. If you get sick, the rest of us will have to look after you. I have told you before that at these altitudes you simply must force fluids and calories."

"I am trying, Vanessa, but—"

Magda joined in for the first time. "Even if what you say is true, Vanessa—and you too, Camilla—do you have to be so hard on her? Remember, this is Cholayna's first trip into the field in many years, and her first experience with this kind of climate—"

"All the more reason, then, that she should be guided by those of us with experience—" Camilla said, but Jaelle interrupted her:

"Do you think it is going to do her any good if you simply stand there and scream at her like a banshee? I don't think I could eat a bite with you standing over me and yelling at the top of your voice!"

Magda held out her hand in a conciliating gesture.

"Shaya, *please*—"

"Damnation, Margali, will you at least keep out of

this? Every time I try to settle something, you want to get into it. If Camilla and I cannot talk without you trying to jump into the gap, as if you were afraid something would slip by without your having a hand in it—"

Magda shut her mouth with an effort. It was so much like what Lexie had said: *Hellfire, Lorne, is there any pie on this planet you don't have your fingers in?* Was this truly how she appeared to people? She started to say, I was only trying to help, and realized, if it wasn't obvious, that she wasn't.

Cholayna had picked up her plate and was making an effort to force down the cold, greasy meat stew.

Can't they even see that if she tries to eat that, and she's already half sick, it's going to make her worse? Jaelle at least should be able to see that. She opened her mouth again, knowing that she risked another set-down for interfering, but Camilla reached for the plate.

"Let me heat that up for you, Cholayna, or if you'd rather, we still have plenty of the dried porridge-powder, which may be easier for you to eat. I'll mix it with plenty of sugar and raisins. There's no sense wasting good meat on anyone who doesn't appreciate it and probably can't digest it properly anyhow. Does anyone want to share the rest of the stew with me while I make up some porridge for Cholayna?"

"And I've been thinking," Vanessa volunteered, "it might be a good thing to save the special Terran high-altitude rations for her. They're almost entirely synthetics, but they're very high-calorie, high-fat, high-carbohydrate, and they won't upset her; the rest of us can make do on the dried meat and fruit from natural sources. Here," she added, handing over the porridge-powder into which Camilla had stirred sugar and raisins, and Cholayna accepted the mixture gratefully.

Magda could see that she had to force herself to eat, but at least it was simpler to force herself when it was simply disinclination to the effort of chewing and swallowing, not an attempt to overcome decades of training, both in custom and ethical preference.

It frightened her to be so aware of what Cholayna was thinking. There had been times, in her early training in the Forbidden Tower, when she had found herself unable to cut out the thoughts and emotions of her colleagues. But they had all been strong telepaths. Cholayna was head-blind and a Terran, and there should be no such involuntary spillage of emotions.

And Camilla, too, had seemed to know—and Magda stopped herself there. No one should know better than she herself that beneath Camilla's rough-talking exterior was a singularly sensitive, even a motherly woman. There was surely no need to postulate that the stress of this trip, or something else she had no way of identifying, was bringing out latent *laran* in Camilla, or even in Cholayna.

Jaelle said sheepishly to all of them at large, "I'm sorry. I can't imagine what got into me. Camilla, forgive me, kinswoman. I meant what I said but I should have been more tactful about it. Margali—" She turned to Magda and held out her arms. "Forgive me, *breda mea*?"

"Of course!" Magda hugged her, and after a moment Camilla came to join them; then Vanessa and Cholayna were there and the five of them were joined in a group embrace that washed away all the anger.

"I can't imagine why I started yelling," Camilla said. "I didn't mean to, truly, Cholayna. I don't want you to get sick, but honestly, I didn't mean to keep on at you about it."

Vanessa said, "This kind of group tension on an

expedition is to be expected. We should be on guard against it."

"Maybe," Camilla said wryly, "the Sisterhood is testing us for our worthiness to be admitted to that place?"

"Don't laugh. We are—" Jaelle looked at them seriously. "The legend says that we *will* be tested ruthlessly, and—we—" she swallowed, searching for words, "Can't you see? We are searching for Sisterhood, and if we cannot keep it among ourselves—" her voice trailed away into silence.

At least, Magda thought as she crept into the tent she shared with Vanessa, they were all speaking again. Magda rejoiced; it would be hard enough to cross Scaravel even with their utmost cooperation.

CHAPTER SEVENTEEN

Jaelle pointed through a light flurry of falling snow.

"The City of Snows: Nevarsin," she said. And Magda picked up her thought—they were almost frighteningly open to one another now—*Will we find Rafaella and Lexie there? And if we do not, what then?* It was beyond belief that Jaelle, at least, would be willing to turn around and go home again. In her mind this journey took on unreal and dreamlike proportions, it would go on forever, farther and farther into the unknown, in pursuit of robed figures, the sound of crows calling, the shadow of the Goddess brooding over them with great dark wings. . . .

Camilla's horse bumped gently into hers. "Hey, there! Are you asleep on your feet like a farmer at spring market, gawking at the big city?"

Nevarsin rose above them, a city built on the side of a mountain, streets climbing steeply toward the peak, where the monastery rose, naked rock walls carved from the living stone of the peak. Above the monastery were only the eternal snows.

They entered the gates of Nevarsin late in the day, and found their way through snow-covered streets, which angled and climbed and sometimes were no more than flights of narrow steep steps, up which their horses had to be urged and their chervines led and sometimes manhandled upward. Everywhere there were statues of the *cristoforo* prophet or god— Magda knew little about the *cristoforo* sect—the Bearer of Burdens, a robed figure with the Holy Child on his shoulders surmounted by what could have been a sun or a world or perhaps merely a halo. Bells rang out at frequent intervals, and once as they climbed toward the top of a narrow street, they met a procession of monks, robed in austere garments of sacking, barefoot in the snow-covered streets. (But they seemed as comfortable, their feet as pink and healthy, as if they were dressed for a more amenable climate.)

The monks, chanting as they came—Magda could make out very little of the words of their hymn or canticle, which was in an obscure dialect of *casta*— looked neither to left nor to right, and the women had to move their horses and pull them to one side of the street, dismounting to hold the reins of the pack animals. The monk at the head of the procession, a balding old man with a hook nose and a fierce scowl, looked crossly at the women, and Magda supposed he did not approve of Renunciates.

So much the worse for him, then; she was going about her own business just as he was, and really with far less trouble to other people; at least their band were not expecting everybody to get out of the middle of what was, after all, a public thoroughfare.

There were a great many of the monks, and by the time they had all passed by, dusk was falling, and the snow was coming down heavily.

"Where are we going, Jaelle? I suppose you know?" Camilla asked.

"Nevarsin is a *cristoforo* city," Jaelle said, "and as I think I told you, women are not welcome at public-houses or inns unless properly escorted by husbands or fathers. I told you about the place; Rafi and I used to make jokes about the Nevarsin Guild-House. They may be there waiting for us."

The house, a large one built from the local stone, was in the remotest corner of the city, and inside had the good smell of freshly worked leather. Inside, the great door opened on a huge courtyard ("Dry-town style," Jaelle whispered to Magda as they were shown inside), where young women in heavy workman's aprons and thick boots were running about. They stopped to greet the strangers with hospitable bows. The mistress of all these women, a small tough old woman with arms like a blacksmith's, came out, looked at Jaelle with a huge grin, then wrapped her in a smothering embrace.

"Ah, Kindra's fosterling!"

"Arlinda, you look no different than when I last saw you —can it have been seven years ago? More than that?"

"It was seven years; Betta had just died, Goddess give her rest, and left the place in my hands. How good to see you, there is always room here for Renunciates to lodge! Come in, come in! Suzel, Marissa, Shavanne, lead their horses into the stable, run and tell Lulie in the kitchen that there will be three, no, four, no, five guests for dinner! Give their horses hay and grain, and their chervines too, and haul all their packloads into the strongroom; I will give you a receipt, no, *chiya*? Just so there's no question. You came across Scaravel? Mercy me, you look thin and tired, and no wonder, after such a trip! What can I do for you first? Hot wine and cakes? A bath? A meal within ten minutes, if you are famished?"

"A bath would be heaven," Jaelle said, to enthusiastic seconding murmurs from all four of the others. "But I thought we would have to go out to the women's bathhouse—"

"My dears, we *are* the women's bathhouse now, it was going downhill, no towels, the attendants with their hands out for tips all the time, and pimps hanging around for so many of the women of the streets that the respectable family men wouldn't let their respectable family women go to it anymore! So I bought it on the cheap, and let it be known that I wanted the street girls certified clean by one of the women's doctors here. And if I caught them making assignations here, out they went. And I chased off all the pimps for good and all. I let the good-time girls know in no uncertain terms that if they wanted baths here, they'd better behave on these premises like apprentice virgin Keepers! And do you know, I think they were glad of it, to be treated just like family women, no difference between them and the wives and daughters of gentlefolk." She shouted. "Suzel, take these ladies to the best guest-chamber, and then straight to the baths, bath's on the house, no charge, these are old friends!"

She drew Jaelle aside but they all heard her whisper, "And when you're bathed and rested, deary, I have a message for you from your partner. Not now, not now, go and have your bath and I'll send some hot wine for you in your guest room."

Jaelle looked pale and strained. "I beg of you, Arlinda, if Rafi is here, send her to me at once. We have traveled from Thendara in the greatest haste we could manage, hoping to overtake her. Don't play games with me, dear cousin."

Arlinda wrinkled up her face, wrinkled and tanned like her own saddle leather. "Would I do that to you, deary? Oh, no, Rafi's not here; they were here three days and went on only yesterday morning. The one who'd been sent to meet them from you-know-where came for them and they left with her."

Jaelle slumped forward and for a minute Magda thought she would faint. She put her arm out and Jaelle leaned on it hard. Through the touch of her freemate's hand Magda could feel misery and dismay.

To come so far, and to miss them by so little . . .

But she recovered herself swiftly. She said with gentle dignity, "You spoke of a message, but if they have gone on before us, it certainly can wait until my companions are bathed and rested. I thank you, cousin."

Arlinda's establishment was nothing if not efficient. In a few seconds, so it seemed to Magda, they had been shown to rooms, given receipts for their packloads and had their personal sacks brought to their assigned room, which was large and light and as clean as if it were a department of Terran Medic. There was a laundry on the premises too, and their soiled and travel-grubbied clothing was whisked away with the promise that it would be returned the next morning. All these things were accomplished by young, energetic, friendly girls, mostly between fifteen and twenty, who scurried around briskly, but with the utmost gaiety, and showed no sign whatever of being driven or intimidated. When Camilla was slow to change her garments (Camilla, because of the scars on her mutilated body, always hesitated to bare herself among strangers) they tactfully offered her a bathwrap to wear while her clothing was being washed, whisked away to fetch it for her, and had her clothes off and the fresh wrap on her body almost, it seemed, while Camilla was grumbling at them that she could manage perfectly well without it.

"Now I know," said Camilla, wrapping herself in the bath garment, which was faded and wrinkled but smelled cleanly of soap, "why Kindra used to call this place the Nevarsin Guild-house."

"It's certainly more efficiently run than many in the

Domains," Magda agreed. One of the young women, beckoning to conduct them to the bath, halted a little and she addressed herself directly to Jaelle.

"You are the leader of this band, *mestra*?"

"I am."

"The tall woman with white hair. She is—does she—is the skin disease from which she suffers contagious in any way? If so, *mestra*, your friend must bathe by herself and may not come into the common pool." Her voice was a little embarrassed, but quite firm, and Jaelle answered in the same way.

"On my honor, she suffers from no contagious ailment. Her skin is that way from birth; she comes from a far country where all men and women have such coloring."

"Well, I never! Who'd have believed it!" the girl blurted in wonder. Cholayna, who had stood behind Jaelle wondering what was going to happen, said, "It is true, my girl. But if your customers in the bathhouse will be bothered or afraid that they will catch something, I am willing to bathe alone, as long as I have a bath somehow."

"Oh, no, *mestra*, that won't be necessary, our mistress has known Jaelle a long time, her word's good," the little girl said, kindly if not tactfully. "It's just that nobody here's ever seen nobody like you, so we didn't know, so we had to ask because of the other customers, you see? No offense meant, none at all."

"None taken," Cholayna said graciously (how she managed it, naked in a bathwrap. Magda never knew). As they went on into the bath cubicles assigned to them, Cholayna said to Magda in an undertone, "I had never thought how strange it would be, in a part of the world where everyone looks very much alike. But then, there are other planets like this, though not many. Skin as pale as Camilla's would be almost as unusual on,

say, Alpha, as I am here. What material is this?'' she
asked, fingering the bathwrap, ''It can't be cotton, not
in this climate; or do they grow it in the south near
Dalereuth?''

''It is the fiber of the featherpod tree; they grow
everywhere in the hills. Woven podwool like this is
costly; it is commoner to treat it like felting or
papermaking, because the fibers are short. But when it
is woven this way, it takes the dyes so beautifully that
many people think it worth the trouble and cost. In the
old days, podweavers were a separate guild, who kept
their craft secrets by living in their own villages and
never marrying outsiders at all.''

Then the bath attendants came in; the child must have
passed on the word about Cholayna, for there was not
even any undue staring as they soaped and scrubbed all
the women; even Camilla's customary defensiveness
relaxed when no one paid the faintest attention to the
scars covering her body, and she laughed like a young
girl as the attendants rinsed them under a hot spray
before sending them out into the hot pool. Magda sank
into it gratefully, though the water was too hot at first
for Vanessa, who yelped aloud as she stepped in.

''You sound like a pig ready for butchering, Vanessa!
You'll get used to it,'' Jaelle advised, lowering herself
into the steaming water. It smelled faintly sulfurous and
seemed to soothe out all the sores and aches of riding.
The women leaned back on the stone shelf in the water,
sighing.

''It feels too good to be true,'' Cholayna said. ''The
last time we were this comfortable, they had us drugged
and poisoned!''

''After this, I feel as if I could handle my weight in
bandits,'' Magda laughed.

Jaelle said seriously, ''We are as safe here as in our

own Guild-house, and much safer than we should have been in any of the public bathhouses, some of which are run by pimps and such people.''

"In Nevarsin? Where the holy monks rule everywhere?'' Camilla was frankly skeptical.

"The holy monks are much too holy to think of such things as laws to protect women traveling alone,'' Jaelle said wryly. "In their opinion, virtuous women do not use such luxuries as public bathhouses where strangers might see their naked bodies, and if a woman frequented such a place she would deserve whatever came to her—disease, unwelcome attentions of whatever kind. There was a time, when the *cristoforo* rule of Nevarsin was absolute, that there were laws to close all the public bathhouses. A few stayed open outside the law, and of course, being run by lawless men, they were lawless places; and the monks used the conduct at such places to justify their closing them . . . *see, baths are wicked places, look at the kind of people who attend them!* Fortunately the laws are more sensible now, but I understand the monks are still not allowed to attend public bathhouses, nor are pious *cristoforo* women.''

Camilla snorted. "If the monks' bodies are as filthy as their thoughts, then they must be a dirty lot indeed.''

"Oh, no, Camilla, they have their own baths, I am told, within the monastery. And many homes also have baths on the premises. But of course those are only the richer folk, and the poorer sort of people, especially poor women, had no respectable place for a clean bath until some women opened them. And of course, the early ones were not overly respectable, as Arlinda told us; she has done the women of this city as much service as any Guild-house.''

"She should be made an honorary Renunciate,'' Camilla said, sinking down to her chin in the hot water.

Jaelle lowered her voice so that the small group of pregnant matrons at the far end of the hot pool might not hear.

"I think she is more than that. Did you hear what she said about Rafaella? *The woman sent from you-know-where* . . . what, do you think, could that be, if not some envoy from the place we are looking for? One of the things mentioned in the old legend was this: if you came far enough, you would be guided. Rafaella and Lexie have come far enough, perhaps, to encounter that guidance. It may be that the message Rafi left me was about the guides sent from—that place."

Camilla's voice was openly scornful.

"And when we get there we will find ourselves among the spicebread-trees and the rainbirds who build nests of scented woods to roast themselves for the hungry traveler?"

But Jaelle was perfectly serious.

"I do not know at all what it is that we will find. The legend says that what each person finds is different, and suited to his needs. There was an old story my nurse used to tell me—oh, I was very little then, a tiny child in the Great House of Shainsa." Magda could hardly keep from staring at her freemate. Only once before in all the years she had known her freemate had Jaelle referred, even fleetingly, to her childhood in the Dry-Towns, and never to anyone in her father's house there. She could tell from Camilla's eyes that this was equally astonishing to her.

"The story said that three men went out to seek good fortune," Jaelle said, in a faraway voice, "and one married a beautiful wife with much gold and treasure, and thought he was fortunate. And the second found an abandoned homestead where he pruned the trees and they grew fruits and mushrooms for him, and he tamed wild cattle, and fowl, and as he labored night and day to build his farm by the hard work of his hands, felt himself the most fortunate of all men. But the third, they say, sat in the sun and watched the clouds, and heard the grass grow, and listened to the voice of God, and said, Never was any man so fortunate and favored as I.''

There was a long minute of silence. Then Cholayna said, determinedly practical, ''As long as I find Alexis Anders alive and unharmed, I have already enough notes on this country and have seen enough strange things that I should be the most ungrateful of women to complain if I find nothing more.''

''I would hope for a mountain to equal Montenegro Summit,'' said Vanessa, ''but one can't have everything.''

''Be careful what you pray for,'' Jaelle laughed, ''you might get it. There are mountains here, I tell you, much higher than Scaravel—though, after this, I could live richly content if I knew I would never again travel above the treeline. Margali, what do you want from that city of legends, should we be guided there?''

''Like Cholayna, I'll be content to find Lexie and Rafaella safe and well. Somehow I can't imagine either of them being very interested in ancient wisdom—''

''And as for legends,'' Vanessa said cheekily, ''you yourself are the legend against which they are measuring themselves, you, Lorne—''

Magda flinched as if Vanessa had struck her. She needed no reminding of that—that in a sense she was to blame that these two women, who should have been her friends, had risked this desperate and dangerous journey.

For all that, would I have wished this road untraveled? I have tested my own strength and found myself stronger than I ever believed. Would I wish this undone?

Leaning back in the clouds of steam, her body at ease in the hot bath, she realized that it did not matter a particle whether she wished all this undone. It *had* happened; it was a part of her, whether for good or bad did not matter either. It was up to her to learn what she could from the experience, and pass on to the next thing in her life.

Just as she suddenly knew that she felt free of the "Lorne legend" which had pursued her for so long. No one, least of all Magda, had required of Alexis Anders that she try to equal or surpass Magda's achievements. *It had been Lexie's own doing, not hers!* Magda felt as if a burden heavier than the chervine packloads had fallen from her back and dissolved in the hot water. She would still help Lexie when she found her; the younger woman had gone into deeper waters than she was trained to handle. Magda was obligated to do anything she could to help her. But only as her vow required her to be . . . in the words of the Renunciate Oath . . . *mother and sister and daughter to all women.* Not from guilt, not because it was her fault Lexie had done this rash and stupid thing. She sighed, a long sigh of pure relief.

"I am getting soggy," Vanessa said. "I think I will get out, and try some of that hot wine they offered us."

"Enjoy yourself," Jaelle said, "but I must have Rafaella's message as quickly as possible."

Clean clothing was as great a luxury as the bath; Magda had saved one set when she let the laundry women take away hers for washing. Food had been brought and smelled most appetizing; but Jaelle hurried off to Arlinda for Rafaella's message.

"Forgive me, *breda*. But Arlinda has known me since before I took Oath as a Renunciate, and she may talk more freely with me alone than with someone else to hear. Save me some of the roast rabbithorn I can smell on those platters.''

Magda conceded the good sense of this, but felt troubled as she watched Jaelle go off alone. Her Amazon trousers had gone for cleaning and she was wearing her old fur-lined bathrobe; she looked small and vulnerable, and Magda wished she could protect her. But Jaelle was not a child to be protected. She went back and watched the others taking covers off dishes with frank greed. Even Cholayna succumbed to a dish of boiled whiteroot seasoned with cheese and pungent spices, with a great dish of four kinds of mushrooms and a side platter of stuffed vegetables. Although she did not touch the roast rabbithorn, she did eat some of the stuffing of dried apples and bread soaked in red wine.

Magda set aside a haunch of the rabbithorn and plenty of the stuffing and vegetables for Jaelle. All through the meal she kept expecting the door to open and her freemate to return, but they had cut into the dessert by the time Jaelle came back.

"I thought I would never eat redberry sauce again, after that place," Vanessa said, dribbling the sweet red stuff across the surface of a smooth custard. "But I find it tastes as good as it did then, and this time, at least, I am sure there is no noxious drug in it."

They all turned to look as Jaelle came in.

"We saved you plenty of dinner," Vanessa said, "but it's probably cold as a banshee's heart."

"Banshee heart, boiled or roasted, is a dish I would never cook," said Cholayna, "but if the rest is too cold, we can probably have it heated up in the kitchens."

"No, that's all right. Cold roast rabbithorn is served at all the best banquets," Jaelle said, as she came and sat down and helped herself to rabbithorn and mushrooms. It seemed to Magda that she looked cold and constrained.

"What was Rafi's message, love?"

"Only to come after her as fast as I could manage," Jaelle said, "but there was another message which Arlinda gave me." But after this she was silent so long that Vanessa finally asked belligerently, "Well? Is this some great secret?"

"Not at all," Jaelle said at last. "Tonight, so Arlinda told me, one will come, supposedly, from that place, and she will speak with us. And I could tell, from the way Arlinda spoke, that she was afraid. I cannot imagine why, if the Sisterhood is as benevolent as I have always heard, a woman like Arlinda would have anything to fear from her. What Arlinda has managed to do, in a city like Nevarsin, is all but unbelievable. Why should the Sisterhood frighten her?" Jaelle poured herself some of the spiced wine, and sipped at it, then shoved it away.

"So, we are to be tried," said Camilla. "That is a part of every search, Shaya, love. The Goddess knows you have nothing to fear. Do you truly think they will find us wanting?"

"Oh, how am I to know that, how do I know what they require?" Jaelle munched cold rabbithorn, as uninterested as if it were packaged field rations, her face stolid and closed-in, betraying nothing. "They will judge me in the name of the Goddess and I do not know what to say to them."

Camilla said, and to Magda she sounded fiercely defensive, "You are what you are, *chiya*, like all of us, and none of us can be otherwise. As for me, I have no more reverence for these women of the Dark Sisterhood than for their Goddess, who thrust me unasked and uninvited into a world which has treated me as I, who am no more than human, would not have treated the meanest of creatures. If their Goddess wishes me evil, I will demand of her why, since when it befell me I was too young to have done anything to deserve it; if she wishes me well, I will ask why she calls herself a Goddess when she was powerless to prevent evil. And when I have heard her reply, then I will judge her as she or her representatives think to judge me!'' She poured herself another glass of wine. ''Nor should you fear anything from these women who presume to speak in Her name.''

''I don't fear,'' Jaelle said slowly. ''I wonder why Arlinda fears, that is all.''

Cholayna had spread out her sleeping bag—the single one of Terran make—on the floor, and, using her saddlebag and her pack as a pillow, was leaning back, writing in a little book. She had, Magda thought, admirably recovered the habits of a field agent. Vanessa was meticulously combing and sectioning her hair for braiding.

Magda was debating following either example, and had started to get her sleeping bag out of its pack when one of the young apprentices came in, carrying an embroidered leather hassock, an elaborate guest seat. Behind the girl came Arlinda herself. Although Magda expected that Arlinda would take that seat, she did not; she backed against the wall and sat down there, legs crossed beneath her heavy canvas apron, her brawny arms akimbo, bristling all over with expectation.

Then a woman came into the room, and they all looked up at her.

She was not exceptionally tall, but she seemed somehow to take up more space than she physically occupied in the room. It was a trick of presence; Magda had met a few people who knew how to use it, but they were seldom women. She had dark-auburn hair, twisted into a tight coil at the back of her head and fastened there with a copper pin or so. She was dressed in clothing of rather better quality than anyone Magda had seen at the baths or in the leather-worker's shop so far, and it fitted her well, something unusual for women in this chilly city of *cristoforos* where women were expected to efface themselves. Her eyes were pale gray, looking out with an imperious commanding presence from under her piled hair.

She took the elaborate seat quite as if it was the expected thing. Magda glanced at Arlinda and noticed that the brawny woman's arms showed signs of gooseflesh, as if she were cold.

What in the name of all the gods on all the planets in or out of the Empire has she *got to be afraid of?* Magda had not believed anything could make this old Amazon— better fitting the name than any Renunciate—afraid.

"I am the *leronis* Acquilara," she announced. She looked them over, one by one. "Will you tell me your names?"

With one accord they waited for Jaelle to speak.

"I am Jaelle n'ha Melora," Jaelle said slowly. "These are my companions." One by one she repeated their names. "We are from Thendara Guild-house in that city."

Acquilara heard them without motion, not a flicker of muscle moving in her face or a flicker of her eyes. An imposing trick, Magda knew. She wondered how old the woman was. She could not guess. Her face was less lined than Camilla's; yet the boniness of her fingers, the texture of her skin, told Magda this was not a young woman. When she moved, it was with an air of complete deliberation, as if she moved only when she had decided to move and never for any other reason.

She swiveled her head to Cholayna and said, "I have

known a woman with your skin color. She was poisoned in childhood with a metallic substance. It is so with you, is it not." It was not a question but a statement. She sounded very self-satisfied, as if waiting for them to acknowledge her cleverness in solving such a riddle.

But Cholayna spoke with equal composure. "It is not. I have known such cases of heavy-metal poisoning, but my skin was this way at birth; I am from a far country where all men and women are like me."

The eyes of the *leronis* flickered and jolted abruptly to Cholayna again. Her face was so motionless otherwise that Magda knew they had really taken her by surprise. *We were meant to be impressed and we spoiled that for her.* Arrogance was a part of the woman. Somehow Magda had expected that envoys from the mysterious Sisterhood would be like Marisela, benevolent and unassuming.

Was this some form of test? The words formed in her mind without volition. She looked at her freemate, trying to send her a warning; *Be careful, Jaelle!*

But she knew Jaelle had not received the warning, her brain felt dead, the air in the room an empty void that would not carry thought. *So we have had a demonstration of her powers, if not the one she expected.*

Arlinda was still cowering by the wall, and Magda looked at the old Amazon with displeasure, not at Arlinda for her fear, but at the arrogant *leronis* for imposing it. Why should an envoy from the Sisterhood try to terrify them? Suddenly Magda remembered the old woman of her dream in Ravensmark Pass. But she was more afraid of this Aquilara than she had been of that old woman.

Acquilara began again.

"I have heard that you are searching for a certain City."

Jaelle did not waste words. "Have you been sent to take us there?"

Magda knew, without being sure how she knew, that Jaelle had displeased the woman. Aquilara shifted her position; after her stillness this motion was as surprising as if she had leaped up and yelled aloud.

"Do you know what you are asking? There are dangers—"

"If we were afraid of the dangers," Jaelle retorted, "we would not have come so far."

"You think you know something of dangers? I tell you, girl, the dangers you have met on the road— banshees, bandits, all the demons of the high passes— they are nothing, I tell you, nothing beside the dangers you still must face before you are taken into that City. It is not I who impose that test on you, believe me. It is the Goddess I serve. You call upon that Goddess, you Renunciates. But will you dare to face Her, if She should come?"

"I have no reason to fear her," Jaelle said.

"You think you know something of fear?" Acquilara looked at Jaelle with contempt, and turned to Camilla.

"And you. You are seeking that City? What for? This is a City of women. How shall you, who have renounced your womanhood, be admitted there?"

Camilla's pale face flushed with anger, and Magda suddenly thought of the Training Sessions in the Guildhouse, when the young women, newly admitted to the Guild, were incited to anger and put on the defensive, to force them to clarify their real thoughts; to get beyond what they had been taught as young girls that they ought to think and feel. Were they being subjected to some such process now, and why? And why at the hands of this woman, this *leronis*, if she was a *leronis* at all?

"Why do you say I have renounced my womanhood, when you find me in the company of my sisters of the Guild-house?"

Acquilara seemed to sneer.

"Where else could you swagger and play the man so well? Do you think I cannot read you as a woodsman reads the tracks in the first snow? Do you dare deny that for years you lived among men as a man, and now you think you can become a woman again? Your heart is a man's heart—have you not proven that by taking a woman lover?"

Magda watched Camilla's face, angry and pained. Surely this woman was a *leronis*, or how could she strike so precisely at Camilla's defenses? Yet she, who had been Camilla's lover so long, knew better than anyone alive how unjust it was. Sexless as Camilla's mutilated body might seem, the body of the *emmasca*, Magda knew better than any other that Camilla was all woman.

"You, who have denied the Goddess in yourself, how will you justify yourself to Her?"

Camilla was on her feet, and her hand was gripping her knife. Magda wanted to jump up, physically prevent her from whatever rash thing she might contemplate; yet she sat as if paralyzed, unable to move a muscle to warn or prevent her friend.

"I will justify myself to the Goddess when she justifies herself to me," Camilla said. "And I will justify myself to her, not to her envoy. If you were sent to guide us to that City, then guide us. But don't venture to test us; that is for her, not her lackeys." She stood over the *leronis*, and for a moment it was a contest of arrogance.

Magda was never sure what happened next. There

was a flash, something like blue fire, and Camilla reeled backward; she fell, rather than sat down, on her sleeping bag.

"You think you know the Goddess," stated Aquilara, and now her voice was all contempt. "You are like the peasant women who pray to the bright Evanda to make their garden bloom, and their dairy animals to drop their calves without blight, and to bring them handsome virile lovers and healthy babies. And they pray to the sheltering Avarra to ease their pains of birth and death. But they know nothing of the Goddess. She is the Dark One, cruel and beyond the comprehension of mortal women, and her worship is secret."

"If it is secret," Vanessa said—all this time she had sat silent on her sleeping bag, listening but not speaking— "why do you tell us about it?"

Aquilara rose abruptly to her feet.

She said, "You girls—" the term was frankly one of contempt now, and included even the mature Cholayna in its scorn—"you think you will use the Goddess? The truth is that she will use you in ways you cannot even begin to contemplate. She is cruel. Her only truth is Necessity. But like all of us, you are grist for her mill, and she will grind you up in it. Your friend saw this, and she has begged a place for you. Be ready when she calls you!"

She turned her back without looking round, and strode out of the room. The apprentice picked up the seat without a word and followed her.

Arlinda was still cowering against the wall in an agony of fear.

"You should not have angered her," she whispered, "she is very powerful! Oh, you should not have made her angry."

"I don't care if she's the Goddess herself," Jaelle said, brusquely, "she rubbed me the wrong way. But if she's got Lexie and Rafaella, we've got to play along with her, at least for a while."

Vanessa had resumed combing her hair and was now braiding it into half a dozen small braids, for tidiness. "Do you think she has Lexie and Rafaella, then?"

Jaelle turned to Arlinda. "Did Rafi go with her?"

Arlinda shook her head and mumbled, "Nay, how am I to know of her comings and goings? She is a *leronis*, a sorceress, whatever she wills, so she will do. . . ."

Magda was shocked, even horrified. Arlinda had seemed so strong, so hearty and tough, and now she was mumbling as if she were a senile old woman. Soon after, she kissed Jaelle good night and went away, and the women of the party were left alone.

"Better get to bed," Jaelle said. "Who knows what might be up for us in this place? Keep your knives handy."

Vanessa looked at her in shock. She said, "I thought you said we were as safe here as in the Guild-house, with Arlinda—"

"Even a Guild-house can catch fire or something. Arlinda's changed from when I knew her ten years ago. Sitting shaking in a corner while the old beldame bullies her guests—ten years ago she'd have slung Aquilara, or whatever that so-called *leronis* calls herself, out into the street on her backside."

"You don't think she's a *leronis*?" Magda asked.

"Hell, no, I don't." Jaelle lowered her voice, glancing cautiously around as if she thought Aquilara might be lurking unseen in a corner.

"She took a lot of pains to impress us with how

much she knew about us already. About Camilla having lived as a man, for instance. Anything she *could* have used against us, she would have used to put us at a disadvantage.'' Jaelle stopped and glanced from Cholayna to Vanessa.

''But she couldn't even guess that you three were Terrans. What the hell kind of *leronis* is *that*?''

CHAPTER EIGHTEEN

"You're right." Magda frowned, trying to decide what this might mean. "She misses things that even Lady Rohana would have picked up. This 'great *leronis*' would appear to be rather lacking in mental abilities, although," she added grimly, "she obviously has some physical ones."

Camilla was still sitting on her bedroll looking stunned. Magda went to her.

"*Breda*, did she hurt you?"

For a frightening minute Camilla did not reply and Magda had a brief memory picture of Arlinda, maundering suddenly like a senile old woman. Then Camilla drew a long breath and let it out.

"No. Not hurt."

Vanessa asked, "What precisely did she do to you, Camilla? I could not see. . . ."

"How should I know? That devil-spawn in the shape of a woman but pointed her finger at me, and it seemed that my legs would no longer hold me up; I was falling through an abyss torn by all the winds of the world. Then I found myself sitting here without wit to open my eyes or speak."

Vanessa said, "If *that* was a representative of your Sisterhood, I do not think very highly of them."

Cholayna, in her guise as a professional, was doing a

mental analysis. "You say, Jaelle, that she hasn't the mental abilities one would expect from most of the Comyn. The physical abilities she displayed could be duplicated by a stunner. She seemed to rely on presence and the old 'I know what you're thinking' trick. She reminded me of someone running a confidence game."

"You're right," Vanessa agreed. She drew herself up and solemnly intoned, "Trust me, dear children! I am the personal representative of the One True Goddess; I see all, know all; you see nothing, know nothing." She dropped the pose and looked thoughtful. "She said we would be *summoned*. What do you suppose she meant by that?"

"I have no idea," said Jaelle, "but I would go nowhere—not out of this house, not to the next room, not to the *cristoforo* heaven itself—at *her* summoning."

"I don't see that we have a choice," Cholayna said. "If she, whoever and whatever she is, has Anders and Rafaella, or even knows where they are. . . ."

Jaelle nodded bleakly. "Right. But we'll hang on here as long as we can. For the moment we should get some rest, be ready for whatever it is they may be planning for us. Want me to take first watch?"

Cholayna put away the little book in which she had been writing. Vanessa tied her braided hair into a scarf and snuggled down in her sleeping bag. Camilla backed herself up against the one wall of the room where there were no doors, and said to Magda in an undertone, "I feel like a fool; yet for the first time in many years I am afraid to be alone. Come and sleep here beside me."

"Gladly," Magda said, positioning her sleeping bag so that Camilla lay protected between her and the wall. "I'm sure that creature—I refuse to call her *leronis*— would send us nightmares if she could manage it."

The fire burned low; Jaelle had kept one of the lamps

lit, and she was sitting up on her sleeping bag, hand ready to her knife. Magda touched the hilt of her own knife . . . Jaelle's knife; years ago, they had exchanged knives, in the age-old Darkovan ritual binding them to one another. It was familiar now as her own hand.

She thought, now that we are safe here I should try and let them know, in the Forbidden Tower, that we are safe. And I would like to know that the children are well and content. She composed herself for sleep, one hand touching the silken bag at her throat where her matrix rested. Drowsing, she let her mind start to range outward. An instant later she was in the Overworld, looking down through grayness at her apparently sleeping form, the motionless bodies of her four companions.

But although she tried to move outward, into the gray world seeking the landmarks of the Forbidden Tower, something seemed to hold her in the room. She hung there motionless, vaguely sensing that something was wrong. She found herself glancing toward each of her companions in turn, tensed for flight but held there by some force she could not overcome. She was not accustomed to this, and while, out of her body, she was free of physical sensation, she felt an anxiety, a hovering fear that simulated real pain.

What could be wrong? All seemed normal; Jaelle, sitting quietly alert; Vanessa and Cholayna, the older woman lying on her side, her face hidden in the pillow and only the pale shock of hair visible, Vanessa burrowed under her blankets like a child. Camilla was asleep too, tossing and turning unquietly and muttering to herself, her face twisted into a frown. Magda silently damned Matera in every language she could think of.

Softly at first, then louder, she heard a small sound in the silence of the overworld; it was the calling of crows. Then she could see them, hooded forms, misty images gradually becoming more defined. For an instant she had a formless sense of well-being. *Yes, this is the right path. We are doing what we were born to do.*

Then the uneasiness came back, stronger than before; the crows squawked their alarm cry, raucous, shrilling through the overworld. Then a sharper scream rang through the room which was not really the room at all. Hawks! From somewhere, dozens of hawks were in the room, angling, stooping down on the crows in every direction. A great wave of emotion, combined of anger, frustration, and jealousy, emanated from the hawks—it reminded Magda of the Terran legend of Lucifer and his fallen angels, cast out from heaven and forever trying to keep others from what they had lost for themselves.

A pair of hawks, feathers falling, speckled with blood, made a dive at Camilla, and Magda snapped back into her body as Camilla woke screaming.

Or had there been any sound at all? Camilla was sitting bolt upright in her sleeping bag, her eyes wild, her arms outstretched to ward off some invisible menace. Magda touched her shoulder, and Camilla blinked and truly woke.

"Goddess guard me," she whispered. "I saw them; ten thousand devils . . . and then you came, Margali, with . . ." she stopped and frowned, and at last said in a confused whisper, "*Crows?*"

"You were dreaming, Kima." The rarely used, rarely permitted nickname was the measure of Magda's disturbance.

Camilla shook her head. "No. Once before you spoke of the emissaries of the Dark Lady as taking crow form. I am not sure I understand it. . . ."

"I don't either." But as she spoke Magda had a sudden vision of Avarra, Lady of Death, mistress of the forces which break down and carry away that which is past usefulness; crows, scavengers and carrion birds, cleaning up the debris of the past.

Hawks; raptors, preying on the living. . . .

Vanessa mumbled in protest, burrowing deeper into her sleeping bag. Magda glanced with compunction at her companions. She should not disturb them. She got up and went to the fireside, kneeling beside Jaelle.

She asked in a whisper, "Did you see anything?" and Jaelle started from an unquiet doze.

"Ayee—! What a guardian I am! We could all have been murdered in our beds here!" She made a nervous gesture at the fire. "I saw in the flames . . . women, robed and hooded, with the faces of hawks, circling about us . . . Margali, I do not like your Sisterhood."

Magda beckoned Camilla forward.

"We saw. Both of us. I think the hawks are—are Aquilara's crew, if that makes any sense to you, and that they have nothing to do with the *real* Sisterhood. But the real ones are near us. They will protect us, if we listen. But if we listen to Aquilara and her threats and summonings. . . ."

"Yes," said Camilla gruffly, "I too have had a warning. If we stay here, we might better have died at the hands of the robbers. It is not our bodies in danger this time; they strike at the inner bastions of our minds. Our souls, if you will. It is not Arlinda or her girls that I fear, but they have somehow let this place be opened . . ." she stopped and said in confusion, "I do not know what I am talking about. Is this what you two mean when you speak of *laran*?"

Jaelle looked from one to the other, dismayed. She said, "What do you suggest that we do?"

"Get the hell out of here," Camilla said, "not even waiting for daylight."

"A poor return for hospitality," Jaelle said, hesitant.

"Hospitality indeed," Camilla said dryly, "loosing such a sorceress—I will not give her the honorable title of *leronis*— upon us."

But Jaelle was still troubled.

"Cholayna was so far right," she said. "If Aquilara has Rafi—and Lieutenant Anders—I do not see how we can afford to leave them in her power. If she can guide us to them—"

"I think she lied, to deceive us into following her," Camilla said.

"But in the name of the Goddess herself, for what reason?" Magda asked. "What would she want with us, and why would she try to deceive us anyhow?"

"I don't know," Camilla said, "but I wouldn't believe a word she said. If she told us Liriel was rising on the eastern horizon I would look at the sky to be certain."

For seven years it has distressed me that Camilla would not use the laran *to which she was born. Now when she does I am trying to argue with her*, Magda thought. Yet from Jaelle she picked up the very real concern; on their actions in the next few hours, the very lives of Lexie and Rafaella could depend.

She thought, *damn them both*, and quickly retracted the thought. She had known for years that a thought was a very real thing. She did not have the *laran* of the Alton Domain, where a murderous thought could kill, but she realized wearily that she did not want any harm to come to Rafaella, who was Jaelle's oldest friend. She felt that she would like to box Lexie's ears, but she did not really want to see her hurt or killed. What they had done was unwise, foolish, and tiresome, but death or damnation would be too great a penalty.

What then was the answer?

"Just supposing that she told the truth—even if her

purpose could have been to confuse us like this," Magda said, "and that she really does have Lexie and Rafaella? What do we do then?"

"Wait perhaps till she comes back, and I will guarantee to get it out of her," Camilla said; she put her hand on her knife, then let it fall, her face grim. "I was not so good at getting it out of her that way, was I?"

Jaelle said, "No. We can't fight her like that. I think that kind of fighting would be the worst thing we could do. She would be able to use the—the emotion of it against us. Do you know what I am trying to say, Magda?"

"She could make us fight among ourselves. Against each other. That may be all the mental power she has, but I am sure she could do that or something worse. Look what she seems to have done to Arlinda."

"But in the name of all the Gods and Goddesses there ever were," demanded Camilla, "what would her *reasons* be? You cannot tell me that she came into our lives, lied to us and sent her demons against us just for amusement! Even if she has a bizarre sense of humor and a taste for lying, what could she possibly hope to gain? Evil she may be, but I cannot believe in the evil sorceress who indulges in wickedness and mischief-making for no reason whatsoever. What does she think she can get from us? If it was theft she had in mind, she would not need to resort to this rigmarole. It would be simpler to bribe Arlinda's dogs and watchwomen."

"Maybe," said Jaelle tentatively, after a long time, "it's a way of keeping us away from the real ones. The real Sisterhood."

Camilla said scornfully, "I can just about manage to believe in one Sisterhood of wise priestesses watching over humankind in the name of the Dark Lady. *Two* of them would strain my credulity well past the limit, Shaya.''

"No, Camilla. Seriously. The legends all say we will be tested. If they are what people say, they must have enemies. Real enemies, or why would they be so secret in their doings? To me it is not hard to believe that there might be—well, others, a rival Sisterhood, maybe, who hate everything they stand for and will stop at nothing to try to keep anyone from getting through to them. And the real Sisterhood let it go on because it—well, it makes it harder for the serious aspirants to get through to them. I mean, I can't imagine they would want to be bothered with the kind of people who would listen to Aquilara, or her kind.''

"You have missed your profession, Jaelle. You should be a ballad-singer in the marketplace; never have I heard such inventive melodrama,'' Camilla said.

Jaelle shrugged. "Whether or no,'' she said, "it leaves our main question still unanswered. Whatever this Aquilara may be, liar, thief, mischief-maker or representative of some rival Sisterhood, the problem facing us is still the same. Does she have Rafaella and Lexie, or was she lying about that too? And if she does, what can we do about it, and how can we tell the difference? If either of you has any answer to *that* question, melodrama or no, I will listen with great willingness. I am reluctant to leave here without knowing for certain whether Rafaella is in that woman's hands.''

It always came back to that, Magda thought in frustration. They were beginning to go around and around without getting anywhere, and she said so.

"You might as well get some sleep, Jaelle. Camilla and I are not likely to sleep much after that—'' she hesitated for a word, reluctant to say *attack*; it might have, after all, been a dream shared among the three of them and born of their mistrust and fear of this place. But Jaelle picked it up.

She said hesitating, "It is not really late. If we had not all traveled so far, none of us would try to sleep this early. Arlinda's apprentices may well be awake, perhaps drinking or dancing in their common-room, or even lounging in the bath, and I will go and try to talk with them. Perhaps one of them spoke with Rafi while she was here."

"A fine idea. Let me go with you, *chiya*," Camilla suggested, but Jaelle shook her head.

"They will speak more freely to me if I'm alone. Most of them are my age or younger, and there are two or three of them I used to trust. I'll see if they're still there and if they'll talk to me." She slid her feet into boots, said, "I'll try to be back before midnight," and slipped away.

CHAPTER NINETEEN

When Jaelle had left them, the night dragged. Magda and Camilla talked almost not at all, and then brief commonplaces of the trail. Magda grew sleepy, but dared not lie down and close her eyes for fear of renewed assault by whatever had attacked her before. She knew it was reasonless, but she was for some reason terrified of seeing again those diving hawks; and although Camilla put a brave face on it she knew Camilla felt much the same.

Cholayna slept restlessly; Magda feared that the Terran woman was undergoing, at the least, evil dreams, but she did not wake her.

Cholayna needed rest. She could certainly survive bad dreams, but there were other worries. She suspected, from the sound of her breathing, that Cholayna was beginning to suffer a few of the early symptoms of mountain sickness. How would the older woman survive the dreadful country past Nevarsin? They had only begun to get into the really high plateau.

Cholayna was tough, she had already survived Ravensmark and the robbers, and had come across Scaravel, exhausted, frostbitten, but still strong. Still, she should ask Vanessa, who knew more about mountains and altitude than any of them, to keep an eye on Cholayna.

As if Vanessa wouldn't, without my telling her! I'm doing it again; trying to protect everyone. That's not my job and I should realize it; other people have a right to run their own risks and take their own chances.

Around them the pulse of the night was slowing; the faint street noises died almost to nothing. She did not know how to read the faraway chime of the monastery bells, but they had rung softly several times, a distant and melancholy sound, before Jaelle came back into the room. Camilla, motionless before the fire, raised her head.

"Well?"

Jaelle came close, dropped on the floor before the fire.

"I found a couple of old friends," she began. Her voice was quiet; partly, Magda felt, not to waken Vanessa and Cholayna, but partly because Jaelle feared being overheard by something that was not in the room at all.

"One of them was a girl I knew when I used to come here with Kindra. I was no more than twelve years old then, but Jessamy remembered some of our games. She recognized Rafaella at once when they came here. They were lodged in this very room."

"They were here; I thought so," Camilla said. "But why didn't they wait for us? And was Anders with her?"

"So Jessamy said. Apparently Lexie had a slight case of frostbite, and they stayed here an extra day, so she would be in better shape to travel. Jessamy didn't talk with Rafi about anything personal, or in private, but Rafi told her that I would be coming—in fact, Jessamy thought they'd intended to wait here for me. Which is why she was so surprised when Rafi left without bidding her good-bye, or even leaving the customary way-gift."

"That's not like Rafaella," Camilla said. "I've traveled with her in the mountains. She has always been generous with tips—it's good business. Up here, everything runs that way—greasing the wheels, so to speak. Even if she was running short of money, she would have been apologetic, made what gifts she could, and many promises. I wonder what happened?"

"Jessamy said Arlinda was not disturbed—they had paid for their lodging, after all, and she never inquires into what tips the girls get. But Rafaella has stayed here before with explorers and climbers and as you say, Camilla, she's always been generous with tips. Jessamy was not complaining or criticizing Rafi, but she did mention that Rafaella must have been in great haste. She didn't even remember the women who repaired saddle-tack and doctored one of their ponies."

Camilla's mouth was grim. "If you wanted evidence, there it is for you. Rafi wouldn't do that kind of thing, not if she ever expected to come back here and get decent service. For one reason or another, they left in a hurry, when they'd been expecting to wait here for us. What more do you want? Probably that Aquilara, or whatever she calls herself, spirited them away in the middle of the night."

"If she was here to speak with us, she didn't go with them," Magda protested.

"Unless she has taken them somewhere and hidden them," said Jaelle. "And if they went willingly, how do you explain Rafaella leaving without the proper way-gifts and courtesies?"

"Might she have intended it as a signal to us that she did *not* go willingly?" Camilla asked.

"And if Aquilara has hidden them nearby," Magda said, "then we can simply wait here, and she will lead us to them. That's what she intends. She said so."

"I know not what you may choose to do," Camilla said, "but I go nowhere in that creature's company. *Nowhere*, understand me? I would not trust her behind me—not even if she was bound and gagged."

"If she has Rafaella and Lexie—" Magda began.

"If Rafaella was such a fool as to trust that evil sorceress, then she deserved whatever—"

"Oh, stop it, both of you," Jaelle pleaded. "This is not helpful. I cannot imagine Rafi trusting that woman at all."

"Jaelle, do you think I am not troubled about her, about both of them? If Camilla feels she cannot trust that woman Acquilara, then if she sends for us, if she says Rafi and Lexie are with her, then perhaps you and I—"

"I trust Camilla's intuition," Jaelle said. "Perhaps tomorrow I shall seek out the woman who doctored their ponies, give her the tip which I know Rafi would have given her, and try to find out who saw them leave, and who was with them."

"That seems reasonable. It will do Cholayna no harm to have an extra day's rest," Magda said.

"I am worried about her too," Camilla said. "If only for her sake, it would be as well if our journey ended here in Nevarsin. The country past here—you know what it is like."

"Only too well. I was born in Caer Donn," Magda reminded her. She yawned, and Camilla said predictably, "If you are sleepy, Margali, go and rest. I will keep watch with Jaelle."

Magda was still reluctant to sleep; yet she knew she would not be able to travel on the next day unless she rested. That was even more true of Camilla, who was not young, and already showing signs of travel-fatigue, but who seemed even more fearful of sleep in this place than she was herself. No more than Cholayna could she travel on without rest.

Camilla's *laran* seemed to be surfacing after all these years when she had attempted to block it, and suddenly, with a pang of dreadful loneliness, Magda thought, *I wish Damon were here. He could show me what to do for Camilla.* It was too heavy a burden to bear alone.

Yet Damon was far away in the Kilghard Hills, and for some reason or other she seemed barred from the familiar access to the Forbidden Tower by way of the Overworld. She had tried, and she knew, deep in her bones, that to try again would bring down upon them the renewed attack of . . . *hawks?*

Damon could even handle that. He is our Keeper.

And then she remembered something Damon had said; *any halfway competent technician can, in necessity, do the work of a Keeper.* Anything she felt she must call upon Damon to do, she could handle for herself. And now she must.

"You must sleep, Camilla. What would you tell me in such case? I am afraid too, *bredhiya*," she added, using the term of endearment deliberately, a way of saying, *trust me.* "All the same, you must sleep. Jaelle and I will ward this room and guard it so that no sorceress or evil influence can come in here, even in dreams. Shaya, help me."

Deliberately, she unwrapped her matrix, watching Camilla's face; the older woman's eyes followed the matrix, looked away.

"Do not try to look into the matrix, you are not trained to it. It will make you ill," she said. "That time will come. For now, don't try—"

"I? A matrix? The Goddess forbid—"

"As long as it is the Goddess who forbids and not your own fear, Kima." Again, deliberately, she used the nickname she had never before spoken in the presence of a third party. "What if it is the Goddess leading you to this? Trust me; I know what I am doing. But turn away your eyes from the matrix for now." She edged her tones gently with what they called *command-voice* and Camilla, obedient and startled by her own obedience, looked away.

"Jaelle—?"

Together they matched resonances until they were working in unison. For an instant the rapport flared, burned between them, a closeness, an intimacy beyond speech or sex, indescribable.

If Camilla could only share this. . . .

Neither of them was sure which mind originated the thought, or which answered, regretfully:

No. She's not ready. Not yet.

As their matrixes flared into resonance, there was a moment of blue fire in the room. Camilla jerked up her head, startled, but it was so brief, Magda knew, already Camilla was wondering if she had really seen it at all.

If the hawks are awaiting any movement out of this room then the true Sisterhood must also be watching over us. They will help us to seal the room. . . .

They cannot interfere. But we have that power. . . .

Jaelle's touch was like a hand clasped in hers, a hand that gripped an Amazon knife that glowed with blue fire. Although Magda knew that she did not move from where she knelt by the fire, her matrix between her fingers, somehow she was walking beside Jaelle, circling the room, a line of blue-white fire trailing them in the wake of the knife. She closed the circle; together, they raised their joined hands in an arch (although they never moved) and between their hands a web of pallid fire ran back and forth.

The old woman was there, with her yelping laughter. So, so, so, you think you can keep me out, silly girls?

Mother, not you. But our friends must rest and shall not be pecked by hawks while they sleep.

Blue fire flamed from the matrixes, weaving like a fiery shuttle, until the room was enclosed in a shimmering dome. Magda ran her consciousness round and round, seeking any chink in their protection. For an instant Aquilara's face was there, menacing, terrible as Magda had seen it for an instant through her pretended good nature and scorn, flaming with rage.

So she is warned, she knows that we know she is not what she seems. . . .

Did you really think we could do this kind of work without warning her?

The hawk was there . . . it was diving for her eyes . . . Magda instinctively thrust her matrix toward it, interposing a shield of fire. The hawk's feathers burst into flame and Magda recoiled from the heat, from the sudden terrible screaming; she felt her fingers go limp and her matrix drop from her hand. Fire and a smell of burning . . . *feathers?* . . . flamed in the room; then her matrix was in her hand . . . had she ever loosed it at all, or was that an illusion?

The fire in the grate had burned to an even bed of coals. The room was silent and peaceful, void of magic, just a quiet room where five weary women could sleep. A few dishes from their supper were still on the table at the center; Jaelle went to the table, brought back a slice of bread, speared it on the end of her knife and held it companionably over the blazing fire. While it toasted, Camilla fetched the last bottle of wine and they shared it, passing it from mouth to mouth.

All Jaelle said was, "Did you see the old woman?"

"I was afraid of her the first time. Now I know she

will not harm us," Magda said, swallowing her share of the wine. For the first time she had no hesitation. Now they were safe. Jaelle split the toasted bread into halves, passed the second to Magda, and they munched in silence. At Camilla's questioning look, Jaelle said, "Food closes down the psychic centers. Are you hungry?"

"For some reason, yes, though I thought I had eaten so much at that fine supper that I would not be hungry for days," Camilla said. She bit into a piece of fruit then flung the core into the fire. For an instant Magda smelled a whisper of burning feathers; then only the fruity smell of the burning apple core.

They slept without dreams.

Magda was wakened by the sound of coughing; deep, heavy, racking coughs, that shook Cholayna's slender body as if by some external force. Vanessa was already at her side with the medikit, checking her, but Cholayna broke away and hurried into the latrine next door, where they could hear her vomiting.

"Bad," Vanessa said briefly. "What's the altitude of this city?"

"Jaelle has the maps. She can tell you; I don't know offhand." Magda understood without being told. Maybe one in forty or fifty people suffered severely at high altitudes. About half of these, given rest and time to acclimate slowly to the new altitudes, got better. Some few developed pulmonary edema, pneumonia, or even cerebral hemorrhaging if they went higher. There was no way to tell how Cholayna would react, except to wait.

Camilla, waking, heard and said, "She has the mountain sickness. I will go and see if in Arlinda's kitchen they have blackthorn tea. If not, almost any tea or fluid will do, but she must drink as much as she can."

"Stop worrying," said Cholayna, appearing in the door. "That dinner last night was too rich for me after days and days of travel rations, that is all."

"Nevertheless," said Vanessa, "you have shown all the symptoms, coughing, queasiness and vomiting. Unless there has been a miracle and you are pregnant at your age, you have a well-developed case of altitude sickness; believe me, Cholayna, that is nothing to take lightly."

Cholayna's eyes were sunk deep in her head. She tried to smile and couldn't manage it.

"I've done it again, haven't I? Delayed you, been the weakest link in the chain—"

"We took all this into account when we agreed to let you come," said Camilla brusquely. "But you must rest today, and your body may adapt itself to the thin air here. I will go and fetch tea, and not forget to tip the kitchen women, which may serve more than one purpose."

Magda had not thought about that. Perhaps Rafaella had spoken with one of the kitchen workers; if Lexie had been suffering from frostbite they would have needed medicines and special hot drinks for her.

Raising her eyes, she crossed glances with Jaelle, who said, "I am going out to the stable. Now that I think of it, one of the ponies looks a bit lame on one side. I will find the woman who helped Rafaella and give her the tip I am sure my partner would have wanted her to have, if she had not been in so great a hurry when she left."

That was an errand only Jaelle could do, and it was best left to her. Camilla went off to the kitchen, and when Jaelle had dressed and gone, Magda persuaded Cholayna to get back into her sleeping bag and rest.

Camilla came back with a steaming kettle and half a dozen little packets of herbs stowed about her person.

"They told us that breakfast would be coming along in a few minutes," she said, "and I smelled a nutcake baking. One of them told me that they had baked one for our Guild-sisters when they lodged here." She poured boiling water over the herbs.

"This is blackroot; it is a stimulant to the heart and will also make red blood; it will help you acclimate to the mountains," she said, kneeling beside Cholayna. "Drink it now and rest. Perhaps by tomorrow your body will be accustomed to the heights here and you can go on with us."

Cholayna drank the bitter tea without protest, only wrinkling up her nose a little at the taste. She asked weakly, "And if I do not?"

"Then we will wait until you are able to travel," Magda said promptly. The excuse that one of their companions was too ill to travel would at least ward off any insistence by Aquilara or any of her cohorts that they should immediately follow the sorceress.

Any further discussion was cut short by the arrival of their breakfast, on several trays which took two girls to carry. Magda tipped the women generously, and sat down to the array of hot fresh bread, scones and nutcakes, plenty of butter, honey and apple nut conserves, boiled eggs and fragrant mushroom sausages. Vanessa and Camilla ate heartily; but Cholayna was too queasy to eat anything. Magda persuaded her to swallow a little bread and honey with her tea, but it was no use coaxing Cholayna to eat the unfamiliar food; she probably could not keep it down anyhow.

Jaelle did not return. No doubt she had decided to breakfast with the apprentices in the stable, to try to find out what they knew. The women who cleared away the breakfast trays were soon succeeded by women bringing back their clean laundry. Camilla went away with them, invited to visit the glove-maker's shops. Magda settled down to mend socks; she liked sewing no better than ever, but she liked wearing socks with holes in them, especially in this climate, even less. Vanessa followed suit, and the women sat quietly mending their clothes.

Cholayna, propped up on her pillows, was writing in her little book. The fire crackled cheerfully on the hearth; the women had brought what looked like an endless supply of firewood. It was peaceful in the room; Magda felt that her nightmares had been no more than that.

But Cholayna's heavy coughing broke the peace of the room. What would Jaelle find out? What would happen if Aquilara summoned them before Cholayna was able to travel? She made some more of the special tea for Cholayna and urged her to drink as much as she could.

"Cholayna, if you are not better in a day or two, it may mean that you are one of the people who simply cannot acclimate properly to the mountains. Now that we know where Lexie and Rafaella are, would you trust me to go on in your place, and let Vanessa take you back to Thendara? You would not have to cross the passes, except Scaravel; you could go by the Great North Road, which is well-marked and well-traveled all the way. I do not want your illness on my conscience—"

"There is no question of that, Magda. I chose to come, no one compelled me, and you are in no way responsible."

"All the same," Vanessa chimed in, "altitude sickness is serious. Tell me, have you any blurring of vision?"

"No, no, nothing of the sort," Cholayna said impatiently. "I am tired and the food is not agreeing with me very well. A day's rest will put me right."

"I certainly hope so," Magda said, "but if not, your only recourse is to go down to a lower level; you will not recover while you stay in Nevarsin. And beyond Nevarsin it is worse, much worse. Couldn't you trust me to do what I can for Lexie?"

Cholayna reached out her hand and touched Magda's. It was a gesture of real affection. "It is not a question of trust, Magda. How long have we known each other? But I trained Alexis, too. I cannot—no, I *will* not abandon her now. You of all people should understand that." She smiled at Magda's look of frustration.

"Let's wait and see. Tomorrow I may be able to travel. I know that some people acclimate more slowly than others. I'm not as fast as Vanessa, that's all."

"But if you don't? At least promise me that you'll agree to go back then," Vanessa said.

"If I do not, then we will decide that then. I make no promises, Vanessa. You are not yet my superior—"

"If I certify you unfit for duty—"

"Leave it, Vanessa," Cholayna said gently. "None of us are here on the same terms as we were in the HQ. I take your advice as mountain expert and I will do whatever you say to try and make up for my slowness in acclimation. Even to drinking that nauseating old-wives remedy Camilla brought me."

"It contains something analogous to—" Vanessa mentioned a Terran drug with which Magda was not familiar—"and they have been using it in these mountains for centuries for just such cases of altitude sickness. Don't be narrow-minded."

"It's not narrow-minded to say I would prefer a couple of capsules of something familiar, rather than this horrid brew." Nevertheless Cholayna swallowed the tea Vanessa handed her, grimacing. "I am doing my best. You were born in these mountains, Magda; and you, Vanessa, have been climbing since you were in your teens. Give me time."

"You're a stubborn old bitch," Vanessa grumbled, and Cholayna smiled at her. She said, with equal affection, "And you are a disrespectful brat."

The bells in the city rang in the distance. Cholayna had fallen into a light doze. Vanessa was restless.

"If only there were something I could *do*!"

"Camilla and Jaelle can do anything that can be done, better than we can, Vanessa. All we can do is wait, and take care of Cholayna." This too was not easy for Magda. In her years as a field agent, she had grown accustomed to handling everything herself so that it would be done her way. The very act of submission, of sitting back and letting someone else do what needed to be done, was foreign to her nature.

It was high noon; Cholayna had wakened, and they had persuaded her to drink more of the blackthorn tea, when Jaelle came back, coming into the room and tossing her old jacket on the chair.

"I talked to the woman who mended Lexie's saddle, and it seems that they left very suddenly—as she put it, at weird-o'-the-clock in the morning, when everyone was sleeping. She happened to be sitting up in the stables to doctor a sick pony. She said the monastery bells had just rung for the Night Office, which is just a few hours after midnight—my brother was educated in Nevarsin and he told me."

"Was Aquilara with them?" Magda demanded.

"No one was with them, at least no one that Varvari saw," Jaelle said, "they saddled and loaded their horses themselves. And she knew which route they were taking because she heard Rafi talking about the dangers from banshees in the pass.''

"Two possibilities, then," said Vanessa. "One, Aquilara scared them away. Two, they arranged to meet her somewhere else. I'm sorry, Jaelle, I don't see that this gets us much further on.''

"At least we know they left the city," Jaelle pointed out. "We could hardly search Nevarsin from house to house. It may not be easy to look for them in the wilderness, but at least there are not so many people to get in the way of the search. And we know that they went northward over Nevarsin Pass, rather than turning southward again, or taking the road to the west, across the plateau of Leng. I have always heard that road was impassable and haunted by monsters next to whom banshees are household pets.''

"That sounds like the Darkovan equivalent of 'here there be dragons,' " murmured Cholayna.

"Nevarsin Pass, and banshees, are dragon enough for me," said Jaelle, the pragmatic. "Sixteen thousand feet; higher than Ravensmark. The road's probably somewhat better, but the question is, is this a bad year for banshees? It depends on a fairly complicated ecological study, or so Kindra used to tell me; if there are enough ice-rabbits, the banshees are well fed above the timberline, and stay up there. If some lichen or other is in the wrong part of its life cycle, there is some kind of population crash among ice-rabbits, the she-rabbits are barren, and the banshees starve, so that they come down below the treeline and look for larger prey. And what I know about the life-cycle of the ice-rabbit could be painlessly carved on my thumbnail. So we'll just have to take our chances.''

"We're going to follow them over the Pass, then?" Cholayna asked.

"I am. I'm not so sure about *we*," Jaelle said. "It's a commitment for me. *You* don't look fit enough to go to the monastery for Evening Prayer, let alone to sixteen thousand feet to fight off the banshee."

"We had this all out while you were away," Cholayna said. "It's a commitment for me too, Jaelle. Rafaella was only following the lead Alexis gave her. Where you go, I go. That's settled."

Jaelle opened her mouth to protest, but something in the tone of Cholayna's voice stopped her.

"All right. Get what rest you can, and try to eat a good dinner. We'll be leaving early."

CHAPTER TWENTY

The afternoon dragged slowly. Jaelle went off again to settle their account with Arlinda, and (she told Magda privately) to make the tips and way gifts Rafaella had not made.

"I suspect she avoided the usual gifting because she felt that might tip off some spy here that she was leaving," Jaelle said. "It's fairly obvious, first, that Arlinda is petrified with fear of Acquilara, and second, that there must be spies, or members of Acquilara's Lodge, or whatever they are, among the women who live here."

"Then don't you run the risk, when you're making these gifts, that you'll warn the very people Rafi was trying to avoid?"

"Can't be helped," Jaelle said. "Rafaella might need to come back here some day; or I might. I'll tell them I'm making the gifts Rafaella would have made if she had had time and ready money. Maybe they'll believe it; maybe they won't. Have you a better idea?"

Magda didn't. She repacked her personal pack with clean and mended clothing; Camilla went to the market, taking Vanessa with her, to purchase extra grain-porridge and dried fruit for Cholayna, since it seemed unlikely she would be able to eat much of the dried-meat bars which were the regular trail ration. She also bought a supply of the blackthorn tea which had done Cholayna so much good.

Jaelle also presented Arlinda with a full packload of the trade goods she had brought for Rafaella. "Rafi won't need them past here; there's nothing to trade and almost nobody to trade with," she said, "though I kept a load of things we might use for gifts or bribes if there are any villages up here; sweets and candies, small tools, mirrors and the like. And the Guild-house needs to be on good terms with Arlinda's establishment; it's the only decent place for Renunciates to stay in Nevarsin."

"I'm not so sure of that, if Arlinda's being watched or dominated by Aquilara's people," said Camilla, packing the fresh supplies into a saddlebag. "We ought to trade off the horses here, and take only chervines into the high country. Horses don't have the stamina."

"Cholayna and Vanessa can't ride chervines," said Magda, "and I'm not sure I could. The mountain horses can go almost anywhere a chervine can go. I suspect if we reach any country too rough for a horse, it will be too rough for us."

While they were loading the saddlebags, Camilla drew Magda aside for a moment and gave her a pair of embroidered gloves, made of the fine leather from the shops covered by Arlinda's establishment. Ever since they had been lovers, Camilla had enjoyed surprising her with little gifts like this, and Magda's eyes filled with tears.

"But these are expensive, Camilla, you shouldn't—"

"I found a few mountain men in the taverns who liked to play at darts and would not believe any woman, even an *emmasca* who had been a mercenary soldier, could throw a knife as well as they could. And when their pride, and their love of gambling, had prompted one man to wager more than he could pay, I generously accepted these in settlement of the debt. I suppose he had bought them for his wife or his lady friend, but she will have to teach her man not to gamble on his masculine pride!'' She chuckled, low in her throat. "They are foolish and frivolous for this mountain city—your hands would freeze in them—but you can wear them when we return to a gentler climate!''

And for a moment Magda felt cheered, aware of optimism again; they *would* return to the comparatively benign climate of Thendara. She had hardly realized till this moment how much her world had narrowed to ice, cold, frostbitten fingers, frozen boots. The thin, frivolous little beaded gloves reminded her of flowers, sunshine, a world where it was possible to dance in the streets till dawn in midsummer; not this austere monastic city where snow lay in the streets all year round.

She pressed Camilla's hand, and Camilla put an arm around her waist. Jaelle looked up and saw them, and as the kitchen-women entered with the dinner they had ordered, Magda saw her frown slightly, as when she was planning some bit of mischief. Then she embraced Vanessa deliberately and leaned over to kiss her on the mouth. Vanessa looked startled, but Magda heard—though she was too far away to hear and knew she was reading the thought behind the whisper, "Play along, silly! Or do you think I am seriously trying to seduce you?''

Vanessa blinked in surprise, but did not protest; she put up her arms around Jaelle, who kissed her long and hard, then turned languidly to the women unloading trays and dishes.

"Don't disturb us till the fifth hour after the monastery bells ring for Morning Prayer,'' she said, and went on to describe an elaborate breakfast, and pay for it, adding a generous tip. When the women went away, full of promises about the expensive delicacies Jaelle had ordered, Vanessa pulled herself free of Jaelle, her face crimson.

"Have you gone mad? What *will* they be thinking?"

"Exactly what I want them to think," Jaelle said, "that we will be long lying abed tomorrow, in various combinations. It will never occur to them to suspect that we are intending to leave the city before the bells ring for Night Office; they won't know we are gone until they bring that fancy breakfast when the sun is high."

"And if Aquilara's spy is not among the kitchen workers but among the girls in the stable?" Vanessa asked.

"Then I will have embarrassed you for nothing," Jaelle said. With a mischievous shrug, she pulled her close and kissed her again. "Did you really object as much as all *that*? I saw no sign of it."

Vanessa only giggled. A few days ago, Magda thought, she would have been angry.

At least she no longer feels that we are a threat to her.

Another leisurely bath; then a plentiful dinner, served in their rooms, and they settled down to sleep as long as they could. But for Magda sleep was slow in coming, even though, with the room sealed against intrusion, she had no fear of nightmares. She was lying between Jaelle and Camilla; after the older woman slept, she tossed and turned and finally Jaelle whispered, "Can't you sleep either? What's the matter? It's going to be a rough trip, but even Cholayna seems better; I think she can make it. You're not still worrying about that old witch Aquilara, are you? I think we've shaken her off. I think Lexie and Rafaella managed to get free of her too.''

"I'm not so sure, Shaya. What bothers me is—who *are* they? What would they want with us, and why?''

"I thought you had a theory about that. That they probably wanted to keep us away from the *real* Sisterhood.''

"But again, why? What would they get out of it? Just for sheer love of mischief-making? I cannot believe that. It must take as much talent and energy to run whatever it is this Aquilara is doing as it takes us to gather and work with the Forbidden Tower.''

"So?'' Jaelle asked. "Perhaps it is simply hatred and jealousy of the powers of the Sisterhood; she does not seem to have very many powers herself, in spite of what she managed to do to Camilla.''

"But even if she hated the Sisterhood . . . no, Jaelle. *We* have a reason to exist, Jaelle. Damon, Callista, Andrew, Hilary, all of us—we're working to bring the good of *laran* to people born outside the Towers, people who don't wish to deny their gifts, but will not live in the Towers, cut off from the real world. We're trying to bring *laran* into the world, prove that it's not necessary to be born Comyn, or aristocrat, or even Darkovan, to have and to use these gifts. We have purpose in what we're doing, but it's hard work, sometimes even painful work, I can't believe she'd go to that much trouble, just to impress us.''

"I don't know what her motive could be, Magda. Does it matter? I want nothing to do with her, *or* with her powers, and I do know this much, that if you go on thinking of her you will pick her up telepathically, and all our precautions will be useless.''

Magda knew Jaelle was right, and she tried to compose herself to sleep as best she could. She thought of her faraway home, of putting her little girl to bed at Armida; Shaya in her nightgown, her soft dark curls tousled. She had not known she remembered so many of the Darkovan folk songs and hill ballads that it had been her mother's lifework to collect, until she began singing them to Shaya as lullabies. Elizabeth Lorne, she knew, had loved her work, and had died thinking that her daughter Magdalen cared nothing for it, knew nothing of it. *How pleased she would have been to hear me singing to Shaya those old ballads from the Hellers and the Kilghard Hills which she so loved. Some day when Shaya is grown, she shall see her grandmother's collected songs and ballads—eight volumes of them, or something like that—in Records, and know a little about her work.*

Perhaps Shaya would be a musician; she remembered that her dark-haired daughter could carry a tune, clearly and sweetly, even before she could talk plain.

Cleindori in the Overworld; *I was surprised when Aunty Ellemir told me where babies come from. I thought they came from the gray world.* What a fascinating light on the relationship of sex education to metaphysics. *She was all grown up, and then she was a baby and I couldn't talk to her, except here in the Overworld.* The Overworld was barred to Magda now, because of the sorcery of Aquilara; or she could reach her child, hold her once more. *If I should die on this trip,* she thought, *if I should never see Shaya again.*

But if what Cleindori said is true, and I have no reason not to believe it, then death might not make any difference either. Curious, that I should learn faith from a child five years old.

She was sliding off to sleep, hearing in the distance the reassuring sound of the calling of crows.

*   *   *

It seemed only moments later that Jaelle woke her.

"The monastery bells have just rung the Night Office. Wake Cholayna; there is bread and dried fruit from supper, which we will eat on the trail." Jaelle was pulling on long wool leggings under her breeches. Magda got into her clothes swiftly, bending to whisper to Cholayna. The Terran woman was sleeping heavily, and it occurred to Magda that if they had wanted to leave her behind, they could have stolen away and left her here sleeping, to be wakened only when the kitchen women came in with the unnecessary breakfast.

No. She is our sister, too. We have to be honest with her, Magda thought, but sighed, wishing Cholayna had agreed to remain here in comparative safety or return to Thendara with Vanessa. She almost wished she were heading south herself, to Armida and family of the Tower and to her child, even to Thendara and her sisters of the Guild-house. She pulled on an extra layer of warm sweater, wordlessly handed Camilla another.

"I'm all right, Margali, don't fuss so!"

She stared Camilla down, and the older woman, grumbling, pulled it over her head. Camilla was so thin, she would be glad of the warmth when they got into the pass.

Cholayna was shivering in the chill of the big room; they had allowed the fire to burn down. Wasting fuel and warmth were a major crime in the Hellers. The breakfast they had ordered would be eaten by somebody, and would be none the worse for being consumed by someone other than the travelers who had paid for it, but keeping a blazing fire all night was a waste the mountain-bred Magda and Camilla could not condone, even though it meant they must sleep under all their blankets. A thin skin of ice had formed over the pitcher of water at the table where they had eaten their supper, and frost rimed the single high, narrow window of the room.

Jaelle muttered in an undertone, "My brother told me once that the novices in the monastery sleep naked in the snow, wearing only their cowls, and run barefoot. I wish I had their training."

"I suppose it is one of your psychic powers," Vanessa said.

"Valentine says not; only use and habit, and convincing the mind to do its task of warming the body."

Cholayna raised a skeptical eyebrow. "I am not convinced. Hypothermia has killed and continues to kill many people. How can they overcome that?"

"Val would have no reason to lie to me; he says that one of the tests for the higher degrees among the monks is to bathe in a mountain stream from the glacier on Nevarsin Summit, and then to dry, with his body heat, the cowl he wears. He has seen it done."

"A conjuring trick to impress the novices with their power?"

"What reason would they have for that?"

"Nevertheless," Vanessa said, "I heard it too when I went into Mapping and Exploring. It has been told before this, in the old days on Terra; before the Empire. Some of the men who lived on the high plateaus, at four thousand meters or more, had lung capacity greater than those who lived at sea level, and their bodies were so adapted that they became ill in the lowlands. I do not doubt that the Nevarsin brethren can learn to do these things. The human animal is amazingly adaptable. Many people would consider your native planet, Cholayna, too hot for human habitation. I visited there once and thought I would die with the heat. Man is not intended to live where the ambient temperature of the air is normally higher than blood heat."

"Maybe not," said Cholayna, forcing on her narrow boot over three layers of thick socks, "but I would rather be there than here." She pulled her heavy windbreaker over her jacket. "Ready?"

Carrying their personal packs over their shoulders, they stole through the quiet halls, and down a long corridor, away from the living quarters, into the stables. The heavy doors creaked, but there was no other sound, except for Cholayna, who went into a sudden spasm of coughing.

"Quiet," Jaelle snarled, half-aloud, and Cholayna tried to muffle the sound in her sleeve, without much success, her whole body shaking with effort.

Their horses and chervines, and their loads, reduced considerably from what they had been when they left Thendara, were stacked in a corner of the same stable.

Jaelle whistled softly with relief. "I suspect Arlinda understood what I meant when I talked with her. Last night, these were stowed away in another set of cupboards in a different stable."

Saddling up her horse, Magda found herself next to Vanessa. She asked in an undertone, "What do you think? Is Cholayna fit for travel?"

"Who can tell? But I checked her as best I could; her lips are a healthy color and her lungs seem to be clear; that ghastly cough is just throat irritation from the dry air and wind at these heights. All we can do is to hope for the best."

They hoisted loads on to the backs of chervines, and in whispers settled their order of march. Jaelle, who knew the city well, was leading; Camilla, who knew it almost as well, bringing up the rear. Magda delayed at the end to help Camilla shove the heavy stable door together and brace it; but they could not bolt it from the inside, and finally Camilla whispered, "Wait, Margali,

I will be with you in a moment." She slipped back inside; Magda heard the heavy bolt slide. She waited in the street so long that she had begun to wonder if Camilla had been captured by one of Acquilara's spies in the house. *We should have left the door alone*, she thought, but just as she was about to try and follow Camilla inside, the tall *emmasca* reappeared from a window. She slid down, turned briefly to blow a kiss, then hurried down the street after Jaelle.

Magda ran after her. "Camilla, what—"

"My gambling friend. Let's not waste any more time; I heard the monastery bell. Let's go." But she snickered as she hurried after Jaelle.

"I wonder what they'll think when they find us gone and the stable still locked from the inside?"

There was no way to silence the hooves of the horses and chervines on the cobbled streets, but leading them was quieter than riding. Still they struck hard, the metal shoes of the horses drawing flinty sparks in the cold. It was icy and clear; stars blinked above the darkened city, and high above, the only faint lights were from the dimmed windows of Saint Valentine's monastery. Bells rang loud in the predawn stillness.

As they climbed the rocky streets, the stars paled above them, and the sky began to flush with the dawn. Magda could see her own breath, the breath of her companions and of the animals, as little white clouds before her. Her hands were already cold inside her warm gloves, and her feet chilly in her boots, and she thought, regretfully, of that breakfast Jaelle had ordered and never intended them to eat.

Upward and upward, the streets growing steeper and steeper; but Magda had been on the road so long now that she was hardly short of breath at the top of the steepest hills, and even Cholayna was striding along at the quick pace Jaelle set.

The northern gate was at the very top of the city, and the road beyond led over the very summit of Nevarsin Pass. At the gates were two men, *cristoforos* by their somber clothing, though not monks, who opened the wide gates to let them through.

"You are abroad early, my sisters," one of them said as he stepped back to let their animals pass through.

"We follow two of our sisters who came this way the morning before last," said Camilla in the exceptionally pure *casta* of a mountain-bred woman. "Did you perhaps let them out this very gate two mornings ago, as early as this, my brother?"

The *cristoforo* guard blew on his bare knuckles to warm them. His breath too was a cloud and he spoke through it, scowling disapprovingly at the *emmasca*.

"Aye, it was I. One of them—a tall woman, dark-haired, a soldier like you, *mestra*, with a *rryl* slung over her shoulder—was she your sister?"

"My Guild-sister; have you news of her, brother, in the name of him who bears the burdens of the world?"

He scowled again, his disapproval of *emmasca* and Renunciate contradicting the inborn freemasonry among soldiers, *cristoforo* or no. And there was no halfway polite way to refuse a request in the very name of the *cristoforo* saint.

"Aye. She had another woman with her, so small I thought for a moment she was travelin' with her daughter like a proper woman. A little thing, wrapped up so I couldn't see much of her but the big blue eyes."

Lexie. So they were still together and Lexie safe and well as recently as two days ago. Magda heard Cholayna's soft sigh of relief. They might even overtake them somewhere in the pass.

"She asked me—the tall one, your sister—if it was a bad year for banshees. I had to tell her, yes, a terrible one; we heard one howling right outside this gate a tenday ago in the last storm. Go carefully, sisters, try to get over the high part before the sun's down again," he warned them. "And saints ride with you. Aye, you'll need them if you take this road by night." He stepped back to let them through, closed the heavy city gate behind them.

Ahead the road led upward, stony and steep, ankle-deep in snow, with heavy drifts to right and to left. Jaelle mounted and signaled to the others to do likewise, and they climbed into their saddles. From the heights far above, like a warning, they heard the shrill distant cry of a banshee.

"Never mind," said Jaelle, "the sun will be up long before we reach the pass, and they're nocturnal. Let's go."

CHAPTER TWENTY-ONE

Three days later, Magda sat on a packsaddle looking at a dried-meat bar in her hand. She was almost too weary to think about eating it; the effort necessary to chew and swallow seemed more than she could imagine.

The harsh winds of Nevarsin summit had blown away such extraneous fears as the thought of sorceresses or psychic attack; none of them had had a moment to think about anything but the raw mechanics of survival. Narrow ledges, a snowstorm which blew away their last remaining tent and left them to huddle in a hastily scooped hole in the snow, fierce winds which stripped away the last pretense of courage or fortitude, and always in the night the terrible paralyzing cries of the lurking banshee.

Camilla put a cup of tea into her hand. How could Camilla, at her age, remain so strong and undamaged? Her eyes looked red and wind-burned, and the tip of her nose had a raw patch of frostbite, but the few hours of sleep they had managed in the snow had revived her. She sat down on another packload, and slurped her own tea, into which she had crumbled the dried meat and bread, but she didn't say anything. At this altitude there was no breath for extraneous words.

"Is Cholayna all right this morning?"

"Seems to be. But if we don't get down to a lower

height, I wouldn't like to guess what might happen. She was coughing all night long.'' But not even Cholayna's coughing could have kept Magda awake last night, after the nightmare of the descent from the pass after dark, by moonlight on the surface of the snow: *kyorebni* looming suddenly from the dizzy gaps of space almost at their feet, wheeling and screaming and then disappearing again: washed-out patches of trail where even the chervines balked and had to be coaxed to step across, and the horses had to be dragged or manhandled, fighting backward, their eyes rolling with terror at the smell of banshee in the crags.

Jaelle had brought them all across, undamaged, without losing a horse or a pack animal or even a load; unhurt. Magda looked at the familiar slight form of her freemate, slumped across a packload, a handful of raisins halfway to her mouth. Her red curls were uncombed and matted under her fur-trimmed hood, her gray eyes sore and wind-burned like Camilla's and her own. Magda wondered at the strength of will and courage in that small body. There had been moments in the pass when Magda herself, a strong young woman in superb physical condition, had wanted to lie down like one of the ponies, without breath or courage for another step; heart pounding, head splitting, face and body numbed with frost. She could only imagine what it had been like for Cholayna, but the older woman had struggled along bravely beside her, uttering not a single word of complaint. It was Jaelle, Magda realized, who had kept them all going.

Magda followed Camilla's example and crumbled the meat bar into her boiling tea. The taste was very peculiar, but that didn't seem to matter. It was astonishing how, at this altitude, she could actually feel the hot food and fluid heating her all the way down, restoring a feeling of warmth to her exhausted and chilled limbs. When she finished the mess she dug into the ration sacks and got out another bar, this one of ground-up nuts and fruits stuck together with honey, and gnawed at it. Cholayna was resolutely spooning up a similar mixture dissolved in her tea.

Vanessa said, "I ought to take my boots off and look at that wretched ankle. But it's too damned cold. Where are we going now, Jaelle?"

Jaelle glanced back at Nevarsin Peak, rising behind them. "The main road branches off toward Caer Donn. If there were any mysterious and unknown cities in that area, one of us would have run across it before this." She fumbled with gloved fingers for the map, and pointed; removing gloves unnecessarily at this altitude was to court freezing. "This little settlement isn't marked on any of the Darkovan maps. It showed up from the satellite picture, and this—" she traced with her outstretched finger—"looks something like a road."

"Something *like* a road," Cholayna groaned. By now they all knew what unmarked roads in this area were like.

"I know, but I can't imagine any other road Rafaella could have taken," Jaelle said. High in the pass, they had come across an abandoned packload, all but empty, with Rafaella's mark on it. "They must be running low on food and grain for the ponies . . . they know we are following them. Why don't they wait for us?"

Magda couldn't imagine, unless Lexie and Rafaella had been given some special guidance to that unknown city of the legend. From the summit of Nevarsin, in a brief moment of blazing sun between storms, she had looked across an endless view of mountain ranges, trackless peaks, toward the remote and inaccessible icewall known as the Wall Around the World. She had glimpsed it only once before and then from a Mapping plane, and never in her remotest dreams had it occurred to her that she would ever travel toward it on foot.

"More tea, anyone?" Camilla asked, and divided the remaining brew into the four mugs held out to her before stowing the kettle and scattering snow over the remaining fire; sheer habit of years on the trail, for there was certainly nothing here to burn.

Vanessa slung packloads on chervines, pulling the straps tight and double-checking them, and Cholayna began helping Jaelle with the saddles. Abruptly she bent over in a renewed fit of coughing, clinging to the saddle-straps and bracing herself against the horse's side. Vanessa's eyes on her were calculating; Magda knew she was wondering if the older woman could make it. But there was nothing to be done. After a moment Cholayna, eyes streaming and the tears already freezing on her cheeks, straightened up and rummaged in her pack for the compass with which she checked the map and the road.

"This way," Jaelle decided. "Let's go."

For a time, then, the road led downhill, then swerved away into an ill-marked trail leading upward between two long slopes. The sun rose higher and higher, and Magda felt sweat streaming down her body under her jacket, and freezing there.

They had ridden about three hours, and Jaelle passed the word back to look for a good place for a rest. The road was steep and narrow; the horses were struggling upward alongside an old glacier, pale with rotten ice. The trail curved, and led across a long snow-laden slope. As they set foot on it, there was a scream as a dozen birds flapped and flew upward in a streaming flight; then a roar like sudden thunder. Jaelle, in the lead, pulled her horse up sharp.

Then, from somewhere above them, tons of rock and ice cascaded down a deep-carved gully in the mountainside. The horses reared upward, neighing. The very mountain seemed to shake beneath them. The pack animals jostled together and their horses crowded close; Camilla leaned over and clutched at Magda, and they clung together as the avalanche roared down and down and down and went on forever.

At last it was silent, though the air was full of crushed ice and dust, and the sound of screaming went on and on. Jaelle's pony had collapsed, struck by a falling boulder. Camilla slid from her horse and hurried, picking her way across the rock-strewn trail. Jaelle, shakily upright, was kneeling beside the stricken pony. Magda looked swiftly around to her companions. Vanessa was hugging herself, arms tight wrapped to her chest, her face very white. Magda could hear Cholayna's breath wheeze in and out as she hung over her pony without even the strength to cough. Silence, except for the screaming of the hurt animal and the shrill cries of the disturbed birds still wheeling in the air.

At last Vanessa said shakily, "They say you can never hear the one that has your name on it. If you can hear it, you're still alive." She picked her way fastidiously over the debris of rock and ice which was all that was left of the trail, to kneel at Camilla's side by the pitiably screaming pony.

"Leg crushed," she said, "nothing to be done."

Jaelle's eyes were streaming tears, which froze on her cheeks, as she struggled to get out her knife. Camilla said, "Let me," and for an instant laid her free hand over Jaelle's. It was almost a caress. "Hold her head, Shaya."

Jaelle held the pony's head in her lap; the struggling animal quieted for an instant, and Camilla's dagger swept down and swiftly severed the great artery in the neck. A few spurts of blood, a final struggle, and quiet. Camilla's lips were set as she tried to brush away the blood from her riding-cape.

"Get the saddle off her. You have ridden stag-ponies before this. Put it on the chervine with the white face; he's the gentlest and most trustworthy," she said briskly, but Magda knew her sharpness concealed real concern. As Vanessa got the saddle off the swiftly freezing corpse (the pony's leg had been crushed under a great rock, it was a miracle Jaelle had not been thrown and killed) Magda went to Jaelle, who looked almost stunned. She took a tube of cream and smeared it over the frozen tears on her freemate's face. Mingled with the splashed blood of the pony, it looked grotesque, but it would keep her cheeks from frostbite.

"Are you hurt, *breda*?"

"No." But Jaelle was limping, and leaned heavily on Magda. "Something hit me in the shins when the pony fell. I don't think the skin's broken, just a bruise." But she threatened to cry again. "Oh, Dancer!" That was the horse's name. "Damon gave her to me, the year Dori was born. When she was a colt she followed me around like a puppy. I broke her to the saddle myself. Oh, Magda, Damon will be so angry that I didn't take better care of her."

The words were meaningless; she was hysterical and Magda knew it. Jaelle was in shock; they were all in shock.

"Get the other saddles off, Camilla, and we'll brew tea; Jaelle needs it after that. We all need it."

At her urging, they moved upslope from the corpse of the pony, around which the *kyorebni* were already wheeling and fighting. Vanessa began to build a fire. Magda sat Jaelle down on a saddle load and surveyed what had once been a road. It had been all but obliterated above them. Nevertheless they were lucky to be alive, to have lost only one mount.

Magda pushed Jaelle down on a load. With the trail gone, there would have to be reconnaissance ahead. But neither Jaelle nor Cholayna was in much shape to forge on for their route. Tea was brewed and drunk; Camilla got the saddle off the dead horse, and tried to fit it on the smallest and most tractable chervine, but the difference in size and contour, even when the bony back of the chervine was padded with a small blanket, made it an almost impossible proposition.

"I have ridden chervines bareback in my day, but I don't intend to try if there's any alternative; that backbone-ridge always splits me in two," Jaelle complained. With hot tea and some sweets from the packloads, some color had come back into her face, but her shin was skinned raw and bruised bone-deep.

"When we come to another village, we will try to trade for a riding-chervine, or at least a proper saddle for this one," Camilla said. Magda finished her food, and stood up wearily.

"It's up to us, Vanessa, to scout ahead and see whether there is a trail anywhere up there." She scanned the map. It was past noon and the day was still fine, but long, narrow, hook-ended clouds were beginning to blow across the sky from the north, and Magda knew, they all knew, what that presaged: high wind at least, perhaps storm and deep snow.

The map showed something like a settlement or a village. She prayed it would not be a village like the last one they had discovered in emergency.

"Put your leg up and rest it while you can, Jaelle.

Vanessa and I will scout ahead.'' Cholayna, she thought, looked worse than Jaelle, her breath coming in heavy rasping wheezes. Yet there was no way to return, and no shelter near. They must simply go ahead and hope they found shelter. Magda was not superstitious, but it seemed that the pony's death was an ill omen. They had had too much good luck on this long trek, and if that good luck had deserted them, who might be next?

Camilla said, ''Let me go with you—''

''You've got to stay here and look after Cholayna and Jaelle. Vanessa is mountain-wise and I'm the most able-bodied one now.'' Magda smiled faintly. She said, ''You have the hard part; it's going to be cold here, not moving. Get out sleeping bags and wrap up in them. At least Vanessa and I will keep warm moving.''

Jaelle said, ''In all of Kindra's old stories, it was made clear that the way to the secret city of the Sisterhood was guarded. I wonder if we are being tested.''

Cholayna said, wrapping a sleeping bag around herself and Jaelle, ''I find it hard to believe that they have that much power. Weather, perhaps—I can just manage to believe that. Avalanche? No, I think perhaps that must be marked up to—'' she interrupted herself with a prolonged paroxysm of coughing, finishing, half strangled, ''to the general cussedness of things. Camilla, is there any more of your witches' brew?''

Magda was oddly reluctant to turn her back even on the makeshift camp. It was her first experience with being roped up, but one look at the debris-strewn, rocky, icy surface above and below them convinced her to let Vanessa make her fast to the rope. They hugged the glacier, picking their way carefully along the heaps of loose rocks, at the imminent risk of breaking an ankle or worse. From the glacier above, walls of ice seemed to tilt forward and hang over them.

Magda was breathless with the altitude—they must, she thought, be somewhere above five thousand meters. The whole of the slope seemed to be strewn with newly fallen snow and old ice. There were several buttresses of rock widely separated by gullies filled to the brim with loose stone and unstable boulders. There seemed no hint of a trail, no suggestion that anyone had ever traveled this way before.

As they climbed, the whole of the great plateau was revealing itself. They were nearing the vast wall of ice which guarded the summit marked on the map; they crossed the gullies in rushes, wary of fresh rockfalls from above, seeking the safety of the natural stone buttresses which stood out from the slopes, clear of the danger.

"Too damned much loose rock and ice this way," said Vanessa, pausing to wipe her face in the shelter of one of the huge boulders. "If we bring everybody up this way, we're going to have to stay awfully close together, which probably means roping the horses and chervines and bringing them up in clusters. Not good. And I don't like the look of that."

She pointed, and Magda, already breathless, felt her heart stop in her throat. They were far to one side, and safe, but the great glacier, an overwhelming mass of tortured formations of ice frozen in the very act of toppling over, loomed high above the other slope, the very end of a great bed of ice sitting almost atop the summit they must cross.

Magda knew little of glaciers; the rock slope was a gentle gradient, but she knew that the ice was in slow, inexorable motion, moving, though imperceptibly, down the slopes they must somehow cross or climb. As the great masses of ice, under immeasurable pressure, reached the edge of the summit, they must break asunder and

roar their way down into the valley. Such was the
avalanche which had killed Jaelle's pony and nearly
taken Jaelle with it. How could they know how soon the
next point of inequilibrium would be reached? Were
their comrades even safe where they were now?

They hurried across another gully of broken stone
and razor-sharp flakes of loose shale which cut at their
boots. The sun had gone behind the thickening layer of
cloud, and Magda, looking down, could only see a
small reddish dot, the sleeping bag Cholayna had wrapped
round herself and Jaelle. Looking upward and across
the valley, they could see, on the next slope, a few
rectangular grayish shapes.

"Now is that the village marked on the map, or is it
just a cluster of stone blocks like these?" Magda wondered aloud.

"God knows; and I'm not in Her confidence," Vanessa
said. "But at the moment I'd take out a nice mortgage
on my soul for a helicopter. I wonder if this might have
been what Lexie saw from the plane?"

"No way of telling. And I don't like the look of the
sky," Magda said. "If it is a village we'll have to make
directly for it. There's nothing else that even looks like
shelter, and I don't like the idea of letting Cholayna
spend another night in the open. Vanessa, I'm worried,
really worried about her."

"You think I'm not? We'd better pray that place *is* a
village or settlement of some sort. I don't think it's
what Lexie saw; it's marked on the maps. But it looks a
little too regular to be a rock formation. Anyway we've
got to try for it. The way that sky looks, we have no
choice. I don't want to bivouac in *that*."

"Who would?" Magda turned to descend the way
they had come, but turned to look at Vanessa, who was
standing at the very edge of the cliff in a way that made

Magda's arms and legs prickle with cramping apprehension.

Vanessa said in an undertone, "God, Lorne, just *look* at it. It makes the mountains of Alpha look like foothills. I was proud of collecting Montenegro Summit. I've never seen anything like this. No matter how this comes out, just the chance to see this—" She broke off, and looked at Magda.

She said softly, "You don't understand at all, do you, Lorne? To you it's just difficulties and dangers and hard travel and rough going, and you can't even see it, can you?"

"Not the way you do, Vanessa," Magda confessed. "I never wanted to climb mountains for their own sake. Not for the love of it."

Unexpectedly, Vanessa reached out and put an awkward arm around her. "That's really something. That you keep going, like this, when it doesn't even mean anything to you. Lorne, I'm—I'm glad we've got to know each other. You're—you're what they always said you were." Her cold lips brushed Magda's cheek in a shy kiss. Abruptly, she turned away.

"We'd better get back down, and tell them what we found. If anything. I'd feel damned funny to climb all the way up to that cluster of gray stuff and find it was just a bunch of rotten old square rocks!"

"Funny isn't exactly the word for what I'd feel," Magda agreed, "but it's the only halfway repeatable word for it."

Going down was easier, though they picked their way carefully to avoid a fall. As it was, Vanessa stumbled and was saved by the rope from a long fall down a debris-strewn slide; putting out her hand to save herself she wrenched her wrist painfully.

The sky was wholly clouded over now, and a cutting wind had begun to blow; Magda was shivering, and halfway down the slope they stopped, sheltering behind one of the rock buttresses to dig out the emergency rations from their pockets and suck on honey-soaked dried fruit. Magda's face felt raw in spite of the cream she had smeared on it. As the sky darkened it was harder to place their feet. How, in heaven's name, were they going to bring horses and chervines, not to mention the ailing Cholayna, up this way? She had no chronometer, but it could not be so late in the day as that sky presaged. Did that mean one of the blizzards, roaring down out of the impassable north?

"How far away would you say that place was?"

"A few kilometers; if we could ride, a couple of hours, no more. Climbing, God only knows," Vanessa said. "Maybe when we get past the bad part, we can put Cholayna on a horse and lead it across, at least." She drew the strings of her hood closer around her face.

It seemed to Magda that the wind was growing fiercer, that it held the very smell of heavy snow. She told herself not to borrow trouble; things were bad enough as they were. As they approached the spot where they had left the others, her mind was tormented with sudden fears; suppose the campsite was deserted, Jaelle and Cholayna and Camilla gone, snatched into oblivion by the hand of the sorceresses who had perhaps led Lexie and Rafaella into some doom in these mountains. . . .

But as they picked their way carefully down the last slope they could see a flash of orange against the rock and snow, Camilla's old riding-cape, and the gleam of a campfire. Then they stumbled into the camp and Camilla thrust mugs of boiling tea into their hands; Magda collapsed on a spread sleeping bag. Nothing, it seemed, had ever tasted so good to her burning throat.

Revived a little by the hot drink, warmed (but not enough), she asked, "How is Cholayna?"

Jaelle tilted her head to where Cholayna was sleeping between piled sleeping bags and blankets. Even from where they sat Magda could hear the rasp of her breathing. Vanessa went and bent her head to listen to the sound at close quarters.

Camilla asked, "Well?"

"Not very well at all," said Vanessa, tight-lipped. "There's fluid in her bronchial passages; I don't know enough to know if it's spread to her lungs. But we've got to find shelter for her before very long. Let's just pray that what we found will *be* shelter."

And I didn't want Vanessa to come. What would we have done without her?

Quickly they told what they had discovered, saddled up ponies and loaded the chervines, roping them together. Cholayna, rousing quickly from her light sleep, protested that she was able to walk with the rest, but they insisted she should ride and set her on her horse Magda took the reins, and they started upward. For the first stretch, at least, they need not be roped up.

But a few hundred feet above the spot where they had camped after the avalanche, the rocks and ice were so loose under foot that Vanessa insisted on getting out the ropes and roping them all together.

"I'm sorry, Cholayna; you'll have to get down. I don't trust any horse's footing here. If you could manage to ride a chervine—"

"No need of that." Nevertheless, Cholayna clung to the chervine's saddle-strap to haul herself along; it was the elderly female, the most tractable of all the animals, and although it whickered uneasily, it did not protest as Cholayna held tight. The other chervines followed their

leader; the horses, too, had to be trusted to pick their
own way over ice and rubble. Magda knew it would be
a miracle if all the animals got across undamaged. Once
Camilla's foot slipped and only the taut-stretched rope
kept her from rolling down the long rocky slope; she
hauled herself to her feet, swearing breathlessly in a
language Magda hardly understood.

"Hurt, Camilla?"

"Only shaken up." She was favoring one foot, but
there was nothing to be done about it here. Slowly, they
forced their way up the long slope, under the lowering
sky, pregnant with undelivered clouds of snow. It was
deliberate, hard going; Magda, who had covered this
upward route already once today, felt her knees would
hardly hold her up; she heard her own breath deepen
and roughen, whistling loudly in and out. Her head
throbbed and her ears ached, but there was no longer
any feeling in her face. She drew up her scarf over her
nose in a rude mask, but the warm breath condensed
and froze so that her face was soon covered in an
ice-mask.

Her world reduced itself to this; one step, then another.
Yet outside the little circle described by the sound of
her own breathing, she was aware somehow of her
companions, could feel the stab of pain in Jaelle's
bruised leg, the knife-edge of pain through Camilla's
foot every time she set it down, knew that the ankle
Vanessa had hurt early in the trip was still paining her
in this cold, felt the dull pain in Cholayna's chest. She
fought to shut it out, knowing that she could do nothing
for the others except to hoard her own strength so that
she needed no help from them. She knew that Vanessa
was crying softly with weariness and pain. She too had
climbed this route once already today.

Just one step and then another. Nothing outside this.

It was a long nightmare. They had been climbing forever and they would go on climbing forever. *I will take ten more steps*, she bargained with herself, *and then I will give up*. And at the end of ten steps; *I will take ten more steps, only ten more, I will not think any farther than that*. She could just manage, breaking it up into these little segments, carefully not thinking farther than this, *seven, eight, nine, ten steps, then I will lie down and never get up again. . . .*

"Magda," it was Vanessa's voice, very soft. "Can you help Cholayna?" Looking up, outside the circle of her own preoccupation, she found that Cholayna had let go the chervine's rein and sunk down in the snow. Vanessa was struggling with one of the horses, fighting to lead it over the rubble, and with one part of her brain Magda wondered why she bothered, while a small detached part of herself knew that if they lost any more horses they would never make it to that village they had seen.

She made her way to Cholayna's side, bent and took the woman by the arm.

"I'll help you. Lean on me."

Cholayna's face was a mottled mess of cream and half-frozen pale patches against her dark skin, her eyes reddened and sunken in her face. Ice clung to loose strands of her hair. Her voice was only a harsh whisper.

"I'm never going to make it. I'm only holding you back. You others go on. Leave me here. No reason the rest of you shouldn't get across. But I'm done, finished."

Magda could *feel*, inside her own mind, the depth of Cholayna's weary despair, and fought against making it part of herself.

"You're only tired. Lean on me." She bent to slip her arm under Cholayna's shoulders. Part of her was angry, she had barely strength enough for herself, but the other part knew that this was a final struggle. "Look, we're only a little way from the summit, you can ride from there."

"Magda, I can't . . . I can't. I think I'm dying . . ."

And for a moment Magda, looking at Cholayna, believed it; she half released Cholayna's hand . . . then something, anger, a final spurt of adrenalin, flooded her with rage.

"Damn it, don't you *dare* pull that on me! You bullied us into letting you come when I *told* you you couldn't make it, I *told* you you couldn't travel past Nevarsin, you wouldn't let us send you back from there! Now you haul your stubborn old rear end up out of that snow, or I'll kick you to the top myself! You've got to do it, I haven't the strength to carry you, and the others are worse off than I am! Get *up*, damn you!" She heard herself, half incredulous. But the anger was flooding her to the point where she actually raised her arm to strike Cholayna.

Cholayna's breathing rasped in and out for a moment, then she stirred, wearily. Magda held out a hand and Cholayna dragged herself upright, clinging to the outstretched arm for a moment. She said between her teeth, "If I had the strength I'd—" but the words evaporated in a spasm of heavy coughing. Magda put an arm round her.

"Here. Lean on me."

"I can manage," said Cholayna, forcing herself to stand without Magda's support, glaring at her with her teeth bared like an animal. She took an unsteady step, another. But at least she was walking. Magda put her arm around her again, and this time Cholayna did not draw away from the offered support.

Jaelle was in the lead; Vanessa struggling with the horses just behind her. Camilla had caught up with the

roped chervines, and was clinging to a saddle-strap as
Cholayna had done for so long, and Magda longed to
go to her; yet she knew Camilla could, if she must,
manage without her help, and Cholayna needed her.

Somewhere below them there was the thunder of an
avalanche and the mountain shook. Magda gasped and
Cholayna clutched at her; but it was far below, and
subsided after a few moments.

*We've got to get across this stretch; it could all go,
any minute!*

"Look," Jaelle called wildly from a few dozen steps
above them. "Look, Vanessa! Across the slope, up
there! Do you see? Lights! Lights, over there! It's the
settlement marked on the map! It's really there, and
we've found it!"

Magda drew in a breath of relief. It hurt her dry
throat, and the icy air burned in her lungs, but it had
come just at the right time. Now they could go on. It
did not even matter that it was starting to snow. With
Cholayna clinging to her arm, they struggled up the last
steps to the peak, and they all clustered there, staring at
the faint glimmer of lights across the valley. From here
it was downhill, and at least part of the way, they could
ride.

CHAPTER TWENTY-TWO

Partway down the slope, it began to snow; they rode through the deepening dusk as the snow thickened, Cholayna and Camilla riding, Jaella leading on foot with Magda and Vanessa behind her. The extra horses and the chervines came after, jostling on the narrow downhill trail. From the position of the lights, Magda could tell that they were well above the valley's floor, and she hoped there would be a road or trail upward. She did not know how Cholayna would fare on another mountain path.

As they went down, the road was lined more thickly with trees, sometimes blotting out the distant lights. The snow fell more and more heavily, and the wind began to rise.

Suppose we cannot reach the village in this snow; suppose it becomes a full blizzard? Suppose they will not take us in, or they are a village of robbers like that one past Barrenscae? But Magda was really too weary to care, to think any further than those welcoming lights. Lower and lower they descended, sheltered somewhat from the fierce wind and snow by the twisted trees lining the road, and there was a faint smell of resins; Magda was so chilled that it was a long time before she could be sure she smelled anything. Down and still down, and then she was certain she smelled smoke and the faint far smell of food cooking, so delicious that it made her eyes stream. The lights flickered faintly far above them, but they seemed too near to be across the valley, as if they were floating in the air.

Magda could no longer see the lights. Then she bumped softly into Camilla's horse, and all the animals jostled together at the foot of a cliff. It was as dark as the inside of a pocket.

"Somebody, strike a light?" It was Camilla's voice. Cholayna was coughing. Jaelle fumbled in the dark and then there was a tiny flare. Gradually, by its light, Magda began to see why they had been so abruptly halted.

They were clustered at the foot of a cliff which rose sheer before them. Someone a long time ago had cut steps into the sheer face, too steep, too far apart, for climbing, as if the original designers had been not quite human.

But beside the steps hung a long rope, with a handle, a plain chunk of wood wrapped in greasy rope. With a quick glance round, Jaelle pulled at it, and heard, a long way above them, the sound of a bell.

Then for a long time nothing happened at all. At least they were in the shelter of the cliff, and out of the wind; but the cold was still fierce and biting. Jaelle and Vanessa stamped about, striking their boots hard against the rock underfoot. Magda knew she should do the same, but had not the necessary strength of will to force herself. Cholayna was coughing and wheezing again, huddled in her down jacket, a thick scarf muffling her face and the sound of her breathing. Magda shivered and waited.

"Do you hear anything, Jaelle? Should you ring the bell again?"

"Something. Up there." Jaelle stepped back away from the cliff, trying to look through the thick darkness and whirling snow. Now they could all hear it, a rough scraping sound.

Jaelle struck another light; then into the tiny circle of flame, crossed with thick-falling flakes of snow, a booted foot descended, then another, quickly followed by trousered legs and a body wrapped in what looked like an assortment of thick heavy shawls. This was surmounted by a face half concealed by matted, ice-rimed white hair, thick and wild, snow lingering on the bushy white eyebrows.

"Ye'll have to lave yer riden' beasts down yere," said a rasping voice in thick mountain dialect. "We got na way to bring dem up. Be ye men or women, strangers?" And in the last sputtering light of the match Magda saw that the deep-sunken eyes were clotted with thick white film. Nevertheless for a shocking instant Magda thought it was the old woman she had seen in the Overworld.

"I am Jaelle n'ha Melora, a Renunciate of Thendara Guild-House," Jaelle said, "and these four women are my Oath-sisters. We are all travel-weary and one of our number is ill. We beg shelter for the night."

"Ay, usn'll shelter ye the night, na worrit to that," said the blind woman. "Shelter ye even be ye men, but men sleep in by the stable wi' dey beasts. This be the hermitage of Avarra, daughters. Men here be curst if dey try to enter, but ye may come up and sleep sound. Bide here just."

She tilted her head upward and gave out a long, shrill, wordless call that resonated in the snow-filled air for a long time. For a minute Magda thought it was a word in her nearly incomprehensible dialect, then realized it was a signal. It was followed by a harsh scraping sound, and then, on a rope, swaying from side to side, a dark shape descended. After a minute Magda realized that it was a great heavy basket, woven of something like wicker, bumping against the edge of the cliff as it came down.

The blind woman gestured.

"Get ye in, girlies. Usn'll stable dey beasts." And indeed as the basket descended farther, Magda could see inside the slender shape of what looked like an adolescent boy but was probably a girl, wrapped in shapeless garments like those of the woman.

Camilla asked, "Shouldn't I stay with the horses?"

The blind woman swiveled her head round quickly at the voice; came and felt about Camilla's head and shoulders, her narrow body.

"Here, ye, be ye woman? Tha' hands be more fit for sword and tha' got nae tits—"

That settled one question, thought Magda dispassionately; this was not the hidden city of the Sorceresses; the woman had no *laran*. Her throat ached with awareness of Camilla's humiliation, but Camilla said quietly: "I am *emmasca*, old mother, and made so as a young girl. Yet I was born a woman, and so I remain. Is there a law of this place that a woman may not bear a sword?"

"Hrrmmphh!" It was an untranslatable sound; Magda did not know whether it was contempt or simply acceptance. The blind woman stood with her hands still on Camilla's shoulders. Then she said, "Na, na, her above shall judge ye, I be not one to do dat. Get ye in." She signaled toward the basket; the young girl climbed down out of it and held it tilted for Camilla to climb in, followed by the others. The blind woman steadied Cholayna with both hands as she clambered shakily into the basket, then sent up that long reverberat-

ing shriek of a signal again. It was answered by a
similar cry from above, and then the basket began to
move upward.

During that terrible bouncing, swaying ascent, up and
up on creaking pulleys invisible in the dark above them,
the rope jiggled and the basket bumped heavily against
the cliff, jostling loose and beginning again the slow
creaking ascent. The wind buffeted the basket, setting it
swaying and spinning with sickening lurches every few
feet. Cholayna peered over the edge with frank curiosity,
trying to pierce through the darkness, but Magda clung
with both hands to the edge of the basket and hid her
eyes in her cloak.

Cholayna murmured, "Fascinating!"

Magda noted, with wonder, that although the Terran
woman's breath was still rasping, her voice weak and
shaky, she had recovered her curiosity and interest in
what was happening around her. She murmured to
Magda, "Do you suppose this is the City of the
Sorceresses?"

Magda whispered back, "I don't think so." She
explained why.

"But the old blind woman is only a kind of gatekeeper or something like that. The people inside might
be quite different," Jaelle murmured under her breath.

Magda didn't answer. The motion of the basket was
making her sick.

How high up is this place anyway? she wondered. It
seemed to her that the basket had been making its slow,
bumpy way upward for at least half an hour, though she
knew realistically it could not possibly be so high. *The
next time I volunteer to go on a journey in the mountains,*
she told herself, *I shall try to remember that I suffer
from acrophobia.*

But even the apparently endless journey bumped and

wobbled and swayed at last to stillness. There were lights, mostly crude torches of tar, which flared and smoked and smelled to high heaven. They were held by women, mostly clothed in coarse skirts and shawls, their hair ragged and uncombed.

"If these are the chosen of the Goddess," whispered Vanessa in Terran Standard—not to be overheard or understood—"I do not think much of them. I never saw such a filthy crew."

Magda shrugged. "Not much fuel or water here for washing. The first thing they did in the robbers' village was to offer us a bath; you can't judge by that."

A pair of the women steadied the swaying basket so that the occupants could climb out. Magda was grateful for the darkness around the torches so that she need not see the long dizzy drop up which they had come.

"Tha' all well come to Goddess's holy house," said one in that barbarous dialect. "May Lady shelter ye safe. Get ye in fra' the snow and wind." Surrounding them, they guided them up a long steep cobblestoned path, into the shadow of a cluster of buildings. The hiss of the storm blew around between the buildings and howled in the cornerstones, but in their lee they were out of the falling snow and sheltered from the wind. Magda remembered seeing the gray cluster of stones from the distance and guessed at their size; they were not built on human scale at all, any more than those steps down which the blind woman had clambered alone in the darkness of the storm.

Their guides thrust them along a sort of corridor between two of the immense buildngs, and abruptly through a great door, into a room where a fire was burning; a tiny fire in a stone fireplace, which hardly lighted the immense dark spaces and corners of the room.

Near the fire, a dark figure shrouded in coarse shawls and veils crouched in the hearth. The women shoved them forward.

"*Kiya*," said one, using the word of courtesy used for any female relative of a mother's generation, usually meaning in context something like Aunt, or Foster-mother. "Here be strangers, and a sick one for your blessin'."

The woman before the fire rose and slowly put back the hood from her face. She was a tall old woman, her face swarthy, with wide-spaced eyes under slender gray eyebrows, and she turned her eyes from one to the other of them slowly.

"A good evening to you, sisters," she said at last. She spoke the same mountain dialect as the other women, but she spoke it slowly, as if the language was unfamiliar to her. However, the pronunciation was clearer and less barbarous. "This is the holy house of Avarra, where we live in seclusion seeking Her blessing. All women are welcome to shelter at need; ye who share our search are blessed. What can this person offer thee the night?" Her voice was deep contralto, so deep it hardly sounded like a woman's voice at all.

Jaelle said, "We seek shelter against the storm; and one of us is ill."

The woman looked them over, one by one. Cholayna coughed in the silence; the old woman beckoned her forward, but Cholayna seemed too weak and lethargic to see the gesture, far less obey it, so the woman went to her.

"What ails thee, sister?" But she did not await an answer. "One knows from thy cough; thee is from lowlands and the mountain air sickens they breath. It is so?" She came and opened Cholayna's jacket, laying her gray head against Cholayna's chest. She listened a moment, then said, "We can cure this, but thee will not travel for a handful of days."

She beckoned to Vanessa. "And thy fingers be frozen, and chance be thy feet as well. My sisters will bring thee hot soup and hot water in a little time, and show ye all a place to sleep safe and dry." Her eyes went to Jaelle and it seemed they sharpened with sudden interest.

"Thy name, daughter?"

"I am Jaelle n'ha Melora—"

"Na', thy true name. Once this one who bespeaks thee dwelt in lowland country and she does well know a Renunciate may call herself to her liking. Thy name of birth, *chiya*."

"My mother was Melora Aillard," Jaelle said. "I do not acknowledge my father; am I a racehorse to be judged by the blood of my sire and dam?"

"Plenty, girl, will judge thee by less than that. Thee does wear thy Comyn blood in thy face like a banner."

"If you know me for a Renunciate, old mother, you know I have renounced that heritage."

"Renounce the eyes in thy head, daughter? Comyn thee is, and with the *donas*"—she used the archaic word, meaning *gift* rather than the more common term *laran*—"of that high house. And thy brother-sister there?"

She beckoned to Camilla, and said, "Why break laws of thy clan, half-woman?" The words were sharp, but for some reason they did not sound offensive, as the question of the blind gatekeeper had been. "Will thee entrust this old one with thy birth name, Renunciate?"

She looked straight into Camilla's eyes.

Camilla said, "Years ago I swore an oath never again to speak the name of those who renounced me long before I renounced them. But that was long ago and in another country. My mother was of the Aillard Domain, and in childhood I bore the name Elorie Lindir. But Alaric Lindir did not father me."

Magda barely managed to stifle a gasp. Not even to her, not even to Mother Lauria, had Camilla ever spoken that name. That she did so now betokened a change so deep and overpowering that Magda could not imagine what it meant.

"And thee has *donas* of the Hastur clan?"

"It may be," said Camilla quietly. "I know not."

"Well ye are come to this house, daughters." The tall woman inclined her head to them courteously. "Time may be for this one to speak wi'ye again, but this night thy needs are for rest and warmth. Make known to these whatever else may be given." She beckoned to the women who had brought them, gave a series of low-voiced instructions in their peculiar dialect. But Cholayna swayed and leaned against her, and Magda did not listen to what she said.

"Come ye wi'us," said one of the women, and led them through the drafty corridors again, then, and into an empty, spacious, echoing old building, stone-floored, stone-walled, with birds nesting in high corners and small rodents scurrying in the straw underfoot which had been laid for warmth. The only furnishings were a few ancient benches of carven stone, and a huge bedstead, really no more than a stone dais. One of the ragged crew laid a fire in the grate and touched her torch to it.

"Be warm an' safe yere," she said in her crude dialect, at the same time making a surprisingly formal gesture. "Usn' will bring ye hot soup from the even' meal, an' medicines for thy frozen feet an' for the sick one." She went away, leaving the women alone.

"They are more generous with fire for us than they were with that old woman, their priestess or whoever she was," Vanessa remarked.

"Of course," said Jaelle, "they are mountain folk; hospitality is a sacred duty to them. The old one who welcomed us—she has probably taken vows of austerity: but they would give us of their best, even if their best was half a moldy pallet and a handful of nut porridge."

"Jaelle, who *are* these people?" Vanessa asked.

"I haven't the faintest idea. Whoever they are, they have saved our lives, this night. If someone told me that Avarra, or the Sisterhood, guided us to them, I would not argue the point." She looked round and saw that Cholayna had collapsed on one of the benches.

"Vanessa, bring the medikit," she said, then hesitated, looked sharply at Vanessa, who had slumped down at once on another of the stone benches and was huddled over, in pain.

"Can you walk?"

"More or less. But I think I have frozen my feet," Vanessa confessed. The words were almost an apology. "They don't hurt. Not quite. But—" she clamped her lips together, and Jaelle said quickly, "You'd better get your boots off and attend to them as quickly as you can. How did you come to do that?"

"I think there may have been a hole in one of my boots—it was cut on the rocks," Vanessa said, as Jaelle helped her off with her boots. "Yes—see there?"

Jaelle shook her head at the cold white toes. She said, "They told us they'd be bringing hot water in a few minutes. Go near the fire, but not too close. No, don't rub them, you'll damage the skin. Warm water will do it better." She glanced around, at Cholayna lying collapsed and oblivious on the stone dais, at Camilla, who was pulling at her boot carefully, and finally pulled out a knife to slit it.

"How many of us are out of commission? Cholayna's probably the worst," Jaelle said. "Magda, you're one of the more able-bodied ones right now. Get her into a sleeping bag—as close to the fire as possible. The old woman said she would send medicines, and hot water, and hot soup—all of which we can certainly use.''

"Now, *that* one—I would willingly believe *her* a *leronis*,'' Camilla said, cutting the boot away to reveal a foot dreadfully swollen, with purplish blood-colored blisters and patches of white. Magda glanced up and saw it, shocked; she wanted to go to her, but at the moment Cholayna was even worse, semi-conscious, her forehead, when Magda touched it, burning hot. As Magda touched her she muttered, "I'm all right. Just let me rest a little. It's so cold in here,'' and she shivered, deep down.

"We'll have you warm in a few minutes,'' Magda said gently. "Here, let me pull off your coat—''

"No, I want it on, I'm cold,'' Cholayna said, resisting.

"Keep it, then, but let's get out of those boots,'' Magda said, easing Cholayna down on her sleeping bag and bending to help her pull them from her feet. Cholayna tried to protest, but her weakness overcame her; she sank back, only half conscious, and let Magda take off her boots and her outer clothes and wrap her in blankets.

"Hot soup and some of that blackthorn tea will help her, if we can't get anything better,'' Magda said. She did not confess her real fear, which was that Cholayna was in the early stages of pneumonia. "What other injuries do we have? Jaelle, that leg you hurt when Dancer fell on you; you've been walking on it. How bad is it? No, let me see it, at once.''

Jaelle's shin was bruised and bloody, but nothing seemed to be broken. It was, however, unlikely that she would walk in comfort for several days; she had already overstrained the damaged muscles and tendons. In addition, there were Vanessa's frozen feet, and patches of white on her hands as well. Camilla's foot was swollen and painful; Magda suspected that one or two of the small bones in the foot were broken.

Magda herself had a patch or two of frostbite on her face, but, although her nose was streaming and her sinuses ached, and she felt she would like to lie down and sleep for at least three days, she seemed to be the only one who had no serious illness or injury at the moment.

Presently the old doors creaked open. Snow and wind blew distantly into the room as a pair of women came in, carrying a couple of great cauldrons of water, with basins and kettles and bandages, and a third followed them with a great pot of steaming soup, which she promptly hung over the fireplace. They smiled shyly at the strangers but did not speak and went away at once, ignoring Magda's attempt to thank them in what she knew of the mountain dialect.

Magda, who was the only one who could walk properly, set herself to get into their saddlebags and ladle hot soup into mugs—first Jaelle and Camilla and Vanessa. Then she got Vanessa's feet into a basin of steaming water—at this altitude, she remembered, water boiled at a temperature quite tolerable to frostbitten or frozen skin.

"This is going to hurt. But keep on with it, otherwise you could—"

"Could lose toes or even fingers. I spent three years learning about altitude injuries and sickness on Alpha, Margali, I know what's at stake here. Believe me." She sipped soup, holding the mug in her uninjured hand—the other was in the hot water—and Magda saw her jaw tighten with pain, but she said with assumed nonchalance, "Damned good soup. What's in it, I wonder?"

"Might be better not to ask," Camilla said. "Ice-rabbit, probably; that's about the only game you find at this altitude, unless somebody's figured out how to cook a banshee."

Magda propped Cholayna's head up and tried to get her to swallow some of the hot soup, but the older woman was unconscious now, her breath rattling through her throat so loudly that Magda had a panicky moment of wondering if Cholayna was really dying.

"If she does have pneumonia," Vanessa said, so quickly that Magda wondered if Vanessa was reading her thoughts, "there are some wide-spectrum antibiotics in the medikit. Hand it here—I'm a little tied down at the minute." She rummaged in the tubes and vials. "Here. This ought to do. I don't think she can swallow, but there's a force-injection dispenser which you can give without any special medical knowledge—"

But before Magda could get the injection device loaded, the door opened again, and, warded by two reverential young women, the old woman who had welcomed them in the entrance chamber came in.

By the flickering firelight she seemed anyone's idea of a witch. But, Magda thought, not the ordinary Terran notion of a witch; something older, more archaic and benevolent, a primitive cave-mother of the human race, the ancient sorceress, priestess, clan-ruler in the days when "mother" meant at once grandmother, ancestress, queen, goddess. The wrinkles in her face, the gleam of the deep-sunken eyes beneath the witchlike disorder of her white hair, seemed wise, and her smile comforting.

She went with ponderous deliberation to Cholayna and squatted down on the dais beside her. Peripherally Magda noted that she was the first person on all their travels who had not shown the faintest surprise at Cholayna's black skin. She touched Cholayna's burning forehead, bent to listen again to her breathing, and then looked up at Magda, bent anxiously beside them. Her smile was wide and almost, Magda noticed, toothless, but when she spoke her voice was so gentle it made Magda want to cry.

"Thy friend be hot wi' the lung-sick," she said, "but fear none, *chiya*, this we can help. Get thee some soup for thysen', thee is so busy with thy friends' ills thee has not tended tha' own. This one is wi' her now; go thee and eat."

Her eyes were stinging; but Magda said, "I was about to give her some medicine, old mother—" she used the title in the most respectful mode—"then I will go and eat."

"Na. Na," said the old woman, "this be better for her than thy outland medicine; strangers here come wi' the lung-sick, but this will help her more." She pulled, from somewhere about her wrapped garments, a small vial and an ancient wooden spoon. Swiftly, she raised Cholayna's head on her arm, pried her mouth open and poured a dose between her lips. "Eat," she said to Magda, gently but with such definiteness that Magda reacted like a child scolded; she went quickly to the big pot and dipped herself a mug of soup. She sat on the bench beside Vanessa and raised it to her lips. It tasted wonderful, hot and rich and comforting, though she had no idea what was in it.

"I don't care if it *is* stewed banshee," she said in an undertone.

Vanessa whispered, "Magda, should we just let that old tribeswoman pour God-knows-what-kind of folk remedies down Cholayna without even asking what they are?"

"They couldn't survive in a place like this without knowing what they're doing," Magda whispered back. "Anyway, I trust her."

She turned to watch what the old woman was doing now; with her two attendants, they were raising Cholayna, piling thick bolsters behind her so that she was half-sitting, and spreading blankets over her for a crude sort of tent, under which they introduced one of the steaming kettles, while one of their number moved a burning brazier under the kettle, so that it was an improvised steam tent. Already, or so it seemed to Magda, between the steam and the old woman's unknown drug, Cholayna's breathing was easier.

The woman took a stick from the fire and with the burning tip lighted a curiously colored candle; it had a strong, astringently pungent smell as its smoke stole into the room.

Then she went to where Magda sat beside Vanessa, checked the hot-water basin where the latter was soaking her feet, and nodded.

"The daughters ha' brought thee bandages and medicine; when the skin is all pink again, bandage wi' this ointment. Use it also for thy bruises," she added, stopping beside Jaelle and Camilla. "It will help the skin heal clean. As for thy friend—" she gestured toward Cholayna—"while that candle burns, keep the pot on a hard boil, that she may breathe hot steam, and here be herbs to strew in the water. The candle will make thy breathing easier as well. When candle burns down, gi' her one more spoon of this—" she produced the small bottle and spoon "—and let her sleep covered warm. Sleep thee also; she will do well enough now."

For a brief moment she bent and peered into Magda's face, as if something she saw there puzzled her; then she straightened up and said, to all of them, somehow even including the semi-conscious Cholayna, " 'Varra bless 'ee all, the night an' ever," and went away.

Vanessa turned the little bottle in her hand, studying

it. It was lumpy greenish glass, hand-blown, with many flaws. She worked out the stone stopper and breathed the strong herbal smell.

"Obviously, a powerful decongestant," she ventured. "Listen; already Cholayna's breathing easier. And the steam tent is more of the same. About the candle, I couldn't say, but it does seem to make it easier to breathe."

"How are your feet?" Magda asked.

Vanessa grimaced, but passed it off lightly. "Hot water docs miracles. I was lucky. This time." Magda, who had experienced frostbite in the Kilghard Hills many times during her travels and knew the agony of returning circulation, took that for what it was worth.

"Don't forget the ointment she gave you, when you bandage them."

"Thanks. But I think I'll stick to the antibiotics in the medikit."

"I've had experience of both," Jaelle said, reaching out for the small jar the old woman had left, "and I think I'll use this. Magda, you're up, will you get me another mug of soup?" And as Magda complied, she added, "The priestesses of Avarra are legendary; according to Kindra, they have been healers for centuries and have a long tradition in healing arts. Some of them have *laran*, too."

And as if that reminded her of that surprising first interview with the old woman, Jaelle turned to Camilla, who was trying to wrap her foot in bandages. She took the foot into her own lap and took over the bandaging.

"So, you are my kinswoman, Camilla?"

Camilla said, very softly—and to Magda's astonishment she spoke in almost the identical mountain dialect—"Truly, did thee not know, *chiya*?"

Jaelle shook her head mutely. "Rohana said something once which made me suspect; though I do not think she knew it was you. Just that a daughter of Aillard had—had disappeared, under mysterious circumstances—''

"Oh, yes," Camilla said grimly, "the fate of Elorie Lindir was a scandal for at least half a year in the Kilghard Hills, till they had something else to wonder at, some other poor girl raped and forgotten, or some Hastur lord acknowledging some other bastard—why, think you, did I live so long as a man, save that I sickened at the gossip of housebound ladies—? Rohana is not so bad as most, but those snows were melted twenty winters past. Leave it, Shaya.''

"You are *her* kinswoman too, Camilla." She stretched her hand to Magda and said, "I hate to keep ordering you around like this, but you can walk and I can't; can you get a couple of pins from my personal kit?''

"It's all right, *breda*," Magda said, found the pins and gave them to Jaelle, who pinned up Camilla's bandages, then got her own bruised leg up on the bench. "One of you, bandage this, will you?''

Magda moved it into her lap and began smoothing the old woman's herbal ointment on the torn and lacerated skin.

Camilla said, with a sudden undertone of fierceness, "I will claim kin with Lady Rohana when she claims kin to me!'' She rose, tested her weight on the bandaged foot, wincing, and went to shake out her sleeping bag by the fire.

"Shall I stay awake to tend Cholayna's steam kettle or will you?'' The flat tone of her voice closed the subject completely.

"I will,'' said Magda, but Jaelle shook her head.

"You've been looking after all of us all day. Go to bed, Magda, I'll look after her now. When that candle burns out—it can only be an hour or two—I can sleep too. At least we needn't keep watch all the time; here we are under Avarra's protection, and all the Renunciates are under her wing."

Magda wanted to protest, but her eyes seemed to be closing of their own accord. She nodded agreement and spread out her sleeping bag beside Camilla's. The fire burned low; outside she could hear the hissing of the thick snow, the wind howling like ten thousand screaming demons around the old buildings.

At the very edge of sleep, Camilla's head lying on her shoulder, she thought again how little she knew this woman she loved. The astonishing words rang in her mind.

My mother was of the Aillard clan, but I was born to the name Elorie Lindir.

And thee has donas *of the Hasturs?* And Camilla's even more astonishing words: *It may well be so.*

CHAPTER TWENTY-THREE

The blizzard lasted for three days.

For the first day Magda did little but sleep; after the exhaustion of the long journey, the stress and fear, her weary body and wearier mind demanded their toll, and for a night and a day and most of another night she spent the hours asleep or in a state of incomplete somnolence, rousing only to eat or drink. They were all in much the same state.

"We thought at first that you too had taken the lung-fever," Camilla told her later, "but that old *leronis* said no, it was only weariness and cold. And, the Goddess be praised, she was right."

This morning Magda had had the energy to wash (at an icy indoor pump where the water was a little above freezing) and to change her underclothing and socks, and to brush her hair.

"How is Cholayna this morning?" she asked.

"Better," Camilla told her, "her fever is down, and she has eaten a little soup. She is still very sick, but her breathing is easier. And she spoke to me in *cahuenga*, which at least meant she knew who I was. What a relief after the last two days of her speaking only in some language none of us could understand, and not recognizing any of us!"

"How are the others?"

"Jaelle has climbed down the cliff—in this snow-storm!—to make sure the pack animals are all right. It is not that she does not trust the women here; but I think she wanted the exercise." Camilla chuckled, and Magda laughed weakly with her. Jaelle always wearied quickly of inaction.

"And Vanessa?"

Camilla pointed; Vanessa was sleeping near the fire, only a few curls of dark hair showing above the top of her sleeping bag.

"Her feet are still very sore and painful, and two toenails came away last night when she changed the bandages, but it is fortunate it is no worse. My feet were almost as bad, but they are healing better. I think it is because Vanessa used only your Terran medicine, while Jaelle and I used what that old *leronis* gave us."

Magda finished the coarse, burnt-tasting porridge, put the bowl away, and slid down wearily.

"I am not sleepy now. But my whole body feels as if I had been beaten with wooden cudgels."

"Rest, then, *bredhiya*," Camilla said. "No one is going anywhere in *that*." The storm was still raging unabated outside; it seemed to Magda that it had raged through her sleep for the last hours and days.

Jaelle came in presently, her outer garments covered with snow, snowflakes clinging to her eyebrows and to her auburn curls.

"You're awake, Margali? Good. I was beginning to worry about you. I climbed down the cliff this morning, and back up, though they said I could ride up in the basket with the grain sacks. It was wonderful even in the snow; when it is not snowing, they tell me, one can see all the way to Nevarsin Peak on the one side, and to the Wall Around the World on the other."

Magda wondered at her freemate's idea of fun. She

remembered that only a few weeks before her daughter was born, Jaelle had insisted on accompanying Damon to the far ends of Armida for the horse-roundup, saying that she knew perfectly well that she had time enough to return before her child was born. She had been in the saddle again before Cleindori was forty days old. Magda herself had been tired and lethargic all during her pregnancy, content to stay indoors and allow Ellemir and Callista to cosset her.

But before she had much time to reflect on it, the door opened and the ancient wise-woman who had welcomed them and brought medicines for Cholayna, came in. She barely nodded to the women but went directly to Cholayna, knelt and felt her forehead; bent her head to listen to her heart and the sounds of her breathing.

"Thee is stronger this morning, daughter."

Cholayna awoke, looked at the wild hair and ragged clothing of the ancient woman, and struggled to sit up. Magda came quickly to her side, so that Cholayna could see that she was not alone and at the mercy of a stranger.

Cholayna demanded weakly, "Where are we? What is happening?"

The old woman spoke a few soothing words but they were in the strange mountain dialect and Cholayna did not understand them.

"Who are you? What is going on?" As the old woman brought out the bottle of medicine and spoon, gesturing to Cholayna to open her mouth, she demanded shakily, "What's this, what are you giving me?" She moved her head from side to side in panicky denial. "What is it? Magda, help me, tell me, isn't anyone listening to me?"

There was real terror in her face, and Magda knelt quickly at her side, taking Cholayna's hands in hers.

"It's all right, Cholayna, you have been very ill, but she has been nursing you. I don't know what she is giving you, but it has made you better. Take it."

Cholayna opened her mouth docilely enough and swallowed the medicine, but she still looked confused. "Where are we? I don't remember coming here."

Questions flooded from her in Terran Standard as she struggled to sit upright, staring wildly about her.

Magda reassured her quickly in the same language.

"Cholayna, no one will hurt you. These people have been very good to us . . . we're safe here—"

"Who is this strange woman? Is she one of Aquilara's people, did they follow us here? I—I think I have been dreaming; I thought Aquilara had captured us, brought us here—"

"Tell un, must not talk, lie down, rest, be warm," the old woman commanded. Magda laid her hand over Cholayna's wrist, gently forcing her back on the pillows.

"You mustn't talk. Lie still and rest, and I'll explain."

Coughing, Cholayna let herself sink back. Her eyes followed the attendants as they rigged again the improvised steam tent. She listened to Magda's simplified explanations, without question; Magda suspected she was simply so weak that she took everything for granted.

At last she whispered, "Then these are not Aquilara's servants? You are sure of that?"

"As sure as I have ever been of anything," Camilla reassured her. "She has been coming in every few hours to make sure your fever was under control. But now you really must lie down and rest, don't think of anything except getting well."

Cholayna closed her eyes again weakly, and the old woman raised her head, glaring at Camilla.

"A name was spoken that is forbidden in 'Varra's holy house. What ha' ye to do wi' that one?"

"Who? Acquilara?"

The old woman gestured angrily. "Silence! Speak not the names of evil omen! This one said, when thy sickness and weariness should be healed, thy story would be heard. Now perhaps is the very time for that hearing; what do ye in these wilds where no women come save in search of Her blessing?"

"Margali will tell thee, Grandmother," said Camilla in the mountain dialect. Magda wondered when she had learned it, and saw in Camilla's mind there was a flash of memory, a year spent as an abused and beaten child, enslaved in a bandit encampment. . . .

"We come in search of Her blessing too." Magda found in her memory the night when first she had seen the image of Avarra during the first meeting of the Sisterhood. "We seek a City said to be inhabited by the Sisterhood of the Wise. Two of our companions were seeking it, and had gone before. We thought, when we saw your lights in the wilderness, that perhaps we had found that place, and perhaps our comrades also."

"This one has read thy mind and memory in thy weakness, granddaughter. We are only sheltering in the shadow of Her wings, *chiya*, and are not of Her sisterhood. Yet thy search does make thee sacred here, where thy companions have *not* come."

The old woman's hand fell on Magda's shoulder. "Yet tell, what of that other name *she* spoke now twice?"

"She came to us by night, promised that she could lead us to our comrades."

"And why did thee not follow her?"

"It seemed to us," Camilla said slowly, "that truth was not to be found in her mouth, and that to follow such a guide was worse than to wander unguided."

"Yet thy companion cried out to her in her unknown tongue—"

"Cholayna was afraid of her," Magda corrected sharply. "Read *her* mind and memory if you can, Old Mother, and you will know I speak truth."

Jaelle asked Magda in Standard, "What's the trouble?"

"She says Rafi and Lexie haven't been here. Which may mean they have fallen into—" she started to say, Aquilara's hands, then looked at the old woman's face and didn't. "I fear, then, that the two we seek may have fallen into the hands of those we count as enemies."

The old woman looked from one to another of them, then said slowly, "Thy friend is better, but still very sick. Watch thee by her a handful of days more," and went away.

Camilla and Jaelle looked at Magda and demanded, "Now what was *that* all about?"

The old woman did not return that day, nor the next, nor the next. Silent attendants came in three times a day, bringing them food: rough porridge morning and noon, thick and nourishing soup in the evening. The enforced rest was good for all of them; Magda recovered her strength, Vanessa's frozen feet healed, and even Cholayna began to sit up for a time during the day.

On the fifth or sixth morning—Magda had lost count of the days, as they slid by with nothing to distinguish them—the snow stopped and the sound of silence woke Magda; the wind was no longer wailing and screaming around the buildings. She stepped out into a bright world, the sun dazzling on roofs and the sky so clear that it seemed she could see across an endless landscape of snowy peaks and valleys far below them.

Perhaps Cholayna would be able to travel soon. Magda

began mentally sorting through their possessions for gifts they could make to the old woman and to the Sisterhood in return for their hospitality. She trembled at the thought of the return journey down the cliff in the basket. And how much farther must they go? Perhaps the old woman could tell them something about Lexie and Rafaella; at least she seemed to know something of Aquilara's people and despised them.

Cholayna was sitting up this morning, and had actually eaten some porridge. She looked better, healthier; she had asked for water to wash her face and dug into her personal pack for a hairbrush; but she was too weak to sit up for so long, so Vanessa had come and taken the brush, and was trying to ease the tangles out of the shock of pale hair.

"I can see that you are feeling better," Magda said, kneeling beside her, and Cholayna smiled.

"I am beginning to feel halfway human again; I can breathe again without knives through my chest! And the snow seems to have stopped. Tell me, Magda, how long have we been here?"

"Five or six days. As soon as you are well enough to travel, we will go on. I think perhaps these people know something of the City. Perhaps, if we ask in the right way, they will tell us."

"But what is the right way?" asked Vanessa.

"One thing we know," Camilla said, joining them, "they aren't in league with—" she stopped, and Magda could read in Camilla's mind the memory of the exaggerated anger the old woman had displayed when she spoke Aquilara's name.

It was as if someone not present spoke, not in words:
The name of evil can summon it and be used as a link . . .

"They aren't in link with that woman who came and

tried to bully us in Nevarsin, in Arlinda's house,"
Magda said. "They have an unholy horror of her very
name, though, so they evidently know what's going
on."

"I wish *I* did," Vanessa complained. "That old
woman gives me the creeps! Inhuman!"

Jaelle protested, "She saved Cholayna's life, and you
could have been permanently lamed. Don't be ungrateful!"

"I know what Vanessa means, though," Camilla
said. "Have you noticed, Margali? I don't expect Vanessa
to understand it, she doesn't know the language as well
as you do; you learned it in Caer Donn as a child. You
noticed she never says *I* at all; just stands aside and
speaks of herself as someone else. I don't begin to
understand it."

"I don't know if it's ever possible to understand an
alien religious practice," Cholayna said thoughtfully.
"Perhaps we should just be grateful that she's well-
disposed toward us."

"We need more than that, though," Jaelle said.
"We've come to the end of the trail. I don't know of
anything beyond here and there's nothing on the maps.
If they can't tell us where to go on, I don't know where
we can go."

"And the old woman hasn't been near us for days,"
Camilla said. "When you spoke—" again the hesitation,
"a certain name, you seemed to put her off. She'd been
so friendly before that, and then—nothing. Not a sign
nor a sight of her." Her smile was bleak.

"Maybe when she found out that some of us had
laran she decided we could find our own way from
here."

"But," Magda said, "that would mean there's something to find. And that it would be possible to find it
from this place."

That night when the attendants came in to rig Cholayna's steam tent again—they indicated by signs that she should sleep in it, even if she could breathe well enough during the day—Jaelle went with them down to see to the animals again. When she came back, she beckoned them all close to her.

"Tomorrow, they said, someone will come to talk with us. I gathered, from what the blind woman—her name is Rakhaila, by the way, that's Hellers dialect for Rafaella—from what she said, there are women here who come and go from—" Jaelle hesitated—"the place we may be looking for. I have a feeling we should be ready to leave at a moment's notice."

"Cholayna's not able to travel yet," Vanessa protested.

"That's another thing we have to talk about. I think perhaps we must send Cholayna back; or leave her here to recuperate further. From something Rakhaila said, this could lead us out beyond the Wall Around the World. There's no way Cholayna's fit enough to make that kind of trip."

Cholayna said doggedly, "We had this all out before. I can manage. I'll do it if it kills me."

"That's what we're afraid of, you stubborn old wretch," Vanessa said. "What good would it do to kill yourself on the trip? Would that do Lexie any good, or you?"

But Magda was not so sure. "We've come this far together. I don't think it would be right to abandon Cholayna here. I think we all go together, or none of us." She did not know why she was so certain.

But when Cholayna had been settled for the night, Jaelle touched Magda's arm.

"*Breda*, we need to talk. Come outside with me for a minute."

They went out into the long corridor between the buildings. Jaelle led the way to a spot at the very edge of the cliff. The pulleys and baskets hung there awaiting the journey down.

"The steps aren't so bad," Jaelle said. "I've been down them twice now."

"Better you than me," Magda said. "Well, Jaelle, do you remember in Thendara you were saying you wanted a year off to go to the mountains? You've had your adventure, haven't you?"

Above them the sky was sprinkled with the stars of a rare, clear Darkovan night. Jaelle looked away north, to where, Magda knew, the Wall Around the World rose, the end of the known world of the Domains. She said, "Maybe it's only beginning."

Magda smiled indulgently. "You're enjoying this, aren't you?"

It was almost a joke; but Jaelle was completely serious. She said, "Yes. Terrible as this trip has been, I loved every minute of it. I wish I hadn't dragged you along, because I know you've hated it—"

Magda said, "No." She surprised herself with the word. "I wouldn't have wanted to miss—parts of it."

The sudden sense of self-mastery when she had accomplished what she had never believed she could do. Cholayna and Vanessa, friends only in the limited sense of co-workers; now, she knew, they were as close as the sisters she had never known. Would she have wanted to miss that? And in a very real sense it was *her* quest. From the day she had first seen the robed figures in their circle, first heard the sound of calling crows, she had known that she must follow them, even if the search led over the roof of the known world.

For a moment she knew this, then practicality took

over again. "Would you go off to this City out of
Kindra's legends, and stay there?"

"I don't know if they'd have me. I think you have
to—well, to study and prepare yourself a long time
first. There seems to be a college of this kind of wisdom and I'm still in kindergarten. But if I decided I
wanted to try preparing to be worthy of it? Or if anything happened that I *couldn't* go back. On a trip like
this, one false step—we've all come that close to the
edge, Margali. If I didn't make it back, you'd look after
Cleindori for me, wouldn't you?"

Magda smiled gently. "I'd have to get in line for the
chance; after Damon, and Ellemir, and Lady Rohana
. . . about all I could do for her would be to sponsor her
if she decided she wanted to work for the Terrans, and
considering that she's Heir to Aillard, I doubt she'd be
given that option. But if you mean, would I love her as
my own—do you doubt our oath, freemate?"

Jaelle touched the hilt of Magda's knife which she
wore at her belt. "Never, *breda*."

"We should go in," Magda said. The great violet
disk of Liriel was rising, almost at full; the largest of
the four moons. The bluish crescent of Kyrddis hung
almost at the zenith of the sky. Stars were beginning to
shine through the clear pallor of the falling night, and
an icy wind was beginning to blow over the heights, a
veritable jet-stream of a wind which tore at their hair
and buffeted them toward the cliffs. Magda clung to a
frost-rimed wall to keep her balance against the fierce
gusts. It was not dark; all round them the growing light
of the moons was reflected from snow everywhere.

"Are you cold? Have some of my cloak," Jaelle
said, putting it round her with her arm around Magda.
Magda smiled as they snuggled together under it.

Jaelle said seriously, "I need to talk to you alone,

just for a few minutes. I wish I didn't have to go back at all, Magda. I'm not needed in the Forbidden Tower. My *laran* isn't that strong; never has been. I'm hardly a competent monitor, and you—a Terran!—you are as powerful a technician as Damon himself. They love me, perhaps, but don't *need* me. In a very real sense I've never been needed anywhere. People don't need me, don't cling to me the way they do to you. Even my daughter comes to you for mothering, instead of me; she sees it too, Magda, the thing that makes people come to you. I've never known—where to go, or why.''

Magda listened, appalled. Ever since she had known Jaelle she had envied what she thought was the younger woman's confidence, sense of purpose, the intensity with which she flung herself into things with a whole-heartedness Magda herself had never known. It had never occurred to her that Jaelle felt this way.

''That's not true, Shaya. You're so much stronger than I am in so many ways. You're braver than I am. You don't hold back and panic, and hash everything over in your mind all the time—''

''Oh—courage,'' Jaelle said, faintly smiling. ''Damon told me once that he thought courage, a soldier's kind of courage, the kind I have, just means I haven't enough imagination to be afraid. Damon himself admits he's a horrible coward, physically, because he has too much imagination. And I have so little. No imagination, not half the brains you have or half the sensitivity either. Maybe what I need is the kind of wisdom they have, these sorceresses of that legendary City. I'm like Camilla. Maybe I need to go and ask them why I was born and what life is all about for me.''

''There are times I've felt the same way, Jaelle. But we both have ties. Duties, responsibilities—''

Jaelle moved restlessly away from Magda. She was

pacing at the very edge of the cliff in a way that made Magda wince. Courage? Or a lack of imagination, knowing she would not fall, so why did she need to worry about what could happen if she did?

"Oh, Margali, can't you see? There's no *reason* for me to go back. In a sense it seems my whole life has been leading up to this, a chance to find out what's real, what's under the surfaces of life. To make some *sense* of it all. Maybe these *leroni* of the Sisterhood know the answers and can tell me. Or help me find out."

"Or maybe they only claim they can. Like Aquilara. To give themselves importance. And it's all tricks."

"No. Can't you see the difference? Aquilara's full of arrogance and—and hates you and me because we really *have laran* and she doesn't though she wanted us to think she did. I'm thinking of—well, Marisela. She doesn't argue about why life happens, or try to convince or convert anyone, she just does what she needs to. I want to know what it is that she knows. The legend says if you get there under your own energies they have to take you in, and if they don't I'll sit on their doorstep until they do."

The idea had its attractions; *to know what life was truly all about, to fling yourself straight at the source of wisdom and demand to know.* Yet there were other duties, obligations, responsibilities.

"Would you really go after this kind of wisdom and leave me alone, Shaya?"

"You wouldn't be alone, Margali. You're not the kind of person to be alone. And anyway, you have Camilla—"

Magda gripped her hands tight.

"Jaelle—*bredhiya*, my love, my freemate, do you really think it's the same thing?" Love wasn't like that, Magda knew, it couldn't be pigeonholed that way. "I

simply cannot believe you are jealous that Camilla and
I—"

"No, oath-daughter." It was rare that Jaelle called
her that now, but it came from the first of their many
pledges to one another. "Never jealous, not that. Only—"
Jaelle held her hands tightly; in the reflected moonlight,
snow-light, her face was very pale, her great dark-
lashed eyes somber in the pale triangle of her face. It
seemed for a moment that a flood of memories reached
out and enfolded them.

*Jaelle looking up at her like a trapped animal, await-
ing the knife-stroke of the hunter; she had saved Jaelle
from bandits who would have killed them both, but now
Jaelle in turn was prisoner, not the captor who had
forced the Amazon Oath on her unwilling; now with a
single stroke of her knife Magda could free herself, she
need not even kill. She need only walk away, leaving
the wounded Jaelle to die of exposure.*

*Jaelle, in the cave where together they had faced
floodwater, death, abandonment, starvation. Jaelle, for
whom her laran had wakened. The exchange of knives,
the oath of freemates.*

*Jaelle, close to her in the Tower circle, bonded by
the matrix link, closer than family, closer than sex,
closer than her own skin . . .*

*Jaelle, clinging to her, her face covered with the
sweat of hard labor, the night Cleindori was born;
rapport between them so close that years later, when
Shaya was born, even the stress of birth was not new to
her; less conscious of agony than of fierce effort, terror,
triumph and delight; Cleindori in a very real sense her
own child, since she too had struggled to bring her to
life. . . .*

Whatever path she chose, always it seemed that Jaelle

*had been there before, and she only a clumsy follower
in her steps. Even now. . . .*

Then the rapport fell away (how long had it lasted? A
lifetime? Half a second?) and Jaelle said quietly, "No,
bredhiya mea, viyha mea, not jealous of Camilla. No
more than you are jealous of Damon."

But there had been a time, Magda remembered, when
she *had* been jealous of Damon, painfully, blindly,
obsessively jealous of Damon. She could not bear that
either, any more than she could bear, after she and
Jaelle had come together as if destined, that any man
could give Jaelle anything she could not. Now she was
ashamed of that brief jealousy, her fear that Jaelle could
love her less because she loved the father of her child.
She had fought through and triumphed, still loving
Jaelle, and loving Damon just as much *because* he
could give Jaelle the one thing she could not, for all her
love.

"The one thing that could make me hesitate would be
leaving you, Margali. Even Cleindori has a dozen who
would be glad to rear her if I could not. But you have
something to return for. I don't. What do I have ahead
of me but to go back, take the Aillard seat in Council
when Lady Rohana is gone? And why should I want to
do that? In the Renunciates, and also in the Forbidden
Tower, we are working so that the Domains need not
depend on Councils, and Comyn, who try to keep *laran*
in their own hands for their own good. The Hasturs who
rule the Council don't want independent subjects, thinking for themselves, any more than they want independent women."

"Then isn't it your job to take that Council seat and
help them change the way they think?"

"Oh, Magda, *breda*, don't you think I've been through

all that in my mind? I can't change the Council because, at heart, the Council doesn't want to change. It has everything it wants the way it is: power, the means to work for its own greed. Now when people don't work for it of their own free will, it bribes them with promises of power of their own, and an appeal to *their* greed."

She turned and paced restlessly along the cliff, her face starkly moonlit. "Look what they did to Lady Rohana! They said to her, 'It doesn't matter to you that you are not free; you have power instead, and power is more important than freedom.' They bribed her with power. I am so afraid that they will do that to me, Magda, find out what I want most, and bribe me with it—I simply cannot believe that all the Comyn are corrupt, but they have power, and it makes them greedy for more. Even the Towers are playing the game of power, power, power, always over other people."

"Maybe that's simply the way life works, Jaelle. I don't like it either. But it's like what you said about bargaining, haggling in the market; it makes each party think he's getting the better of the other." Magda's smile was strained. "You said you liked haggling."

"Only when it's a game. Not when it's real."

"But it is a game, Shaya. Power, politics, whatever you call it—it's simply the way life works. Human nature. Romantics among the Terrans think the Darkovans are immune to it because you aren't part of an interstellar Empire, but people *do* operate because of profit, and greed, as you say—"

"Then I don't want any part of it, Magda. And I know they will try to bully me into taking that Aillard seat in Council, and within ten years I should be as bad as any of them, using power because they have convinced me that I am doing good with it. . . ."

"I think you would be incorruptible, Jaelle—" Magda began, but Jaelle shook her head with a wise sadness.

"Nobody's incorruptible, not if they let themselves be tricked into trying to play those power games. The only thing to do is to stay outside them. I think maybe the *leroni* of Avarra, the Sisterhood of the Wise, could show me how to stay outside. Maybe they know why the world works that way. Why good and evil work the way they do."

Jaelle turned restlessly, her cloak flying.

"Look at Camilla. She has a right to hate—worse than Acquilara. Did you hear her say she was a Hastur, at least that she had Hastur *laran?* And look what they did to her! But she's such a good person, such a *loving* person. And Damon, too. Life has treated him badly— but he still can love. The world is so rotten to people, and people keep saying it isn't fair—"

Magda murmured, "The *cristoforos* say it: 'Holy one, why do the wicked flourish like mushrooms on a dead tree, while the righteous man is everywhere beset with thorns . . . ?' "

"Magda, did you ever think? Maybe the world isn't *supposed* to be a better place? Maybe it goes on the way it does so that people can *choose* what's really important." Jaelle spoke passionately, striding to and fro into the face of the wind, her auburn curls flying from under the hood of her cloak. She had forgotten the cold and the jet-stream wind.

"Let the Council, and the Terrans, play power games with each other. Andrew walked out and did what he could somewhere else. Let the Towers have their political struggles, under that horrible old hag Leonie Hastur—I don't care what Damon says, he may love her, but I know she is a tyrant as cruel and domineering as her twin brother who rules the Council! Between the Council, and the Towers, where is there a place for the use of *laran?* But Hilary and Callista found another way, even though the Towers were corrupt. Let women wear chains in the Dry Towns, or be good wives in the Domains, unless they have the courage to get out of it—real courage, not my kind that's just lack of imagination. Courage—to get out of the Dry Towns, or their own chains, the way my mother or Lady Rohana did, or the way you did when you found the Guild-house—"

"But your mother didn't get out of it, Jaelle. She died." For years, Magda knew, Jaelle had concealed this knowledge from herself.

"Sure she died. So did yours. So will you and I some day. Since we're all going to die anyhow, no matter what we do or don't do, what sense does it make to go around scared all the time, crawling, and putting up with a lot of rotten stuff just to hang on a little longer? Look at Cholayna. She could have stayed nice and safe in Thendara, or accepted your offer to send her back from Nevarsin. Even if she died here, wouldn't it have been better than turning back at Ravensmark and knowing she'd failed in what she set out to do? Living is taking risks. You could have stayed in the Guild-house and obeyed orders. My mother could have stayed in the Dry Towns and worn chains all her life. She might have died when Valentine was born even though, but she'd have died in comfort, and I'd still be there. In chains." She looked pensively at her bare wrists.

"It's all there is, Magda. We can't change life. There's too much greed and profit and—and *safety.* Human nature, like you said. We can only get out of it. Like Damon when he founded the Forbidden Tower. He could have been *blinded*—his *laran* burned out, because he wouldn't back down and promise to use his *donas* only in the way the others, the ones with the power, said he should. But if he'd done that he'd have been blinded anyway; he'd have done it to himself. And he knew it.''

Magda knew Damon's story. She knew she did not have that kind of strength. *Except, sometimes, when Jaelle forces me to follow her into some mad challenge . . .*

"So don't you see, Magda? I can go back and play dreary games of power in the Council, or I can go *ahead,* to whatever these *leroni* can teach me—''

"You said that courage was needed to set up the Forbidden Tower, and we have a place there—''

"That was Damon's trial of integrity, Margali. Not mine.'' Jaelle turned and faced her freemate. "Only I can't go if it's going to hurt you *that* much. That's the one thing that could stop me. I won't do it over your—your dead body.''

There was such a lump in Magda's throat she could hardly speak. She didn't have to; she gave Jaelle her hands again.

Shaya, my love, my treasure, do what you must do.

And you'll come too, Margali?

Suddenly Magda knew that Jaelle's quest had become her own. But she had, perhaps, stronger ties. A weakness, now, not a strength, but:

I don't know. I must see Cholayna safe. I brought her here and I cannot abandon her now. I'm not sure, Jaelle. But I won't try and hold you back.

"I had hoped we could go together,'' Jaelle said aloud as they turned back toward the buildings. "Margali, we must go in, we'll freeze.'' And indeed it was growing colder, the cold no longer bracing and stimulating but deadly. "I suppose you're right; if you're not ready, it wouldn't be right for you. But, oh, *breda,* I want to say, we go together or not at all. I couldn't bear to leave you behind.''

But always, Magda thought, Jaelle was that one step ahead of her.

"Lead on," she said lightly, and I'll follow as far as I can. But just now I'd prefer to follow you in out of the cold.''

CHAPTER TWENTY-FOUR

Magda was dreaming. . . .

There was a circle of robed figures around a fire; dark hooded figures, gathered around something that lay at their center. Magda could not see what it was, nor see what they were doing to it; only that there was a sound like the screaming of hawks, and with every cry of the hawks there was a pitiable crying, so that for a moment Magda thought in horror, *it is Shaya, they have my little Shaya there, they are hurting her.* The fire at the center shot up and surged high, and Magda could see that it was no child, but the naked figure of a woman, lying bound in their circle.

Magda tried to rush forward to her, but it seemed that she was held in place by invisible bonds; chains like the chains of a Dry-Town woman.

"For the love of God, help me, Lorne! You got me into this, now you have a duty to get me out of it!"

It was Lexie's voice. She had known all along somehow that it was Lexie lying there helpless, and that she had been responsible for the act or omission that had landed Lexie there.

She struggled against her bonds, but the hawks went on screaming. She could see what they were doing now; with every surge upward of the flame, the hawks swirled, borne on the currents of fire, and swooped over Lexie's inert figure, and with every downward swoop they tore into her naked flesh, carrying away great dripping hunks of blood and skin, while Lexie screamed, terrible screams that reminded Magda horribly of the time she and Jaelle had been marooned in a cave with rising floodwater, and Jaelle had miscarried Peter Haldane's child. She had been delirious, not fully aware what was happening much of the time, and in her delirium she had screamed like that, as if she were being torn asunder, and Magda had not been able to help her. They had come so close to dying there.

And now it was Lexie screaming. And it is my fault; she was competing with me, and that was how she got into this.

Again Magda strained against her bonds to rush forward to Lexie, but there was a curious blue fire in the air, and in that evil glow she could see the face of the black sorceress Aquilara.

"Yes, you always want to ease your own conscience by being so ready to help other people. But now it is your task to learn detachment; that her troubles are not of your making, and that she must take the consequences of her own actions," Aquilara explained callously. It sounded so rational, so reasonable, and yet the screams tore at her as if every stroke of the razor talons and cruel bloody beaks fell on her own heart.

"Yes, that is what they are doing," Aquilara went on explaining. "They will tear and tear at that false and sentimental conscience of yours which you think of as your heart, until it is gone from your breast." And Magda, looking down, saw a great bleeding hole opening in her chest, from which a screaming hawk carried away a piece of flesh . . .

No. Think. This is a dream. Slowly a sense of reality penetrated Magda's mind; slowly, slowly. She felt herself pull free, free of the invisible bonds, raised her arms, jerked herself up, and found herself sitting bolt upright in her cold sleeping bag. Her heart was still pounding with the nightmare. She heard Jaelle cry out, and reached over to shake her freemate awake.

"Shaya, Shaya, are you having a nightmare too?"

"Zandru's hells," Jaelle whispered, "it was a dream, a dream, I was only dreaming—Aquilara's sorceresses. They were torturing Rafaella, and they had chained me up to Rafi's big *rryl* and were making me play ballads on it, and she was screaming—ah, how she was screaming, like a girl of fourteen in childbirth—and the demons all kept yelling, 'Louder, play louder, so we cannot hear her scream . . .' " She shuddered and buried her head against Magda's shoulder.

Magda stroked Jaelle's soft hair, comprehending what had happened. Even the themes in the nightmares they had shared had been all but identical.

She wondered if Camilla and the others were suffering nightmare too. She was almost afraid to try to sleep again. "I thought this place was guarded," she said, "that even the names of that witch and her people could not be spoken here. . . ."

"I think that was only while we were sick and exhausted," Jaelle ventured. "Now that we are well again, and there are decisions to be made, nightmares can move in our minds, those demons—" she hesitated, said tentatively ". . . torturing us?"

But Magda could not attend to the question. A wave of horror swept through her, making her physically ill with its impact.

She was lying on the ground, chained hand and foot at the center of a ring of robed and hooded figures . . . no; they were men, scarred bandits, wielding knives, naked, their gross hairy bodies and erect phalluses

*touching her everywhere, intruding into her everywhere,
and they were like razors, like knives shearing off her
breasts, invading her womb, tearing her womanhood
from her. One of them, an evil hawk-faced man with a
scar, held up the body of a naked, bleeding child, a
fetus half-formed, shrieking,* "Here is the Heir to Hastur
that she may never bear!" *Slowly, slowly, the face of
the bandit changed, became, not gross and scarred, but
noble, pale, detached, the face of the sorceress Leonie
. . . No; it was a man's face. The face of the regent,
Lorill Hastur.* "How can I acknowledge as my own
child a girl who has been so treated, so scarred?" *he
asked coldly, and turned away. . . .*

"Magda!" Jaelle clutched at her in horror; Magda
freed herself from the terrible paralysis of nightmare.
Once before during the waking of her own *laran* she
had become a part of Camilla's nightmares. A dreadful
time; and the worst of it had been Camilla's horror and
shame, that she could not barricade these memories and
horrors from her friend and lover.

She bent over Camilla and shook her awake.

"You were crying out in your sleep, love. Were you
having a bad dream?"

Magda had seen this before: how Camilla struggled
up from the paralysis of terror. With shaking hands, she
wiped the sweat of nightmare from her face, fighting to
compose herself.

"Aye," she whispered at last. "My thanks for waking me, oath-sisters." She knew, and she knew they
knew, what she had been dreaming. But she could trust
them to ask no questions, and she was grateful.

The next morning, Cholayna's color was good, and
her breathing so easy that the women who came to
bring the breakfast porridge dismantled the steam tent

and took it away. Cholayna sat up and dressed herself, all except her boots, saying she felt perfectly well.

But Magda knew this raised again the question they had been avoiding while Cholayna's life was in danger, and she found herself dreading the debate. Cholayna could face no more rough weather and exposure.

Yet how likely was it that she would agree to go back, and could she turn over the search for Lexie to Vanessa and Magda? *Would* she? Magda doubted it.

So they carefully avoided the subject, and Magda felt the enforced silence fraying away at her nerves. It was a fine bright day, and Vanessa went out to walk along the cliffs, trying to scan out a route ahead. Magda walked with her a little way.

"Tell me, Vanessa, did you have bad dreams last night?"

Vanessa nodded, but she turned her face away, her cheeks crimson, and did not volunteer to say what she had dreamed, and Magda did not ask. They were under attack again; the Sisterhood of the Wise was most effectively guarded by the Sisterhood of the Dark or so it seemed . . . or could it be that the two were inextricably intertwined? Her own nightmare and Jaelle's had come from their own inner demons and flaws, not from anything anyone had imposed on them from the outside.

But Camilla? This was no nightmare based on something she had done wrong, no background of mistake or cruelty or omission coming back to haunt her, as with Jaelle and Magda, but something done to an innocent child who had no way deserved any of it. . . .

Jaelle had asked the unanswerable question: *Why do the wicked flourish?* But even the *cristoforos* had no answer to that question; they framed the question itself in poetic language and called it a mystery of their God.

Vanessa was involved at the moment not in philosophical speculations, but practical realities.

"We'll have to go on from here, on foot. A couple of chervines might make it, but I can't imagine taking a horse over those trails."

"Do you think Cholayna can make it?"

"Hellfire, Lorne, I'm no mind reader. But she'll insist on trying, and I don't think I'd be able to stop her. You want to try convincing her? No? I thought not."

When they went back to the building where they had spent the last few nights, Camilla was on her feet, bowing to someone in the lee of the fireplace. Magda and Vanessa came in, and Jaelle said, as if completing an introduction she had begun, "and these are our companions Vanessa ryn Erin and Margali n'ha Ysabet."

Magda came around the fire and saw a small, slight young woman, with her hair in a long braid down her back, as the countrywomen around Caer Donn wore it. She wore a simple knee-length tunic, dark saffron-color, embroidered at neck and sleeves with a childish pattern of leaves and flowers, and simple unadorned brown riding breeches. Otherwise she wore no jewelry or ornament except for a plain copper ring in her left ear.

She said, "My name is Kyntha." She spoke the ordinary *casta* of the hill country, but slowly and carefully.

"I have been sent for, and I must go soon. Tell me why you have come into this country, so far beyond Nevarsin?"

Jaelle leaned forward and whispered so softly that no one else could hear, "This is the woman Rakhaila told me about." Aloud she said, "We came after friends of ours. Now we have cause to think they have met with catastrophe, or captivity."

Kyntha said nothing, and Jaelle dug into a pocket and pulled out Rafaelle's letter, which had started them on their travels.

"I do not know if it is the custom in your country for women to read and write—"

"I can read, yes," said Kyntha, stretching out her hand for the letter. She read it slowly and carefully, her lips moving as if it were in some other language.

Then she said, "What do you want of me? If it is the Sisterhood of the Wise that your friend seeks, I think you know she failed before she started."

"Can you help us rescue her?" Jaelle asked.

"No." It was flat, final, left no room for discussion or argument, and had more impact than a dozen protestations or excuses.

"Nevertheless, for the sake of our friendship, I must attempt it," said Jaelle.

"If you must, you must. But beware of being dragged into the causes which she set in motion. And if you save her from the effects of her own folly, what then? Will you safeguard her all her life lest she fall again into error?"

Vanessa began, "If she has trespassed unwittingly on your sacred Sisterhood, would you punish her for ignorance?"

"Does the snow punish the child who strays into it without cloak or hood or boots? Is the child less frozen for that?"

That was, Magda thought, another conversation-stopper. At last Jaelle asked, "Can you help us find the way to the City where the Sisterhood dwells?"

Kyntha said, even more deliberately:

"If I knew the way to that place, I should be sworn

never to tell. I think you know this much. Why then do you ask?''

"Because I know that there are some who have come and gone," Jaelle said, "and why should I look for a key to a strange lock when, perhaps, knocking politely on the door will gain me entrance?"

Kyntha smiled fleetingly for the first time.

"Some have gained entrance there. It is not for me to say you would not be welcomed. Who told you of that place?"

"My foster-mother, for one," Jaelle said. "Though I never thought I would seek it. But now it seems to me that the time has come."

"And your companions? Do you speak for them?"

Jaelle opened her mouth, then shut it again. Finally she said, "No. I will let them speak for themselves."

"Good." Kyntha looked at each of them in turn, but there was a perceptible silence. At last Cholayna said, "I have no wish to trespass upon your City. My interest is in one of the young women mentioned in the letter."

"Is she your daughter or your lover? Or is she a child that you seek to keep her from the consequences of her own actions, daughter of Chandria?" Magda was surprised that Kyntha, after the hasty mass introductions, remembered Cholayna's name.

"None of those. But she was my student; I trained her. I accept responsibility for her failure."

"Arrogance," Kyntha said. "She is a grown woman. The choice to fail was her own, and she is entitled to bear her own mistakes."

Vanessa interrupted in an argumentative tone, "If it is forbidden to help a friend in your city, I hope I may never go there. Dare you tell us that it is forbidden, or unlawful by your rules, to help a friend?"

Kyntha's eyes met Vanessa's for a long moment.

Then she said in the same serious manner, "Your motives are good. So with the child who wanted to help the tigercat move her kits to a warm and cozy den in his own bed. You do not know what you are doing, and you will not be spared because your motives were admirable."

Her eyes moved on to Camilla. "Do you seek the City, or are you here only from an ill-conceived desire to share the fate of your friends?"

"If you scoff at friendship, or even at love," Camilla retorted, "then I care not what you think of me. My reasons for seeking that city are my own, and you have not yet convinced me that I should entrust them to you. What evidence have I that the key is in your hands?"

"Good," Kyntha remarked. "There are many who know the way to that place, but some of those who offer to show you the way do not know it as well as they think they do. It is not impossible that permission would be granted for you, and perhaps for this one—" she indicated Jaelle with a faint movement of her head. "I don't know. If it is ordained that you shall be allowed to seek that end to your journey, then you may be guided or even helped. But many have been offered help and turned back, and some who persevered could not finish the journey, for one reason or another. You must be wise and wary." She turned to Magda and said, "And you?"

"Twice I have encountered the Sisterhood, or so I believe," Magda said. Kyntha's eyes on her were oddly compelling; Magda felt it would be unthinkable to lie before those eyes. "Once they saved my life and the life of my freemate. One of these women who in your words, *trespassed*, has also, in great crisis and at the point of death, encountered these same Sisterhood. Therefore I believed that I—and perhaps she too—had been summoned. How do you know that we have *not* been summoned, but assume immediately that either of us has chosen to trespass?

"Because I read her companion's letter," Kyntha replied. "Even if she had been summoned, anyone who could concur in the motives of that letter would never find the place they sought. It would be for her, at that particular time, and in that particular company, an act of trespass. As for you, I have no way of knowing whether you have in fact been summoned, or whether you suffer from a delusion. If you have in truth been summoned, help will be forthcoming. And you will be left in no doubt."

Silence. At last Jaelle said, "May I ask you a question?"

"Or a dozen. I cannot promise to answer, though. I was not sent to you for that, and I am not learned or wise."

"Are you a member of that Sisterhood?"

"If I should claim to be so, how would you know I told you the truth? Anyone might make such a claim."

Camilla interrupted, "There are those among us with *laran*. Enough, at any rate, to know a liar from a sooth-teller." Her voice was hard, but Kyntha only smiled. Magda got the definite impression that she liked Camilla.

"Another question," Jaelle said. "We met with—" She hesitated, and Magda guessed she remembered they were not to speak Aquilara's name. "With one who presumed to try and give us commands in the name of the Goddess. Tell me, was she one of your Sisterhood?"

"Why do you question your own instincts, Shaya n'ha Melora? Will you let me counsel you a little, as much as I may?"

"Certainly," said Jaelle.

"Then this is what I advise you. Be silent. Speak to no one of your objective, and never, thrice never, name the evil you distrust. It would be simpler for your little daughter to cross Ravensmark pass in her silken indoor slippers and armed only with a wooden spoon against the banshee, than for you to enter into that place in the wrong company. And there are some who, if you are summoned, will attempt to stop you out of jealousy, or from the sheer love of mischief-making. If help is sent to you, trust your instincts." She bowed, somehow including all of them in the gesture.

"I wish you good fortune, whether you believe it or not," she said, and without any more fuss or any kind of leavetaking, went away.

"Well," said Cholayna, when it was obvious that she would not return, "what are we to make of *that?*"

"I've no idea," Jaelle said. "But I wouldn't count on hospitality from these people much longer. We've had our warning, we're rested and well again, now it's up to us to decide whether we are going on, or back."

"I am not going back," said Camilla. "I gather from what she said that the city we seek is near, and as for a city of Avarra's Sisterhood, it would be safer to assume it is nearer Avarra's holy house, than farther. She said nothing of sending us back."

"And I think perhaps she was sent to determine how determined we are," said Jaelle. "She certainly did her best to discourage us."

"That wasn't the idea I got at all," Magda protested. She thought Kyntha had been admirably straightforward. "However, if she's gone to make some sort of report to her superiors, maybe we ought to wait until the report's gone through and the verdict delivered. She said help might be forthcoming, even guides."

"I gather we all agree on one thing, that she was sent, and that she is not a member of—the *other* crew," Vanessa said. "She acted, though, as if there was no question of letting me, or Cholayna, near the place. Just you two and maybe Magda." She looked, mildly startled, at Magda. "I noticed she treated you as if you were one of the Darkovans yourself."

Magda felt she should have noticed that herself. *Yes surely, she had a right to be considered among the Darkovans.* But did she really, or was that merely a flattering assumption? And why was she worrying about this, questioning her own motives, at this late date? She had surely gone too far to turn back now.

"I think we should leave as soon as we can, then," said Jaelle.

"I think we should wait to see if the help they hinted at is offered," Magda demurred.

"I don't agree," said Camilla, "and do you know the reason why? She said she could give us no help in rescuing Lexie and Rafaella. She treated Cholayna and Vanessa as if they were slightly unwelcome intruders, in spite of the kindness and hospitality they had been offered. My guess is this: if we wait for their help, it will come at the price of sending you two—" she nodded at the two Terrans, "back at once, and on abandoning all hope of rescuing Rafaella. I'm not ready to do that."

"Nor I," said Magda. "I think we should pack at once, and go as soon as we possibly can." She added, diffidently, "None of us has been ready to try this, but I believe it's our last resort; I am willing to try to follow Lexie and Rafaella with *laran*, no matter in whose hands they may now be. You, Jaelle?"

"I would be afraid of picking up—that *other*," Jaelle said, troubled, but Camilla shook her head.

"If they're in *her* hands, as I have begun to suspect, we have no choice. I see Lexie and Rafaella, and I see—*her*. Shaya, is this what happens when you call it *laran*?"

But there was no leisure to answer the question. First a couple of the attendants came in, scurrying. Then the old woman who had tended Cholayna walked in with kindly assurance, and took her seat among them.

And behind her a small sturdy woman at whom they blinked for a moment, disbelieving. If the Terran Legate himself had walked in, Magda could not have felt more amazement, more disruption of everything she had expected.

"Well, this looks like a meeting of the Hellers branch of the Bridge Society," the woman said. "Isn't anyone even going to wish me good day?"

But they were all too astonished to speak. It was Cholayna, at last, who croaked, in a voice still hoarse and rasping, "I should have known. Hello, Marisela."

CHAPTER TWENTY-FIVE

"Marisela! How did you get here?" demanded Jaelle.

"Same way you did; riding when I could, walking when I couldn't, climbing when I had to," Marisela said. "Of course, since I knew where I was going, I took the straight road as far as Nevarsin.

"You might have told us," Camilla said.

"Yes," said Marisela dryly, "I could have held your hand every step of the way. Don't be a fool, Camilla. What I said to Margali is still true, I was not and am not free to discuss the affairs of the Sisterhood with outsiders, and that includes their abode, and the necessary search, unaided, to reach them."

"If they demand this much effort to reach them," Camilla asked, "how do we know it is worth this kind of suffering?"

"You don't. No one forced you to come. Be very clear about that, Camilla. At any moment you could have turned back to safety and to known rewards and everything you have claimed for yourself from life. There is no reason to renounce any of it, and for you, less reason than most. Yet I notice that none of you chose to turn back."

"This is all beside the point," Vanessa said. "Whatever psychic search you are talking about, Camilla, our interest is only in finding Lexie and Rafaella."

But it was Marisela who answered.

"Are you very sure of that, Vanessa? I notice you have not turned back, either. Have you gained nothing from this trip yourself? Is your search entirely unselfish?"

"I wish you'd stop talking in riddles," Vanessa complained. "What's that got to do with it?"

"Everything," said Marisela, "think carefully, now. Because on your answer may depend whether or not you are allowed to go on. Friendship may carry you far, and please don't think I am deriding the good instinct to help your friends. But in the long run, Vanessa ryn Erin—" Magda was startled and shocked that she used, not the Guild-house name by which Vanessa was known there, and in the Bridge Society, but Vanessa's Terran, legal name—"In the long run, nothing matters but your own motives for this quest. Have you gained nothing?"

"Is that wrong?" Vanessa asked aggressively.

Marisela hesitated and looked for a moment at the old priestess in her bundled rags, seated impassively on the stone dais. The old woman raised her eyes and looked sharply at Vanessa. For a moment Magda expected that she would attack, with those quick harsh words she could use and demolish Vanessa with some sharp answer. But the ancient's voice was surprisingly gentle.

"She does not question thee about right or wrong, little sister. Thee seeks right, us knows that, or thee would be outside in the storm, whatever thy need; shelter is not offered here to those who actively seek to harm their fellow beings. Thy sister asks thee, of many good things, has thee found something which is thy own and to thy liking? Speak sooth now and fear nothing."

"I can't believe that you are asking me this," Vanessa said impatiently. "Yes, one of the reasons I came on this trip was because I wanted to see these mountains, wanted a chance to climb some of them, and I knew I'd never get the chance otherwise, and I was prepared to put up with a lot for that chance. That doesn't mean I wasn't sincere about helping to find Lexie and Rafaella.''

''I didn't know you were so fond of her,'' Marisela observed.

''*Fond* has nothing to do with it,'' Vanessa said angrily. ''She's not my lover or my bosom friend or confidante, I'm not—well, I know it's the custom here and there's nothing wrong with it, but I'm not *interested* in women as lovers. But we were in training school together, and she's in trouble. She needs friends, and she doesn't have many. I suppose if I was in trouble she'd give me a hand. Or what else is all your talk about sisterhood—and I don't mean all this stuff about secret Sisterhoods and societies, either—what's it supposed to mean, if I can't try to help out a friend? And Rafaella, well, she's a mountaineer. I *respect* her. Can't you understand that kind of thing?''

The old woman was smiling, but Vanessa took no notice of her. Marisela nodded to Vanessa, almost a formal gesture of recognition.

She said, ''Rafaella and I were housebound together in Thendara Guild-house; it seems a long time ago. I am worried about her myself; she was one of the reasons I came so far. She has a right to her own search, even if what she seeks is riches, but I was afraid she was getting into deep waters where she could not swim, thinking only that she was doing legitimate business. I knew Jaelle was concerned about her, and if it was only a question of bad weather and a rough trail, Jaelle, with you to help her, could have been left to the search. But there were other things involved and I hoped to keep her from getting into them without a clear idea of what she might be facing." She sighed heavily. "So, you have not caught up with her?"

"As you can see, we have not," Camilla said dryly. "As if you did not know, being a *leronis* . . ."

"I'm no more omniscient than you are, Camilla. Until I actually came here, I still hoped. But if she was not safe *here* during that great storm, there are two possibilities; either she is safe *somewhere else* . . ." she spoke the words with a careful intonation and a hesitant glance at the old woman, and Magda knew suddenly that she was speaking of Acquilara and her followers, "or she is dead. For there was no other shelter and nothing could have lived unsheltered in these hills. I can't bear to think they could be in the hands of—" She blinked angrily, and Magda noticed she was trying hard to stifle uncontrollable tears.

The old woman bent toward her and said soothingly, touching Marisela's hand, "Thee may hope she is safe dead, granddaughter."

Cholayna, who had been following all this with close, concentrated attention—Magda, who had been through the same kind of training, knew what effort it would take her to follow this conversation in the language they were using, though Cholayna had had the best and most effective language training in the whole of the Empire— spoke up for the first time.

"Marisela, I'm like Vanessa, I can't believe I'm hearing this. Are these people so jealous that they'd really hope Lexie and Rafaella are *dead*, rather than involved with some religious heresy? I've heard of religious bigotry, but this beats anything I ever heard of! I'm not ungrateful to these people. They saved my life, saved Vanessa from being lamed for life—they saved us all. But I still think that's *terrible!*"

It was the old woman who spoke, slowly, as if—she

were trying to make Cholayna understand across an insurmountable barrier.

"Thee is ignorant. This old one canna' give thee a lifetime wisdom in a few minutes on this floor. But if thee canna' imagine worse than simple dyin' thee is worse than ignorant. Are there na' things thee would die rather than do? Those whose names we would not speak—" she stopped, frowned, shook her head in frustration almost tangible.

"How to say to thee? Would thee rather die, or torture a helpless child? Would thee rather die, or betray thy innermost honor? It is their joy, those ones, to see others do that which they thought they would rather die than do, out of their weak fear of dyin' because they know nothing an' believe less about death." Her head shook with wrath. "An', an', to speak their name is to invite them into thy mind. Think this old one hates thee, that she takes that risk for thee and thy ignorance, sister, to try an' teach thee a crumb's worth of wisdom."

Magda looked at Jaelle, and for one blazing instant, whether it was *laran* or something deeper, it all came together in her mind. It was all one with what Jaelle had said the night before: *We're all going to die anyway*.

Magda was remembering dreadful things done, in the history of the human race, by men to their fellow men—and women—because they so feared death: guards who had forced their fellow creatures to death in concentration camps; the immense slaughter of war where the killer justified himself by fear of being killed in turn; infinite terrible betrayals out of that most ignoble fear— *I'll do anything, anything, I don't want to die . . .* It was bad enough to do these evils because in some demented way you thought they were good, like the religious monsters who burned, hanged or slaughtered others to save their souls. But what possible justifica-

tion could there be for anyone who did these things
because the alternative was personal death? In a single
blazing moment, Magda felt a fierce joy. It suffused her
with a flush, an almost physical rush of total awareness,
knowing how strong was life and how little death had to
do with it.

In a great rush she felt totally involved and caught up
in it; aware of her intense love for Jaelle, *of course, this
was why I risked my life for her;* her wholly different
love for Camilla. Love reached out for no reason even
to encompass that ridiculous old woman, *she doesn't
even know Cholayna and she is risking what she thinks
of as a very real spiritual death for her, she fears she's
inviting Aquilara and her crew into her very head to
play games with her, and because she loves us. . . .*

*They could only kill me, and that wouldn't matter.
Dying hurts, but death won't.*

And then she snapped out of it, astonished at her own
thoughts. There was no question—nobody had asked
her to die for anything! *What's wrong with me? I don't
want to die any more than anyone else, why am I
indulging myself in heroics?*

And then she wondered if it had all been imagination;
for Cholayna was saying, with polite strained patience,
that she didn't really think the question had any application here.

"No one has offered me that choice. And with all
respect, I find it hard to believe that these rival
sisterhoods, or whatever they are, will behave like some
old legendary dictator or brainwashing expert and offer
them a choice between death or dishonor. How absurdly
melodramatic!" Then Cholayna bent toward the old
woman, very serious.

"Whenever I hear anyone say there are things more
important than life or death, I find myself wondering

whose life they are planning to risk. I find it is seldom their own.''

The old woman's toothless smile was gentle, almost despairing.

"Thee means well, but thee is ignorant, daughter of Chandria. 'Varra grant thee lives long enough that thee may one day learn wisdom to match thy good strength and will.''

Marisela stood up, as if gathering up the scattered threads of her discourse.

"It's time to go, while the weather holds, and the only way to go is to get going. Are you ready to leave?''

Jaelle said quietly, "I told you, Magda. We were warned to be ready.''

Camilla thrust her hands into the pocket of her tunic, and demanded, "Go where?''

"To the place you have been seeking. Where else?''

"To the City of—''

"Hush,'' Marisela said quickly, "don't speak it aloud. No. I am serious. Word and thought have power.''

"Oh, in the name of the Goddess, or of all Zandru's demons, Marisela, spare me your mystical rubbish!''

"Do you dare to tell me that? You know better, however you have tried to barricade it, *Elorie Hastur*.''

Camilla actually laid her hand on her knife.

"Damn you, my name is *Camilla n'ha Kyria*—''

Marisela stared her down.

"And still you say names have no power, Camilla?''

Camilla folded herself abruptly into a seat, her voice gone.

Magda began matter-of-factly to gather their possessions. The enforced stay of days in that room had made it a gypsy-camp clutter, though they had tried to keep what order they could. The old woman rose stiffly; Marisela stooped to assist her. Camilla strode toward her.

"Grandmother of many mysteries! Is a question permitted the ignorant?"

"How else shall they be instructed?" asked the old woman mildly.

"How did you know—" she stopped and swallowed and finally said, "all that?"

"To those who see beyond surfaces, little daughter—" her voice was infinitely gentle, "it is written in thine every scar, every line of thy face. In the energies which surround thy body it can read as clearly as a hunter of the wild chervine reads the poor of his game. Fear not; thy friend—" she nodded at Marisela, "broke not thy confidence. This one swears it."

"She couldn't," said Camilla brusquely. "She didn't have it." She stared quizzically at Marisela, and Magda could almost hear the words: *did she read me too, does she know everything about me?*

Then she asked, her voice abrupt and harsh, but speaking clearly in the mountain dialect the old woman spoke, "Thee makes it thy task to search out old names and buried pasts. May I then ask thine own, Mother?"

The toothless smile was serene.

"This one has no name. It was forgotten in another life. When thee has reason to know, *chiya*, thee will read it clear as I read thine. Avarra bless thy long road, little one. Few of thy sisters have had such trials. How shall the fruit grow unless the blossoms are pruned from the tree?"

. She smiled benevolently, and closed her eyes as if falling into the sudden light sleep of senility. Marisela looked at Camilla almost in awe, but didn't speak.

"How soon can we get out of here? It's a fine day; let's take advantage of it."

In a surprisingly short time they were ready to leave. The sky was cloudless, but the wind blew across the heights as they approached the cliff. They went in two shifts, and Magda, edging unobtrusively back to wait for the second, watched with horror as the basket jerked and wobbled and bumped against the cliffs. The rope looked too small to hold it, though it was a mighty cable of twisted fibers almost three fingers thick. She turned away her eyes, knowing if she did not she would never have the courage to get into the contraption.

Jaelle, Cholayna and Camilla, with Marisela, had gone in the first load. As the basket came bumping back to where she stood with Vanessa and the old blind woman Rakhaila, Magda recoiled; coming up in the dark was one thing, but in broad daylight, she could not, she *could not* force herself to step into it.

Rakhaila felt her cringe, and guffawed.

"Haw! Haw! Ye rather climb down cliff, missy? I be old an' blind, an' I do so every livin' day. Steps be right yonder." She gave Magda a push toward the edge, and Magda cried out and fell to her knees, grabbing for safety; in another moment she might have stumbled over that terrifying edge.

Vanessa caught her arm. She whispered, "It's perfectly strong, really. There's nothing to be afraid of, Magda, they've evidently been going up and coming down here for centuries and it's never failed them yet." She steadied Magda's arm as she managed, carefully turning her eyes away from the narrow dizzying gap between basket and ground far below, to step over the edge, and sink in, her eyes on the floor of the basket, strewn with bits of straw and grain.

Where do they get their food and grain up here? Does it all have to be hauled up in this one basket? she asked herself, knowing that it was just a way to keep herself from being afraid. And then she was sourly amused at herself.

All my fine theories about not being afraid of death, and here I am almost wetting my breeches with fright because of a primitive elevator that's probably just as safe as the ones in the Terran HQ!

Acrophobia, she reminded herself, was, by definition, not a *rational* fear. But surely it hadn't been nearly as bad as this when she first crossed Scaravel with Jaelle seven, no, eight years ago. And she remembered positively enjoying her first trip to Nevarsin with Peter when they had both been in their twenties.

With unbelievable relief she felt the basket touch ground and scrambled out.

"You're going with us, Marisela?"

"Of course, my dear. But I don't know all the ins and outs of the trail; Rakhaila will guide us. The horses will have to stay here. We'll take one pack animal and leave everything else for the return journey."

Wondering vaguely how a blind woman could guide them on a confusing trail which even Marisela could not find, Magda volunteered to lead the pack chervine for the first stretch. Down here the wind was not the jet stream of the heights, but still blew so strongly that old Rakhaila's matted hair blew out behind her magnificently as she set off in the teeth of the gale.

The snow was slushy under foot, and the wind cut hard; but Magda, wrapping her woolly scarf over her face, was grateful that it was not freezing. Vanessa, she noticed, was still limping a little. She followed Rakhaila close; behind her came Jaelle, then Camilla with Cholayna at her side; at least at the start, Cholayna set off fresh and strong and rested, and her breathing was good. Perhaps she had managed to acclimate to the altitude by now. They would not have let her go, she told herself, if there had been any sign of continuing pneumonia.

They set off along a trail which led across the knife-edge of a ridge, with a long drop to either side. Magda, leading the chervine behind Cholayna and Camilla, looked to the right, where the slope was gradual and gentle, and did not make her dizzy. The trail was just wide enough for one, but looked quite well-traveled; where the snow had melted Magda could see that it had been beaten down hard as if by generations of feet.

Behind Magda and the chervine was Marisela bringing up the rear. The fierce wind prevented much talk, and they went on at a smart pace.

An hour on the trail; part of another. The five days of rest had done Magda good; her heart no longer beat furiously with the altitude. Lower down she could see the tops of trees. A good place for banshees, she thought dispassionately, looking out over the icy wastes below her, on either side of the ridge, but even they would have starved to death centuries ago.

Rakhaila flung up her arm with a long shrill cry and they came to a halt.

"Rest ye here; eat if ye ha' need." Rakhaila herself, thought Magda, looked as if she had been battered into stoicism by all the winds of a hundred years; as they got out the camp stove and brewed tea she hunkered by the trail, immobile, looking like a random bunch of rags, and when Camilla offered her a mug of the brew she shook her head contemptuously.

Camilla muttered, "Now *there's* an Amazon who makes us all look like puppies!" She gnawed on a half-frozen meat bar.

Cholayna had one of the cakes made from ground-up

nuts and fruit stuck together with honey; she munched at the stuff with determination.

Magda heard her ask Camilla: "Do you really think they are dead?"

"Marisela isn't given to exaggeration and I've never known her to lie. If she says they're probably dead, she means it. Or else, as she said, they're in the hands of Acquilara, or whoever else is hanging around."

"And we're still looking for this, whatever it is, this city of sorceresses? I think we ought to try and trace where the *others* have gone, try to find out where Acquilara could have taken them. If they're being held for ransom, we can pay it. And if they want to fight, well, I'll try that too."

Rakhaila's old filmed eyes turned to Cholayna. She said, "Ha' ye a care what ye ask, sister; the goddess may gi' it to ye."

"I'll take that chance, if you will guide me there," said Cholayna quietly. "Marisela can take these others on to the City, or wherever they prefer to go. *Will* you guide me to whatever place Marisela believes our friends are being held?"

Rakhaila only gave a contemptuous, "Haw!" and turned away.

Jaelle and Camilla were sitting on their packs, eating meat bars. Magda heard them talking about Kyntha.

"She said, 'Never name the evil you fear.' Does that mean such things as weather? Is it wrong to discuss the storm that's coming?" Jaelle asked.

"Wrong? Of course not. Wise? Only if you can do something to avoid it. Certainly it is sensible to discuss precautions you can take. Apart from that, it only creates a self-fulfilling fear of something that can't be helped. Don't talk of how terrible the storm might be; think of what you can do to ride it out undamaged."

"Then why did she tell us not to talk about Acquilara or even mention her name?"

Marisela smiled. Magda noticed it was the same cheerful, dimpled smile she used when she was instructing the young Renunciates in the Guild-house.

"I have spent too much of my life as a teacher," she remarked, "I must be getting old; I am glad that there are wiser heads than mine to instruct you two. In brief, naming them could attract their attention; thoughts, as we know, have power."

"But who *are* they, Marisela? I can just manage to believe in one benevolent Sisterhood demonstrating some interest in the affairs of women—"

"Of humankind, Camilla. Our sisters and our brothers as well."

"But the idea that there is a rival organization dedicated to doing harm to humanity strains my belief!"

Marisela looked troubled. She said, "This is not the wisest place to discuss their doings. Let me say only that—Jaelle, you must have heard this among the Terrans as I heard it when I was in nurse's training there— *for every action there is an equal and opposite reaction.*"

"So they are a reaction to the good sorceresses, and do evil?"

"Not that simple. I can only say that they care not enough to do evil to humankind; they want what they want, that is all. They want power."

"Is that a bad thing?" Jaelle argued. "You are always telling the young girls, in training session, that women have a right to claim power—"

"Power over *themselves*, my dear! That kind of power is in accord with the Sisterhood. We have only one aim; that in the fullness of time, everyone who comes to this world shall become everything that he or she can be or do or accomplish. We do not fall into the error of thinking that if only people would do this or thus, the world would thereby be made perfect. Perfection is for individuals, one at a time, we do not determine the way they choose to live. Nevertheless, when the Sisterhood sees long-term trends and dangers, they nurture— how shall I put it—tendencies which will break these patterns and give people a chance to live another way." She smiled gently at Camilla and said, "I do not know; perhaps it was a part of the pattern that you should not have grown up to be the powerful Keeper you were so obviously born to be."

"Keeper? I?" Camilla snorted indignantly. "Even had I grown to womanhood in my father's house—my *real* father, that is, and after this I should be a fool if I did not suspect who he was . . ."

"Right. Can you imagine yourself in the sorceress Leonie's position?"

"I would rather—" Camilla began, drew a long breath, and said on a note of surprise, as if she had just this moment thought of it, "I would rather have wandered the roads all my life as a bandit's sword-mate!"

"Exactly," said Marisela, "but had you been reared in the silks and privileges of the royal house of Hastur, I doubt you would have felt that way, but would willingly have followed Leonie into Arilinn. Ah, Camilla, Camilla love, don't fall into the error of thinking this was your destiny, ordained in stone before you were born. But if some God or well-meaning saint had put for his hand to save you from your fate, where would you be today?"

Of course, Magda thought. It was the totality of her life that had made Camilla what she was.

Camilla asked, "Did you know? Before this?"

"I knew of you, till this very day only what you chose to tell me, Camilla, and what once I read in your mind and heart when you were—broadcasting; believe me, I have never invaded your privacy. What you *were* is of no interest to me."

Jaelle said aggressively, "I suppose now you will say that the Sisterhood chose to save my life and Magda's for some reason—"

"I am not privy to all their reasons! Shaya, child, I am only one who serves them, one of many messengers. I am free to guess, no more. Perhaps they felt some long-term purpose would be served that the daughter of Aillard should bear a child lest her *laran* be lost to the world forever. Perhaps they wished some psychic gift of the Terrans to be strengthened in the Forbidden Tower and thus brought Magda there after she had decided she wished for a child, so her little Shaya would be reared among those who would foster her *laran*. Perhaps some one of them succumbed, as I do even when I know it might be better not, to the simple wish to save a life. Who can tell? They too are only human, and make mistakes, though they can see further than we do. But no one is perfect. Perfectable, maybe, in the fullness of time. Not perfect."

"Yet after they went to all the trouble of saving Lexie's life they let her fall into the hands of—Acquilara? I'm sorry, Marisela, I just can't believe that."

"I never asked you to believe anything," said Marisela, suddenly indifferent, and rose to her feet. "Except that just now, I believe Rakhaila wants us to move on, and my legs are cramped from sitting down. Can I help you pack the kettle?"

As they went on Magda had plenty to think about. If what they said about *laran* in those of Terran blood was true, she thought, I am surprised that I was not somehow pushed into having Andrew's child; heaven knows, he has about the strongest *laran* of any Terran I have ever known. But evidently they allow total free will. They left me to destiny. And I have heard that the Syrtis are an old Hastur sect; so Shaya is kinswoman to Camilla by blood as wlll as to Jaelle by the laws of a freemate's oath.

That was reassuring. *If anything happens to me, Shaya will have kinfolk who will care for her. She and Cleindori are sisters indeed.*

Jaelle said, "I'll take the chervine now for a bit, *breda*," and Magda relinquished the rein, moving forward to walk at Marisela's side. The path was leading upward now, edging alongside a mountain trail with long switchbacks, hugging a stone cliff from which, sometimes, loose rocks bounced downward; but the trail at this point was covered with an overhang and Rakhaila strode confidently along it as if she could see every step of her way.

"Want to walk on the inside?" Marisela asked. "As I remember, heights bother you."

"A little," Magda said, and accepted, and they strode along side by side for a time, without talking. At last Magda asked:

"Marisela, these—I won't name them; you know who I mean—" the picture of Acquilara was in her mind, in the curious bluish glow of her nightmare, "May I ask just one thing? Why would anyone—want to go that way? Are they the ones who, maybe, tried to—to look for the *real* Sisterhood and failed? And this was easier?"

"Oh, no, my dear. It takes much, *much* more strength and power to do evil than to do good, you see."

"Why is that? I heard that evil was just being weak, taking the path of least resistance—"

"Goodness, no. That's just being weak, fearful, selfish . . . in a word, human, imperfect. If being weak

were a crime we'd all stand before the judges. That's
excusable. Terrible sometimes, but certainly excusable.
The thing is, people who are good, or are *trying* to do
good the best way they can, they're working with nature,
see? To work up the power to do positive evil, you have
to go *against* nature, and that's much, *much* harder.
There are resistances, and you have to work up momen-
tum against the whole flow of nature."

This was a new idea to Magda, that good was simply
fulfilling nature's plan and evil was anything which
worked against it. She was sure she did not entirely
understand it, for Marisela was a midwife and a nurse
and, taken to extremes, this could be interpreted as a
prohibition against saving lives, which Marisela had
spent her whole life doing. She decided she would have
to talk further about it some time with her friend. She
was never to have the chance.

They were taking a long dip now, along the steep
trail, into a long valley below the timberline. Before
they dipped into the trees, Marisela called softly to
Rakhaila to halt a moment, and pointed upward. Across
the valley was a long line of steep ice cliffs, shining in
the crimson brilliance of the sun.

"The Wall Around the World," she said.

They drew together, watching, stunned. Vanessa drew
a long, overawed breath. But all she could find to say
was, "They look—bigger than they do from a plane in
M-and-Ex."

That was an understatement. They seemed to go on
forever, far past sight. Magda thought, God, we're not
going over *that*, not on foot, are we?

Rakhaila gestured impatiently and set off at a swinging pace that took her out of sight among the trees.
Camilla and Jaelle followed, but Cholayna dropped back
beside Magda and Vanessa.

"I shall be glad to be going downhill," she said.

"Tired?"

"Not as much as I thought I should be." Cholayna smiled at her. "In a way I am more glad than ever that I came, if I could only stop worrying about Lexie."

"This must have been what she saw," said Vanessa. "It was worth it, just to see this. And we're going across it!" She made a small sound of incredulous delight.

"And in line of duty too," Cholayna said dryly. "Who was talking about rewards and wangling a working holiday, Vanessa?"

It was a pleasure Magda could gladly have dispensed with, but she would not spoil Vanessa's enjoyment. They were between the trees now, some growing at crazy angles on the slope below, others hanging thickly over the trail, darkening the bright sunlight; but it gave some shelter, too, from the wind. Rakhaila, with Camilla and Jaelle, were out of sight. Marisela turned back to gesture toward the three Terrans to hurry, and for a moment her face, smiling gaily, was frozen for Magda in sudden horror and then blotted out in a shower of blood. Her eyes were still staring; in a split second of shock Magda remembered reading somewhere that the eyes of a corpse could see for some twenty seconds after death.

Then somewhere Acquilara's gloating laugh echoed in her ears and she was dragged backward and down without a chance to struggle. She heard Cholayna's smothered gasp, the only sound she could hear—Marisela had died without a chance to scream.

I had no chance either, she thought, insanely aggrieved, before the world became dark and silent.

CHAPTER TWENTY-SIX

The first thing she remembered was, *Dying hurts, but death won't.* But it did, she thought. Her arms and back felt battered, and she was sure at least one leg had been skinned.

I thought, if I died, I'd find myself in the Overworld. Cleindori said she was there before she was born. Or was that a child's dream?

Too bad. It was a beautiful idea. She was sure now that the reality would be less pleasant. But where was Marisela? If they had been killed together, shouldn't they be together now?

After a long time there began to be an orange glow, and from the distance she heard a voice.

"You bungled it, as usual. I especially wanted the other one alive, the midwife."

Acquilara's voice. *Of course. What else?*

"Shall we kill this one now, then?"

"No. I can find a use for her."

After a measurable interval Magda thought, *but they're talking about me.*

The next thought came also after a perceptible time. *If they are considering killing me, then, obviously, I'm not dead.*

And then she did not remember anything more for a long time.

*   *   *

When she woke again she was afraid she was blind. Darkness surrounded her, and silence except for a far-away dripping of water. Magda listened carefully, and after a time she heard soft raspy breathing. There was someone else beside her, sleeping. *Sleeping,* she thought indignantly, when Marisela has been killed, when I have been captured and beaten. How can they sleep? Then she remembered she had been sleeping or unconscious herself for a considerable time. Maybe she wasn't blind. Maybe it was dark where she was, she and the other sleeper. She didn't know . . . her eyes were closed.

As soon as that thought occurred to her, she opened her eyes.

She was lying in a cave. Above her great pale stalactites stabbed down from the roof, shadowing each other for as far as she could see, like pillars of some great Temple. In the distance there was a glow of fire flickering and throwing strange images and shadows.

She was covered with a thick fur blanket, but not tied up, as far as she could tell. That made sense. Who could run away, where could anyone go in this climate? She turned over; by the dim flickering light she could make out two blanket-wrapped forms sleeping beside her on the floor. Captors? Or fellow captives? There was not really enough light to recognize anyone. She felt at her waist and found that her dagger was gone.

"Shaya?" she whispered, and one of the motionless bundles stirred.

"Who is it? Is there someone else here?"

"Vanessa, it's Magda," she whispered. "Did they get all of us?"

"They have Cholayna. She hasn't stirred; I think they may have hit her too hard." Magda could tell that

Vanessa had been crying. "I can't hear her breathing. Oh, Magda, they killed Marisela!"

"I know. I saw." Magda's throat was tight. Marisela had been her friend since almost the very first day in Thendara Guild-house; they had worked together to found the Bridge Society. She could not believe the suddenness with which that innocent life had been snuffed out.

Why, why?

She said they were evil. She was right. I cannot remember that Marisela ever harmed anyone, or so much as spoke an unkind word; not in my hearing, anyhow.

And now they might have killed Cholayna as well. She crawled closer to Vanessa. "Are you hurt, *breda*?" She wondered why she had never called Vanessa by this simple sisterly word before this.

"I'm—not sure. Not badly, I think, but there's a lump on my head. They must have hit me just hard enough to put me out. As far as I can tell most of my reflexes are intact. Everything works when I wiggle it."

Magda's eyes stung. How practical, and how like Vanessa. "Are any of the others here?"

"If they are, I can't see them. They could—" again Vanessa's voice quavered and Magda knew she was crying again, "they could all be dead, except us. If they'd kill Marisela—"

Magda hugged her gently in the dark. "Don't cry, *breda*. It's terrible, *they're* terrible, but we can't do her any good now with crying. Let's just make sure they don't have a chance to do any more killing. Did they take your knife?"

Vanessa managed to stop crying. *She can cry for Marisela*, Magda thought. *I can't. Yet I loved her*. She knew she had not yet really begun to feel the loss. And she faced the knowledge that Jaelle and Camilla might be dead as well. All the more reason to care for Vanessa, and Cholayna if she was still alive. She repeated softly, "Did they take your knife? They took mine."

"They have the knife I was wearing in my belt. I have a little one in my coat pocket and as far as I know they haven't got that one, not yet,"

"Look and see," Magda whispered back urgently, "and I'll see if Cholayna is—is breathing."

Vanessa began groggily searching her pockets, while Magda crept toward the inert bundle that was Cholayna Ares.

"Cholayna!" She touched the woman's hand warily. It was icy cold. The chill of a corpse? Then it occurred to Magda that it was very cold in the cave—though not nearly as cold as outside in the wind—and her own hands were nearly freezing. She fumbled to open Cholayna's coat, thrust her hand inside and felt warmth, living warmth. She bent her head close, and could hear, very faintly, the sound of breathing.

Perhaps asleep, perhaps unconscious but Cholayna was alive. She relayed this information to Vanessa in a whisper.

"Oh, thank God," Vanessa whispered, and Magda feared that she would begin to cry again.

She said hastily, "We can't do anything until we know what kind of shape she's in. I'll try to wake her."

With a possible head injury she did not dare shake her. She murmured her name repeatedly, stroked her face, chafed the icy hands between her own, and finally Cholayna stirred a little, with a painful catch of breath. She opened her eyes and stared straight at Magda without recognition.

"Let go of me—! You murdering devils—" It was obvious that Cholayna was trying to scream at the top of her voice; but the scream was no more than a pitiful whisper. It was equally obvious to Magda that if she did manage to scream, she would alert their captors, who could not be far off. She hugged Cholayna in her arms, trying to restrain the woman's struggles, saying softly and insistently, "It's all right, Cholayna. Be quiet, be quiet, I'm here with you, Vanessa's here, we won't let anyone hurt you." She repeated this over and over until at last Cholayna stopped fighting her and recognition came into her eyes

"Magda?" She blinked, put her hand to her head. "What's happened? Where are we?"

"Somewhere in a cave," Magda answered in a whisper, "and I think Acquilara and her crew have us."

Vanessa crept close to them in the dark. "I have my little knife. Are you all right, Cholayna?"

"I'm still in one piece," Cholayna said. "I saw them kill Marisela; then they hit you over the head, Magda, and grabbed me; I think I may have stabbed one of them before they got the knife away from me. Then that damned bitch Acquilara hit me over the head with a ton of bricks, and that's all I remember."

"And then we woke up here," Vanessa summed up, clutching at them both in the darkness. "Now what?"

Magda laughed, mirthlessly. "Well, you tried to bribe Rakhaila to bring you here. She *said*, be careful what you pray for, you might get it . . . and here we are. Right in Acquilara's stronghold. At least, if Lexie and Rafaella are still alive, we're in a prime position to rescue them. Or ransom them."

Cholayna nodded; her dark face contorted in an expression of pain and she clutched her head again and held still.

"Who knows? Sooner or later, they're sure to come

back for us; if they thought we were all dead, they would hardly have wasted blankets on us. I don't see Marisela laid out here awaiting proper burial, or anything so charitable.''

Magda shuddered. "Oh, don't," she implored.

Cholayna leaned toward her and held her close. "There, there, I know you loved her, we all loved her," she said, "but there's nothing to be done for her now, Magda. Though if ever I get that filthy sorceress at the end of my knife . . . but now we have to think of ourselves, and what we can do to get out of here. What about Jaelle and Camilla? Do you know if they are alive or dead?''

Magda could remember nothing more than Marisela falling in a shower of blood. Then nothing.

"I saw you fall, Magda, and Cholayna," Vanessa repeated. "Jaelle and Camilla were out of sight, round a bend in the road; they may have gotten clean away, and never known we were gone until they stopped on the trail and we didn't catch up.''

"Do you know how long ago that was?" Cholayna asked. But neither of them had the slightest idea of elapsed time, or even whether it was night or day. Nor did they know how many their opponents were, nor how they were armed, nor what their plans might be, or whether Jaelle and Camilla were dead.

Yet Magda had an almost totally irrational conviction . . . "I think I would know if they were dead," she said. "I think, if either of them had been killed, I am *sure* I would know.''

"Being sure isn't evidence," Vanessa said, but Cholayna interrupted her.

"You're wrong. Magda has had very intensive psi-tech training. Not the kind they give in the Empire, but probably even more effective. I'd say her feelings *are* evidence, and evidence of a very high order."

"You may be right," Vanessa conceded after a moment, "but I don't see how that helps us much, since they obviously don't know where we are, or how to rescue us."

It was enough for Magda at that moment, after seeing Marisela murdered before her eyes, to be certain that both her lover and her freemate had escaped that fate. Yet she and her two Terran compatriots were in the hands of a cruel and unscrupulous woman, possibly one with some kind of *laran* —she remembered how Acquilara had struck down Camilla with a look.

She would as soon kill us, too, as look at us!

Vanessa felt the shudder and her arms tightened about Magda.

"Are you cold? Here, put my blanket round you. We might as well relax while we can; for all we know it could be early evening and they'll get a good night's sleep before they come to fetch us here. We may as well try and do likewise."

They huddled together, silent, under the blankets. Magda could pick up the dread and apprehension of the other women, the pain that crept, with the cold, into Cholayna's bones and muscles, as if in her own body. She wanted to shelter her, to protect them both, yet she was powerless.

Time crawled by; they never knew how long. Perhaps an hour, perhaps two. Magda kept falling into little dozes, where she would hear incoherent words at the very edge of hearing, see blurs of light that turned into strange faces, then jerk awake and know that none of this had happened at all, that she was still huddled between Cholayna and Vanessa in the dark and cold of their prison. She thought it was another of these tiny dreams when she began to see a light, but Vanessa stiffened at her side and whispered, "Look! They're coming!"

There was the light of a torch, bobbing up and down as if being carried, waist-high. It moved closer. It was no illusion. It was not fire on the end of a long stick. It was a small, brilliant flashlight, and in another minute she could see who was carrying it.

Lexie Anders bent over them and said, "All right, Lorne, get up and come with me. Do you see this?" Briefly, she showed Magda something that made Magda gasp; this was breaking every lawful arrangement between Terrans and Darkovans.

"It's a stunner," Alexis explained. Magda could see all too well what it was.

"For your information, it has a lethal setting. I would rather not be forced to use it, but I swear that if you try to make trouble, or attempt any silly heroics, I will. Get up. No, Van, you stay where you are, I don't choose to try to handle you both at once."

"Anders, in heaven's name, are you working with these people?" Cholayna sounded outraged. "Do you know what they are? Do you know they killed Marisela in cold blood?"

"That was a mistake," said Alexis Anders. "Acquilara was very angry about it. Marisela got in the way, that was all."

Cholayna said with hard anger, "I'm sure Marisela would be glad to know that."

"It wasn't my doing, Cholayna, and I refuse to feel guilty about it. Marisela had no business to interfere."

"Interfere? Going about her lawful business . . ." Magda cried.

Lexie moved the stunner. "You don't know a damn thing about it, Lorne, you don't know what's at stake here or what Marisela was involved in. So keep your mouth shut and come with me. If you're cold, you can bring the blanket."

Magda crawled slowly out from between Vanessa and Cholayna. Cholayna put out a hand to hold her back.

"For the record, Anders. Insubordination; defection; intrusion into closed territory without authorization; possession of an illegal weapon in violation of agreements between the Empire and duly constituted planetary authorities. You *do* know you're throwing your career away—"

"You're a stubborn old bitch," said Lexie. Shocked, Magda remembered Vanessa saying the same thing; but she had said it affectionately. "You don't know when you're beaten, Cholayna. You can still get out of this alive; I'm not bloodthirsty. But you'd better keep your mouth shut, because I don't think Acquilara is particularly tolerant of Terrans. I warn you, shut up and stay shut."

Another peremptory gesture with the stunner. Magda touched Cholayna's hand, saying in an undertone, "Don't put yourself on the line for me. This is between us. I'll see what she wants."

When she rose to her feet, she found that she was shaking all over. Was it the stunner pointed menacingly at her, was it the cold, was it simply that they must have struck her on the exact site of the previous concussion? She saw the glint of satisfaction in Lexie's eyes.

She thinks I am afraid of her and for some reason that pleases her. Well, let Lexie continue to think that. Magda realized that while she was a little bit afraid that the stunner in Lexie's hand might go off by accident, she was not at all afraid of Lexie herself.

She didn't turn a hair when Cholayna was throwing that list of indictments at her. That means one of two things. Either she's resigned to throwing her career away—or she has no intention of leaving Cholayna alive to testify against her.

Lexie waved the stunner again.

"This way."

She took Magda across the great cave filled with stalactites, gestured to her to walk down a slippery ramp, wet with falling water from somewhere, and pushed her through into another cave.

This one was lighted by torches stuck in the wall and smoking upwards; randomly Magda noted the direction of the smoke and thought, *there must be air coming in somewhere from outside.* At the center was a fire burning; at first Magda wondered where they got wood for fire, then realized from the smell it was not a wood fire at all, but a fire of dried chervine dung; a stack of the dried pats was at one side of the fire. Around the fire was a rough circle of hooded figures, and for an instant of awful disillusionment Magda thought, *is this the Sisterhood?*

Then a slender familiar figure rose from beside the fire.

"Welcome, my dear," she said. "I'm sorry my messengers had to use so much force. I told you to be ready when you were summoned, and if you had listened to me, you could have saved us a great deal of trouble."

Magda drew a deep breath, trying to compose herself.

"What do you want, Acquilara?"

CHAPTER TWENTY-SEVEN

But Acquilara did not do business that way. Magda should have known.

"You are hurt; let us bandage your wounds. And I am sure you are cold and cramped. Would you like some tea?"

Magda sensed that to accept any offers from the black sorceress would be to yield to her power. She started to say proudly, *No, thank you, I want nothing you can give*. She never knew what stopped her.

The most serious obligation she had now was to stay as strong as possible, so that she could get away, could help get Vanessa and Cholayna out of this. She said deliberately, "Thank you." Someone handed her a foaming cup of tea. It was faintly bitter, and smelled of the dung-fire, and a lump of butter had been stirred into it, which gave it a peculiar taste, but added, in the bitter chill, to its strengthening quality. Magda drank it down and felt it warming her all through. She accepted a second cup.

Two women came from the ring around the fire to help bandage her wounds. On the surface they were somewhat more prepossessing than the women of the hermitage of Avarra; they seemed clean enough and wore under their long, hooded cloaks the ordinary dress of village women from the mountains, long tartan skirts, thick overblouses and tunics, heavy felted shawls and boots. The bandages they used were rough, but seemed clean. Magda realized that skin had been stripped from her leg—she never knew how it happened, though she surmised that in the fight she must have rolled down a slope covered with sharp rocks. There were abrasions on her face too; she had not noticed them before.

With the scrapes and bruises salved and bandaged, she did feel better, and the tea, even with its faintly nauseating taste, had strengthened her so that she felt prepared to meet whatever might come next.

"Feeling better?" Acquilara was almost purring. "Now let us sit down together and discuss this like civilized women. I am sure we can come to some agreement."

Agreement? When you have murdered my friend, imprisoned my companions, and for all I know you may have killed my freemate and my lover? Never!

But Magda had more common sense than to say this aloud. If this woman was half the *leronis* she claimed to be, she would sense Magda's antipathy and know how little likely Magda would be to accede to her plan.

"What do you want with me, Acquilara? Why have you, as you put it, summoned me?"

"I am the servant of the Great Goddess whom you seek—"

Magda started to say, *Nonsense, you're no such thing*, but decided not to antagonize her.

"Very well then, tell me what your Goddess wants with me."

"We should be friends," Acquilara began. "You are a powerful *leronis* of the Tower called Forbidden, which has refused to play into the hands the Hasturs, or to submit to that terrible old *teneresteis* Leonie of Arilinn, who keeps all the people of the Domains paralyzed under the iron rule of the Arilinn Tower. As one who has helped to free our brothers and our sisters, you are my ally and my comrade and I welcome you here.''

And Marisela? But Magda said nothing. Perhaps if she waited long enough Acquilara would tell her what really was going on. As Camilla had pointed out, even an ''evil sorceress'' did not go to all this trouble simply to amuse herself.

''Your friend has told me that you are from another world, and she has said something about the Empire,'' Acquilara began over again. Magda's eyes strayed to Lexie where she stood in the corner. She had put the stunner out of sight. ''You are a powerful *leronis*, but you owe nothing to the Comyn. And among your companions are two others of Comyn blood. Am I not right?''

''You have been correctly informed,'' she said. *Casta* was a stiff language and Magda wasted none of its formality.

''Nevertheless, I cannot imagine what all this has to do with the fact that you have murdered one of my friends and imprisoned others.''

''I told you, Acquilara, you wouldn't get anywhere with her that way,'' said a voice from the shadows where Lexie stood. Rafaella n'ha Doria did not have a stunner, or any weapon Magda could see except for the usual long knife of a Renunciate.

''Let me talk to her. In a word, Margali, she knows you have had *laran* training in your Forbidden Tower, or whatever it may be. But you are Terran. On the other hand, Jaelle, born Comyn, has renounced her Comyn heritage, and as a Renunciate she is free to use her powers as she will.''

She stood waiting for Magda to confirm what she said; instead, Magda burst out in anger.

''I would not have believed it if they had told me,

Rafi! You, whom she loves as a sister, to sell her out this way! And Camilla, too, calls you her friend!''

"You don't know what you are talking about," Rafaella said angrily. "Sell her out? Never! It is you who have induced her to betray herself, and I am trying to remedy that." She came all the way forward and stood facing Magda.

"You have not even let Acquilara tell you what she is offering. No harm is intended to Shaya, or even to Camilla—"

"That is the red-headed *emmasca*?" Acquilara nodded with satisfaction. "She has Comyn powers, perhaps Alton, perhaps Hastur, there is no way of telling but to test her. That's easily enough done. She may balk a little at the testing, but there are ways of handling that."

The words of the Monitor's Oath flashed through Magda's mind: *enter no mind save to help or heal and only by consent*. These people had never heard of this obligation. The thought of Camilla, forced unwilling to enter, undesired, that painful openness, made her shake with rage. At that moment, if she had had a weapon, she could cheerfully have killed Rafaella.

Did Rafaella even know what she was proposing or how painful it would be?

"Listen to me, Margali," said Rafaella earnestly. "We are sisters in Bridge Society—perhaps we haven't been as good friends sometimes as we might, but just the same, we're working for the same objectives, aren't we?"

"Are we? I don't think so. It seems to me that if your motives are the same as the Bridge Society you would have brought your proposal to Cholayna, or to me, or even to Jaelle or Camilla herself. Lieutenant Anders—"

she used Lexie's official rank deliberately, "is *not* a member of Bridge. Why go to *her*?"

"It was she who came to me with this proposal. And if you do not know why she would not come to you or to Cholayna with it—I should have known, of course, you would never admit anything could be done, in Bridge, or in the Empire, without your being a part of it." Rafaella's words were an angry torrent, but a brief gesture from Acquilara cut her off.

"Enough. Tell her what the proposal is. I am not interested in your personal grievances against her."

"Jaelle has had some training in the Forbidden Tower but these women can complete her training until she is more powerful than Leonie of Arilinn. Camilla, too, will be trained to the maximum of which she is capable. If she truly has Hastur blood, she may be the most powerful *leronis* for many years. Real power awaits them—"

"What makes you think that is what they are looking for?"

It was Acquilara who answered. "For what else did they come into these hills in search of the old crow-goddess in her abandoned shrine? Was it not to seek the full potential of what powers they might one day have? They may not know it, but that is what they were doing. This is the end of every quest; to become what you are, and this means power, real power, not philosophy and moral lectures. From the crow-people they will get austerities without number, and at the end, a pledge never to use or indulge their powers. They will be told that the end of all wisdom is to know and to refrain from doing, for actually *doing* anything would be black sorcery." Acquilara's face was savage with contempt. "I can offer them better than that."

"While if they are taught here by Acquilara," said

Rafaella, "at the end of their training they will be sent back to Thendara, armed with the means to make some real changes in their world, to turn it to their own real advantage. Jaelle on the Council, as she could have been, *should* have been all along. And Camilla—there's no end to what Camilla might do. She could rule all the Towers in the Domains."

"That's not what Camilla wants."

"It is what, as a Hastur, she ought to want. And when I am done with her, she will want it," said Acquilara with unshakable confidence.

This woman had power. Magda could feel it in her very stance, her gestures. Acquilara gestured to Lexie to go on.

"You are very naïve, Lorne," Lexie added. "That is why you have meddled in so many things and never achieved anything real. Have you seen your file in personnel at HQ? I have. Do you know what they say of you? You could be in a real position of power. . . ."

Magda found her voice.

"I can't presume to tell you what Camilla and Jaelle want," she said, "but I can tell you that power, in that form anyhow, is not what I want."

"And I can tell you that you are a liar," Lexie said. "For all the talk, there is really only one real game, only one thing anyone wants, and that is power. Pretend, be a hypocrite if you like, deny it, lie about it, I know better; that is what *everybody* wants."

"Do you judge everybody by yourself?"

"Unlike you, Lorne, I don't pretend to be better than everybody else," Lexie said, "but it doesn't matter. When the new cooperation between Terran and Darkovan begins, it will take a whole new turn; and this time it will not be Magdalen Lorne's name at the head of it, but Alexis Anders's."

"Is that what you want more than anything else, Lexie?"

"It's what you wanted and what you got, isn't it? Why say it's unworthy of me?" Lexie demanded.

Again Acquilara brought the talk to a halt with one of those imperative gestures. Magda, watching her carefully, realized that she was uncomfortable whenever the focus of the discussion moved away from herself.

"Enough, I say. Magdalen Lorne—" like all speakers of *casta* she mangled the pronunciation of the name, diminishing her dignity; she knew it and tried to look all the more imposing, "promise me that you will help me to convince Jaelle n'ha Melora and the other comynara, the red-haired *emmasca*, to work with me, and I shall find a use for you too among us. It would be a good thing to have a Terran intelligence worker as one of us. This would be a truly powerful *Penta Cari'yo*, not a ladies' lodging society and dinner club. Once our influence was entrenched in Thendara, it would be easy to have you as head of Terran Intelligence—"

"What makes you think that is what I want?"

"Damn it, Acquilara, I told you more than once, that is not the way to get anywhere with Lorne," Lexie interrupted.

"You presume on your importance, *terranis*," snarled Acquilara. "Don't interrupt me! Well, Magdalen Lorne, think it over."

"I don't need to," Magda said quietly. "I'm not interested in your proposition."

"You cannot afford to refuse me," Acquilara said. "I am making you a very generous proposal. *Terranan* are not popular in these hills. I need only reveal who you are in any village to have you torn to pieces. As for your friend, the woman with the black skin, what would they think of her? A pitiful freak, to be exposed on the hills for the banshee and the *kyorebni*. Yet if you are one of us, you are under my powerful protection anywhere in these hills.''

She motioned to two of the women.

''Take her back, and let her think it over. Tomorrow you will give me your answer.'' She signaled to Lexie. ''Guard her with your weapon.''

One of the women stepped up to Acquilara and whispered to her. She nodded.

''You are right. If she is as powerful a *leronis* as we've heard, then she will lose no time in warning the *comynaris*. Give her some *raivannin*.''

Raivannin! Magda thought in consternation. It was a drug which paralyzed the psi facilities and *laran;* sometimes it was used to immobilize a powerful telepath who was ill or delirious and could not control his or her destructive powers. She sought, quickly, to leap into the Overworld, to align herself with Jaelle, to cry out a warning, *Jaelle, Camilla, beware* . . . a few words. A few seconds of warning. . . .

She had underestimated these people. Someone seized her—not physically; no hand touched her—but she discovered that she was ice-cold, she could not move or speak. She felt she was falling, falling, though she knew she stood motionless; her body and mind were buffeted by raging ice, wind, as if she stood naked in a blizzard. . . .

She heard Lexie say, ''Let me take care of her. I can set the stunner to keep her out for a few hours.''

''No, she needs freedom for the decision,'' said Acquilara smoothly. Suddenly Magda was seized by two powerful sets of hands and held motionless, physically this time. Rafaella forced her mouth open and poured something icy and cloyingly sweet down her throat.

"Hold her about half a minute," Acquilara said from out of the darkness. "It's very fast-acting. After that she'll be safe enough."

An incredible flush of heat pulsed across Magda's face, making her sinuses pound and a hot flare of pain fill up her head. Only a moment, but she wanted to scream aloud with its impact. Then it ebbed slowly away, leaving her feeling dull and empty, and suddenly deaf. She blinked, letting herself lean on the women who were holding her; she could hardly find her balance; all the peripheral awarenesses were gone, she was shorn and blinded, naked in her five senses, she could see and hear and touch, but how little, how inadequate the world seemed; nothing, nothing outside herself, the universe dead . . . even her ordinary senses felt dulled, there as a film over her sight, sounds came dulled as if from far away, and even the cold on her skin seemed remote as if she had been dipped in something heavy and greasy, insulating her from the world.

Raivannin. It had sheared away all her expanded senses, leaving her head-blind. A powerful dose; once she had taken it when she was ill and Callista felt she should be shielded from a Tower operation; but it had only blunted her awareness of the matrix work going on around her, so that she could shut it out if she chose. Nothing like this total insulation, this closing and clogging of her senses.

"You gave her too much," said one of the women holding her—even her voice sounded indistinct, or was this the way ordinary voices sounded, un-enhanced by the psychic awareness of their meaning? "She can hardly stand up. She may never recover her *laran*, after a dose like that."

Acquilara shrugged. Magda realized, in despair, that she could not even hear the malice and falseness in

Acquilara's voice any more, it sounded like anybody's voice, she even sounded pleasant, how did the head-blind ever know whom to trust?

"Small loss. We can manage without her, and she might be easier to handle that way. Take her away, back to the others."

CHAPTER TWENTY-EIGHT

As the women hauled her away from the ring of fire-light and back to the first cave where she had waked in captivity, Magda was conscious only of despair. She could not even warn Jaelle or Camilla.

She tried to convince herself that she should not be worrying. Jaelle and Camilla did not know where she was, or even where to look. Now that she was drugged with *raivannin* they could not even hunt for her with *laran*.

And if Acquilara tried to persuade them to join her plans, they could always refuse. There would be no way to force them, and no danger that Jaelle or Camilla would find Acquilara's offer tempting enough to be worth deserting their own principles. So why was she worrying?

They dumped her unceremoniously in the first cave and went away. Magda huddled down on the floor in misery.

Lexie is certainly intending to kill Cholayna or have her killed, or she would not have dared to speak that way to her.

Cholayna raised her head as Magda slumped down on the floor.

"Magda, are you all right? What did they want?"

"To make me an offer, of no particular interest to

377

me," Magda said dully. "Nothing's wrong. I told them, in essence, to go to hell. Go to sleep, Cholayna."

She had made a fatal error of strategy. She should have pretended to play along, pretended to be impressed with Acquilara's plans; then they would have left her free, and she could have put herself in touch with Jaelle or Camilla with her *laran*. Now it was too late.

"You're shaking all over," said Vanessa. "I don't think you're all right at all. What did they do to you, really? Here, come under my blanket, get yourself warm. You look like hell."

"Nothing. Nothing you'd understand. Let me alone, Vanessa."

"Like hell," said Vanessa, pulling Magda by main force under her blanket and wrapping it around her. She took Magda's hands in hers and said, "They're burning hot! Come on, Lorne, what did they do to you? I've never seen you like this before!"

Magda felt dulled, exhausted, and yet she just wanted to cry and cry until she dissolved in tears. Vanessa's hands on hers felt like a stranger's hands, no sensation but the raw physical touch. What must it be like to have only this to share with another person, however dear; how could you tell friend from stranger or lover? And she could be like this forever. It would have been better to die. She let herself fall against Vanessa, and to her despair and shame she was aware that she was sobbing helplessly.

Vanessa held her and patted her back.

"Sssh, sssh, don't cry, it's going to be all right, nothing's so bad it can't be helped. We're here, right here . . ." and Cholayna, hearing them, arose and took Magda's burning hands in hers, rubbing them.

"Come on, tell us, what did they do to you? You'll

feel better if you tell us, whatever it was. Let us help you.''

"There's nothing anyone can do," Magda muttered, despairing, through her sobs. "They—they drugged me. With *raivannin*."

"What the hell is that?"

"It—it shuts down—*laran*. So that—I couldn't—it's like being deaf and blind—" Magda felt her own words stumbling on her tongue, lifeless, conveying nothing of her real personality or her true thoughts, dead noises, like the mouthings of an idiot.

Cholayna put her arms around Magda, holding her tight. "What a ghastly thing to do! Can't you see, Vanessa? It was so that she couldn't warn Jaelle, or even reach her—do you understand? What a *fiendish* thing to do to anyone with psychic talent! Oh, Magda, Magda, my dear, I know I can't really understand what it means to you, I can't really *imagine* it, but I can understand just a little what it must mean to you!''

Magda was completely discomposed; but, held warmly and comforted between her friends, she managed after a time to stop crying.

"It might even be a help somehow," Vanessa said in a whisper. "I notice that when they brought you back they didn't bother to send Lexie and her stunner. They evidently thought that with your *laran* inoperative you couldn't be dangerous to them. I get the feeling that they didn't even bother to worry about us—me and Cholayna—because we *didn't* have any kind of psychic powers.''

Magda had not thought of that. She had been, she realized, so deeply in shock that she had not thought of anything.

Have I, she wondered, come to rely so deeply on my

laran that I forget everything else? That's not right, either.

"You're right," she said, pulling herself together and sitting upright, wiping her tears on her sleeve. What Vanessa said was true; they were unguarded. Something might be done. Without food, packs, or maps, and not even knowing whether it was daylight or dark outside, escape would be difficult; but it need not be impossible.

Vanessa had her knife, a small affair, razor sharp, with a blade as long as her hand; it folded up, and perhaps they had not even recognized it as a knife. Cholayna was unarmed.

"But I'm not afraid of anyone I can see," she said grimly, making a gesture Magda recognized; she too had been trained in unarmed combat. Magda had not, until they were attacked in the robber's village, used it to kill; but she had been impressed with Cholayna's fighting skill.

"It must be night outside," she said, making an effort to rally her ordinary strengths. They might have disabled her *laran*, but after all, she had lived almost twenty-seven years without any hint that she possessed it; there was more to Magdalen Lorne than just *laran*.

"Acquilara told them to guard me—at first—so that I could think over my answer till tomorrow; I had the idea they were winding things up for the night. Sooner or later, even this crew must sleep; they're not some sort of Unsleeping Eye of Evil, they're just women with some nasty powers and nastier ideas about using them. If we're going to make a move, it should be while they're sleeping."

"We might not even have to kill them," Cholayna said. "We might be able to sneak out past them. . . ."

"If we knew the way out," Magda said, "and I

suspect there will be guards, unless they are dangerously over-confident—"

"They just might be," Cholayna said. "Think of it,
Magda, the psychology of power. This cave is isolated
in the most godforgotten part of these isolated and
godforgotten mountains. No one knows the way here.
No one ever comes here at all. They probably guard it
psychically from the rival crew, the Wise Sisterhood,
but I'd bet a month's pay that there won't be any
physical guards at all. They've immobilized you. They'll
take precautions about the rival Sisterhood tracking them
down by *laran*. But they don't even bother to guard
Vanessa and me. Just you, and just your *laran*."

Cholayna was right. So they had only two problems:
to wait until Acquilara and her cohorts were sleeping,
so that they could find their way out of the cave (she
had felt a draft of outside air blowing from the outer
cave where they had challenged her, so it must be
nearer the exit) and second, how to survive outside.

The second was the most important. Vanessa was
already ahead of her: "Supposing we do get out? We
don't have food, outer clothing, survival equipment—"

"There's sure to be food and clothing somewhere in
these caves—" Cholayna protested.

"Sure. Want to go to Acquilara and ask her to give
us some?"

"Another thing, even more important," said Cholayna
with a quiet determination, "Lexie. I'm not going to
leave without her."

"Cholayna, you saw," Vanessa protested. "She held
a gun on us. Rescue, hell, she's *one* of them!"

"How do you know that there wasn't a gun, or
something worse that we couldn't see, being held on
her? I'd want to hear from her own lips that she wasn't

coerced before I'd abandon her here," Cholayna said. "And Rafaella—did you see her, Magda, is she alive?"

"Alive and well," said Magda grimly. "She held me while they poured the drug down my throat. And I'll guarantee nobody had a gun on her, or anything like that. She explained to me at considerable length what Acquilara was doing and why Jaelle and Camilla ought to be convinced to join them rather than the Sisterhood. I wasn't convinced, but she seemed to be. I honestly don't think we ought to waste time trying to rescue them, I got the impression that they were exactly where they wanted to be and it would be no use at all to try to persuade them to leave."

"I can't believe that of Alexis," said Cholayna in despair. "But then, I would never have believed she would hold a stunner on me, either."

Even without *laran* Magda could feel Cholayna's sorrow. How hard it must be, to accept that Lexie was not a prisoner here, but a willing accomplice.

But Cholayna brought herself sternly back to duty, and was searching her pockets. She brought out from the depths a wrapped package.

"Emergency field rations. We need the fuel." She broke the bar into three parts. "Eat."

Magda shook her head. "They gave me some hot tea with butter in it; I'm all right. You two share it." She accepted only a mouthful of the dry, flavorless, but high-calorie ration, chewing it slowly. *I'll never complain about the taste of this stuff again, after butter-flavored tea smelling of dung-fire.*

Vanessa opened her little knife, had it ready. They folded up the blankets and slung them across their backs; they might need them as basic shelter, if they found their way out of the caves. Their eyes had adapted so well to the faintest of light within this cave that they could see the glow that came from the outer cave which was apparently the meetingplace and headquarters of Acquilara and the women of her cult.

Magda was wondering: Acquilara's people, where do they come from? Do they live here all year round, or meet here occasionally? They can't live in these wilds, because there's nothing to live *on*.

There was no reason to waste time now in speculation. Magda didn't care if they came here out of necessity, imitation, or sheer perversity, or because like Vanessa they had a passion for climbing mountains.

They stole noiselessly toward the orange glow of the fires in the outer cave. Magda was aware of the dung-fire smell, of a flow of cool air on her cheek—these caves were well ventilated. This might in part explain why there was so little marked on the map in the Hellers, if some inhabitants lived in caves. But people needed more than simple shelter; they needed fire, clothing, food or some place to grow it. If there were many people living in this area, there would be more signs than this. She did not for a single moment believe Lexie's theory about a city in these wastelands, made invisible to observers by some unknown technology. A few isolated hermits, withdrawn here for spiritual purposes, perhaps. Not any great population.

There were a couple of intermediate caves, one with steps leading downward into a vague glow. Probably torchlight somewhere, Magda thought. She had once seen a geological survey indicating that there were several active volcanoes in the Kilghard hills—which would have been obvious anyway from the presence of hot springs all through the countryside. There must be dormant ones here too, but nobody would be living in them.

Vanessa whispered, "We should search these caves. There might be storerooms of food and clothing."

"Can't risk it," Cholayna said in an undertone. It was surprising, Magda thought, the way in which Cholayna, without discussion, had become their leader. "We could stumble on all them, sleeping down there. We need to get out fast and not be weighed down. We'll manage somehow. Straight out, fight our way if we have to; don't kill unless there's no alternative, but don't mess around, either." She adjusted the blanket she had strapped across her back, making sure her arms and legs could move freely, and Magda remembered how she had dealt with the robbers in the village.

Another few steps and they were in the rear mouth of the main cavern, or at least what Magda supposed to be so; the great cavernous room where she had spoken to Rafaella and Lexie under Acquilara's eyes. She looked at the ring of scattered coals which had once been a fire, and shuddered, here they had held her . . . *drugged her, a violation worse than rape, afflicting her very selfhood. . . .*

"Steady." Vanessa gripped her shoulder. "Easy, Lorne, you're all right now."

Vanessa did not understand, but Magda firmly took hold of herself. They had stopped her, wounded her, but she was alive and still in possession of her senses, her self, her integrity.

Yet if Acquilara was right, if they overdosed me to the point where I am permanently blinded of laran. *. . .*

I can live without it. Camilla chose *to live without it.* She bemoaned the thought that she might never share with Camilla what she shared with Jaelle, with her companions in the Tower, but if she must, she could accept that. *Camilla lost more than that.* She looked warily around the great cave.

At first it seemed empty. They had withdrawn to whatever deeper caves they used, whether for sleeping or for whatever mysterious rites occupied their time. *When they're not murdering or drugging people. I don't care if they're all down there consorting sex with demons or banshees. I wish them joy of it. So long as it keeps them busy while we get the hell out!*

"But there must be guards somewhere, even if it's only at the outside doors," Vanessa whispered. "Be careful! Can you tell where that draft's coming from, Magda?"

She turned her head from side to side, trying to decide from which direction the air flowed. Now *laran* would have been useful, though clairvoyance was not her most outstanding talent. Cholayna touched her arm silently and pointed.

Someone was sleeping on the floor, at one side of the cavern, by the light of the guttering torches. A woman's form, wrapped in a blanket. One of Acquilara's sorceresses. A guard, at least. Vanessa had her knife out. She started to bend over, her hand poised for the stroke, but Cholayna shook her head, and Vanessa shrugged and obeyed.

Magda had identified the airstream. She hesitated a moment; some such caves, she knew, were ventilated by long chimneys of rock, and taking that direction might lead them into an impassable labyrinth. But they had to risk something. Anyhow, it was most likely that a guard would be posted, even if she was sleeping, across the doorway an escaping prisoner must take to reach the outside world. She pointed.

One by one they stepped carefully over the sleeping form of the woman. But if Magda had hoped that the next cave would lead to the outside world with a blaze of daylight and a few steps to freedom, she was doomed to disappointment, for the next cavernous chamber was larger than the last, totally empty, and all but lightless.

CHAPTER TWENTY-NINE

They could wander in these caves for days; except that Acquilara's gang would find them sooner or later, more likely sooner, and bring them to a quick and messy end. Acquilara had wanted to use her, but she did not deceive herself that there would be any kindness or forbearance shown.

Not drugging, this time. Death.

Vanessa was making her way very slowly around the walls, feeling every inch with outstretched hands before her. She slipped, recovered, let herself down on one knee and beckoned. They came on tiptoe to join her. She had fallen over a cluster of large sacks, one or two of which had been opened and folded over at the top.

One held dried fruit; the second held a kind of grain, millet, probably intended as food for pack animals. At Cholayna's gesture they filled their pockets from the sacks. It might mean, in that bitter cold outside, the narrow razor edge of separation between life and death.

Beyond the piled sacks rose a long stairway; dimly they made out that the steps were carved in part from the soft limestone, filled in with a kind of rock and cement and smoothed over just enough to climb without falling. The steps were wet, slippery and treacherous, and Magda hesitated to set foot on them.

"Do you think this is the way out? Or does it go farther into the caves?"

"Let's find out first." Cholayna began slowly groping her way around the rest of the wall. Magda tried, automatically, to reach out with her *laran*, to try to see past the opening of the stairs, but there was only a dull ache.

In her . . . eyes? No. In her heart? *I can't identify what's missing, but I'm only half there.* She banished the thought, forcing herself to go slowly around the dripping walls. Back at the feed sacks she bumped gently into Vanessa.

"There's a big door over there," Cholayna murmured. "I'd like to get out of here before that guard over there wakes up and we have to kill her."

"I think it's the stairway that leads out," Vanessa argued. "I can feel air blowing from up there."

"I'm not so sure. Think, Vanessa. Could they have carried all of us down these stairways without at least one of us waking up?" Cholayna sounded persuasive. Vanessa said, "You're the boss."

"No. It's too serious for that. You and Magda have a stake in this too. Magda, what's your best hunch?"

Grimly Magda reminded herself that Cholayna had no idea how that question would seem a wounding prod of her loss; Cholayna meant it at strict face value.

"Don't have any just now, remember? But I'd like to have a look at that doorway before we try climbing the stairs."

"But hurry," Cholayna fretted, and Magda began silently feeling her way. It was very dark. She could hardly make out her spread fingers before her face. Vanessa murmured something and slid away into the darkness. After a heart-stopping time she came back, carrying one of the low-sputtering torches.

"I had to step right over her. I took this one. It seemed to have more time left on it than the others, but none of them looked all that great. I wish I could find where they keep their stash of fresh ones."

"That's another thing," Cholayna said between her teeth. "Unless we find our way out damn fast, we're going to need light; we could, literally, wander the rest of our lives in these caves."

"Hold this," Vanessa said, thrusting the low-burning torch into Cholayna's hands and slipping away again. After another long time and some curious soft scraping sounds, she returned, breathless, her arms filled with the torches. One or two had a coal or so on the end; the others had been extinguished.

"Sorry I was so long about it," she whispered. "I had to pull them down off the wall. Now we'd better get moving—one look at the place and anybody will know we passed through. Let's move."

Cholayna reached out and gripped her wrist. She said, "Good thinking. But get one thing straight, Vanessa: from this very minute, we stick together, we don't get separated. Understand? You may know mountains; I know something about caves. You stick close; better yet, we stay in physical contact all the time. If one of us gets lost or separated we can't even yell to find each other!"

"Oh. Right," Vanessa said, sobered.

Magda took the burning torch from Cholayna's hands. "I won't go out of sight. But I'm going up to see where these steps lead. There's no sense of all of us coming if it's a blind chimney, or another empty chamber."

"I doubt it's blind; the stairs look too well-used for that," said Cholayna, bending low to scan the marks on the roughly floored surface.

Holding the torch before her, Magda slowly climbed the steps.

She looked back at Cholayna, standing at the foot of the crude stairway. It was not blind. It led into some kind of chamber above, and there was light there. Daylight, already? She thrust her head up over the edge and instinctively recoiled.

She thrust the torch behind her to conceal its light. At least two dozen women lay sleeping in the chamber above; Magda could see at the far end of the room Lexie Anders's curly blond head. She did not see Acquilara. Slowly she began to withdraw down the steps, placing each foot carefully on the stair below.

The woman nearest the stairhead opened her eyes and looked straight at Magda.

It was Rafaella n'ha Doria.

Magda never knew how she stifled a yell. She withdrew swiftly down the stairs, and Vanessa, watching her precipitate retreat, snatched out her knife and stood braced.

But nothing happened. Silence; no outcry, no rousing of the legions, no outraged hordes pouring down the stairs with weapons raised. *Was she fast asleep? Didn't she see me? Did she decide to let me go for Jaelle's sake or because we used to be friends?*

Then, stealthily, Rafaella came down the stairs. Vanessa held her little knife at the ready, but Rafaella gestured to her to put it away and motioned them all to a safe distance from the stairway.

"You can put it away, Vanessa n'ha Yllana," she said. "If you are leaving, I'm going with you."

"You had me fooled," Magda said in an undertone.

"Oh, don't deceive yourself," Rafaella said sourly. "You haven't converted me to the rightness of your cause, or anything like that. I still think Jaelle would be better advised to work with them than with that other crew. But I don't like what they've done to Lexie and I don't want them doing it to me.''

"Do you by any chance know the way out?''

"I think I can find it. I've been in and out twice since the storm.'' Rafaella led the way swiftly through the other large doorway and into a chamber strewn with rubble and rocks. Phosphorescent fungus shed an eerie light from the walls, and the torchlight wavered on giant formations of limestone, pale and gleaming like bone, folded and layered most marvelously. "Careful here. It's wet and dripping all through here, but at least the water's pure and good drinking, and there's plenty of it.'' She scooped up a handful from a little stream that ran downhill beside where they were climbing.

"If you get lost again in here remember to follow the stream *uphill*. If you follow it down it leads *way* down— I've only been down three or four levels; they say there are at least ten levels below this, and some of them are filled with old books and artifacts from a time—they must be thousands of years old. Lexie went down and saw a few of them and said there had evidently been a time of very high technology on Darkover, though none of it looked Terran. Which surprised her. She said Darkover was once a Terran colony, but this was completely different. Then Acquilara told her that it was *before;* that there was a whole civilization before humans colonized this world. You're the specialist, Margali, all that stuff would interest you, and Mother Lauria would go crazy over it, but it's not for me.''

At the far end of this chamber lay a gleam of light— not daylight, but a faint glimmer somehow different in quality from the guttering torchlight. From it they could all feel a faint breath of the terrible chill outside. Magda shivered, buttoned up her heavy jacket, drew on her gloves. Vanessa arranged her blanket snugly over her shoulders like a mountain man's plaid. Four abreast, they moved stealthily toward the entry.

Magda always swore that for what happened next there was no natural explanation. Vanessa said she came from the staircase and they never stopped arguing about it. Magda saw a faint blue flare, a shrill faroff shrieking like a hawk, and Acquilara stood in the doorway before them.

"Are you leaving us? I'm afraid I can't relinquish your company so soon." She raised her hand, and Magda realized there were women warriors all around the entrance chamber. They struck the torches from Cholayna's hand, knocked Vanessa to the ground, took her knife, then dragged them along with Magda and Rafaella back into the chamber of fires, where all four of them were held securely.

The room filled up with women, some of them, Magda was sure, hastily roused sleepers from the chamber above.

"I am too lenient," Acquilara said. "I can tolerate no traitors. *Terranan*—"

Lexie came forward through the crowd.

"I underestimated her strength and intelligence," Acquilara said, indicating Magda. "Once she is broken, we can find a use for her. But I must make an example of what happens to those who mock my clemency. This one betrayed us."

She went to Rafaella and took the knife from her belt; handed it to Lexie.

"Prove yourself loyal to me. Kill her."

Cholayna cried out sharply. "Lexie! No!"

With brutal deliberation Acquilara backhanded Cholayna across the mouth. "It should be *you*, freak," she said. "*Terranan*, I wait."

Lexie barely glanced at the knife and dropped it.

"To hell with your tests of loyalty. If you need them, to hell with *you*." She let the knife lie where it had fallen.

Magda thought Acquilara would strike Alexis down where she stood; she had defied her, risked letting the sorceress lose face before her women. Acquilara stood frozen for a moment, then evidently decided to salvage what she could from the incident.

"Why, *Terranan*?"

"She knows the mountain roads. She is competent. She will be needed to escort them back to Thendara when the time comes; by that time she will know better than to defy or disobey. Killing her would be waste. I abhor waste." Lexie spoke coldly, without the slightest emotion.

Now is she telling the exact truth, or is it some latent loyalty in Lexie? After all, they traveled over the mountains together, and they must have some kindness and respect for one another after sharing an experience like that. Magda ached for the touch of *laran* which would make it possible to know.

Soon they found themselves back in the cavern from which they had come. Rafaella was dragged along with them, and unceremoniously dumped there. Their hands were tied, and Acquilara ordered her women to go around and take their boots off, one by one.

Cholayna protested. "You have not even told us why we are your prisoners. And without our boots we will surely freeze."

"Not if you stay in these caverns, where the temperature all year round is sufficient to keep water from freezing,'' Acquilara said. "Only if you try to leave them will you suffer the slightest harm. I should really take all your outer garments as well.''

But she did not carry out that threat; she even left the blankets. She also posted a pair of guards, armed with knives and daggers, at the door of the chamber. She would not, Magda thought, underestimate them again.

Cholayna wrapped her blanket around herself, clumsily, using her long, prehensile toes, and told the others to do the same. "We need to keep warm, stay as strong as we can.''

"Jaelle—they didn't kill her, did they?'' Rafaella asked, shrugging into her blanket as best she could with her hands tied.

"As far as I know she got clean away. And I hope she stays so.''

"By the paps of Evanda, so do I, I swear it! I would not have harm come to her for all the metal in Zandru's forges. I truly believed we would find—'' she broke off. "I did not know the *terranan* woman was quite so bloodthirsty. For a moment I thought Lexa' really would kill me.''

"I had hoped not,'' Cholayna said gravely. "I cannot believe that of her.''

Rafaella said, "I don't suppose this is what Lexa' really meant by a *city of wisdom*. Still, if we could get at the ancient artifacts under the mountains, I dare say your Terrans would call it a fortune.''

"I wouldn't mind seeing them,'' Cholayna said, "but I'd prefer to get out of here with a whole skin. I don't know if we can manage another escape attempt. Still, if any kind of chance comes we should be ready.'' She wriggled around, lying close to Magda. "See if you can manage to get my hands loose, Magda. Vanessa, see what you can do for Rafi's.''

"The guards—" Magda gave an uneasy glance over her shoulder.

"Why do you think I suggested we all do a lot of moving around getting ourselves wrapped up in blankets and so forth? The guards won't pay any attention if we move discreetly and behave as if we were still tied up."

Magda started slowly easing the knots loose. They had been well tied, and it took a long time, but she had nothing else to do anyhow. At last she slipped free the last cord, then thrust out her own wrists, to let Cholayna fumble with her bonds.

"It must be daylight outside," said Vanessa, lying full length and shamming sleep while Rafaella picked at a difficult knot.

Daylight. If she had had sense, or *laran*, not to go up those stairs, to take the doorway, they could by now have been miles away.

Rafaella asked, "This Acquilara. Do you think she is a powerful sorceress?"

"She's not much of a telepath. I don't know what else she has or doesn't have, and right now I'm in no position to judge," Magda said.

"*Laran!*" Rafaella's voice was scornful, but suddenly Magda was aware of the overpowering reason behind Rafaella's jealousy. It took no psychic powers to read; since Jaelle's childhood, Rafi had known Jaelle to be a daughter born into the powerful caste of Comyn, who ruled all the Domains, all Darkover, with their powers. Nevertheless, Jaelle had chosen the Guild-house over her Comyn heritage, blotting out the great distance that would otherwise lie between Rafaella and Jaelle. They had been friends, partners; even, for a brief time in their girlhood, lovers.

And then Magda, who was not even Darkovan and

should have had no more *laran* than Rafaella herself, had come between them, and it had been Magda, the alien, who had lured Jaelle back to her *laran* and to her heritage.

I should have had imagination enough to see this before.

"*Laran* or no," Cholayna said, "I know one thing about this Acquilara: she is a psychopath. Any little thing can touch her off, and then she can be dangerous."

"You think she's not dangerous now? Would a sane woman have tried that business of trying to make Lexie kill Rafaella?" Vanessa asked.

"A sane woman might well have tried it. But a sane woman would not have been diverted so easily from it," Cholayna warned. "I am more afraid of her than of anything so far on this trip."

The day, or night, dragged on, and they had no way of marking it. What did it matter? Magda wondered. It was unlikely that they would get out of this one. Either Acquilara would kill them in a fit of psychotic frenzy, or they would escape, to be followed by a swift death from exposure, or a slow one from starvation. She only regretted that her *laran* should die before she did. She would have liked to be able to reach Callista, Andrew, and especially her child. The Forbidden Tower would mourn her, never knowing how she had died. Perhaps it was as well they should not know.

She wondered if it was an ethical question peculiar to women. There were some, even in the Guild-house, who would have said that she should not, with family responsibilities and a child to raise, have undertaken such a dangerous mission. Terran HQ, at least in Intelligence, usually reserved such missions for unmarried men with no families.

But Intelligence was a special volunteer service. In

Mapping and Exploring, in Survey, for instance, a man's marital status did not affect what he was expected or allowed to do. Was it so much worse to raise motherless children than fatherless ones? She longed for Shaya and wondered if she would ever see her again. If Jaelle had gotten clean away, Jaelle would look after her daughter. If Jaelle had been killed too—well, at least the children were safe.

"I don't suppose they'll bother to send in anything to eat," said Vanessa, "but I still have a pocketful of the stuff we got out of those sacks. Here. . . ." She passed it from hand to hand, out of sight of the guards. "We might as well eat and keep up our strength."

Magda was chewing prosaically on a raisin when it happened, a flare like a light exploding in her brain and Callista's voice:

. . . as an Alton one of my talents is speech to the head-blind. . . .

It was as if she were speaking in the next room, but perfectly clear. Then it was gone, and nothing would bring it back; Magda reached out desperately, trying to touch Jaelle, Camilla, to reach for the Overworld and the Forbidden Tower . . .

But her mind was still filled with the insidious inhibiting power of *raivannin* and she had no idea how that voice had gotten through to her.

If I could only pray. But I don't believe in prayer. She didn't, she thought, even believe in the Goddess Avarra, even though she had seen the thought-form of the Sisterhood. She tried to summon that image, the brooding goddess with wings, the robed figures, to fill her mind with the sound of calling crows, but she was all too aware that it was only an image, mind and memory, nothing like the sureness of contact with her *laran*.

She slumped in her blanket, munching wretchedly on dried fruit, which, like everything else in these caverns, smelled of the dung-fires they burned here.

She looked up, and Camilla stood before her.

But not the real Camilla. She could see the wall through her body, and her eyes blazed with supernatural fires. Her hair, in the real world faded and sandy, seemed alive with the brightest of copper highlights. Not Camilla. Her image in the Overworld. Yet Magda's head was still filled with the sick fuzzy strangeness of *raivannin*. So she was not seeing Camilla with her *laran*. Somehow Camilla had come to her. Then she saw, standing next to Camilla—but her feet were not quite touching the floor of the cave, and she was surrounded by a curious dark aureole—the slight, modest young woman who had come to the monastery to speak with them.

She heard the words with her ears. They were not in her head.

"Try not to hate them," Kyntha said, matter-of-factly, "this is not a spiritual recommendation, but a very practical one. Your hate gives them entry to your mind. Tell the others."

Then she was gone and Camilla was standing before her again.

Bredhiya, she said, and vanished.

CHAPTER THIRTY

It had happened. She could not use her *laran* to cry out to Camilla; drugged with *raivannin* she was head-blind, insensitive, unreachable. Jaelle, alone, without helpers from the Tower, was all but powerless. And so Camilla had made the breakthrough, done the thing that she had been avoiding all her life.

Magda felt a confusion beyond words. On one level she was filled with pride for Camilla, that she had overcome her dread and distaste for this long denied potential. On another she was almost immeasurably humbled that Camilla would do this for her sake, after so many years of denial, of rejection. On yet another, she felt pain that was almost despair. Camilla would never have come to this, except for me. It would have been better to die than to force this on her.

She was so filled with mixed joy and sorrow for her friend, that for a moment she did not realize what it meant. Camilla had found her, by *laran*. One way or another this meant rescue was on the way, and they must be ready.

She crawled toward Cholayna and whispered, "They've found us. Did you see Camilla?"

"Did I—*what?*"

"I saw her. She appeared to me. No, Cholayna, I wasn't hallucinating. I saw Kyntha, too. It means that since I could not search for her, she came looking for me, and it means an attempt at rescue. We must be ready."

Vanessa listened with a skeptically raised eyebrow.

"Talk about psychological defense mechanisms! I suspect you're out of your mind temporarily, Lorne, and no wonder—giving you all kinds of strange drugs, without the slightest reason—"

"You haven't been on this planet as long as I have," Cholayna said, overhearing this. "It happens and it's no delusion, Vanessa. I didn't see anything. I didn't expect to. But I don't doubt Lorne did and we should be ready."

"They won't get us away without a commotion of some sort," Vanessa said. "Not without our boots."

Rafaella, who had been dozing, sat up, and the good news was relayed to her in a whisper.

"And Jaelle? What of Jaelle?" she asked. "Any word?"

Magda said dryly, "Not going to try persuading her this time that Acquilara's gang would be more useful in the long run? Changed your mind about what kind of solid citizens they are?"

Rafaella's face was white.

"Damn you, Margali, is it any wonder I didn't want you in this? You always have to twist the knife, don't you? And you of course, you never make mistakes, you're always so right, so perfectly absolutely smug-faced *right!* All these people who are so damn awed by you because you never do anything wrong—some day Jaelle's going to realize what you're doing to her, what you do to everybody you say you care about, and break your neck, and I hope I'm there to see it and cheer!"

She turned her back on Magda and buried her head in

her blanket. Her body shook, and Magda realized she was crying.

For a moment Magda was almost too shocked to draw breath. *Rafaella and I have quarreled before, but I always thought she was still my friend. Is that what I am like? Is that how people see me?*

Vanessa had heard; more, she had seen Magda's face. She leaned close to Magda. "Never mind," she said in a voice that could not be heard a foot away, "she always calms down sooner or later. Remember her own judgment of people's just turned out not to be so great, after all. She gambled on Anders and lost."

It's as if this whole thing had been my fault, my fault Lexie Anders did what she did, my fault Rafaella followed her.

She remembered what Kyntha had said. *Try not to hate.* Her mind was still clouded, but she knew that she did not hate Rafaella. *I'm angry with her. That's different.*

Lexie? That was more difficult. However she tried, she could not exonerate Lexie from the blame for this whole miserable expedition.

"What is it?" Cholayna whispered, and Magda remembered that Kyntha had said, *Tell the others.*

"I'm trying hard not to hate Lexie." She repeated what Kyntha had said. Her feelings about Rafaella were her own affair, and she could not share them with Cholayna, but Lexie was another matter.

"You can leave the hating to me," Vanessa said implacably. "She's come so close to getting us all killed—"

"But she didn't kill Rafaella," Cholayna argued. "Not even with a knife in her hand, and an admiring audience standing around watching."

Rafaella stuck her head out from under her blanket. "I knew she wouldn't. I know Lexa' pretty well by now.'' Magda was astonished at herself, realizing that even in this adversity she still thought like a linguist, noting that Rafaella said *Lexa'*, using the Kilghard Hills dialect, rather than the *Lexie* that the rest of them, the Terrans, used.

"She would never have killed me," Rafaella insisted. They might all have been sitting around in the music room of the Guild-house, arguing a point in Training Session for the young Renunciates. "She wouldn't have killed Margali, not even when she had the gun—blaster? Stunner—on her."

If she can forgive Alexis *that,* how can I possibly keep on hating her? How can I keep on being angry with Rafi? We've quarreled before. Yet she'd speak up for me just the way she did just now for Lexie. She wanted suddenly to hug Rafaella, but she knew the other woman was still angry with her.

Well, she has a right to be. What I said *was* nasty, under the circumstances.

But if she can forgive Lexie, then I should be able to stop hating her. Magda made herself remember Lexie at her best; explaining Survey work to the young women for the Bridge Society; Lexie in Training School on Alpha, sharing experience with the younger students; Lexie, regressed to her early years . . . *a little fair-haired girl, Cleindori's age. I walked hand in hand with her like a younger sister.* . . . She sought the sympathy she had found for her then.

I don't know if it will do any good. But I'm trying.

Vanessa said grimly, "I can just manage not to hate Lexie, if I have to. But don't try asking me not to hate that woman Acquilara. That's carrying good will too far. She'd have killed us all—"

"But the fact is that she *didn't* kill us," Cholayna said. "She even left us the blankets. 'One who does good, having an infinite power to do evil, should have credit not only for the good she does but for the evil from which she refrains.' "

"What in hell are you quoting?"

"I don't remember; something I read as a student," Cholayna said. "Remember, too: the woman's psychotic. She can't help herself."

"I've never believed in diminished responsibility," said Vanessa, frowning.

Magda wondered: did this in any way exonerate Acquilara, who was at least guilty of searching for power by any means she could grab it? Jaelle had defined that as evil. She didn't know.

"Listen! What's going on?" asked Cholayna, suddenly raising her head. At the far end of the cavern there was a stirring, women running in and out. Alexis Anders came up to one of the guards; they spoke urgently for a few minutes. Then the guards hurried toward the prisoners.

They held out four pairs of boots.

"Get into them! Hurry, or it will be the worse for you!"

"What are you going to do with us?" Vanessa demanded.

"No questions," said one of them, but the other had already said, "You're being moved. Hurry up."

They hurried into their boots, afraid the guards would lose patience and force them to move without the boots. The guards prodded them to their feet with long sticks, urged them ahead. Cholayna found an opportunity to whisper to Vanessa and Magda, "If you're right about Camilla organizing a rescue, this could be it. Keep alert and seize any chance to fight our way out!"

Magda tried to get her bearings—which way was she being taken into the labyrinth? The darkness made her nervous, with no light but that from the smoking torches, making wavering images on the uneven shapes of the walls. Something sticking to her sock inside her boot hurt her foot. She recognized the slippery stairway up which they had tried to escape.

Cholayna was breathing hard. She was not, after all, long out of bed after pneumonia. Rafaella grabbed her rudely around the waist. "Lean on me, Elder." The respectful Guild-house term rang strangely here.

Vanessa bumped into her from behind. Magda felt the younger woman's breath on her neck as she whispered hastily, "I'm going to try and get that stunner away from Lexie. It could even the odds against us."

Magda's first impulse was to protest—she had lived long enough as a Darkovan to be appalled at the thought of any weapon longer than arm's reach. Also, Terran law prevented high-tech weapons on low-tech planets. But Alexis Anders had already used, displayed, the weapon here. And they were desperately outnumbered, four or five to forty or more. And—the final convincer— she didn't think her protest would stop Vanessa anyway. She muttered back, "Get me to testify at the court-martial when we get back."

But at first, when they were herded into a corner of the upper chamber, she did not see Lexie at all. She heard shouting, noise, commotion below, but they were in the dark, lighted only by one torch on the walls, sending out tarry choking smoke, and another wavering in the hands of an old woman, who stood against the cavern wall.

Then there was a clash like the sound of metal and Magda saw a press of people crowding around the head of the staircase. She could not see what was going on.

The Sisterhood do not kill. That was the one thing that was in all the legends, both Jaelle and Camilla had repeated that. Would they fight even for a rescue? Someone was screaming on the staircase. There was a new glare of freshly lit torches, and by their light Magda saw Camilla at the stairhead fighting.

It was time to act. She dashed at one of their guards; shoved her so hard that the woman toppled toward her, and she grabbed the sword out of her belt; as the woman scrambled up, she knocked her down again with a kick she had learned on another world. Her own violence spun her around and she saw that Cholayna and Rafaella were trying to follow her example, but she had no time to see what happened, as she ran toward Camilla, shouting. Where was Jaelle? In the torchlit shadows it was all but impossible to tell friend from enemy.

Camilla grabbed her hand, pulling her down the stairs, and they ran together. Somebody rose up in front of them and Magda struck out with the edge of her hand. She did not think to use the snatched-up sword instead. They ran right over her. Camilla was shouting, in a ringing voice that echoed through the caverns:

"*Comhi' letzii!* Here. Gather here!"

Somebody came up and grabbed Magda; she almost struck her down before she realized it was Jaelle, in a thick pointed cap shoved down over her bright hair.

"They're here." Magda gabbled at her, breathless. "Rafi. And Lexie. Rafi's all right. She's on our side. Lexie has a stunner. Be careful. I think she'd use it."

Acquilara's women were crowding down the staircase. Magda heard Vanessa scream and whirled. Lexie had the stunner and was holding it almost in Cholayna's face, in an attitude of wordless threat.

Cholayna's foot swept up in a *vaido* kick and the stunner went flying, scooting over heads like a soaring ball. Magda ran for it, sliding, snatching it up before

Acquilara's hands closed on it. Acquilara had a knife; Magda kicked it out of her hand.

A woman with an evil scar halfway across her face closed with her. Magda kicked, fought, scrabbled, thrust the stunner inside her own tunic. It felt icy cold against her bare skin and she was suddenly terrified that Alexis had taken off the safety catch and it would go off. Where was Lexie? Frantically, Magda sought her in the flickering torchlight, where women were pushing and crowding and screaming. Cholayna. Where was Cholayna? Magda pushed back through the press of people to find her. Cholayna was lying on the ground and for a frightful moment Magda, seeing Alexis Anders standing over her, thought that Lexie had struck her down.

But Cholayna's rasping breath could be heard halfway across the cavern. She struggled to rise, and realization swept over Magda. Cholayna was poorly acclimated to the altitude; she had been fighting like a woman half her age. Lexie was unarmed.

I have the stunner! And she hasn't been checked out for the field here—she's had unarmed-combat training, but against a knife—unarmed, Alexis was holding off two women with knives who were trying to get to Cholayna. Magda thrust frantically through the crowd toward them. *Rafaella was right*—Vanessa grabbed Cholayna, hauling her to her feet. The three of them backed off, slowly, toward the daylight that could be seen at the edge of the big chamber. The knife-bearers made a final rush, and Lexie went down in a sprawl of bodies.

Magda fought her way toward them, and saw Camilla rise upward, throwing off assailants. Vanessa dragged Cholayna up to her feet, gasping, leaning heavily on her arm. Camilla's face was pouring blood from a slash on her forehead.

Lexie Anders lay motionless on the floor of the cavern, and for a moment Magda thought she was dead. Then she stirred, and Vanessa leaned down and grabbed her. She fought her way up, clinging numbly to Vanessa's arm.

She wouldn't let them kill Cholayna, I knew it. How badly is she hurt?

Magda's throat was hurting, and she paused a moment, painfully catching her breath. Then she ran across the big chamber to where Cholayna and Camilla found shelter, with Vanessa supporting Lexie. Now Magda could see the great splotch of blood on the back of Lexie's tunic. It looked bad. They were enormously outnumbered. Rafaella and Jaelle were back to back, trying to hold off another threatening rush by Acquilara's women, who were all armed with knives and looked as if they would have no hesitation about using them. For the moment they were hanging back, but any second they might attack again.

The slash across Camilla's forehead poured blood into her eyes turning her face into a bloody mess. Magda reminded herself that all head wounds, even minor ones, bled like that and if it was that serious Camilla would not still be on her feet. Still the sight terrified her, and she ran to join them. In this lower chamber they could dimly see daylight from the cave-mouth, but, before that, there seemed to be dozens of women with knives. Cholayna's breath was still coming so hard that Magda wondered how she stayed on her feet. Vanessa, herself limping, was holding Lexie upright, half conscious.

Then as if from nowhere in a glare of light—*torchlight? No, too bright!*—half a dozen strange women, hugely tall, veiled in dark blue, with high-crowned vulture headdresses suddenly appeared. They bore great curved swords with gleaming edges, such swords as Magda, who had made something of a study of weapons, had never seen on Darkover anywhere, swords that glittered with a supernatural light. Magda knew they could not possibly be real. Acquilara's women retreated. Even the one or two who had courage to try to rush up against the glare of those lighted swords fell back, cowering and screaming as if wounded to the death, but Magda could see no blood. Were they entirely illusion, then?

A familiar voice said, "Quick! This way!" and rushed her, a hand on her shoulder, across the lower chamber toward the daylight outside. Magda flinched at the paralyzing chill, the gust of wind, but Kyntha said in her ear, "Hurry! The fighters are illusion; they cannot hold long!" She pushed Magda along what looked like a concealed trail leading between the cliff wall and the caverns.

A swift glance behind her showed Magda that all her companions were gathered in that crevice, Camilla still trying to wipe blood from her eyes. Magda hurried back toward her, shaking Kyntha's hand from her elbow. The wind flung her, slipping and sliding, toward the edge of the cliff; she brought herself up, terrified, clutching at the wall.

Camilla was all right. Where was Jaelle? Cholayna's breath, rasping and harsh, could be heard even over the shouts from inside the caverns. Vanessa was limping. Two of the tall women in vulture headdresses were guarding the rear, covering their escape. *Where was Jaelle?*

Magda saw her now, behind the vulture-crowned women warriors. Illusion? How could it be? She hurried back toward her freemate. Suddenly there was a dreadful glare of pallid light, like ultraviolet, and Acquilara rose up behind them. She had a dagger, and struck out at Vanessa, who was at the rear. One of the tall, robed women in the vulture headdresses was there with her blazing sword, but Acquilara made some strange banishing gesture and the woman in the vulture headdress exploded into blue light.

Jaelle flung herself at Acquilara, her sword out. Magda started to rush to her freemate's side, her hand on her sword. The path was narrow, but she thrust herself through the others, uncaring.

Acquilara pointed. Another of the robed, vulture-crowned women warriors—*illusion?*—flared horribly into blue light and was gone. Magda tried to rush her.

"No! No!" Magda never knew whether Jaelle screamed the words aloud or not, "I'll hold her back! Get the others away!" She flung herself on Acquilara with the knife.

Acquilara feinted with her long knife, and Jaelle brought up her arm in guard. Her sleeve was covered with blood. Then the sorceress's knife came up, and Magda rushed forward—

And stopped, sick and dizzy with terror of the cliff edge before her. Jaelle's knife went into Acquilara's breast, and the sorceress shrieked, a frantic dying howl of rage, and jumped at Jaelle. Her arms locked around Jaelle's neck.

Then the two slid together, slowly, slowly, with the dreadful inevitability of an avalanche, toward the edge, together slipped over the edge and fell. Magda screamed, rushed toward the cliff-edge; Camilla's strong arm snatched her back as she tottered, shrieking, on the very brink.

From below came a rumble, a great shattering sound like the end of the world, and a thousand tons of rock and ice ripped away from the cliff and roared down to bury them both a long, long way below.

Camilla's cry of horror and grief echoed her own. But even while Magda still heard the shaking of the avalanche, Kyntha pulled them away.

"Come! Quickly!" And as Magda turned back to where Jaelle had fallen, Camilla shouted, "No! Come! Don't make her sacrifice useless! For the children—for *both* the children—*bredhiya*—"

But it was already obvious that the fight was over. With Acquilara gone, the remnants of her group were scattering, throwing down their arms, screaming in terror, like an anthill kicked over. The phantom women warriors rose up over them, triumphant.

Cholayna had sunk to her knees, gasping, unable to breathe. Magda looked back at them, numbly.

Jaelle. Jaelle. The fight was over, but too late. What difference did it make, now, if they all died? *My own cowardice. I couldn't face the cliff. I could have saved her.* . . .

She was too numbed even to cry. But in the icy blast of the wind, the last sound she had expected to hear broke her out of her frozen despair.

In all the years she had known her she had never known Camilla to weep.

CHAPTER THIRTY-ONE

Camilla's eyes were swollen almost shut with unaccustomed tears. She had refused to let the old blind woman, Rakhaila, tend her wounds, the slash across her forehead, the knife wound in her hand that had nearly severed the sixth finger on her right hand.

Magda sat close to her, in the upper room in the cliff-top retreat of Avarra, where Kyntha had taken them when the battle was over. All the way up in the basket she had forced herself, self-punishing despite the the vertigo, to look down into the dizzying chasm.

Too late. Too late for Jaelle.

Less than an hour after the fight was over, she had felt the numbness leaving her; the *raivannin* was wearing off, her *laran* reasserting itself. Now, as she held Camilla, she felt the redoubled pain, her own and Camilla's anguish. She had longed for so many years to share this with Camilla; and now it was only loss and bereavement they could share.

"Why couldn't it have been me?" Magda was not sure, again, whether Camilla's words had been spoken aloud or not. "She was so young. She had everything to live for, she had a child, there were so many who loved her . . . you at least tried to save her, but I couldn't even *see*. . . ." She struck, with a furious hand, at the slash on her forehead, a dreadful matted mess of hair and frozen blood.

411

"No, Camilla—truly, *bredhiya*, you have no reason to reproach yourself. It was my—my cowardice—" Again, in despair, Magda relived the moment when she had held back, in fear of the unguarded cliff-edge. Could that moment have saved Jaelle?

She would never know. For the rest of her life she would torment herself, in nightmares, about that memory. But whether or not—she forced her mind away from her own anguish, it was too late for Jaelle, nothing she did could change that now, but Camilla was still living, and it seemed that Camilla's grief was worse than her own.

"Kima, *bredhiya*, love, you must let me care for this." She went and fetched hot water from the kettle over the fireplace, sponged away the frozen blood, revealing an ugly, but not dangerous slash.

"It needs stitches," she said, "but I cannot do it, and I do not think Cholayna can. Not now, at least."

"Oh, leave it, love, what difference does it make? One more scar," said Camilla. Passive, uncaring, she let Magda bandage the wounded hand. "I did not even know they had kidnapped you—Acquilara and her crew— imagine, it was the blind woman who insisted we turn back, to find you gone. And Jaelle—" Camilla's throat closed and her grief threatened to overwhelm her again. "Jaelle—tried to follow you with *laran*, and was not strong enough, she could not find you. So she—" Camilla bowed her scarred head on her hands and cried again, while Magda heard in her mind that shattering scene. Jaelle, crying, begging. . . .

I can't, Camilla. I am not strong enough. Only you can find them. They could be anywhere in these mountains, dead or alive, and if we do not find them soon they will starve, freeze, die . . .

I am no leronis. . . .

Will you cling to that last lie to yourself until they are

all dead? Is there no end to your selfishness, Camilla?
For myself I do not care, but Magda—Magda loves
you, loves you more than anyone alive, more than the
father of her child, more than her sworn freemate. . . .

As she heard those words in her mind, Magda felt
that she too would be overcome again with weeping.
Had it been true? Had Jaelle gone to her death believing
that Magda loved her less?

Then, resolutely, Magda forced herself to abandon
that lacerating train of thought. She told herself firmly:
Either Shaya knows better now, or she is someplace
where it makes no difference to her. She's gone beyond
my reach. Painful as it was, she could do nothing more
for Jaelle. She brought her full awareness back to Camilla.

"So she persuaded you—and you came for me! But
where did Kyntha come from?"

"I do not know. Jaelle—" Camilla swallowed and
resolutely went on—"Jaelle said to me, *I am a catalyst*
telepath, I have little skill myself, but I am told I can
awaken it in others. She touched me, and it was as
if—as if a veil fell from me. I saw you, and I *knew* . . .
and I came to you."

"She saved us all." But not herself. Magda knew
she would never cease to grieve; nor would Camilla.
She had only begun to feel the pain that would come
back to haunt her at odd hours for the rest of her life,
but for now she must put it aside. When she thought of
Jaelle now she saw the Jaelle she would always
remember, her wild hair streaming behind her, in the
wind of the heights, turning to say, *"I don't want to go*
back. . . ."

She shared the picture with Camilla, saying softly,
"She told me that. She didn't want to go back. I think
she knew, I think she saw her life as a finished thing. . . .
She had done all she wanted to do."

"But I would so gladly have died instead—" Camilla said, choking.

Rafaella's hand fell on her shoulder. "So would I, Camilla. The Goddess knows—if there is a Goddess—" She had been crying, too; she bent and hugged Camilla hard.

Kyntha was standing beside them. Her voice was compassionate, but matter-of-fact as always.

"Food has been prepared for you. And your companions' wounds have been cared for." She bent to examine Camilla's forehead.

"If you wish, I can stitch it for you."

"No. Not necessary," Camilla said. Wearily she rose and followed Kyntha to the end of the room near the fireplace. Magda hung back a little, looking curiously at Kyntha. She said, "You do not speak the mountain dialect of these women. Where did you come from?"

Kyntha looked a little chagrined. "I can speak it when I must, and here I try to remember to do so, but I am—young and imperfect as yet. I grew up on the plains of Valeron, and served five years in the Tower at Neskaya before I found a more meaningful service, Terran."

"You know?"

"I am not blind; Ferrika is known to me, and Marisela was my sworn sister in service to Avarra. There was a time when I too thought that I would cut my hair and swear the vows of a Renunciate. Do you think we come out of mysterious cracks from the underworld? Come and have some soup."

One of the women tending the kettle put a mug into her hand. She thought, *how can I eat, with Jaelle. . . .*

But she forced herself to drink the soup, which was hearty and thick with beans and something like barley. It seemed to melt, a little, the icy lump at her heart.

One of the beshawled attendants she had seen in her previous stay in this place was kneeling by Vanessa, rebandaging her injured leg. Rafaella seemed uninjured, though Magda had seen her in some close-quarters fighting, and her heavy cloak was cut and slashed and badly torn. Cholayna had been propped up on pillows; Magda knelt beside her.

Cholayna stretched out her hand toward Magda.

"I'm all right. But oh, I'm sorry about Jaelle, I loved her too, you know that—"

Magda's eyes filled. "I know. We all did. Let me get you some soup." It was all she could do. She looked at Lexie, lying on a pallet made of coats and spare blankets, still unconscious.

"Is she—"

"I don't know. They've done what they could for her, they say." Cholayna's voice was tight. "Did you see? They—those women—I was down. They were kicking me to death. Lexie saved me. That was when they stabbed her."

"I saw." So Rafaella had been right about Lexie. Magda knelt and looked at the younger woman, pale, like a sick child, her feathery fair hair lying on her childish neck. Her eyes were closed and she was breathing in long shuddering gasps.

Rafaella came and stood behind her. She whispered, almost inaudibly, and it was like a prayer, "Don't die. Don't die, Lexa', there's been too much dying." She raised her eyes to Magda and said defiantly, "You never knew her. She was a—a good friend, a good trail-mate. She fought like a mountain-cat to get us over Ravensmark after the landslide. I—I never thought I'd ask this of you, but you're—you're a *leronis*. Can you heal her?"

Magda knelt beside Alexis Anders. There had been

too much death. She reached out to Lexie's mind, trying to reach the child she had sensed there for a moment, thrusting gently for contact—

Lexie's eyes opened; she turned over a little, her breath rasping in her throat. At the back of her mind Magda took notice: *lungs pierced. I doubt if Damon and Callista with Lady Hilary to help them could heal this*. Yet she knew she must try.

Lexie's eyes held awareness for a moment. She whispered, "Hellfire! You again, Lorne?" and her eyes closed, deliberately. She turned her head away.

"I can't reach her," Magda whispered, knowing it was the truth. "I am no magician, Rafaella. This is far beyond my powers."

For an instant Rafaella's eyes met her own, acknowledging the truth in what Magda said. Then, still defiant, she turned her back and moved past her. Magda had not seen; the old nameless priestess sat there in her bundle of shawls, her toothless, creased face regarding them all silently. Rafaella knelt before the ancient shamaness and said, "I beg you. *You* can heal her. Help her, please. *Please*. Don't let her die."

"Na', it canna' be done," said the old woman. Her voice was gentle, but detached.

"You *can't* just let her die . . ." Rafaella cried.

"Does thee not believe in death, little sister? It comes to all; her time comes sooner than ours, no more than that." The old woman patted the seat beside her, almost, Magda thought, as if encouraging a puppy to curl up at her side. Rafaella numbly sunk down in the indicated place.

"Hear 'ee, that one dying *chose* her death. Chose a good death, saving her friend from dying before her time—"

Cholayna turned as if galvanized. She cried out,

"How can you say that? She was so young, how can she be dying before her time when I, I am old and still alive, and you helped me—"

"This one told thee before, thee is ignorant," said the old priestess. "That one dying there, she chose her death when even for a moment she allied herself wi' the evil."

"But she turned back! She saved me," Cholayna cried, and burst into a fit of coughing, half strangling with it, tears running down her face. "How can you say she was evil?"

"Was not. Better to die turning away from evil, than die with it," said the old woman. "Rest thee, daughter, thy sickness needs not these tears and cries. Her time was on her; thine will come, and mine, but not today or tomorrow."

"It's not right!" Rafaella cried out in despair. "Jaelle died saving us all; Lexie tried to save Cholayna. And *they* died, and the rest of us lived—any of us deserved death more than Jaelle: *they* deserved to live—"

The old priestess said very softly, "Oh, I see. Thee thinks death a punishment for wrong-doin' an' life the reward for good, like a cake to a good child or a whip to a naughty one. Thee is a child, little one, an' thee canna' hear wisdom. Rest thee all, little sisters. There is much to say, but thee canna' hear in thy grief."

She rose creakily from her seat; the old blind woman, Rakhaila, came to her and offered an arm, and she tottered slowly from the room.

Kyntha remained a moment, staring at them with resentment. Then she said, "You have grieved her beyond words. You have brought blood here, and the deaths of violence." She stared with distaste at Lexie. "Rest and recover your strength, as she has bidden you. Tomorrow there are decisions which must be made."

*   *   *

Lexie died just before sunset. She died in Cholayna's arms, without recovering consciousness. As if they had known, four of the old woman's attendants came in silently and took the body away.

"What will you do with her?" asked Vanessa apprehensively.

"Gi' her to the holy birds of Avarra," said one of the women, and Magda, remembering the high vulture-headdresses of the women warriors of illusion, knew that their Sisterhood paid reverence to the *kyorenbi*, whose task it was to deal with matter which had outlived its usefulness. She explained this quietly to Vanessa and Cholayna, and Cholayna bowed her head.

"It does not matter to her now. But I wish she had not come so far to die. Poor child, poor child," she murmured.

Vanessa rose and put on her heavy coat. "I'll go and watch. I can do that much for Personnel. No, you stay here, Cholayna, if you go out in this cold you'll have penumonia again and hold us up another ten days. It's my job, not yours."

They seemed to know what she intended, and waited for her.

Rafaella rose and said roughly, "My coat's torn to pieces. Lend me yours, Margali, you're about my size. I'll go, too. We were comrades; if she'd lived, we would have been—friends."

Magda nodded, with tears in her eyes.

"No, Camilla, you stay here, she was nothing to you. We loved her."

Camilla and Magda came by instinct to kneel by Cholayna's bed, holding her hands as Alexis Anders' body was borne away by the priestesses. After a long time Rafaella and Vanessa came back, silent and subdued, and had nothing further to say that night. But Magda heard Rafaella crying far into the night, and after a long time Vanessa got up and went to her, lay down beside her, and Magda heard them whispering to one another till she fell asleep.

Magda woke before the others, and lay listening to the soft hiss of the snow outside the building. Jaelle was gone; their search was ended. Or was it? They had found Lexie and Rafaella; Lexie was dead. Jaelle, who had come to seek a legendary city, had preceded her into death. Marisela, who knew the city and the Sisterhood, was dead too. Were they nowhere, lonesome spirits on the wind, or were they together, seeking something tangible? Magda wished she knew. She could not even guess.

The Sisterhood. They know. Marisela knew. If Jaelle had lived, Magda now knew, they would have sought that knowledge together; perhaps with Camilla, whose quest was to demand of the Goddess, if there was in truth a Goddess, the reasons for her life and her suffering. Now she had another grievance against the Goddess who had taken Jaelle from her. If she could find or fight her way in, Magda knew Camilla would go on.

And Magda should go with her. It was her destiny. But as she listened to Cholayna's hoarse breathing, Magda knew she was not free to follow. Cholayna might already have penumonia again, and would not be fit to travel for many days. She could not follow them to the city; she would not be admitted. A search for wisdom was not her destiny; she would return to the Terran HQ, as Vanessa must. And she, Magda, must take them back.

She had a swift vision of Jaelle—head bent against the wind, face against the storm, leading—leading the way on some madcap adventure—

Now Jaelle had gone before her again, where she could not follow. She must persuade Camilla to go on; but Magda must go back with her Terran compatriots.

Day dawned fully, and after they had cooked and eaten some breakfast, the old woman came back, ceremoniously seating herself on the stone dais, accompanied by the blind woman Rakhaila and by Kyntha.

"Did ye all sleep well? Medicines 'ull be given thee, sister," she added to Cholayna, then turned to Kyntha.

"Thee shall speak, what must be said."

Kyntha faced them. There was an odd ceremoniousness in her voice. She spoke the mountain dialect this time, though she spoke it slowly.

"Thy sister Marisela should ha' said this to ye all. Her duty, which I do with grief. Thee has come to seek the Sisterhood, and Marisela was leading thee to a place where thee might be questioned as to thy will. We ha' no heart to make thee travel again that path, so I ask thee here. What does thee seek?" She turned toward Camilla.

Camilla said, harshly, "Thee knows I seek those who serve the Goddess, that I may ask them—or her—what her purpose is for me."

Kyntha said gently, "She answers not such questions, sister. It will be thy own task to gain wisdom to hear her voice."

"Then where do I start looking for this wisdom? In your city? Take me there."

Blind Rakhaila erupted with a guffaw.

"Jes' like that, thee says? Haw!"

"Thee has lived a life of much suffering and travail, seeking wisdom," Kyntha said. "Yet look on Rakhaila here. She is older still; she has endured as much as thee; yet she has not been admitted there. She is content to dwell at the outer gates as servant to the beasts who carry the servants of the Sisterhood."

"Has she asked it?" Camilla said. "There are different paths to the Sisterhood; furthermore, I think you have the duty to do so, because I have demanded it. Do your duty, my sister, that I may do mine."

The old shamaness beckoned to Camilla. She patted the seat beside her, as she had done with Rafaella the day before.

"To one who asks, all is answered," she said. "I bid thee welcome, granddaughter of my soul."

Magda felt a sharp pain at her heart. Jaelle had gone before her, with Marisela. Now Camilla had outstripped her and was to be taken from her.

Kyntha said to Rafaella, and her voice was not harsh, but faintly sarcastic, "Now you know the city is no place of riches and jewels, do you still wish to go there?"

Rafaella shook her head. She said, "I accepted a lawful commission. It is ended badly; my companion is dead. But I do not regret the search. I have no desire to be a *leronis*. I leave that to others."

"Go, then, in peace," Kyntha said. "I have no authority over you." She turned to Vanessa. "And you?"

Vanessa said, "With all due respect, I think it's all moonshine. Four moons' worth of moonshine. Thanks, but no thanks."

Kyntha smiled. "So be it. I respect you for your loyalty in following others where you had no interest in the quest—"

"You're giving me too much credit," Vanessa said. "I came because there were mountains to climb."

"Then, I say to you, you have had your reward and you are welcome to it," Kyntha said. Then she bowed to Cholayna.

"Sister from a far world, you have all your life

sought wisdom beneath every strange sky. You hold life in reverence and you seek truth. The Sisterhood has read your heart from afar. If it is your will to enter, you too may come, and seek wisdom among us.''

For the first and last time, Magda felt the touch of the Terran woman's thoughts; she could not read them as words, but she touched the expanded sense of their import, the knowledge that in her own way Cholayna had sought this all her life.

Then Cholayna sighed, with infinite regret.

''My duty lies elsewhere,'' she said. ''I think you know that. I cannot follow my wishes in this matter. I have made another choice in this life, and I will not turn away from it.''

Again Kyntha bowed, and turned at last to Magda. ''And you? What is your will?''

Magda knew her own sigh was an echo of Cholayna's. She said, ''I would like to come to you. I wish—but I too have duties, responsibilities—I am sorry. I wish—''

But she knew she must return with Cholayna and Vanessa, to the world on the far side of those mountains. If this wisdom was meant for her, then some day she would have another chance, and be free to take it. If not, it was not worth having. She must return to her child, to Jaelle's child as well. . . .

Kyntha took a single step toward her. She put her hand under Magda's chin and lifted it. She said, ''This is the place of truth! Speak!'' It was like a great gong. ''The tides of thy life are moving. *What is thy truest will?*''

Magda heard what Andrew had said to her, when she came to the Forbidden Tower. *There isn't one of us here who hasn't had to tear their lives up like a piece of scrap paper and start over. Some of us have had to do it two or three times*. Far off it seemed that she could hear the calling of crows.

Would she ever return? She dismissed that. If she should never return, then that was her destiny. She had abandoned the Guild-house when the time came for that, and returned to build a Bridge Society between her two worlds. Jaelle had ruthlessly run ahead, knowing she had worn out the challenges of the past, looking ahead. Magda would have courage to follow.

"I would like to follow Camilla to the City. But I have a duty to my companions—"

A brief silence in the room. Then Rafaella said roughly, "Isn't that just like you, Margali? You think I'm not fit to take Cholayna and Vanessa back to Thendara? You stay here and do what you damn please. I'm the mountain guide. Who needs you?"

Magda blinked. Rough as the words were, what she heard in them was pure love; what Rafaella had said was, *sister*.

"Hell, yes, Lorne. That's settled. When Cholayna's able to travel, you go." Vanessa went and stood beside Rafaella. "We decided that last night when you were asleep."

Almost disbelieving, Magda looked round. The ancient sorceress beckoned to her. She went and numbly sat on the dais beside her, feeling Camilla's cold hands in hers.

The end of a quest? Or a beginning? Did all quests end like this, a final step upward to the pinnacle of a mighty mountain, which gave way to reveal a new and unknown horizon?

A note from the publisher concerning:

THE
FRIENDS OF DARKOVER

So popular have been the novels of the planet Darkover that an organization of readers and fans has come into being, virtually spontaneously. Several meetings have been held at major science fiction conventions, and more recently have been organized around the various "councils" of the Friends of Darkover, as the organization is now known.

The Friends of Darkover is purely an amateur and voluntary group. It has no paid officers and has not established any formal membership dues. Although the members of the Thendara Council of the Friends no longer publish a newsletter or any other publications themselves, they serve as a central point for information on Darkover-oriented newsletters, fanzines, and councils and maintain a chronological list of Marion Zimmer Bradley's books.

Contact may be made by writing to the Friends of Darkover, Thendara Council, Box 72, Berkeley CA 94701, and enclosing a SASE (Self-Addressed Stamped Envelope) for information.

(This notice is inserted gratis as a service to readers. DAW Books is in no way connected with this organization professionally or commercially.)